I was born in Stockport in 1947. After leaving school and college, was employed in numerous capacities including owning my own businesses, and being a professional yachtmaster.

In 2012, my novel *Maria's Papers* was released, and I am now writing more stories following historic researcher Naomi Wilkes (née Chance) and her intrepid and unusual bunch of allies, as she becomes embroiled in ever more baffling and precarious adventures!

# THE MATTHEW CHANCE
## LEGACY

This book is dedicated to my wife Jay, for everything.
L.L.L.

Stephen F. Clegg

---

# The Matthew Chance
# Legacy

AUSTIN MACAULEY
PUBLISHERS LTD.

A CIP catalogue record for this title is available from the British Library.


ISBN 978 184963 398 7


www.austinmacauley.com

First Published (2013)
Austin Macauley Publishers Ltd.
25 Canada Square
Canary Wharf
London
E14 5LB


Printed and Bound in Great Britain

# Acknowledgments

I would like to thank my special band of readers, Jean Dickens, Jayne Miles, Michele Norton, Lorraine Middleton, Ted Wylie, and especially Nicola Drake, whose ingenious idea inspired one of the central themes of the story. Thanks guys, I am indebted to you all.

I would also like to thank my 95-year-old mother Jocelyn, who made my earlier life so much richer by the expanse of her mind.

# Preface

Naomi checked her mirror and then pulled over to where she'd stopped on her first visit. She took out her binoculars, walked across the lane to the dry-stone wall, and looked down Lark Hill. She put the binoculars up to her eyes and tried to see if she could spot the remains of any digging near the side of the lake.

For several seconds she scanned the area, looking for signs of latent activity, and then every hair on her body stood on end.

The same gaunt looking figure that she'd glimpsed before stepped out of the trees at the bottom of the hill and looked right back at her through another pair of binoculars.

Her first instinct was to drop hers and to look the other way, but she was made of much sterner stuff; she kept them trained on him and waved. The man, whom she presumed to be the sinister and creepy Les Spooner, didn't respond, but kept on looking.

Naomi tried waving again but still drew no response.

The Chance family throughout history had been known as the 'Iron Chances' because of their inherent resolve and tenacity, and some of that kicked in. She knew that she had permission to be on the site, and ignoring the voice in her head that kept repeating *'No, don't...'* she walked back to her vehicle, put the binoculars inside, and locked it, with a steadfast determination to climb over the wall and confront the gamekeeper.

She turned to cross the lane and her heart leapt into her mouth.

Spooner was standing behind the wall that she had seconds earlier been leaning on.

The shock of his appearance was so great that she jumped back, yelped "Jesus Christ!", and banged into the side of her car. There appeared to be no way that he could have got to the wall in such a short time.

As her heart rate slowed she stared at his fearsome appearance. He was wearing a long black coat and wide-brimmed hat, his skin was thin and pallid, and appeared to be stretched over his bony face and hands. His dark, sunken eyes looked weird, more like an animal than human, and he looked as though he had been dragged out of a Victorian mausoleum.

In a raspy, hollow sounding voice Spooner said, "Don't you ever step onto this land again, or I'll shoot you where you stand..."

# Chapter 1

"'Tis the same each time you look at it boy; 'tis but a box and not much of one to look at either."

Alexander Chance lifted the tails of his day coat, clasped his hands behind his back, and strode across to his son in the 'unstately' drawing room of the run down but spacious Chance Hall, on the Scarred Earth Estate near Rochdale in the District of Spotland.

Fourteen-year-old Valentine looked at the chest on the sideboard; it stood in the same space that it had occupied for as long as he could remember. It tantalised him beyond measure, but he had never been allowed to touch it, let alone see inside it.

It wasn't very large, measuring just eighteen inches long by eight inches wide and twelve inches high. It was unremarkable except for one thing – carved into the lid was the depiction of a cow's head with horns that had been pollarded, leaving only a couple of small stumps.

"But grandfather told me that my inheritance is in there," he said, looking up at his father with his large appealing brown eyes.

Alexander looked down at his son, thought for a second, and said, "Well, in that at least, he was imparting the truth."

"Then if it truly is my inheritance, why may I not see inside?"

The feeling of discomfort spread through Alexander once again. He closed his eyes for a second and wondered how long he would be able to keep the vile secret.

He looked down at his son and said, "You may not see, Val, because therein lies the Caput Mortuum, and as long as you don't ever open the lid you will be spared the brute consequences of your grandfather Matthew's legacy."

Valentine stared at his father's face devoid of understanding.

For a while neither spoke and then, with a slight nod of his head, Alexander walked towards the drawing room door.

"Father," said Valentine, "what is the Caput Mortuum?"

"Ah!" said Alexander.

He returned to where his son was standing and bent down. He looked into his son's face and lowered his voice to give it just the right amount of gravity.

"Caput Mortuum, Valentine, – 'tis Latin and means, 'Head of the Dead'."

Valentine gulped as his father remained motionless just inches in front of his face. He cast a nervous glance in the direction of the chest and decided against opening it.

Alexander could see from his son's reaction that he'd instilled the correct level of foreboding, and drew himself up.

"Good," he said. "Now that that is settled, I shall withdraw to..."

The conversation was brought to an abrupt halt as they heard the unmistakable sound of a cane banging on the ceiling above.

Alexander looked up and shut his eyes.

"Would you like me to go, father?"

"No, thank you son," said Alexander heading for the door. "'Tis probably nought but another of your grandfather's whimsies, which I swear he is able to conjure up with unerring accuracy each time your mother and the servants go to market."

Upstairs the floorboards creaked as he walked towards his father's bedchamber. The carpet was threadbare beneath his feet and the wallpaper hadn't been replaced for years. The colours were yellowing and becoming monotone, showing clear signs that the grand old lady that had been Chance Hall had not only reached the top of the hill, but had gone a considerable distance down the other side.

He reached the bedchamber, turned the door handle, and stepped in.

"Father," he said, "what is your desire upon this beautiful morning?"

"I want a shit and my pot's full, so get down on your knees and get it from under my bed. It needs emptying."

Alexander recoiled at the thought of such an odious task, and his father was quick to spot it.

"We all do the same," he said with harshness, "so stop being such a bloody namby-pamby, and get on with it."

"Can't it wait until the maid gets back?" said Alexander in near total despair, "I do have..."

"No it can't!" cut in Matthew, relishing his son's anguish.

Alexander took a deep breath, walked across to his father's bed, and retrieved the object of his total disgust.

With perverse pleasure, Matthew watched as his son cautiously made his way to the bedchamber door and then said, "And be sharp about it or you'll be cleaning shit out of my bed too."

Alexander could feel his top lip curl. He wanted to say, "Why don't you hurry up and die, you repulsive old bastard?" But that was out of the question, his whole future depended upon his father. He'd threatened many times over to leave the Scarred Earth Estate to Valentine alone, and that would have had serious consequences upon his ability to repay his numerous debts.

Ten minutes later he returned to the bedchamber with the clean pot, and in an effort to distract his father from his stated intent said, "Valentine's becoming more inquisitive about the contents of the chest."

Matthew stared with contempt at Alexander for a moment. He couldn't believe that his wastrel of a son had produced such a fine upstanding boy as Valentine.

"Well take his mind off it," he said. "Give him some work to do."

"You know that that will only distract him for a short while. We should confide in him."

"He doesn't even know about the Whitewall Estate, so what is there to confide?"

"Now you are just being evasive," said Alexander. "So far, providence has been on our side with Cousin Joseph knowing nothing of his true inheritance, but should Valentine ever learn the truth, we will be undone and he will never trust either one of us again."

Matthew looked out of his chamber window. The moors always looked their most stark at this time of year. They hadn't had any significant snowfall so far, but it was just a matter of time.

Images started to flash before his ageing eyes; images of boyhood, of joyful days playing in the snow with his brother John. He could hear the tinkling laughter of his beloved mother and recall the long happy hours they'd spent together as a family, – a privileged, moneyed family.

And then he recalled the fateful day that their father had informed him and John about their joint inheritance, Whitewall.

He shivered at the thought. Whitewall that had ripped apart his family; Whitewall that dogged every day of his life, and Whitewall, the one place on earth about which Valentine must never learn.

He looked across at his son. It was too late for him, but maybe not for his grandson.

"Then we'll have to send him away," he said.

"*Away*? What do you mean, *away*?"

"I mean away from here, from us, from Spotland."

Alexander was mortified.

"You cannot be serious, father. I won't hear of it! Think of the effect it would have upon him if we were to suggest such a terrible course."

Even the idea of sending his thoughtful and gentle son away horrified him. Valentine may not have had all the privileges that he'd had as a child growing up in Chance Hall, but in general terms it was superior to most children of his age.

"Think about it boy," said Matthew, cutting through Alexander's thoughts. "It makes sense. He doesn't seem drawn to our way of life; he's never shown any interest in the running of the estate, and he's always got his head into one book or another."

Alexander looked at his father and had to admit that that was true. Valentine could always be found in the library during his numerous periods of self-imposed solitude immersed in books about travel, and adventures in far off, exotic places.

He said, "Where did you have in mind for him, Oxford, Cambridge...?"

"The Royal Navy," said Matthew.

Alexander didn't think that he could have been more shocked; the suggestion rendered him speechless.

"I have an acquaintance that has influence at The Admiralty. He owes me more than one favour, so we shall contact him and see if we can get Valentine aboard one of his vessels."

Alexander was dumbfounded, and stood looking at his father with an open mouth.

It had been a donkey's age since he'd seen him so animated. Indeed, over the last five years his father had become so insular and selfish that he couldn't wait to get out of his company, and now here he was talking about "having an acquaintance with influence at The Admiralty"!

His father still had the power to shock, and it was almost too much for him to take in.

"It's the perfect solution," said Matthew. "With young Valentine gone from here, it'll take his mind off speculating about his future, and it may give us some time to make amends for those things that we should not have done."

Alexander found his tongue and said, "Have you taken leave of your senses? Have you not read the newspapers and been following the events around us? Good Lord above, father, Valentine could be posted anywhere! Perhaps you'd like him to go to the New World where there's considerable unrest with the French, Spanish and colonial Americans, – or how about France, where the common rabble have started a revolution?"

Matthew was uncompromising.

"Listen to yourself boy!" he said. "Whose fears are you giving voice to – your own, or Valentine's? Do you deem me to be such a bad judge of character? He's made of much sturdier stuff than both of us are, he is cooler headed, and brighter. This could be just what he needs."

Alexander's volatile emotions began to settle; he conceded that the idea *did* have merit. Maybe his father was right – it could give them time to make amends, and it would have the ability to take Val's mind off of things at Chance Hall. Furthermore, it had the potential to lift him out of the rural environment and allow him to live his adventures, instead of reading about them.

He turned to face his father and was surprised to see him staring back. They looked into each other's eyes and, with the briefest nods, agreed upon something for the first time in years. Both men lapsed into a comfortable silence, happy to be in one another's company.

Neither man, however, could have known on that cold January morning, that by those simple actions, they had set in place a chain of events that would not only result in Valentine never being able to return to England again, but one that would generate greed, rivalry and murder for more than the next two hundred years.

# Chapter 2

The telephone rang on Naomi's desk and caused her to jump. She'd been immersed in filing endless reams of paperwork and lamenting that being a historical researcher was to a lesser degree a researcher, and to a much greater one, a filing clerk. Even in her absence, the paperwork had built up to such an extent that for fear of it toppling and scattering across her office floor, she'd been forced to dedicate time to filing it.

The phone rang a second time; she reached over her mini-Mount Everest and picked up the handset.

"Good morning, Walmsfield Historic Research Department, Naomi Wilkes speaking."

"Ah, Naomi," There was a fleeting pause on the telephone. "Er, I hope that you don't mind me calling you by your Christian name instead of Mrs Wilkes?"

"You can call me anything you like, as long as it's not late for dinner!" said Naomi with a smile on her face.

"What? Oh, of course – yes, very droll," said the caller. "We haven't been introduced, but my name is Craig Brompton. I'm a Professor and close friend of Gordon Catchpole, whom you may recall…"

"Led the investigations into the findings at Whitewall Farm," said Naomi. "How could I ever forget?"

"Hmm, it was one of the, er, more fascinating cases, I recall." Brompton paused for a second and then said, "Yes, well, now, I seem to recall from those days that not only were you involved in the historical research, but you are also a member of the Chance family by birth. Is that correct?"

"Yes, it is."

"Good. And would I be right in assuming that you are still the person to contact with reference to historical research relating to your area, including the Whitewall Farm?"

"You would."

"Excellent!" said Brompton now satisfied with the antecedents. "Then I have something here that may interest you."

Ten minutes later, the door to Carlton Wilkes' office burst open as Naomi charged in.

"Whoa! What the devil…?" said Carlton.

"Cal. Cal. Shush!" Naomi quelled her husband's objection. "You're not going to believe this. Over in Newton, they're building a new complex called the Vical Centre, and part of the site is being recorded for posterity. There's a team of archaeologists and conservators there who have been recording and cataloguing the entire finds…"

"Darling," interrupted Carlton. "This is all very interesting but I have a hellish schedule and…"

Naomi leaned over her husband's desk and pinched his lips together with her forefinger and thumb.

"Shush!" she said brimming with enthusiasm. "You're going to be just as excited about this as I am."

Carlton adored his wife. No other woman he had ever known did the same silly, affectionate things that his wife did. He no longer resisted and was happy to sit there with her fingers still pinching his mouth shut.

"Mm, mm," he mouthed, accepting defeat through half-smiling lips.

Naomi frowned and said, "Shush! I've told you, you are going to be just as excited by this as I am!"

She stopped speaking for a second until she realised that she had her husband's full attention.

"Now," she said, "during the excavations, a hidden wall safe was unearthed in one of the cellars and it was taken to the conservators intact. They sent for a specialist team who got it open within a couple of days, and once open, they discovered some documents in there, proving that the wall safe once belonged to a firm of Solicitors named – wait for it – Josiah Hubert and Sons!"

Her deep brown eyes sparkled with exhilaration as she removed her fingers from her husband's lips.

Carlton could see the look of expectancy on his wife's face. He knew that it should have meant something to him, but the lift had stopped short of the top floor.

"And that means…what?"

"Josiah Hubert and Sons – Whitewall – durr!" said Naomi.

The penny dropped.

"What, *the* Josiah Hubert and Sons?" said Carlton, almost disbelieving his own ears.

"Yes! And if you thought that was good, listen to this. One of the documents in the safe was an unopened letter with 'John and Matthew Chance – Cestui que Vie' written on the rear *and…*" Naomi paused enjoying the sheer deliciousness of being able to tell her husband the electrifying details. "… it says 'Matthew's Copy' on the front!"

She couldn't help herself, she let out an involuntary shriek of delight and clapped her hands together.

As an ex-Army Officer and the current head of the Planning Department, Carlton was a dignified and controlled person, but even he could feel the excitement. He sat bolt upright and said, "Good grief, Mimi, that's amazing!"

The memories flooded in. In May 2002, on behalf of the Historic Research Department, he had forced open an old travel case known as the Whitewall File and had discovered two items. One was a faded blue envelope addressed to 'the incumbent Mayor and District Clerk' dated from 1869, with the inscription 'John & Matthew Chance – Cestui que Vie' written on the rear, and the other was a leather document folder, containing lots of old notes and correspondence.

As per the instruction on the envelope, he'd handed the unopened documents to the incumbent town clerk Giles Eaton, and he had never seen them again.

Through a process of deduction, he and other members of the Chance family had concluded that the envelope had contained a copy of the Deeds and a Tenancy Agreement relating to the old Whitewall Estate on nearby Wordale Moor, which indicated that the estate, now named Whitewall Farm, had once, and maybe still did, belong to them.

Had the case been proven in Court however, it could have had disastrous consequences for Walmsfield Borough Council, because it could have proved that their predecessors, the old Hundersfield District Council, had illegally purchased some of the Whitewall land for their own ends. And it would also have been possible that it could have been required to repay an inestimable amount of money to the Chance family, by way of recompense.

But events had conspired against them. Before anybody had been able to prove anything, the documents had disappeared and all of those who'd seen them had died in questionable circumstances including Giles Eaton, the man thought at the time to be the main instigator of the documents' destruction, and the mysterious deaths.

During that period, Eaton had become associated with Adrian Darke, a local multi-millionaire businessman whose forebear was also believed to have illegally purchased some of the Whitewall land. For a while, suspicion had fallen upon him too, but nothing had ever been proven, and all of the investigations into his involvement had been dropped following the death of Eaton.

Once it had been accepted that John Chance's copy of the documents had been destroyed, all had seemed lost, until a discovery had been made in America by another branch of the family.

An old chest, believed to have contained Matthew's copy of the documents, had been inherited by Alan Farlington, Matthew Chance's direct descendant. He'd invited Naomi and him to Florida to supervise opening it, but once again they'd been thwarted, because amongst the scraps of deteriorated parchment they'd found inside, only one had had the words 'eus immit' written upon it, and nobody had been able to fathom what that had meant.

He looked up and saw Naomi deep in thought.

"So," he said shaking them both out of their reminiscences, "when you opened the old chest in Florida, the remnants that we saw must have been something else and not the remains of Matthew's copy of the documents."

"Well let's not be too hasty in assuming that," said Naomi. "We've been here before, and I've learned that when it comes to Whitewall nothing is ever straightforward, but I must admit that I always harboured doubts about the contents of that old chest."

Carlton nodded and sat back in his chair. It had been on the trip to America in 2002 that he had fallen in love with Naomi. He looked at her pretty face and dark brown eyes and adored her more every day.

"So what now, beautiful?" he said.

A huge grin lit up Naomi's face.

"What do you think?" she said. "It appears that a whole new chapter in the Chance family saga may be about to open up. I'm off to Newton this afternoon to get that envelope!"

# Chapter 3

*The Vical Centre, Newton*

The mud squelched beneath the tyres of Naomi's red Honda CRV as she entered the confines of Newton's Vical Centre construction site. She drove to the parking area and stopped. She was buzzing with excitement at the prospect of opening the mystery envelope, and had speculated over the contents so much that she hadn't noticed the journey.

She switched off the engine, checked her appearance in the rear view mirror, and sat back in her seat to gather her wits.

The whole Whitewall affair had taken a back seat since the madness and mayhem of 2002, when all of the investigations, revelations, and experiences had come to an ignominious end as every last scrap of evidence supporting the Chance family claim to the estate had come to nothing.

Bodies dating from the mid-1800s had been discovered there, all of whom had been murdered, and then when most of the people who'd seen the contents of the file in 2002 had died in suspicious circumstances too, it had seemed like a curse. She'd known since her childhood that some great mystery had surrounded the estate, but every time that she'd got closer to uncovering it, something had happened to snatch it away from her again.

Her hitherto unknown psychic side had sprung into life during that time, and despite a lot of scepticism on the part of Chief Inspector Crowthorne, who had led the investigations, it had proved to be invaluable in helping to discover the whereabouts of several of the bodies and even he'd had to concede that there appeared to be more to the subject than first met the eye.

She now rarely mentioned her psychic occurrences to anybody but Carlton, but she had come to trust in them more and more as the years had passed by.

The feeling of a thumb pressing down on her left shoulder either heralded the start of one of her experiences, or told her that she was not alone. And it was pressing down now.

She opened the door of the car and stepped out. Several green portable office cabins stacked three high occupied an area adjacent to the car park. She picked her way through the underfoot detritus until she reached a signboard with 'Conservation Suite – Level 3' written upon it, and then made her way to the foot of the open plank-on-scaffold steps. She looked at them full of suspicion, and wondered whether the conservation team, which nine times out of ten consisted of women, had been placed in an upper cabin in order to afford the local workmen the odd chance of seeing a well-shaped leg or two.

She held the back of her skirt and ascended, ruing that she'd opted to wear a mini that day – but once she'd reached the top, she couldn't resist the urge to turn and see if she'd attracted any admirers.

"Afternoon, love!" called one of four workmen who'd appeared by magic at the bottom of the steps. "Would you like a bite of my Jammy Dodger?"

"No thank you," called Naomi. "I prefer a nice chocolate roll!"

She heard the workmen burst into laughter and shout back all sorts of responses as she knocked on the Conservation Suite door and entered.

"I see that you've already met the local cavemen!" said Helen Milner, one of the trio of conservators based at the site.

"I grew up with a brother," said Naomi, "so those meatheads are no bother!"

She walked around the office and introduced herself to the girls.

"Professor Brompton said that you might call today," said Helen. "He asked me to give you this."

She pulled on a pair of white cotton gloves, extracted an envelope from a box file on her desk, and offered it to Naomi.

"The legend on the rear was a new one on me," she said as she handed it over.

Naomi took the envelope and turned it over.

"Ah yes, 'Cestui que Vie'. I take it that you know now?"

"Yes I do," said Helen. "'Cestui que Vie' means, 'the person for whose life any lands or hereditaments may be held' – or perhaps more precisely, 'he for whose life, land is held by another person.'"

"Bravo!" said Naomi smiling and pulling on her own cotton gloves.

She turned the envelope around and noticed a faint pencil score across the 'Matthew's Copy' inscription, and the name 'Daisy' written below it.

She frowned and then said, "Okay, let's take a closer look."

Despite being blessed with 20/20 vision, she removed a small folding magnifying glass from her pocket and examined the envelope in minute detail.

The three conservators watched in silence until Naomi said, "This envelope has been opened and then resealed."

"Well I hope that you don't think any one of us was responsible for that!" said an indignant Charlotte Southwell, one of the more punctilious members of the team.

"No, of course not," said Naomi, smiling across at her and trying to dispel any kind of awkwardness. "Judging by what I can see through the glass, I would say that it had been opened well over a hundred years ago, maybe more."

The three conservators relaxed.

"Whoever resealed it did a very good job though. I doubt that I would have ever seen it with the naked eye."

Charlotte and Nina Clements the first member of the team to have examined the letter, got up from their positions and walked over to where Naomi was sitting.

Naomi held up the envelope for both to see.

"Gosh you're right," said Nina. "I still can't see the break, even though I know one's there!"

Charlotte remained silent, still unsure of whether Naomi had been questioning their professionalism.

"Will you open it here, or would you prefer to take it back to your office at Walmsfield?" asked Nina.

Naomi felt like a girl with an unopened present. She knew that the contents would be good, but there was just that period of time when savouring the moment was better.

She pondered Nina's question for a few seconds and then said, "Let's do it here!"

Unaware of the enormous significance this moment had for Naomi, the three conservators gathered around as first she removed a digital camera from her bag and took two macro images of the front and rear of the envelope. She then re-examined the wax seal with the aid of her magnifying glass. The impression was unremarkable and consisted of a simple upright cross with the letters 'J' and 'H' either side of the upright. She presumed that that represented the name 'Josiah Hubert'.

Next she undid a soft chamois leather roll, containing a set of shiny stainless steel implements and spread them before her. She extracted a small scalpel, inserted the tip of the blade under the flap of the envelope, and teased it across in both directions until all but the wax seal had given way. Not daring to breathe, she slid the scalpel under the seal, exerted some upwards pressure, and was rewarded seconds later as it became detached intact.

With a hammering heart she prayed that she would be confronted by two documents; the original Deeds to the Whitewall Estate showing that the Chance family had once owned the property, and a Tenancy Agreement proving that her long dead great-great-great aunt Maria, who'd first initiated the battle to reclaim ownership, had always been right in her assertions.

Glancing up, she saw the three conservators looking at her, and felt that she needed to explain.

"I'm expecting these papers to refer to a property on Wordale Moor, once called the Whitewall Estate, and you cannot know how important they are. The simple existence of these documents has been responsible for unbelievable amounts of intrigue, acts of unwarranted cruelty, and numerous murders. God knows how many back in the nineteenth century, and we suspect at least three only as far back as 2002."

She now had the undivided attention of everybody and Charlotte's initial suspicion had long since melted away.

"And if they are what I think they are, then let me paraphrase our own ex-town clerk who died not long after opening another copy of these papers."

"Died?" said Charlotte.

"It's a long story," said Naomi, "and I will tell you all one day, but this is what he said after opening the other set. 'The revelations held within these documents for the last one-hundred-and-forty years are of such monumental concern to us that if they are not handled properly, the whole of Walmsfield Borough Council could go into financial meltdown. The consequence for thousands of people could be disastrous, and the collateral damage to parts of Lancashire and Yorkshire County Councils would be so great that it would make the national news'."

The shocked silence that followed was broken by Nina. "My God!" she said, "What on earth is in there?"

Naomi let the question hang in the air; she looked at each face in turn and then said, "Let's see."

She replaced her cotton glove and opened the envelope. There was only one document inside.

With minute care she opened it up. It was a letter. She spread it out on the desk and read the neat handwriting.

*To Mrs Daisy Hubert,*
*High Farm Cottage,*
*Cragg End,*
*Rushworth,*
*Lancashire.*

*19th March 1869.*

*My Dearest Daisy,*

*I trust that you are reading this because some ill has befallen me, and if it has, I entreat you not to judge your devoted brother-in-law too harshly for the act of desperation mentioned in my previous dispatches.*

*The documents that I sent you last week are those that you need to keep concealed from those most heinous characters, Abraham and Caleb Johnson of the Whitewall Estate, and to whom you may attribute my demise. They should be taken at once to Rochdale Police and not to the local Magistrate, whom I believe to be in the pay of the Johnson's closest companion, Hugo Darke of Brandworth Manor.*

*Now please heed my grave counsel. Until you are ready to hand those documents to the police, commit them to the safe confines of 'Larkland Fen'. Only remove them when you need to, and be aware that prying eyes could be watching all of your movements from this day henceforward.*

*I beseech you dear sister-in-law, do not enter into any correspondence with the Johnsons. Do not go anywhere near them and do not under any circumstances attempt to blackmail them with the knowledge that you now have, for they will hunt you down like a dog and extinguish your life.*

*Should you not hear from me again, the money in the wall safe is yours to keep, and I will pray for your safekeeping every day of my life left here on God's good earth in this your most perilous of undertakings.*

*Your loving brother-in-law,*
*George.*

Everybody in the Conservation Suite read the letter at least three times before Charlotte broke the silence and said, "My God, that's so sinister!"

Naomi put the letter to one side and said, "This is not what I expected to find."

"It would explain the pencil score and name Daisy on the front of the envelope, though," said Helen.

"True," said Naomi. "It's obvious that George Hubert removed the original documents, placed them somewhere else, and re-used this envelope."

Helen nodded in agreement and then returned to her seat deep in thought.

"Do you think that the original documents are lost?" asked Nina.

"Maybe they are now," said Naomi.

"And do you know what happened to Daisy?" said Charlotte.

"No, I don't, but I will look into it."

"And what documents did you expected to find?" said Nina.

"I hoped that one would have been the original Deeds to the Whitewall Estate and the other an old Tenancy Agreement which would have confirmed that the Johnsons were not the rightful owners. The proving of that alone would have been enough to have them prosecuted, – but I have no idea whether there were any more or not."

"It's obvious that Daisy never got this letter," said Charlotte, "but are there any records of the Johnsons ending up in police custody?"

"Not that we are aware of. I do recall being told by a local amateur historian and friend of mine that Abraham Johnson's disfigured body was found near an old mine shaft in Rochdale in 1869, but we have no record of what befell Caleb. We have lots of evidence of his wrongdoings, but as far as justice is concerned, it's as though he disappeared off the face of the earth sometime in 1870."

"This is a hell of a story," said Charlotte. "Did you know about Daisy Hubert?"

Naomi looked up and said, "No. I hadn't ever heard of her until I read this letter."

"Well do please try to find out and let me know," said Charlotte. "You have me hooked here. I want to know if she crossed swords with those Johnsons!"

"I'll try, but that could prove to be one heck of a task." Naomi paused for a second and then said, "Thinking about it though, I suppose we also have to ask ourselves why she never received this letter either."

"Perhaps the Johnsons got her in the end," said Nina.

Naomi expelled a long "Hmm…"

She thought about why Daisy's full name and address hadn't been written on the front of the envelope, and concluded that George had either planned to hand deliver it, or that he had been expecting her to collect it.

Nobody had noticed that Helen had been studying an Ordnance Survey book in the opposite corner of the room until she spoke. All heads turned in her direction.

"This is curious," she said. "We know that folk didn't travel far in the mid-nineteenth century and I presume that would have been the case with Daisy Hubert, yet I can't find any mention in our somewhat limited reference books relating to anywhere named Larkland Fen."

She paused for a second whilst twisting a few curls of her hair.

Nobody else spoke.

"I mean," she continued, "George Hubert wrote, 'commit the documents to the safe confines of 'Larkland Fen' and only remove them when you need to.'

"He made it sound more like a depository than a place; he even placed the words Larkland Fen in inverted commas which, to me, hints that there is more to this reference than a simple straightforward location."

All eyes turned to the letter and sure enough, Helen was right – there were single inverted commas around the words 'Larkland Fen'.

They all fell into silence until Helen spoke once more.

"If Larkland Fen was a place known to Daisy Hubert, I doubt that she would have travelled any great distance to it, especially if she was going there to store sensitive documents.

"We need to get more detailed historic reference material within a five mile radius of where she lived, and try to establish where it was, or indeed may still be. That way we will be able to eliminate possibilities like banks or solicitors' offices."

She turned to face Naomi and said, "Daisy is the key. She was the last known person to have received the documents. You need to find out more about her. For example, when and how she died, and if High Farm Cottage still exists on Rushworth Moor. It might provide us with further clues to progress matters."

Being a professional historic researcher and in charge of her own department, Naomi needed no lessons on how to proceed, but she listened with interest to Helen's ideas and lateral thinking, and to her use of the term 'us,' instead of 'you,' when she referred to progressing the investigation.

"Furthermore, if we are lucky enough to find a clue referring to the whereabouts of the mysterious Larkland Fen," said Helen oblivious of Naomi's thoughts, "we may then find out what it was and whether or not it still exists."

She paused for a few seconds and then said, "And if it does exist, and it is a depositary, whether or not it still contains those documents."

Helen's bold assertion stunned everybody into temporary silence.

It struck Naomi that she hadn't mentioned any of the latest revelations to her family, and she knew that they'd be galvanised into action once again. A new game was afoot, and the prospect of bringing together all of her old friends and family to help with the new investigations thrilled her to the tips of her toes.

"My father spoke very well of a woman curator in charge of a local cottage museum somewhere near the old estate. I'll give him a ring when I get home tonight and see if he can tell me who it was; maybe she can help."

Glances were passed between the three conservators, but nobody spoke.

"What?" said Naomi.

Silence ensued.

"Come on – if you know something, spill it."

Helen looked at her two colleagues and said, "It may be Daphne Pettigrew, the curator of Wordale Cottage Museum – and let's just say that she's a one-off."

Nods of agreement were passed between the three conservators.

Naomi looked at each face and then said, "Alright – it's obvious that you aren't going to elucidate, so I'll make the call tonight."

Half an hour later she bid farewell to her new friends, and promised to keep in touch. As she turned to wave goodbye to them all, she noticed Helen poring over her reference books, still deep in thought.

Charlotte and Nina smiled and waved back and seemed to be the friendliest, but as she looked at Helen, the thumb pressed down upon her shoulder and she knew that it would be her that she would be seeing a lot more of in the future.

A future that would, within one calendar month, bring them into contact with a brutal and heartless killer intent on murdering them both.

# Chapter 4

*May 1790. Chance Hall, Lancashire*

On the day of Valentine's departure, his mother and father stood at the door of the coach that would take him to Liverpool. His mother was in tears, and although his father appeared to be unmoved, Valentine could hear the breaks in his voice and knew that he too was very emotional.

"Valentine, wait!" Matthew's voice called from the front door of Chance Hall.

One of the male servants helped the old man across to the coach.

"This is for you." Matthew handed Valentine the chest.

Valentine couldn't believe his eyes. He looked down at it and noticed that his initials had been carved into the lid with the 'V' to one side of the cow's head and the 'C' to the other.

It was unreal! He had it, the object of so many years' desire. He placed it upon his lap, put his hands on each side of the lid, and lifted, but it was still locked.

Looking puzzled he said, "Thank you, grandfather. I shall treasure it and keep it with me wherever I go – but where is the key?"

Matthew said, "There isn't one."

"Then how should I open it?"

"You shouldn't."

Valentine frowned and looked at his grandfather.

Matthew said, "I have never lied to you about the contents of that chest. Your inheritance, as such, is in there, but I beg you, for mine and for your father's sake, please don't look inside until you bring it back here to Chance Hall."

"But why?" said Valentine.

"Because the contents are a curse upon this family and will reign misery and despair upon you unless you keep that chest sealed. That is why I haven't given you the key."

"A curse?" Valentine looked down at the chest. "Then what is the point of carrying this with me if it is both cursed and not to be opened? Why should I not leave it in its place upon the sideboard?"

"Because," said Matthew, "when you take that chest with you, you take from your father and me a burden – one of our doing, yet one to be borne by you; and if you can resist temptation and bring it back here unopened, the curse will be lifted."

Valentine looked at his grandfather's troubled face and said, "Very well. I'll take it with me and I won't open it, nor will I allow anybody else to open it, until the day that it's returned to Chance Hall."

Matthew smiled, and as tears of emotion welled up in his eyes, he felt a steadying hand take hold of his. He looked down and saw that it was Alexander's. He held onto it and felt closer to his family than he had for as long as he could remember.

Valentine saw what passed between his father and grandfather, and hoped that his departure would bring them closer together.

"God go with you," said Elizabeth as the coach driver slapped the reins and urged the horses forward.

Three days later, the young midshipman Valentine Chance complete with unopened chest, stepped aboard *HMS Spartan* at the Liverpool docks under the watchful eye of Captain Edward Telford, bound for the Americas.

Sitting in the loneliness of his bedchamber, Matthew realised how empty Chance Hall was without Valentine; he couldn't admit to having given much of any twenty-four hours to the boy, but that was not the point. His departure had created a vacuum that was not being filled. His new understanding with Alexander was agreeable enough, but it was as though somebody had thrown away his favourite old jacket – it had left a hole.

As he stared out of the window across the moors, he realised that his life had been filled with holes, all of which had been of his own making. He hadn't cared; in fact, when he wanted his way he'd never considered consequences. And if people got hurt, it was of no importance to him.

He dropped his gaze and lapsed into a short period of contemplation.

"Bovi!"

From across the endless realms of time, he heard it. His eyes narrowed almost imperceptibly as though the sound had been coming from within his bedchamber.

*"Bovi!"*

He heard it again, the name that his family had given him. 'Bovi' indeed! He still hated it.

Controlling his volcanic temper had always been an issue. His closest of kin used to reckon that he had the shortest fuse of anybody they knew, and all had fallen foul of it at one time or another.

His immediate family had consisted only of his mother, father and twin brother John. He'd named him 'Saint John' because of his persistent and consistent goodness. It was as though God had taken all of his virtues and given them to John, whilst conversely taking all of John's vitriol and giving it to him.

He remembered the occasion that he'd been given the chest that Valentine now had.

Following the loss of a simple game of croquet on the lawn of the Selhurst Estate, he'd gone armed with a pair of scissors to his brother's bedchamber where he knew that he kept a glass vivarium containing six newts. John had cared for them, and had given them all names.

He'd removed each one from the tank and had cut them in half.

John had been heartbroken. His parents had been beside themselves with anger, and he'd received a sound beating from his father for his act of wanton wickedness.

One week later, on Christmas Eve, they'd gathered around the tree and swapped presents and he'd been presented with the chest. He'd seen the carving of the cow's head with pollarded horns, but had associated nothing with it. Filled with excitement he'd turned the key in the lock, expecting his present to be inside, but he had been confronted only by a piece of rolled-up parchment. Unsure of what to expect, he'd opened it up and seen the Latin aphorism;

*'Dat Deus immiti cornua curta bovi.'*

He recalled staring at it and then saying, "What is this?"

"It is your Christmas present," his father had said.

"But I don't understand it, it doesn't make sense."

"I was expecting you to say that," his father had said. "It now is your task to find out the meaning of the proverb, and when you have, not only will you have learned a valuable lesson, you will also understand why we gave it to you."

It had taken him two weeks to establish the meaning, but one of his tutors had at last translated it for him.

"It means young sir, 'Curst cows have curt horns,' or perhaps, 'angry cows have cut horns'."

"And what is that supposed to mean?" he had said.

"It means that angry men cannot do all the mischief they want. It's true to say that the Latin version proposes more that God gave angry cows cut horns, but whether tendered in Latin or in our northern English dialect, the meaning is the same. Angry men cannot do all the mischief they want!"

That evening he had stood in the parlour holding the parchment, contemplating the day's revelations when his father and brother had entered. They had seen that he'd been made aware of the meaning of the proverb.

"I see that the 'cornua curta bovi' is now cognisant of the worth of our gift," had said his father.

He recalled looking at them both and nodding.

"And you should be always aware, Matthew," his father had continued, "that though you and John were both endowed with the same length of horn at birth, people like me will make it their business to see that your horns remain cut short if you cannot control that vile temper of yours. Hence the depiction on the lid of your chest, placed there as valuable aide memoire from your devoted parents."

The nickname 'cornua curta bovi' or 'cut-horned cow' had stuck until, through prolonged usage, it had been reduced to just 'Bovi.'

Fifty-eight long years ago that had happened, and until he had had Valentine's initials carved into the lid of the chest, it had neither changed, nor been out of his sight for even one day. His father had been right too – the cow's head carving did remind him of his parents' warning about his temper, but that had not been enough for him to curb it, and that had been no more apparent than with the events that had unfolded after he and John had inherited the Whitewall Estate.

In January 1747, his catastrophic temper had overtaken him. What had started as a failure to agree over rent increases had ended up in the final break-up of the Chance family, and the removal of him and John from Whitewall.

His mother and father had never forgiven him for what had ensued, and by the time that they had both died, they had expressed their disgust by bequeathing the Selhurst and Hilltop Estates in their entirety to John alone.

He could remember that morning as clear as day. Cold and crisp it had been; a fog had hung over the moors, and everything had appeared to be grey and claustrophobic looking.

John had won the argument over the percentage amount of increase that should be applied to the crofter's annual rents, but the disagreement had deteriorated and he had become insulting; and as usual, John had risen above it. This, of course, had aggravated him even further, until just as one of the young maidservants had walked in, John had accused him of being puerile and ridiculous.

Knowing that the maidservant had heard his rebuke had pushed him over the edge. He couldn't explain why, but on that day it did.

He knew that John took the horse and trap to the local suppliers at 10am daily and so, armed with a pistol, he had secreted himself behind one of the large sandstone gateposts adjacent to the courtyard, and had awaited his brother's appearance.

As the trap had approached the narrow gateway he'd stepped out, aimed the pistol at his brother's chest, and fired. The sound of the shot had been magnified by the stillness of the air, and as the horse had reared up, he'd seen John fall backwards clutching his chest.

Pandemonium had ensued. Various members of staff had attended either John or the petrified horse, and he'd just stood, with the gun in his hand, watching in silence as the chaotic world had carried on around him.

Life in those few minutes had been dreamlike; he'd felt detached from it. Nobody had looked at him or spoken to him – it was as though he'd been invisible. And then, through the mists of surreal reality John had appeared before him, standing, and looking.

He could see the hole in his brother's waistcoat and the blood around it, and in a moment of supreme self-doubt he'd looked at the gun in his hand to see if it had ever been there.

For several seconds they'd stared at each other in silence until John had proclaimed, "Bovi, – we are brothers no more."

And from that day, until the day he'd died in 1762, not another word had passed between them.

It transpired that the ball from the pistol had struck his brother's combined thick leather wallet and pocket book inside his equally thick overcoat pocket; and though it had split the skin of his chest and knocked him off of the seat of the trap, no more serious damage had been done.

But to him it had. In that one defining action, he'd ostracised himself from the entire Chance family. He'd been despatched to live life alone at Chance Hall on the Scarred Earth Estate, and apart from his necessary staff, that was how he'd remained until he'd started a family of his own.

On the strict proviso that he had never tried to regain tenure, he'd been allowed to retain his half of the Whitewall Estate as his father had always promised, but only as the silent owner with his estranged brother John.

And following that disastrous episode, he hadn't thought that things could get worse, but they had. What he had done in 1762 following John's death had been unforgiveable. Every night he felt the presence of his mother and father staring down at him with contempt, through the mists of time, and he knew that once they were reunited in the next life, he would be brought to account.

Even when he'd had the opportunity to make amends with his beloved grandson, he hadn't, and now the sum result of his despicable behaviour lay in the chest that Valentine so misguidedly cherished.

# Chapter 5

*Tuesday 28<sup>th</sup> March 2006. Rushworth Moor, Lancashire*

It was a beautiful spring day as Naomi cruised along Cragg End Lane, looking for anywhere that could resemble High Farm Cottage. The driver's window was wound down and all the sights, sounds, and distinctive countryside smells pervaded her senses. To the left and right of her trees and hedges of varying height offered little in the way of seeing over them, and as the lane meandered up the Moor it narrowed until it was just wide enough to allow two small vehicles to pass.

The road began a low descent for a short stretch, and as its full extent came into view before the next bend, she saw a grand looking drive veering off to the right, up to two high and imposing wooden gates. She slowed down to see if she could see a house name or number as she glided past, but there was none.

Onwards and upwards the lane snaked through the trees for another half-mile or so until it broke out into open rolling moor top. Five minutes later, the lane terminated one hundred yards ahead at High Farm.

The scenery was breathtaking. In front was the farm; to the left, the cultivated moorland rolled downhill affording her a spectacular view for miles around; to the right, the fields were filled with horses and different breeds of cattle, and it undulated down to a lake, by which, she could see a small red sailing dinghy pulled up onto the bank.

She had to get a photograph or two. Camera in hand, she stepped out of her CRV and was about to start snapping when she heard the toot of a car horn. She stepped backwards as a Range Rover approached and then stopped beside her.

The passenger window wound down and a cheery looking man said, "Good morning! Lovely view isn't it?"

"It's delightful," said Naomi. "I hope that you don't mind..."

"Not at all love," said the man. "I only stopped in case you'd lost your way or something."

Naomi hesitated and then said, "I'm not lost, but I am looking for something."

"What's that then?"

"Perhaps I'd better explain. My name's Naomi Wilkes, I'm a professional historic researcher with Walmsfield Borough Council, trying to locate a building named High Farm Cottage in Cragg End Lane, but there appears to be no sign of it. Have you ever heard of such a place?"

The man lifted the peak of his tweed flat cap and scratched his head for a second.

"Sorry love," he said. "I can't say that I have and I'm very well acquainted with these parts 'cos I'm the local farmer."

"Maybe it was knocked down some years ago," said Naomi, "but thank you for giving me some of your time."

"No problem, sorry I couldn't help," said the farmer.

He smiled, put the Range Rover into gear, and pulled away.

Naomi waved as he departed and was then surprised to see him stop again.

He reversed to where she was standing and said, "I've just thought of something. About a mile back up the lane there's a house with a large driveway and big wooden gates..."

"Yes," said Naomi, "I saw that; the cottage isn't in there, is it?"

"No, I don't believe so, but there's the shell of a small building in the trees opposite. One of the old farmhands told me that it was used to store hay bales and such, but the roof came off it years ago so it's never used now, and it's become overgrown."

"And can I get access to it?"

The farmer looked Naomi up and down and said, "Well, you're not dressed for foraging, but if you don't mind clambering through the foliage, you should be able to get to it."

Naomi recalled the width of the lane and said, "Can I park there okay?"

"No, not really, it's too narrow, and all sorts of idiots fly along there. Park in the large driveway opposite; the house belongs to the local landowner and he only goes there for odd weekends now and then."

Naomi thanked the farmer and turned to walk back to her CRV.

"Hey – my name's Dave Brown by-the-way. If you need anything more come up to the farm and give me a knock. Who knows, I might even have the kettle on!"

Naomi smiled and promised to let him know if she needed anything more.

Once again, Dave pulled away with a cheery smile and wave.

Naomi took one or two snaps of the exquisite scenery and then drove back down the lane to the large driveway, pulled in and stopped.

The minute that she stepped out of her CRV, the thumb pressed down on her shoulder and she heard a sort of muffled grunting sound. She stood stock-still and tried to understand it. It sounded feminine, but because it was muffled she couldn't make it out.

As though aiming a radio aerial, she turned around hoping that she might see something that would focus what she was hearing, and in doing so noticed the pair of imposing gates a short distance in front her. She walked up to them and saw a small coat of arms on each one; there was no family name but the legend below each stated, 'Aquila Non Capit Muscas'. She made a mental note of it and then headed back towards the lane.

It became obvious why she hadn't noticed the old building on the way up to High Farm, because apart from her attention being drawn to the driveway and gates opposite, the whole structure was ninety percent overgrown.

She turned right and walked down the lane, here and there parting the foliage as she moved along; until the small golden sandstone building gave way to a low stone wall. She followed that for another fifty yards or so looking for some kind of entrance, but when none was apparent, she gave up and turned back.

Heading up the incline she followed the wall past the building until it terminated at a single small gatepost. There was no corresponding gatepost opposite, so she checked the ground below her feet for mud, and then pushed her way into the tangled trees.

She found it difficult to proceed because of the way that the branches had grown; they appeared to be wrapped around one another, twisting and arcing left and right or up and down in wild confusion. Every step she took was hampered – it felt as though the boughs were restraining her and urging her not to press forwards – but within a few minutes she broke through and was confronted by the shell of the old building.

Dave had been right; it was small, and she doubted that it had been a cottage at all. There couldn't have been enough room within its confines to accommodate more than two very small rooms on the ground floor, but there were the familiar niches in the walls above the windows, indicating that a second floor had at one time been in situ.

She took a couple of paces towards the doorway, and a sudden gust of wind blew into her face. The trees sprung into life and started to generate a strange groaning sound as the boughs grated against one another. She cast a wary glance around and took another step forwards.

The thumb pressed down on her shoulder and the muffled, grunting sound started again; this time it was much closer and it sounded like a person who had been gagged.

An irrational fear started to manifest itself in her and she started to feel uncomfortable. The wind seemed to grow in intensity, and the closer she got to the building the more restless the branches became. They seemed to prod and poke her at every step.

She ducked below them, retrieved her camera from her handbag, took several photographs, and then stepped into the building. She stopped. The ground below her feet felt springy and soft as though she was on rolled up carpet. She took a couple more steps and found that it was the same wherever she trod; it felt weird and unnatural, but it was covered in compacted soil and was impossible to determine.

Something touched her on the shoulder. She wheeled around in alarm but nothing was there. She felt as though she was being watched and the urge to leave swept over her again.

"Get a grip!" she said out loud. "It's nothing but a bunch of old trees."

She took a couple of deep breaths, and then walked to the opposite side of the building.

Through an open portal she saw the remnants of an overgrown garden surrounded by a low, dry-stone wall. She peered through the dense foliage and noticed a narrow gateway opposite that lead into the trees. In the far left-hand corner was a small, tilted gravestone.

She stepped into the garden, took a few more photographs, and then set the camera to movie mode. She got down on her haunches and commenced a three-hundred-and-sixty degree sweep around.

Suddenly the foliage behind her erupted at ground level. It sounded as though an army of small creatures was sweeping towards her in a wave. She jumped up in alarm and dropped her camera. Goosebumps formed on every part of her body, and her breath came in short gasps. She strained her eyes waiting for something to appear, but it didn't.

She couldn't stand any more. She snatched up the camera, clicked it off, and stuffed it into her handbag. She then fought her way back through the foliage. With a huge sigh of relief, she stepped out into the relative calm of Cragg End Lane. Almost at once the thumb lifted, the muffled, gagged sounds stopped, and the breeze ran out of steam and died.

She returned to her CRV, climbed in, and locked the door. Following several minutes of self-grounding and rationalisation, she decided that she wanted to know a lot more about the cottage. She switched on the engine and drove back up to High Farm to speak to Dave.

She wanted permission to dig the site and to carry out a small geophysical survey and she also wondered whether or not he'd heard of Larkland Fen.

"Larkland Fen, you say?" Dave frowned and said, "Are you sure you don't mean Lark Hill Fen?"

"I don't think so," said Naomi, "but then again I have no means of verifying it one way or the other."

Dave made a 'hmm-ing' sound and said, "The hill leading down to the lake is named Lark Hill, and years back there was a very marshy area at the bottom. I recall as kids we used to call it Lark Hill Mire, or Lark Hill Fen."

Naomi put down her mug of strong tea and said, "Oh."

Silence ensued for few seconds as both mulled things over.

"I'm not absolutely positive because it's been years since I was there," said Dave, "but I also seem to recall that there were the remains of some sort of dilapidated old building there too."

"That sounds compelling..." said Naomi.

"Yes," but as I said, it's been years since I was there so I may be mistaken."

"Could you take me down there this afternoon?"

"No, I can't because it's not part of my land and we'd need permission from the landowner."

"And what if we were to hop over the wall and take a quick peek without anybody knowing?"

"Because trust me, it wouldn't happen. He has security cameras installed everywhere and there's the spooky Les Miserables."

"Les Miserables?" said Naomi. "Don't you mean *Les Miserables,* as per the stage show?"

"No," reiterated Dave. "It's Les Miserables as it sounds; his Christian name is Les, or maybe Leslie, and he's a miserable sod."

Naomi couldn't help smiling; she shook her head and said, "Priceless!"

"Not only is he miserable," said Dave, "he's dangerous too. Rumour has it that whenever he finds anybody on the owner's land, he looses a couple of barrels off over their heads and then threatens to shoot them if they don't vacate straight away. And as if that wasn't bad enough, he's been nicknamed 'The Dark Spectre', because it doesn't matter where people have trespassed

– he's reputed to have appeared from nowhere within minutes. He really is spooky!"

Naomi raised her eyebrows and decided that hopping over the wall wasn't such a good idea after all. She thought for a second and then said, "Could we get permission from the landowners to have a look?"

"I can ask."

Naomi thanked him and said, "Now, can I have your permission to carry out some exploratory tests in and around that old building in Cragg End Lane?"

"What kind of tests?"

"Nothing serious; perhaps a couple of small test pits no more than one metre square below the floor, and a geophysical survey of what appears to be the back garden. It would involve clearing away some of the shrubbery and foliage that has overgrown the place, but it wouldn't have a lasting effect and it wouldn't be seen from the lane."

"It sounds okay to me," said Dave, "and I can't see any reason for objection, but that bit of land is also owned by the same people who own Lark Hill."

Naomi's heart sank. She said, "Well, that's that then, I can't do anymore."

She reached into her handbag, extracted one of her business cards, and handed it to Dave.

"Those are my contact details, and I'd appreciate it if you could get me permission to visit those sites."

Dave looked at the business card and said, "Okay – I'll give them a call after milking tomorrow morning, – then I'll ring you."

Naomi finished her tea, thanked Dave for his hospitality, and left.

She drove out of the farmyard and then pulled up close to where they'd first met. She wound the passenger window down, placed her travel binoculars up to her eyes, and scanned the land around the lake at the bottom of Lark Hill.

Out of the blue, the thumb pressed down upon her left shoulder; the pain was so intense that she stopped what she was doing and rubbed it for a few seconds with her right hand.

"Go! Go now," said a quiet female voice with a strong northern accent.

Naomi tried to rationalise what she'd heard, but couldn't see any reason why she should leave. She wasn't parked in a dangerous or illegal position, and she was alone. High Farm was just one-hundred yards away and she had her mobile phone. She'd learned to trust the voices over the years, and she always heeded them in potentially dangerous situations, but just sometimes she wanted to make her own decisions.

"Go," urged the voice once more. "Go now."

Naomi ignored it and scanned the area at the bottom of Lark Hill one more time. She saw nothing discernible until she reached a small wooded copse; then the thumb pressed down once again and the voice repeated, "Go." She ignored it and kept on looking.

As her gaze alighted upon one section of the copse she noticed something small and black; she stared at it for a few seconds but couldn't make it out. She adjusted the focus wheel of the binoculars and looked again.

She was looking at another pair of binoculars looking at her. She snatched hers down and tried to appear like a tourist taking in the view. She allowed several minutes to pass and then looked down at the copse without the aid of the binoculars. She saw nothing. She scoured the land around and still saw nothing. The pressure from the thumb was almost unbearable, but unable to resist temptation; she picked up the binoculars and looked at the copse once again.

This time a figure stepped into view and stared straight at her through his binoculars.

Naomi only caught a fleeting glimpse of the man before she feigned looking elsewhere, but his appearance had an immediate effect on her. He looked very tall, was wearing a full-length black overcoat down to his shoes, his collar was turned up and he wore a wide brimmed hat similar to a Homburg. He also appeared to be thin and gaunt.

Within seconds she returned to her CRV and set off back down Cragg End Lane.

In much less than five minutes, she swept up the incline adjacent to the shell of the cottage in the trees, when to her utmost astonishment, she saw the same gaunt figure staring straight at her from the opposite driveway.

It had been impossible for him to get from the bottom of Lark Hill to where he was in the short time that it had taken her to drive there. She was staggered.

As she drove past he raised a bony, pale hand and pointed his forefinger at her. It felt as though she'd been stabbed by ice; it spread through her like a cold wave and manifested itself in the worst threat that she'd ever known.

It only lasted for a few seconds, but she knew from the look of his skeletal, sallow face and deep-set black eyes that the experience would remain with her for a long time afterwards.

# Chapter 6

*Wednesday 29<sup>th</sup> March 2006. Christadar Property Holdings, Manchester*

"And why does she want to carry out the research, Mr Brown?" Dominic Sheldon, the Estates Manager, settled back in his chair and listened with interest.

"According to Mrs Wilkes, she is researching people who lived in the locality and wants to try to build up a picture of everyday life in the mid-1800s."

"So she isn't looking for anything specific?"

"No. She is aware that a couple of buildings on the estate once housed local working people, and she wants to dig a couple of test pits and carry out a couple of geophysical surveys to see if she can discover anything more about them, their domiciles, and their way of life."

"And it won't disrupt anything?" said Dominic.

"Not according to her. She promised that she would return the sites to their previous appearances and said that any minor foliage clearance would soon re-grow."

Dominic pondered the situation for a few seconds and then said, "I'll have to run it past Christiana, but I can't see it being a problem."

"Okay," said Dave. "I promised to give her a ring and let her know your decision."

Dominic paused and then said, "Alright – leave it for an hour, and if you don't hear from me, you can ring her and say that it's okay to proceed. Tell her that she'll need to send Mr Spooner the proposed locations and a planned itinerary, by email, with a copy to this office at least one week before she commences work."

"Mr Spooner?"

"Yes, Leslie Spooner, the gamekeeper at Cragg End."

"Ah, Les Miserables!" said Dave. "I didn't know his name was Spooner."

"Well, now you do," said Dominic, showing no sign of amusement.

Dave cleared his throat and said, "Yes, of course – sorry Mr Sheldon. I'll wait an hour and then make the call if I haven't heard from you."

"Very well. Goodbye."

Dave put the telephone receiver down and muttered, "Touchy…" He looked at the old grandfather clock in the corner of his living room and made a mental note of the time.

Thirty miles away, Naomi jumped up from behind her desk and opened her office door as Postcard Percy approached.

Percy smiled, cast a furtive glance at Naomi's mini-skirt, and said, "Good afternoon, my dear. What a pleasurable sight you are for these old eyes."

He loved visiting Naomi. Most of the other Council employees showed little or no interest in his copious bundles of memorabilia, his old newspaper cuttings, local historical artefacts and of course his numerous old postcards from which he had gained his nickname, but with her it was different; it was always a rewarding and satisfying experience, and one from which they both benefitted.

Naomi sat Percy down, gave him a cup of tea, and brought him up to date with the events on Rushworth Moor. She also told him that she was awaiting an answer from Dave Brown about the request to carry out further research.

Percy frowned when he heard the part about Les Miserables' inexplicable and scary appearances in Cragg End Lane and said, "I'm sorry to interrupt you dear, but could you confirm his name again for me?"

"Dave Brown the local farmer said that his name was Les Miserables but I suppose that it could be anything."

Percy wrote it down on a pad and then said, "You know, the incident with the wind-blown foliage near the cottage could have a rational explanation, but that spooky gamekeeper sounds much more interesting."

"Dave said that he was known as The Dark Spectre..."

"The Dark Spectre? What a delicious name; I look forward to researching him."

"And the rest," said Naomi. "I'd appreciate you digging into your material and seeing if you have anything on either of those locations."

Percy frowned and said, "I will look, but I've tended to concentrate my research around Wordale and Rochdale, and my notes may be sparse."

"I telephoned my parents at the weekend and they have promised to come up and give a hand..."

"How is Sam and...?" interrupted Percy.

"Jane. They're both very well thank you."

"Please send them my regards, and tell them that I'm looking forward to working with them again."

"I will," said Naomi. "Dad also told me about a curator named Daphne Pettigrew at Wordale Cottage Museum, but he's asked me to leave her to him. It sounds as though he really likes her."

"Well, she's a character. I'll vouch for that."

Naomi frowned as she took on board the second reference to Daphne Pettigrew being odd, but she guessed that all would be revealed soon enough.

"Gasworks!" said Percy.

"Gasworks?" repeated Naomi, "Which gasworks?"

"Not *which,* dear – it's who."

"So who is he? And why is he named Gasworks?"

Percy faltered for a few seconds as he chose his words.

"He's a good friend of many years acquaintanceship. He has a huge knowledge of Rushworth and district, and he's nicknamed Gasworks because, because..."

"He has I.B.S.?"

"I.B.S.?"

"Irritable Bowel Syndrome," said Naomi,

"Well, I don't know about that. I just know that he has a bad habit of treading on ducks."

"Treading on ducks?" said Naomi, "What on earth...?"

"Try to link his nickname with the sound that could ensue from such an activity..."

Naomi thought for a second and then burst out laughing. "What are you like, Percy?" she said. "And where on earth did you get that analogy?"

Percy shrugged his shoulders and gave in to some light laughter himself.

A few minutes later he said, "Okay, joking aside, I'll contact him as soon as I can and put him to work, and I'll give you a call if he comes up with anything."

He looked down at his watch and said, "Got to go, dear."

He pulled himself to his feet and then remembered something. He said, "By-the-way, if Gasworks ever mentions his machine, just go along with it and I'll explain it to you later."

Naomi smiled and said, "Okay – I think..." She shook her head as she waved goodbye. Life was always interesting and unpredictable with Percy and his band of weird and wonderful associates.

Just before lunch the phone rang and Dave Brown confirmed that he had received permission for her to be able to proceed with the investigations on Rushworth Moor. She thanked him and promised to send the required details to Les Miserables and to the Christadar offices.

She glanced up at the clock on her wall, jotted down a few initial notes and then went to join Carlton in the Ryming Ratt for lunch.

On the way over to the nearby pub, she recalled that she hadn't told Carlton what had happened to her on Rushworth Moor. He had brought home some pressing work and by the time that he'd finished, he'd been exhausted. She'd mentioned the visit, but she hadn't gone into detail.

She stepped into the warm and comforting atmosphere of their favourite lunchtime venue, picked her way through the tables, and caught sight of Carlton studying a menu.

The light from the window behind him highlighted the grey that was starting to creep into his full head of dark hair. Despite being at the wrong end of his forties, he still looked strong and muscular. His expensive dark blue suit, crisp white shirt, and perfectly matched silk tie gave him the appearance of being a man on top of his game. She was still impressed and pleased by him, even after four years of marriage.

"I don't like the sound of that place in Cragg End Lane and I don't like the sound of that creepy gamekeeper either," said Carlton as they sipped their coffees after lunch. "And his nickname, The Dark Spectre, it's enough to give you nightmares! Why on earth didn't you tell me about him along with all the other stuff last night?"

"Because you were busy and I knew that you'd react like this."

"So what's different now?"

"Now I've got Percy and Gasworks onto the case, and it's out of my hands."

"Gasworks?" said Carlton.

Naomi leaned close to her husband's ear and said, "He's a friend of Percy's, and he treads on ducks!"

Carlton laughed out loud and nearly spit his coffee across the table. "Damn it Mimi," he said, "the stuff you come out with…"

They chuckled for a while until Carlton said, "On a more serious note, promise me that you won't go anywhere near those places on Rushworth Moor without letting me know first."

He knew that Naomi was careful and levelheaded, but he couldn't help feeling protective.

Naomi smiled up at him; it was part of what made her love him.

"I won't, I promise," she said.

Halfway through the afternoon, the telephone rang on Naomi's desk. She picked it up and said, "Good afternoon Naomi…"

"Ah yes, Mrs Wilkes, Naomi – er, Craig Brompton here."

"Yes, Professor, how can I help you?"

There was a slight pause. "Well, it's all rather embarrassing, and I most sincerely apologise. Nothing has ever happened to me like this before."

Naomi opened her mouth to speak but was cut off.

"And let me assure you that nothing like this will ever happen again!"

"Professor," said Naomi. "What is it?"

"We've found another letter addressed to the Chance family."

Naomi's heart raced. She said, "Where? In the old wall safe?"

"Well that's just it, you see," said Brompton. "It was in the safe and we found it a few days ago but we, er, just found it again ten minutes ago."

"I don't understand," said Naomi. "What do you mean you found it again ten minutes ago?"

There was no avoiding it. Brompton cleared his throat and then said, "It had somehow dropped down behind my desk, and upon my return yesterday I thought that the girls had given you both envelopes, but then I dropped my rubber..."

"Dropped your *rubber*?" repeated Naomi wickedly.

"No, no, I didn't mean... I meant my pencil rubber."

Naomi couldn't help smiling to herself, but remained silent.

"It was then that I noticed it on the floor in front of my feet..."

"Your rubber?" said Naomi turning the screw some more.

"No, the other letter."

Naomi could hear Brompton's obvious discomfort and said, "It's all right, Professor – this sort of thing can happen to anybody."

"Not to me it can't!" said Brompton with conviction. There was a slight pause and then he said, "Well not until today, that is... Anyway, we have the letter here for you whenever you're ready."

"Who is it addressed to, Professor?"

Naomi heard movement at the other end of the phone as Brompton retrieved the envelope.

"To a Mr Alexander Chance of Chance Hall in the District of Spotland."

Naomi puzzled for a few seconds but couldn't recall mention of an Alexander Chance in her previous investigations into the family history.

"Very well," she said. "I'll be over for it tomorrow."

She put down her phone and tried to place Alexander in the family tree. She recalled reading his name somewhere, but couldn't place it.

Following several seconds of conjecture about what could be in the letter, she shrugged and decided that speculation was a waste of time. She would have the answer soon enough.

# Chapter 7

*March 1792. Chance Hall*

Matthew was awakened by a voice.

"Begging your pardon, sir…"

He stirred, but it was as cold as the grave in his bedchamber and he had no inclination to respond.

"Mr Matthew, sir!"

This time the voice was more insistent. He ignored it and remained still.

"Please Mr Matthew, – sir," said the voice. "We have a visitor in a fine looking uniform and he's asking for you…"

Matthew thought for a few seconds then lifted his head up and looked across the room. He recognised the young maidservant, whose shapely backside had always caught his eye.

"What kind of uniform, girl?"

"I don't know, sir, but it isn't like my father's militia outfit."

Matthew huffed and said, "What colour is it, for pity's sake?"

"It's a blue coat, white shirt and white breeches with…"

Matthew interrupted her flow.

"Damn it, girl, that's Royal Navy. Go and put him in the library, offer him a drink and tell him that I'll be down presently."

The maidservant nodded and turned to leave.

"Wait!" said Matthew. "What time of day is it, and where are my son and his wife?"

"Just after eleven of the clock, sir. Mr Alexander has taken the trap into Bury and Mrs Elizabeth is with cook."

"Very well, go and ask Elizabeth to meet me in the library."

Matthew pulled himself out of bed and shuffled across to his wardrobe. He pulled out his finest shirt, breeches and coat. If he was to receive news of Valentine from a Naval Officer, he wanted to make sure that he looked like a proper country gentleman and not a shabby old scarecrow.

In the library, Fourth Lieutenant Christian Gartside stood up and bowed his head as first Elizabeth and then Matthew entered. The formal introductions were completed and they all sat down.

Elizabeth asked the question that had been upon the whole family's mind.

"What news do you have of Valentine?"

Lieutenant Gartside looked with gravity at both faces and said, "I am sorry to say this, madam, but there is none."

"What do you mean, none?" said Matthew, "He's an officer in the Navy; it's your business to know!"

Gartside cleared his throat and said, "That's as maybe, Mr Chance sir, but it changes nought. I have, as Valentine's closest friend, been despatched here by my Captain to inform you that he is missing."

Elizabeth clasped her hands to her mouth.

"You're not implying…?"

"No, madam, I am not."

"Damn it all man," said an exasperated Matthew. "Explain yourself; can't you see how upsetting this is for his mother?"

Gartside cast a sideways glance at Elizabeth.

"It was not my intention to come here and upset you, madam; on the contrary, if it's of any comfort to you at all, I'm of the firmest conviction that he is fine. Time and again Valentine has surprised us with his ingenuity, honesty, and clear head – qualities that are often wanting in much older men. Unfortunately, it was because of those admirable virtues that we find ourselves in this hapless situation."

Elizabeth and Matthew looked at each other, and then with a slight shake of her head Elizabeth said, "Lieutenant Gartside, we know nothing of our son's successes or failures; indeed, you are the first person to whom we have been able to speak about him, so please tell us everything that you know."

Gartside nodded and sat back in his chair.

"Very well, I shall do my best to stick to the salient points.

"I met and befriended Valentine aboard *HMS Spartan*, where we were both Midshipmen under the command of Captain Edward Telford. We departed Liverpool in June 1790, bound for the Colonies, and our orders took us to various destinations along the eastern coast of America, until early in November of the same year we arrived in Charleston, Carolina.

"There, and following my promotion to Fourth Lieutenant in the latter part of 1790, both Valentine and I were transferred to *HMS Discovery* under the command of Captain George Vancouver, with instructions to proceed to the north-west coast of America to chart the waterways and to establish peaceful trading relations with the local Indians."

Matthew rocked back in his chair and grinned from ear to ear.

Elizabeth was the first to notice this most unusual occurrence from a man she considered to be of a stern and intolerant disposition.

Gartside looked too, and stopped talking.

Seeing both faces staring at him only served to heighten Matthew's enjoyment.

"Gracious me, father!" said Elizabeth, "What takes you so?"

Matthew continued chuckling until he said, "Well, listen to young Gartside here talking about himself and Val in such a matter-of-fact way! Crossing oceans, charting new waters and trading with American savages, if you please!"

"Sir, I must protest," said Gartside. "They are not savages, they…"

"Yes, yes – I know," said Matthew, sweeping aside the protestation, "but wasn't it just a short while past when the lad's only adventures were to be gleaned from books in the library? And now, listen, he is seeing things and experiencing life in a way that we would never dream about!"

Gartside reflected upon his account, realising that those things he considered to be a part of normal Navy life had to sound like high adventure to the uninitiated.

Elizabeth too lapsed into silence, until she realised that Matthew's observation had stopped their visitor's narrative.

"Well thank you for that, father," she said, "but we should not impose upon Lieutenant Gartside's time; he may have more important matters to attend to than regale us with this account."

Gartside said, "Not at all, madam. I have devoted this day to these proceedings and have no other items to attend to."

"Then you must lunch with us before you go. I insist." Elizabeth's invitation left no room for dissent.

Gartside accepted and said, "And I would be very happy if you would call me Christian instead of Lieutenant Gartside."

Elizabeth nodded, sent for a maid, and then imparted instructions to her about the revised numbers for lunch; after which, she asked Gartside to continue.

"Very well," he said. "In September 1791, we entered the Strait of Juan de Fuca, south of what is now named Vancouver Island, and there met with an American Merchantman under the command of one Captain Robert Gray.

Following an amicable meeting and exchange of information, Valentine was called for. It transpired that Captain Gray had some weeks hence had to put down a revolt instigated by a member of his crew, which had resulted in two of his officers being killed. He'd made it known to Captain Vancouver that he was in need of the services of a reliable, honest, and levelheaded young officer as a temporary substitute for one of his own murdered officers, and Valentine had been deemed to be the most suitable.

It was agreed that the two vessels meet the following November, near the estuary of the great west river which Captain Gray had named the Columbia River, – but we never saw them again.

Captain Vancouver sent several parties ashore and established that Captain Gray had been trading animal pelts with the local Indians in return for iron objects and that he had departed.

Several more weeks we sailed those waters, but with never a sight of Captain Gray's vessel, the *Columbia Rediviva*, until in accordance with our orders, we left."

Matthew was stunned by the cavalier way that a vessel of the Royal Navy had sailed away and left Valentine.

"But surely you couldn't just abandon him like that?" he said.

"We had no option, sir. We were under strict orders to return to St. Augustine in Florida, where we were to pick up and escort a local dignitary back to Boston. Captain Vancouver stayed several weeks longer than he should as it was."

Unable to conceal her anguish, Elizabeth said, "But did you hear *nothing* of his fate?"

Gartside shot a glance downwards and appeared unsure of how to answer.

"Well, Christian?" said Elizabeth.

The young officer looked into the eyes of the mother of his best friend, and decided upon openness.

"It seems, madam," he said, "that the local Indians had traded pelts with Captain Gray fifteen months earlier in 1790, following which he'd sailed across the Pacific Ocean to China to trade."

"Yes, but what has that got to do with Valentine?" asked an aggravated Matthew.

Gartside hesitated for a second and then said, "Well... This is entirely unofficial, you understand?"

Elizabeth and Matthew nodded.

"I overheard Lieutenant Puget telling Captain Vancouver that Captain Gray had returned to Canton in China to trade their pelts for tea."

Normally dignified and reserved, Elizabeth couldn't help herself; a tear rolled down her left cheek, she dropped her head and said, "No!"

"That's downright outrageous, Gartside!" bellowed Matthew. "Going off and leaving him to his fate when you had a notion he could end up in China, for pity's sake!"

"Sir, it was not my decision to make! I did not command the *Discovery*."

"Nevertheless, I'll be having strong words with my contact at the Admiralty, you just see if I don't!"

Gartside regretted his frankness and said, "But sir, I beseech you, my last comments were only what I overheard and formed no part of the official explanation for Valentine's current situation. It was because he and I were such good friends that I decided to tell you everything that I know. In truth, if you do now take my Captain to task over my witless comments, he will both deny their validity *and* have me put on a charge!"

Elizabeth brought her emotions into check and realised that, despite Gartside being a naval officer, he was still young, and that although he may be lacking in the art of discretion, he was indeed being honest with his best friend's family.

She calmed the blustering Matthew, thanked Gartside for his frankness, and assured him that his comments would go no further.

During the enjoyable lunch that followed, Gartside recounted some of his and Valentine's adventures to his enthralled hosts until at last it was time to leave.

At 15:00 hours he bid farewell, and departed for Liverpool.

The sound of the grandmother clock in Matthew's bedchamber seemed to permeate every part of his brain. *Tick*, the pendulum swung; *tock*. *Tick*, the pendulum swung; *tock*. The ticking and the tocking were a mirror image of his heart. Each sound echoed a beat, and like the beats of his heart, as each one passed it drew one beat closer to the time that both would stop.

*Tick* – the sound spread through the stillness of his chamber like the ripples on a disturbed pond – *tock*.

Matthew lay huddled beneath the heavy bedclothes and pondered the day's events. Fate, he thought, seemed determined to deny him happiness; he'd hoped that the officer visiting that day would be bringing news of Valentine's return, but he had not.

"China indeed!" he thought as he lay between the cold cotton sheets. "My poor lad, half way around the world and trading animal skins for tea! Bah!"

His only consolation had been his last minute decision to speak to Gartside before he'd left for Liverpool.

"If you ever see Valentine again," he'd said, "or ever find yourself in a position to be able to get a message to him, please tell him that his grandfather Matthew said this – 'Ignore your box; your inheritance is the Whitewall Estate.'"

64

Lying there, he determined that if it was to be the last thing that he did in his life, he would put those things right that he had promised to do time and time again.

He and Alexander would do it on the morrow, for certain.

The carriage bearing Gartside clattered across the sets inside Liverpool Dockyard and awoke him. Despite the lateness of hour, he recalled Matthew's garbled but impassioned plea and determined to pass on the message that he'd been given for Valentine.

He pulled out the piece of paper that he'd scribbled it upon before leaving Chance Hall, and read the words once again.

'In your box is your inheritance, the Whitewall Estate.'

# Chapter 8

*Thursday 30<sup>th</sup> March 2006. The Vical Centre, Newton*

As Naomi ascended the steps to The Vical Centre, this time dressed in a skirt that terminated below the knee, she waited for a comment, and true to form it came.

"Good morning love, I've just cooked a fry-up – would you like to sample my sausage?"

Naomi couldn't help smiling to herself. She didn't feel in the least threatened, and enjoyed the repartee. She turned around and saw several workers standing at the bottom of the steps, one of whom had a small frying pan in his hand.

She called back, "I only like jumbo sausages, and looking at the size of your equipment, it would appear that you're a chipolata man!"

A peal of laughter broke out at the bottom of the steps as several of the other workmen ribbed the one that made the comment.

Smiling to herself, Naomi knocked on the door of the Conservation Suite and entered.

"Are those idiots bothering you?" said Nina, "'Cos if they are, I can report them."

"No, of course they're not," said Naomi. "I know that some women could take offence, but I think it's only a bit of light-hearted banter."

Nina nodded and said, "Alright, if you say so. I'll go and put the kettle on. Helen has your letter."

Naomi walked across to a vacant place and sat down as Helen deposited the letter in front of her. Once again she took a couple of close-up photos of the envelope, put on her cotton gloves and then opened it.

Nina and Charlotte joined Helen and peered over Naomi's shoulder as she removed the letter and spread it on a muslin cloth on the table.

The script was neat and precise.

*Alexander Chance Esquire,*
*Chance Hall,*
*Clough Moor,*
*Spotland,*
*The County of Lancashire,*
*England.*

*10th February, 1829.*

*My Dearest Father,*
*I pray that this missive finds you in good health and spirits and that Captain Gartside has safely delivered it into your hands.*

*I am well, as are Agnes, James, and Nathan. I regret not having written sooner and more often, but the time flies by at an ever-increasing rate and though this is the poorest of excuses, I hope that you can forgive me for my lapses.*

*First, I have a confession to make!*

*A few months ago I gave in to curiosity and opened Grandfather Matthew's chest. Even after all these years it was in good condition; the wood was neither affected by worm, weather or age, and is a testament to the quality of good old English oak.*

*Here I must admit that I found myself astounded that I have no recollection of you ever telling me that you were aware of the contents of the chest, but they were a great surprise to me.*

*Inside was a parchment scroll, showing some evidence of deterioration, upon which was written the Latin aphorism 'Dat Deus immiti cornua curta bovi'.*

*I was at first mystified by the words, but with the help of a local academic soon learnt the literal meaning; but the significance of it and how that relates to my inheritance of the Whitewall Estate is a complete mystery to me.*

*I now beseech you to enlighten your perplexed son and throw some light upon that anomalous dictum!*

*Now I have something of great import to pass on to you. You know that I am now a very wealthy man; my family here in America is very well provided for, but of late I have begun to despair about the level of indulgence practised by my two sons, who appear to be doing everything in their power to drink and gamble away the family fortune.*

*As a consequence, and unknown to them I have placed a very large and very rare ruby in a secret place.*

*I first came by this stone in 1806 whilst visiting the Marquesas Quays, a group of islands south of Florida. At the time I was a 2$^{nd}$ Lieutenant in the US Navy, and had come upon a bunch of ruffians trying to rob an old lady of the pitiful amount of coins that she possessed. I despatched them and accompanied her back to her home and was invited in. In an incredible gesture of kindness, she gave me the stone; a stone that she told me had been recovered by her husband, a native diver of the Marquesas, from a sunken Spanish treasure ship named the Santa Margarita. She told me that the stone was named 'El Fuego de Marte' (The Fire of Mars), and that the Spanish had employed local divers to try to recover it and any other treasure that they could find, but because they were paid such a pitiable sum by the Spanish, many of them kept what they found. She told me that when her husband found the one piece that they were all looking for he brought it home and hid it, but that he had never been able to sell it for fear of being branded a thief and hanged.*

*I tried to insist that she keep the stone, but she argued that she had no children and was too old and too afraid to sell it, and that I should have it in the hope that one day it may benefit my family in a way that it could not hers.*

*In the end, I accepted it, and insisted that she take all the coin I had on me. Later that day we parted company.*

*I have not until this dispatch ever told anybody, including my wife and sons, about this stone but now feel it necessary to inform you of its whereabouts, as I will my sons, – but their letter will only be able to be opened upon the occasion of my death.*

*And so that the whereabouts of the stone cannot be found by somebody waylaying and reading this tome, I have devised two contrivances that can only be solved with what appears to be Grandfather's chest.*

*I hope that by doing this I will secure the longevity and fortune of the family here, but that should something overcome us all in America, there will also be the opportunity for somebody to come from England to recover it.*

*The contrivances are thus –*

*"First the – chest you must obtain, then seek the truth within. Grain o' truth on topmost board, when first you order all discord."*

*And upon solving that, this is the second –*

*"Grandfather's name 'after deed', 'tween here and there and then proceed, to go below 'mid soil and seed. Now at last the gift discover, oh joyous day beside the river."*

*Because of the first rate quality of Grandfather's chest, I have used that to secrete the stone. I have transferred the old parchment scroll to a pine chest of similar design, and I have even had the original carvings recreated.*

*No doubt time and familiarity will lead my subsequent heirs to think that this is the chest from Chance Hall, but you and I will know that it is not. We will also know that the trail to 'El Fuego de Marte' stems from that reproduction; and I also like to think that the eventual discovery of the stone will be further enhanced by knowing that it is contained within the original chest.*

*Now at last it is an immutable truth that an inheritance lies within that place that Grandfather Matthew always promised it would be!*

*Take good care of yourself, my dearest father. I look forward to hearing from you soon.*

*I remain your devoted son,*
*Valentine.*

Silence reigned for several minutes as each person re-read the letter.

"Wow," said Nina. "How intriguing."

Naomi's mind had gone into overdrive. She sat pondering for a few moments as comments were passed between the other girls. She too had thought that the chest she'd seen in Florida had been the original, but it hadn't.

"I love puzzles," said Helen reaching for a pen and pad. "I'm going to write down those 'contrivances' and see if I can work them out."

Naomi didn't give Helen's statement a second thought; the possibility of Valentine inheriting Whitewall had thrown her mind into confusion.

She knew that Valentine's grandfather Matthew had at one time owned Whitewall with his twin brother John, but she hadn't ever questioned why no member of Matthew's side of the family had ever attempted to assist her Great Aunt Maria in re-acquiring ownership of the Estate once the hitherto unlocated Tenancy Agreement had expired. She was also aware that Valentine and his successive heirs had remained in America, but the inconvenience of being on a different continent didn't explain why neither he, nor any other member of his family, had ever pursued that right of ownership. Whitewall had been a substantial piece of real estate in the early 1800s, and would have been worth a lot of money.

When she'd opened the chest in America in 2002, she'd seen the fragments of parchment lying in the bottom and only one small piece had conveyed the partial words 'eus immit' upon it. She now understood that she had been reading the remains of the 'anomalous dictum' that Valentine had referred to – 'Dat D*eus immit*i cornua curta bovi'.

She sat back in her chair and tapped her right fingernails on the table. She now needed to know the meaning of that aphorism, and how it related to Whitewall.

Her train of thought was interrupted by Charlotte.

"I love the name of that ruby, 'El Fuego de Marte'! Do you think that they ever found it?" she said.

Naomi looked at her, ordered her mind, and said, "I don't know. You'd think so."

"Is there any way of verifying that?"

Naomi thought for a few seconds and then said, "Well, Valentine's descendants do have that reproduction chest in Florida, so I could convey the first of the contrivances to them and ask them if they can make any sense out of it."

"Yes," said Helen joining in the conversation. "Please do. Valentine stated in his letter that the trail to it stems from that so it would be fascinating to see if they could find any more clues."

Naomi promised to do as she was asked, and half an hour later bid farewell with an undertaking to keep in touch.

She drove away from The Vical Centre with two things to do; a light-hearted request to the Farlingtons in Florida, and an altogether more serious need to talk to Percy about the 'anomalous dictum'.

At 7:30pm that evening, the Chief Executive Officer of Christadar Property Holdings, Christiana, sat sipping a dry martini with her prominent businessman and multi-millionaire husband Adrian Darke, prior to having dinner at one of Manchester's top city centre hotels.

She placed her glass down on the table in front of her and said, "I had an unusual request about our place at Cragg End yesterday."

Adrian glanced across the table at his beautiful and elegant wife. She still had the innate sexiness about her that had attracted him in the first place; her flawless olive skin and dark curly hair showed her Italian ancestry, but unlike some of those ageing Italian 'mommas', she had matured into a very sophisticated, confident, shapely and sensual woman who always attracted male attention wherever she went.

"Oh yes," he said. "What was that about then?"

"Some local historical research group requested permission to carry out a geophysical survey, followed by a few small digs on two areas of our land."

Adrian frowned and said, "Why?"

"It would seem that they are trying to establish how the common man lived in the 19<sup>th</sup> century, and we have the remains of two workers cottages that they want to look into."

"And where are these old cottages?"

"One is that overgrown shell of a building opposite our gates in Cragg End Lane and the other is somewhere near the lake at the bottom of Lark Hill."

Adrian shrugged and said, "Well, well, whatever next? Did you give them permission to proceed?"

"Yes," said Christiana. "I didn't see what harm it could do."

Adrian said, "That'll keep Les occupied for a bit, then!"

Christiana flashed a look at her husband, "I wish you'd get rid of him," she said. "He makes my skin crawl…"

Adrian thought for a few seconds and then said, "I can't do that; he's been on the estate longer than we have. And who knows? Generations of his family may have lived in that old cottage."

"Have you ever been inside it?"

"No, I haven't – but then again, why would I?"

Christiana gave an involuntary shiver as she thought about their gamekeeper. Every time that she'd tried to take a quiet walk on any part of the estate, he'd appeared out of nowhere, always dressed in the same dark clothes.

He hadn't spoken to her at any time; he'd just raised his hat with his long bony fingers and nodded an acknowledgement. She'd responded as best as she could each time without looking into his fearful eyes, and then he'd seem to disappear without a trace, but as she'd progressed along each of her walks, she'd had the distinct feeling that she was being followed.

A thought popped into her head; she looked up and said, "How old is he? Maybe he's passed his retirement age…"

Adrian looked at her face with a semi-resigned look and said, "I've no idea, but you know that doesn't make a difference. Even if we tried to retire him what would we do, ask him to vacate his cottage?"

Christiana shrugged and said, "Maybe…"

"We couldn't do that and you know it; and besides, he's very effective at curbing trespassers."

A waiter appeared out of nowhere, leaned down, and said, "Madam, sir, your table is ready in the bistro."

Both acknowledged him, finished their drinks, and stood up.

As Christiana followed the waiter, she turned to her husband and said, "I'm not surprised that we don't have any trespassers up there. He scares the shit out of me, and we own the place."

Adrian waited until his wife was facing forwards again; he then looked down and smiled to himself.

# Chapter 9

*Friday 31ˢᵗ March 2006. Naomi and Carlton Wilkes' house*

Just before 11:45pm, Naomi tapped the last full stop on the keyboard of her laptop and sat back in her cream leather office chair.

The house was silent, Carlton was in bed asleep, and since the central heating had switched off at 10:30pm, everywhere had started to feel chilly. She'd been determined to complete an important report before retiring, and because she only needed six hours sleep per night, the pending 12:30am bedtime was just another of her regular occurrences.

She read through her text and, satisfied that it was okay, hit the 'Print' button. The printer sprang into life and deposited the report into the document tray; she retrieved it, reached down to put it into her briefcase, and then jerked backwards in alarm.

The black silk hem of a full-length dress swept past her right hand and then disappeared.

With a thumping heart, she sat bolt upright and looked around the dimly illuminated room. She jumped up from her seat and switched on the main overhead light. Nothing was there.

She placed her right hand on her left shoulder, but felt no psychic indication. For several minutes she stood waiting for anything, but when nothing happened, she decided that it must have been her mind playing tricks.

Fifteen minutes later she climbed into bed alongside Carlton and switched off her bedside light. She turned onto her right side, pulled the duvet into her neck and prepared to let sleep overtake her.

Seconds later her eyes sprang open. She turned onto her back and looked down at the foot of the bed.

Standing in the darkness was a woman in a black full-length dress. She had on a pair of black gloves, an old-fashioned bonnet and she carried a small umbrella or something similar. Naomi didn't feel afraid. She stared back at the figure that was staring down at her.

For what seemed like several minutes, they looked at each other in total silence until the woman moved around the bed and bent closer.

The orange glow of the outside street lamp shone through a crack in the curtains and illuminated the woman's face as she passed it, causing Naomi to wonder whether she was real or not, but before she could respond the woman leaned closer and mouthed something. It appeared to be a two-syllable word that she was trying to say, but no sound was forthcoming.

Naomi lifted her head up from the pillow and looked closer.

The woman opened her mouth and once again mouthed what appeared to be "bad dog" or "mad dog", or something similar. She repeated this several times over and then stood up straight and nodded.

Naomi closed her tired eyes and rubbed them for the briefest of seconds, but when she opened them, the woman had gone. The only thing that remained was a strong scent of violets.

She didn't know how long she remained awake after that. She didn't try to rationalise what she had seen, she didn't feel perturbed, and she felt calm, – calm, and deeply comforted.

At 7:15am Carlton leaned over Naomi, kissed her on the cheek, and said, "It's quarter-past-seven, pet, time to get up."

Naomi rolled over, opened one eye, and said, "Do I have to?"

"Yes, you do. You've got to present that report to the Rochdale Historic Society this morning." He paused for a second and then said, "Did you manage to finish it last night?"

The memory of the previous night's visitation flooded back. Naomi opened her mouth to speak but was cut off.

"And have you been using a new perfume or deodorant?"

Naomi frowned and said, "No, why?"

"It smells like violets in here. I noticed it as soon as I woke up. I opened the window a bit more before my shower, but it still smells as strong now. What did you use?"

Naomi sat up and slid her feet out from the warmth of the duvet; she reached across to her bedside shelf for a glass of water and took a sip.

"It wasn't me," she said. "It was somebody else."

"What? What do you mean somebody else?" Carlton stopped tying his customary Windsor knot and turned around to face Naomi.

"Last night somebody, or perhaps something, appeared at the end of our bed and stared at me…"

"What?" said Carlton. "And you said nothing?"

"No, it wasn't like that. She wasn't a real person, she was a… a…"

"A what?"

"Well I hesitate to say it, but I think that she was a…"

"A ghost? Is that what you are trying to say?"

"Well, yes, and no – she was more like a visitor from the past."

"A visitor from the past?"

"Yes, or more to the point, a visitor from *my* past."

Carlton sat down on the edge of the bed and looked at his wife. He'd had to come to terms with all sorts of strange goings on since falling in love with her, but she'd never reported seeing anything or anybody in their home before.

"And didn't you feel afraid or alarmed?" he said.

"No, on the contrary. I believe that she was here to tell me something."

Carlton expelled a long breath and stared at his wife.

"She came close to me as I lay in bed, leaned over, and appeared to say, "bad dog" or "mad dog", or something like that."

Carlton frowned and repeated, "Bad dog? Mad dog? What on earth is that supposed to mean?"

"I've no idea because I couldn't hear a word she was saying. She appeared to be trying to speak, but it never happened. She mouthed the phrase once or twice more, I closed my eyes to rub them, and when I opened them again she'd gone. That's when I noticed the smell of violets."

"Good grief, pet," said Carlton, turning to stare out of the bedroom window. "That sounds hellish spooky to me." He sat in silence for a few seconds and then said, "You said that you thought she was a visitor from your past; have you any idea who?"

Naomi pursed her lips and hesitated before replying. She knew that her answer would be unsettling, but from what she had seen, she'd been convinced.

"It was Maria," she said.

Carlton wheeled around and said, "Okay, now you've got me worried! During all of the troubles that we experienced at Whitewall Farm four years ago, you never once told me that Maria had tried to contact you, yet now, within days of finding more documents relating to the Chance family, you tell me that she's come here in the middle of night, trying to warn you about someone named 'bad dog' or 'mad dog', or something."

He paused for a second and then said, "What if it's that blasted Sugg rearing its ugly head again, or something else equally nasty?"

Naomi felt her heart miss a beat at the thought of the fearful Sugg reappearing in her life.

Sugg had been a huge and deformed Irish wolfhound that had lived in the 19$^{th}$ century; whose ghostly antics and fearsome barking had scared hundreds of people. His 'presence' had also alerted Naomi to the site of numerous bodies at Whitewall.

She pondered the previous night's events and then said, "Wait, Cal. I didn't say that Maria had warned me about anything. I told you that she had mouthed 'bad dog' or 'mad dog' or something looking like that, but that doesn't mean that it was bad or mad dog, does it? There must be numerous combinations that look the same when you think about how it's formed in speech."

Carlton calmed and said, "I suppose so."

He remained silent as he tried to think of a few, but then caught sight of the time.

"Alright," he said. "Maybe I was being a bit hasty, but you have to ask yourself this; what on earth is so crucial that it's brought Maria back now? If she hadn't felt the need to make contact during all of the weird and dangerous stuff that went on at Whitewall in 2002, what could be so important that it requires her to try to tell you something now?"

He looked at the clock on the bedside shelf and said, "I can't stop now or I won't have time for a coffee, let alone brekky."

He got up and walked into the bathroom to finish getting ready.

For several minutes Naomi stayed where she was, deep in thought. Carlton's comments had concerned her.

She remembered feeling at ease with whom she believed to be Maria, and she couldn't recall thinking that Maria had been trying to warn her about anything, – but two things did bother her.

The first was Carlton's comment about what was so important that it now required Maria herself to make contact, and second, if it had been the hem of Maria's dress that she'd seen in their office, how had she been able to appear twice without her getting any kind of prior psychic warning?

Which in turn meant that if Maria had been able to slip undetected below her psychic radar, could someone – or something else – be capable of doing that too?

In the end, she had to concede that there could be more worrisome things out there than she had ever considered before, and for the first time since acquiring her unique capability, she wasn't as confident about its infallibility.

At 10:30am Eastern Standard Time, in the Farlington house, in Dunnellon, Florida, Alan Farlington, the distant cousin of Naomi descended from Matthew's side of the Chance family, sat down on the edge of his bed and inspected the exterior of the old sea chest. Nothing looked different; he couldn't remember how many times he'd seen it before, but it looked just the same as it had always done.

He picked up the email from Naomi and read what she'd named "one of Valentine's contrivances," again.

*'First the – chest you must obtain, then seek the truth within. Grain o' truth on topmost board, when first you order all discord.'*

He re-read it and then looked back at the chest; the words *'Grain o' truth on topmost board'* made him re-examine the lid several times over, both inside and outside, but there was nothing of any significance to be seen.

Next he turned his attention to the words *'then seek the truth within'*. He inspected every inch of the interior of the chest, but as before found nothing to link it to Valentine's contrivance.

Finally he read the words *'when first you order all discord'*. He re-examined the whole chest again; he looked at the hinges and lock to see if they had been tampered with, he studied the small dovetail joints and even the worn studs on the base, but try as he may, he still saw nothing unusual.

In mild frustration he closed the lid, locked it, placed it on the floor, and pushed it under the bed with his heel.

He went downstairs, switched on his laptop and emailed Naomi, reporting that he'd found nothing whatsoever to link the chest to any part of Valentine's contrivance.

# Chapter 10

*18th November 1871. The Whitewall Estate, Wordale Moor, Lancashire*

"Don't you dare to talk to your aunt in that tone!" said Silas.

"It's all right dear," said Maria. "Harland has a right to be heard."

Silas looked with disapproval at the dapper figure of Maria's twenty-eight-year-old nephew, and wondered how two people from the same family could be so different.

"You had no right to give those papers to Aunt Charlotte," said Harland. "Am I not my father's son, and wasn't he the eldest in our family?"

"Yes, but…"

"But nothing, Aunt Maria! You are living here at Whitewall and it should be me and my family, not you and the… the…" Harland looked with disdain at Silas and then said, "…cabby!"

This time it was Maria's turn to be incensed.

"You offensive boor! You call yourself a gentleman? Apologise to Silas this instant, or get out of my home."

"I'll do no such thing. You know that my father – and indeed your father – would never have approved of you marrying out of your class."

"And it was nobody's business but my own whom I chose to marry, and both my eldest brother and father, had they been alive, could have gone to blazes if they hadn't approved. None of you will ever know what Silas had to endure to help me, and I'll never be able to repay his kindness, so keep your ill-mannered comments to yourself. He is my husband now, and as such, demands your respect! Do you understand?"

Silence reigned for a few seconds until she repeated, "Harland, do you understand?"

Harland looked at Silas with contempt and then nodded.

Maria ignored the look and said, "Good – then apologise."

Harland thought about it for a few seconds and then turned his head to one side. He said, "Sorry."

"That's not good enough, Harland! Look him in the eyes and say it."

Harland looked up and saw Silas' startling green eyes boring into him.

He swallowed hard and then said, "Very well! Silas, I apologise. I should not have been so discourteous. Please forgive me."

A short silence ensued as Silas stared at Harland. He then nodded and said, "Very well, apology accepted."

"But this changes nothing," said Harland turning to face Maria. "I am the rightful heir to this place, not you."

"And I am not here as the heir to Whitewall. I am here as the wife of the incumbent tenant." She paused for a second, allowing time for her words to sink in, and then said, "But you are aware of the circumstances that led to me being here, so why are you being so obtuse?"

"Because the end result is the same – you are now living here, and it should be me and mine!"

Silas couldn't contain himself any longer and said, "Harland, what is it that you can't comprehend? Your aunt is only living here because I took up the tenancy of this place and she is married to me. She didn't succeed in her quest to return Whitewall to Chance family ownership; indeed, if anything, all she succeeded in doing was to put herself into a position whereby she can no longer admit to who she really in case she is re-incarcerated at Parkway."

Harland looked at Silas and said, "And how do you know that for sure? We all know that Aunt Maria was committed through corruption – we could fight her case in a court of law."

"And who would pay for that, you?"

"It's not about money Silas, it's about principal."

"And I repeat, who would pay for that – you?"

Silence ensued as Maria watched the altercation from across the room.

"And what if we lost the case?" continued Silas. "Would you be willing to risk your aunt being returned to the asylum?"

Harland opened his mouth to speak but thought better of it.

"Yes, right!" said Silas.

Harland seethed. He didn't like being beaten in an argument; indeed, he didn't like being beaten at anything, and especially by somebody whom he considered to be an intellectual inferior.

Silas was angry too; he disliked Harland with everything he had, and he watched his every move. He recalled that after each of his previous visits, things had gone missing – nothing of real importance maybe, but missing nevertheless; a small porcelain ornament, his favourite penknife, odd pieces of kitchen cutlery, and on one occasion, even the contents of his tobacco jar.

Harland broke Silas's cogitation and said to Maria, "That still doesn't explain why you gave your documents to Aunt Charlotte instead of to me. You know that I have two daughters and another baby on the way, and even they have more of a claim on Whitewall than she does, presuming, of course, that she will even try!"

Maria wanted to say, "Because they are a darned sight safer with Charlotte," but in the interests of trying to maintain a semblance of decorum and not prompt further argument said, "I gave them to Charlotte because I knew that they would be safer in a place that was a permanent home. And besides, I always promised that I'd give them to her if ever I had to abandon my pursuit of ownership."

Harland stood up, walked across to the window, and, after several seconds of brooding silence, turned to face Maria.

"Well, I demand that you retrieve them from her and hand them over to me. Thereafter I shall take up the gauntlet and attempt to return Whitewall to our family."

"And what would you do if you were successful in proving Chance family ownership?" said Silas. "Have your Aunt and me evicted from here?"

"You don't belong here anyway," said Harland.

Silas fumed. With blazing eyes he turned to his wife and said, "Get him out of here, Maria; otherwise I shall not be responsible for my actions."

"Ah, so there we have it," said Harland. "Class will out. When it comes to reasoned argument or discussion, the lower orders will always resort to violence."

Now Maria was angry too; she jumped to her feet and pointed towards the front door.

"You heard Silas, you insulting creature – get out of my house and don't come back until you've re-learned some of the manners that you profess to have."

The gloves were off. Harland had only ever tolerated his aunt and had always considered her to be way above her station, so when she'd re-emerged into the family after escaping from a lunatic asylum, *and* with a common cabby turned tenant farmer for a husband, he had missed no opportunity to air his disdain and contempt.

He'd been aware of Maria's attempts to regain Whitewall but he, and his father before him, had considered it to be a futile attempt to regain past glories. Now though, to find her settled on the family estate was too much to bear. His father had been Maria's elder brother; therefore, as far as he was concerned, Whitewall was his by birthright, whatever the circumstances.

He looked with barely controlled anger at Maria and said, "Don't you dare dismiss me in such a manner... especially in front of him!" He nodded towards Silas and said, "I am not one of your, your... hoi polloi!"

"Oh, and you consider yourself to be hoi oligoi, do you, Harland?"

Harland diverted eyes, and in doing so noticed a delicate silver necklace atop the sideboard.

"Because," continued Maria unaware of Harland's sudden interest, "you are not! You have always been a ne'er-do-well; a leech on your immediate family and a leech on your relatives, and it is only due to the strength and fortitude of your long-suffering wife that you still do have a family..."

All of Harland's disputatious tendencies had given way to his desire to pocket the necklace, until Maria touched a nerve.

"… and your father would have been ashamed of you coming here and behaving as you have."

Harland wheeled around and blurted out, "Pah! At least I don't have to spend my time hiding away with a common cabby in case I'm returned to a lunatic asylum!"

Silas leapt to his feet, charged across the room, and grabbed Harland by the lapels of his jacket.

"I swear that I shall shoot you if you ever set foot on our land again!"

"On my land, don't you mean?"

Silas pulled Harland even closer causing him to stand on his tiptoes.

"No sonny! My land – and don't you ever forget it. Now, do as your aunt says, and *get out*!"

As Harland was pushed away, he steered himself towards the sideboard and feigned stopping the momentum by placing his hands on top of it. He felt the necklace below his left palm, scooped it up, and then turned to face Silas.

"Very well, I'll leave – but don't make the mistake of thinking that this is over, because it is not. Regardless of the circumstance, Whitewall is mine by right, and I swear that one day I shall have it."

"Over my dead body!" said Silas.

Harland gave Silas a withering look and then turned to Maria.

"You just mark my words!"

Silas grabbed Harland by the arm, propelled him to the front door, pushed him into the yard, and then slammed it shut behind him.

"You haven't heard the last of this!" yelled Harland, "Lex talionis, cabby!"

Silas returned to the parlour and saw Maria sitting and seething.

"Are you all right, May?"

Maria looked up and said, "He's trouble, Silas, and we might have made a bad enemy out of him."

Silas thought about the encounter in the early part of 1870 when Caleb Johnson had broken into their home, intent on murdering them both.

"We've had worse," he said.

He dismissed the thought and headed for the door. It was close to milking time and he needed to get on.

"Oh by-the-way, what does 'lex talionis' mean?"

Maria looked up and said, "Lex talionis?"

Silas nodded.

"It means, 'an eye for an eye'."

# Chapter 11

*Monday 3<sup>rd</sup> April 2006. The Town Clerk's Office, Walmsfield Borough Council*

"Rushworth Moor is inside the Walmsfield Borough boundaries," said Naomi, "and the new documentation that I've got may help to clear up the mystery that surrounded the Whitewall fiasco back in 2002."

Gabriel Ffitch leaned back in his chair and looked at Naomi. He recalled the 'Whitewall Fiasco' and had hoped that nothing to do with Whitewall would ever emerge again.

"And how does digging up two cottages help?" he said.

"I'm not proposing that we dig up two cottages. I just want to carry out two small geophys' surveys and sink four one-metre square test pits. The whole exercise could be over in two days – three at the most."

Ffitch placed his elbows on his desk and brought his hands together as though he was praying. He leaned his face forwards and proceeded to tap his lips with the tips of his forefingers.

"The cost of the exercise is well within my budget," said Naomi, feeling aggravated that she was having to justify her proposed plans with somebody uninvolved in her type of work, but following the death of Ffitch's predecessor Giles Eaton in 2002 and his possible implication in the loss of historical Whitewall documents, procedures had been put in place that required her to inform the incumbent town clerk whenever anything relating to Whitewall Farm or the Chance family was to be pursued.

"I need time to think it over," said Ffitch.

Naomi seethed. "I beg your pardon?" she said. "I am required by standing orders to inform you what I am doing and where I am going when it comes to Chance family or Whitewall research. I am *not* required to obtain your permission!"

"Nevertheless," said Ffitch, "I still need time to think it over."

Naomi was stunned by his obstinacy. She frowned and said, "There is nothing to think over! I am going to Rushworth Moor on Wednesday to carry out this research."

She got up from her chair, turned and headed for the door.

"Wait, Mrs Wilkes," said Ffitch. "I didn't mean to antagonise you…"

Naomi stopped and turned around.

"You know how difficult things were after the last investigation into the Whitewall affair. The rumours about disastrous findings circulated around these offices for months afterwards, we had the police crawling over every bit of paperwork we had, and the disruption was horrendous."

Naomi nodded but held her tongue.

"And when you mentioned Whitewall earlier, all of that flooded back into my mind. I found myself wondering whether or not I wanted to live through anything like that again, and that is why I was being recalcitrant."

Naomi empathised and softened, but said, "I can understand that, but what are we to do when we're faced with difficult decisions? Jam our heads where they don't see daylight and hope that they'll disappear?"

"Well of course not," said Ffitch. "It's just…"

"It's just nothing, Mr Ffitch. I cannot possibly know where any of my research will take me, but I won't be put off doing it because it might lead me to an unpalatable truth."

"Yes, I agree…"

"Good," said Naomi. "Then that makes two of us!"

She turned to head for the door, but was stopped.

"You didn't say where the cottages were," said Ffitch.

Naomi turned once again and said, "I told you – Rushworth Moor."

"Rushworth Moor is a large place, Mrs Wilkes. Where exactly are we talking about?"

Naomi thought for a second and then recalled what Dave Brown had said.

"The two cottages are on the Cragg Vale Estate, and I've already received permission from their management company to proceed."

Ffitch's heart sank at the mention of the Cragg Vale Estate, but he didn't show it. His day had just taken a turn for the worse.

"Alright, Mrs Wilkes," he said, without giving anything away. "Thank you for letting me know."

Naomi stood looking at the town clerk for a few seconds longer than she should have because the thumb had pressed hard down onto her shoulder.

Ffitch saw her looking and said, "Is there something else?"

"What aren't you telling me?" said Naomi.

Ffitch became disorientated. It felt as though Naomi had climbed into his head and had read his thoughts.

While trying his best to control his emotions he said, "Nothing, why do you ask?"

Naomi looked at him and said, "Just take it from me, Mr Ffitch, I know when something is amiss, and right now I know it."

Ffitch felt as though he was back at school and that he'd just been discovered lying. It was intimidating and unpleasant.

"I'm sorry, Mrs Wilkes," he said. "I don't know what you are talking about. Now, if you don't mind, I do have other pressing things…"

Naomi stared at him for a while longer and then nodded and departed.

As soon as the office door closed, Ffitch snatched up the phone and spoke to his feisty secretary Morag.

"Mo," he said, "don't put any calls through to me for at least fifteen minutes, and don't let anybody disturb me."

"Okay Gabe, got it."

Ffitch disliked her use of the name 'Gabe' but given their unique and intimate history and her less than approachable character, he couldn't bring himself to broach the subject, let alone ask her to alter it. It would have been akin to feeding wasps to a Doberman Pinscher with mouth ulcers.

He retrieved his personal mobile from his briefcase and rang the number that he hoped he would never have to ring. Within seconds there was a response.

"Mr Darke," he said. "Gabriel Ffitch here; you told me that I had to ring you if anybody from the Chance family ever started prying about in any of your businesses or holdings..."

Ten minutes later, Ffitch emerged from the elegance of his office and entered the domain of Morag Beech.

She ruled her world from her office chair with a rod of iron. She was blowsy and overweight but she was happy with herself. She almost always dressed in black trouser-suits with flat-heeled shoes, and her ruddy face and neck appeared to be over-inflated because of her short dark, style-less hair. A faux diamond stud glistened from her left nostril, and she looked intimidating.

Empty crisp packets, pork pie and biscuit wrappers lay in the overflowing wastebasket, and an unopened box of cream cakes sat waiting to be devoured on the corner of her desk.

All of that aside, she was an excellent secretary; she was mega-efficient, a brilliant timekeeper, she never got sick, and she was loyal and devoted to Gabriel Ffitch.

She knew that her surname was Beech, but she always referred to the two of them as 'Ffitch and his bitch'.

"Yo Gabe," she said as he appeared through her door. "You look a bit peaky, what's up?"

"I just had to put a call in to you-know-who."

"Shit, why?"

"Because Naomi Wilkes is planning a couple of digs on their Cragg Vale Estate."

Morag retrieved the cake box from the corner of her desk, extracted a cream horn, and said, "Here, sit and get this down you."

Ffitch walked over to her office chair, sat down and took the cake.

"You always knew that that was the deal babe," said Morag. "Neither of us would be here if it hadn't been for Adrian."

Ffitch took a bite of the cake, swallowed it, and then said, "I know, but as the years have passed we've done a good job, and I hate feeling that we're only here because of him."

Morag nodded.

"Okay, so maybe you rang Adrian to advise him that the Wilkes woman was coming, but that's not so bad, is it? It's not like you were arranging a contract hit on her."

Ffitch finished the last of the cream horn and raised his eyebrows.

"We are talking Adrian Darke here. You know that crazy son-of-a-bitch. Once he starts getting involved, nasty things start happening to people…"

"Cragg Vale, you say?" said Morag, "Isn't that where…?"

"… that mad-as-a-sodding-goose gamekeeper is? Yes, it is!"

"Well, bloody good luck to her, that's what I say. I'm no slouch when it comes to confrontation, but that geezer would make me think twice."

Ffitch wiped his mouth with a clean tissue and looked at his secretary. They had never been intimate in the true sense of the word, but he loved being in her company. They'd first met whilst being employed by Darke Industries early in 2001; he was a Business Promotions Manager and she'd been his secretary, and they'd hit it off from day one.

Following one or two brushes with Naomi Wilkes and her obsession to discover the truth about Whitewall ownership, Adrian Darke had nearly lost a £4.5 million deal with the Highways Agency because some doubt had arisen about the validity of his ownership of a piece of land purchased from the Whitewall Estate in the 19th century. As a consequence, he'd determined that he would never be caught blind-sided by her again because he still retained thirty percent of the land in question.

Within a few months he'd 'managed' to get Gabriel and Morag installed into Walmsfield Borough Council as the town clerk and his PA, principally to keep an eye on things, and to warn him if anything untoward was surfacing.

And in return for this service a small annuity always landed on each of their hall floors every Christmas.

Neither Ffitch nor Morag was married, but they'd spent a lot of time together in and out of work, and though both suspected that one day something might happen, but to date it had not.

"Come on Gabe," said Morag, "chin up; it may not amount to anything."

Ffitch got up and walked to the office door, opened it and stepped through. Just before closing it he leaned around, looked at Morag, and said, "Maybe…"

"Do you know who is behind those requests to dig on Cragg Vale?" Adrian Darke was livid.

"Calm down Adrian!" said Christiana from her office at Christadar, "You'll give yourself a heart attack."

"It's only Naomi bloody Chance, or Wilkes, or whatever her name is now!"

Christiana paused for a second until the penny dropped.

"Oh, bugger," she said, "I had no idea…"

"Well, now you do, and she's told Gabriel Ffitch that it's something to do with her family history, so you'd better fix it!"

"I…"

The telephone went dead and Christiana stared at it in disbelief; she put it down on her desk and sat back in her chair to consider her options.

One hour later she telephoned Adrian and said, "It's fixed. I've sent instructions to the Wilkes woman that she can proceed at Cragg Vale, as long as she is accompanied by our own professional researcher at all times."

"Our own professional researcher?" said Adrian. "We haven't got one of those."

"We have now."

Adrian paused for thought and then said, "Who on earth do we have that fits that bill?"

"Hayley Gillorton."

Adrian burst out laughing and said, "Hayley, 'what-are-you-fucking-looking-at' Gillorton?"

"You've got it," said Christiana.

Adrian chuckled with unadulterated mirth and said, "Good choice honey, good choice."

# Chapter 12

Naomi checked that everything was in place for the visit to Rushworth Moor the following week. The vegetation clearance team would get to work at High Farm Cottage on the Monday, and the geophys' team would commence their soundings early Tuesday. Mid-morning the same day, the archaeologists, and diggers would arrive and start work there too.

She planned to join them and meet the Cragg Vale Estate historic researcher Hayley Gillorton on the Tuesday, where they could discuss tactics and assess any finds as the dig proceeded.

And once the clearance team had finished at High Farm Cottage, they would proceed to the site at the bottom of Lark Hill and commence a similar programme of works there.

She gathered up all the necessary paperwork, including copies of the emails sent to the gamekeeper at Cragg Vale, and to Christadar Property Holdings outlining their plan of action, and placed them in a file in her pending tray.

She looked at the clock on her wall; it was 2:30pm and bang on time there was a knock on her door.

"Come in Percy!" she called.

The door opened and Percy waddled in with an unkempt looking man. They made their way to the seats in front of Naomi's desk and sat down.

"Good afternoon, dear," said Percy. "Please let me introduce you to Gas... er, Pat."

Pat lifted up off his seat and extended his right hand, and in doing so emitted a suspicious sound.

Naomi shook the offered hand and shot a glance at Percy who just smiled awkwardly and shrugged.

"Now," said Percy, "Pat has been busy looking into the history surrounding that old cottage on Cragg End Lane and trying to discover which building used to stand at the bottom of Lark Hill, so I'll pass you over to him and he can tell you first hand."

Naomi said, "Okay" and turned to face Pat.

Pat remained silent at first, and then looked over his left and right shoulders, almost as if he was expecting to be overheard divulging some great secret.

He leaned forwards and in a lowered tone said, "Sorry – can't help."

Naomi didn't know who was more surprised, she, or Percy.

Percy wheeled around and said, "But you told me that you had something to say to Naomi!"

"I did," said Pat, "and I've just said it."

"But…"

"But nothing. I can't help!"

Percy looked at Naomi and said, "Well, I'm sorry dear. I thought that Pat had learned something about those places, otherwise I wouldn't have wasted your time."

Naomi opened her mouth to speak but was cut off by Pat.

"I didn't say I don't know anything. I said I can't help."

Naomi felt as though she was caught up in some sort of bizarre lunacy; everybody seemed to be confused with each other.

"I mean, I know that there's nowhere local named Larkland Fen, I know that High Farm Cottage was lived in by Daisy Hubert up until the time of her death some time in June 1869. I know that she was found tied to a chair and had been beaten to death…"

Naomi put her hand up to her mouth and said, "My God."

"… and I know that at end of July 1869 it was leased to a guy named Caleb Johnson…"

For a second time Naomi said, "Oh my God!"

Pat gave her a quelling look and continued. "…it was leased to guy named Caleb Johnson for twelve months, but he disappeared sometime in February 1870 and was never seen again."

Naomi was amazed by what she was hearing. Two mysteries solved in one sentence by a guy who said he couldn't help.

"That's wonderful Pat, I..."

Pat put his hand up and said, "I haven't finished!"

Percy looked at Naomi and shook his head; he too was astounded by what he was hearing.

"There never has been any habitation at the foot of Lark Hill. There is a boatshed marked on small-scale maps of the area dating from the late 1800s, and although it appears to be quite a distance from the current lake, that was because the lake was larger in the 19th century.

"The boatshed, which had a corrugated iron roof, was struck by lightning late in the afternoon of May the 28th 1893, killing two people and a pig who were taking shelter in there. The building was destroyed and never rebuilt, and all that's left now are the ruins."

Even the verbose Percy was amazed and stunned into silence.

Naomi said, "Well, for somebody who can't help..."

Pat stuck his hand up again and said, "I haven't finished!" He looked at Naomi and Percy and then said, "My research also threw up something very unusual."

He stopped speaking, leaned forwards, and waved his right hand to draw both Naomi and Percy closer.

They both leaned forwards.

Once again Pat looked over his left and right shoulders and then leaned closer and said, "What do you have to do to get a cup of tea in here?"

For the second time in quick succession, Naomi was flabbergasted; she sat back in her chair and stared at Pat.

Percy was surprised too, but was quick to jump on the bandwagon.

"I'll have one too if I may – white, no sugar, I'm..."

"I know," said Naomi getting up from her desk, "you're sweet enough."

Five minutes later, with all the tea orders sorted, Naomi looked at Pat and said, "You mentioned earlier that your research had thrown up something unusual?"

"It did," said Pat. He took a sip of tea and then said, "It was about the gamekeeper from the Cragg Vale Estate, Les Spooner."

Naomi recalled him and shivered inside.

"During my investigation, I checked the names of the incumbents from Cragg End Lane in the 1861 and 1871 local census records. That gives you a fair indication of the movement of people over a ten-year period, and whilst scanning over the addresses listed, I noticed a property named Cragg Vale Cottage. At first I wondered whether it was that small building in Cragg End Lane, but it was not. That was shown as High Farm Cottage.

"I then noted the name of the person residing at Cragg Vale Cottage, and saw that it was Leslie Spooner! After that I checked every census record up until 1911, the most recent one to be released, and on each document Leslie Spooner was named as the gamekeeper and sole occupant."

"But…" said Naomi.

"And I checked the date of birth shown for him. It was listed as February 29th 1832. Now I know that he only had a birthday once every four years, but how do you explain that?"

Naomi and Percy exchanged glances and then Naomi said, "It must have been a name that was passed from father to son."

"But there wasn't anybody else listed on any of the census records living there other than him," said Pat.

"But that's highly misleading," said Percy. "The census records only give a snapshot of who is living where on the night of each census; it doesn't record any movement of folk in between, and suspicious as though this may appear, it can easily be explained away."

"Maybe so," said Pat, "but my waters tell me different." He looked through slitted eyes at Naomi and Percy and then said, "And I always listen to two things – my off-licence manager and my waters. That's why I can't help."

Naomi looked puzzled about the reference to the off-licence manager, but shrugged it off and said, "But you've been an enormous help."

"No," said Pat. "I mean I can't help you if you if you want me to go with you to Cragg Vale, 'cos I won't go."

Once again a brief silence ensued until Naomi said, "Well, I'm very grateful for all of the information that you've supplied." She looked at the notes she'd jotted down and saw that she'd recorded all of the salient points. "They will be most helpful, especially your mention of Caleb Johnson living at High Farm Cottage. That was a surprise."

Pat nodded and finished his tea.

"Gotta go, Perse," he said turning to Percy. "I've got to check that those idiots have sorted my machine out this time."

Naomi recalled Percy's earlier warning about Gasworks' mention of his machine. She couldn't help herself and said, "And what machine is that Pat?"

Percy's mouth opened and then closed in resignation.

"You know," said Pat, "for my work."

Naomi frowned and said, "For your work?"

"Yes – it helps me with all the difficult bits."

Percy put his left middle finger up to his forehead, rubbed it from side to side, and looked down.

"What difficult bits?" said Naomi.

"The difficult bits with the curves."

Naomi frowned and said, "Curves?"

"Yes, that's what I already told you. That and the grooves – you know!"

He made an arcing movement with his right hand as though he was stroking a football, and then turned to Percy again.

"Come on, Perse," he said. "They close at 4:00pm on a Thursday and I need you to drop me off at the bus stop."

Percy raised his eyebrows, looked at Naomi in despair, and then said, "Right-ho."

"Before you go, Percy, I have another saying for you to look up for me if you can."

Percy pointed to a desk pad and said, "Write it down for me dear, and I'll see what I can do."

Naomi wrote down 'Dat Deus immiti cornua curta bovi' and handed it over.

"Better go," said Percy rising to his feet. "We can't stand in the way of progress if Pat's going to get his machine back."

Pat nodded and stood up and another suspicious sound erupted from the trouser department. He looked straight at Naomi and said, "A bit more choke and I should get that started."

Naomi giggled and shook her head. She walked them to the office door, thanked them again, and returned to her office chair.

There is never, ever, she thought, a dull moment with Percy and his cronies!

Following their departure, she looked at her notes and couldn't believe her luck; like the pieces of a jigsaw, they all seemed to fit together.

She had the letter from George to Daisy Hubert warning her not to approach the Johnsons with the information that she possessed, because they would kill her; and there was Caleb, the tenant of High Farm Cottage in July 1869, just one month after her body was found beaten to death.

She already had evidence that Caleb had abandoned the Whitewall Estate after the death of his father Abraham sometime around the middle of 1869, and now she knew where he'd gone.

There could only be two conclusions; either Caleb had discovered where his documents had been sent by extracting the information from George Hubert before killing him – George had written that his life was in danger from the Johnsons – or that Daisy had tried to blackmail him with the incriminating evidence that she had.

The big question was, did Daisy tell Caleb where the documents were before succumbing or not? The odds were that she had, but as long as the issue remained unresolved, there was a need to investigate.

Half an hour later, she had just finished tidying up her notes and double-checking her itinerary for the following week when the telephone rang on her desk. She picked it up and said, "Historic Research Department, Naomi Wilkes speaking."

"Naomi, it's Helen from the Vical Centre. Are you passing this way anytime soon?"

Naomi checked her diary and said, "No, but I do have time tomorrow. Why?"

"Because I think that I've worked out the meaning of Valentine's first contrivance."

# Chapter 13

*20th November 1871. Rochdale Police Station, Lancashire*

Harland stood on the pavement outside the Rochdale Police Station and looked at the forbidding entrance. The customary dark blue lamp hung over the large front door, and everywhere inside appeared to be in darkness.

He knew that he was about to take a precipitous step but over the weekend he'd convinced himself that it was the right thing to do for his immediate family. Furthermore, he was still smarting from the unceremonious way in which he'd been ejected from Whitewall by Silas.

He took a deep breath, straightened down his jacket and stepped inside.

"Good morning sir," said Desk Sergeant Graham Banks with a smile on his face. "What can we do for you?"

Harland walked up to the wooden counter and said, "I'd like to report the whereabouts of an escaped inmate from the Cheshire Lunatic Asylum at Parkway, Macclesfield."

The affability dissolved and Banks said, "An escaped inmate from Parkway, you say?"

"That is correct."

He watched as the Sergeant bent down to retrieve a pad and pencil from a drawer under the counter, and noted that as he stood back up, his burly six foot two inch frame seemed to occupy most of the space behind it.

Banks licked the tip of the pencil, leaned forwards, and said, "Name?"

"What, mine or the inmate?"

"The inmate, sir."

"Maria Chance."

Banks commenced writing and then paused. He looked up and said, "That with a 'C' or an 'S'?"

Harland frowned and wanted to say something caustic about the policeman's lack of education, but remained calm and collected.

"With a 'C'."

"Hmm," said Banks. "I don't recall receiving any reports of anybody being wanted by that name, but then again Parkway Asylum is in Macclesfield, so that would come under the jurisdiction of the Cheshire Force, not us." He paused for a few seconds and then said, "And just where is this lady now, sir?"

"At the Whitewall Estate on Wordale Moor."

The mention of the Whitewall Estate had an immediate effect on Banks; some of his most unpleasant official duties had been experienced there, and he had no desire to go near the place again.

"They still got that bloody mad dog up there?" He paused for a second and then said, "Begging your pardon, sir – I didn't mean to swear."

"It's fine," said Harland, "and the answer to your question is 'yes', but I do believe that his behaviour has modified since the death of the Johnsons who previously owned him."

More bad memories flooded into Banks' brain. He shook his head and looked up into the air.

"The Johnsons – by God, there wasn't a person round these parts didn't breathe a sigh of relief to hear that those buggers had gone…"

Harland allowed Banks his moment of reflection and then said, "About the matter in hand?"

Banks looked down and said, "Yes, sir, sorry, years of service have made me wary as a cat, and everything about that place rings my alarm bells. Now, this er…" He looked down at the name on his pad, "… Maria Chance – how do you know that she's an escaped inmate?"

Harland realised the awkward spot that he'd placed himself in. He'd never considered what he'd say if he was asked how he knew his aunt. He lost concentration and said, "I, er…"

Banks stood watching, and as the seconds ticked by, another little warning bell started to ring.

"Sir?" he said.

Harland felt cornered. He reached into his waistcoat pocket, retrieved his watch, and looked at it.

"I'm sorry, Sergeant," he said. "I'm a bit pushed for time – got a train to catch. Isn't what I've given you enough to be going on with?"

"No sir, I'm afraid not. I can't just turn up at the Whitewall Estate and accuse somebody of being an escaped lunatic without some evidence to back it up."

"Couldn't you get that from Parkway?"

"I could, but then again why would I need to when you seem to know what's going on?"

Harland began to feel desperate; the walls seemed to be closing in on him.

"Because I told you I have a train to catch!"

Banks knew that something was amiss and could see the rising panic in the informant. He decided to try a softer approach.

"Alright, sir, we'll send an officer up to investigate." He lifted up the pad, licked the end of his pencil once again and said, "Now, If I could just have your name and address?"

"Why is that necessary?" said Harland.

"So that we can send one of our constables round to your house to take a full statement when you've got more time."

"This is preposterous," said Harland. "What would you do if you'd received an anonymous tip off?"

"But I haven't, have I, sir?" Banks waited for a second and then said, "Come on, sir, why don't you be a good gentleman? Just tell me your name and address and then we can all go about our business."

"Because I'm late! Look, I've already told you – Maria Chance is an escaped inmate from the Lunatic Asylum at Parkway, and she's hiding at the Whitewall Estate. Surely that's enough?"

"And what is your connection to this lady, sir?"

"What?"

Another thought flashed through Harland's brain, 'What if the Sergeant asks me how long I've known about this?' Panic broke out.

"Look, Sergeant, I've told you all that you need to know for now. I have a train to catch and I'm not prepared to stand here and answer any more unnecessary questions, so good day to you!"

He doffed his hat and disappeared through the front door.

Banks watched the retreating figure and scratched the back of his head.

"That sounded interesting."

Banks turned and saw the slight figure of Detective Inspector Jack Brewster standing in the doorway of the Information Room.

"Yes sir, it was, in more ways than one."

Brewster, who'd heard the entire exchange, pondered for a few seconds, and then said, "We'd better follow it up. I'll either go myself, or I'll send an officer to Parkway to find out if they have any reports of a missing inmate, and if they do, we'll take a trip up to Whitewall."

Banks drew in a deep breath, put his hand up to his mouth, and uttered a long "Hmm."

"Problem, Sergeant?"

"No, sir, – well maybe, it's the thought of going up there again. I thought that we'd finished with that place once the Johnsons had gone, and now here it comes, rearing its ugly head once more."

The two men stood in silence until Brewster said, "There's more to this than meets the eye, Graham. We need to find out who that informant was and what his connection to Whitewall is."

Banks nodded and said, "Yes, sir."

Brewster turned to walk away and then stopped and looked back over his shoulder.

"And I hope that he was right about that bloody dog."

Further down the High Street, Harland made his way into a bar and ordered a large whisky. He paid for it and walked across to an empty table by the open fire. He unbuttoned his coat, sat down and took a sip. As he put it down on the table, he castigated himself for going into the Police Station unprepared. It was obvious that he would have been questioned about where he'd received the information relating to his aunt's escape, what his connection with her was, and why he hadn't reported it earlier – and they were all questions that he could have explained away. Instead, he'd made himself look foolish – foolish and suspicious.

He picked up the whisky glass, took another deep draught, and then slammed it back down on the table too hard.

The barman looked and called over, "Another, sir?"

Harland nodded in his direction and then stamped his foot in frustration.

"God damn them!" he muttered, "Another reason for getting those thieving bastards out of Whitewall."

# Chapter 14

*Friday 7<sup>th</sup> April 2006. The Vical Centre, Newton*

For the third time in two weeks, Naomi parked in the allotted space by the portable cabins. She couldn't help smiling to herself because she knew that some banter would ensue with the workmen. She'd been careful to wear jeans for the ascent up the steps, but she did have a short jumper on and she knew that she looked good.

Concealing her smile, she ascended the steps and nearly made it to the top.

"Good morning beautiful!"

Naomi turned and smiled at the same man who'd greeted her each time that she'd arrived, "And good morning to you too," she called back. "Anything on offer today?"

"Funny you should say that," called up the man as two or three of his amused mates appeared, "I was just about to prepare some lunch for the lads. Would you like to join us and sample my meat and two veg?"

The men laughed out loud and waited for a response.

"What size shoes do you take?" called Naomi.

"Size seven – why?"

"Small feet, small everything," called Naomi, "Sorry, your portions won't be big enough!"

Laughter broke out as she turned and made her way to the Conservation Suite, and as before, she heard the guys taking the mickey out of their mate.

She knocked on the door and entered.

"I don't know who enjoys the banter most," said Nina shaking her head, "you or the guys!"

"They're never like that with us," said Charlotte. "Are you sure that you're okay with it?"

"Course I am," said Naomi. "I enjoy a bit of good-humoured repartee, as long as it doesn't go too far."

As with previous visits, Helen appeared to be immersed in her work and oblivious to the goings on around her.

"Morning Helen," said Naomi.

Helen lifted up her head and said, "Morning, come and sit by me." She looked at her colleagues and said, "Whose turn is it to get the teas?"

Charlotte said, "Mine." She took everybody's requirements and walked over to the dispenser. "We think that Helen's cracked that first contrivance," she said, "but there's no way that we can crack the second one unless the first leads us to some other clue."

Naomi walked across to Helen's desk and perched on the seat that had been drawn up for her. She saw the first contrivance written on the top half of a folded piece of A4 paper.

"It's the 'order all discord' thing that had me thinking," said Helen, "that and the hyphen after the words 'First the'." She turned the contrivance around to face Naomi and said, "See?"

Naomi looked at the words.

*'First the – chest you must obtain, then seek the truth within. Grain o' truth on topmost board, when first you order all discord.'*

She had to admit that she hadn't put any effort into trying to solve the contrivance, but she didn't say so to Helen.

Oblivious of Naomi's thoughts, Helen said, "First the, hyphen, doesn't make any sense when you read it as a whole; but if you take the first two words and read them literally, it states, 'First the'. Do you get it?"

Naomi didn't and said, "What do you mean?"

"First the!" repeated Helen.

The penny still didn't drop, and Naomi said, "I'm sorry; I must be thick or something. Explain it to me."

Helen picked up her pencil and wrote down the words, 'the first'.

"Don't you see?" she said. "I think that the words 'first the' are a cryptic instruction to put 'the' first!" She looked at Naomi and said, "Now we have this…" She wrote down, 'the first chest you must obtain'.

"Ah," said Naomi. "That makes sense; we know from Valentine's letter that there were two chests…"

"Right," said Helen, "now we continue with the discord thing. When you read both contrivances it is obvious that Valentine wrote them in a rhyming format." She pointed down and said, "if you look at the last sentence, the words 'board' and 'discord' rhyme, but so too do the words 'obtain' and 'grain.' So, if you move the position of the first full stop to behind the word "within," the first sentence becomes discordant."

Naomi looked again and saw that Helen was right.

"So if we order all discord and move the full stop from the word 'within' and move it to behind the word 'grain', the two sentences rhyme once more, and the discord is ordered…" She looked at Naomi, smiled in triumph, and said, "… and we are left with this!" She turned over the piece of paper and pushed it in front of Naomi.

*'The first chest you must obtain, then seek the truth within grain. O' truth on topmost board, when first you order all discord.'*

"Good grief, Helen," said Naomi, "you're a genius! So your theory is that 'the truth', whatever that happens to be, is within the grain of the topmost board, or lid?"

"Right!"

A memory flashed into her mind. She recalled examining the lid of the chest whilst she was in Florida, and the only other distinguishing feature apart from the carvings had been an indentation that looked like the result of a hammer blow.

"So," she said, "I need to be contacting the Farlingtons to ask them to re-examine the lid?"

"Yes!"

Naomi had a thought and brought a hand up to her mouth.

Helen noticed and said, "What?"

"I've just had the wildest notion…"

"And?"

"Well…" said Naomi feeling the excitement build up inside her. "What if the Farlingtons do find something?"

"That'll lead us to understanding the second contrivance."

"Yes, of course it would, but that's not the point."

Helen frowned, and looked at Naomi.

Charlotte and Nina, who'd been listening to the conversation too, stopped what they were doing and walked over to Helen's desk.

"The point is," said Naomi, "if the Farlingtons do find anything within the grain of the lid, that means that 'El Fuego de Marte' has not been found."

"But Valentine's letter stated that he was sending the same contrivances to his sons in a letter to be opened after his death," said Nina, "so the odds must be that they've already discovered it."

"But the contrivances were the same in both letters," said Naomi, "and both led to the lid of the first chest, so if the Farlingtons do find something, that means that Valentine's sons didn't discover the ruby."

"My God, you're right!" said Charlotte.

"And what if Valentine outlived both of his sons?" said Helen, "It's possible that his descendants never have received that letter for any number of reasons."

Charlotte was beside herself with excitement.

"Oh my God," she repeated, "this could be just like that film 'National Treasure'!"

"Oh, come on," said Helen. "One single ruby, however large it is, doesn't constitute a national treasure!"

"Nevertheless," said Naomi, "this could turn into something altogether more serious here."

All three conservators stopped speaking and turned to face Naomi.

"I know that this is all speculation, but if 'El Fuego de Marte' is as yet undiscovered and we do find it, whose would it be? Was it that native woman's stone to give to Valentine? Would the Spanish still know about it and would they try to reclaim it? Would the country from where it was plundered, probably Mexico, want it back? Or could it be, as Charlotte hinted, American national treasure, and then would we all get a cut?"

"Or more to the point," said Helen, "do we keep this between ourselves until we know whether the first contrivance leads us to something more?"

Out of the blue, something flashed from right to left across Naomi's vision. She looked to the left with such speed that everybody looked left too.

For a few seconds, everyone found themselves staring at the cabin door in total silence.

Charlotte said, "Did you see something Naomi?"

Naomi, who was still disorientated, said, "Sorry, I thought I saw something."

"What?" said Charlotte.

"I don't know; maybe it was…"

Naomi felt her heart rate start to increase and knew that she wasn't alone anymore; her breathing began to shallow, and she was overcome by a feeling that something was approaching her from the rear. She turned around and looked behind her.

Everybody else did too.

"What is it, Naomi?" said Charlotte. "You're beginning to spook me out here."

Naomi was about to speak when she noticed a black shadow in the corner of the room; she didn't think she could take anymore. Her eyes widened, and everybody turned to look at where she was staring.

The black shadow shot towards Naomi at such a speed that she leapt out of her seat and sprang to one side.

Her chair crashed to floor and Charlotte jumped back in alarm.

"Jesus Christ! What…?" yelped Charlotte.

It all happened so quickly that Naomi couldn't make out what or who had rushed towards her, but she was convinced that whatever it had been had rushed at something behind her.

"Naomi! Naomi!"

Naomi looked up and saw Helen staring at her with a perplexed look upon her face.

"Naomi, are you all right?" Helen turned to Nina and said, "She looks in shock. Get her a biscuit and a glass of water."

Nina responded as Helen once again turned her attention to Naomi.

Naomi realised that she'd been making a spectacle of herself and thought of something.

"I'm sorry to upset you, girls. I thought that I saw a bee in here, and if I get stung I go into anaphylactic shock, so I'm extremely nervous around them."

Charlotte looked around and said, "There aren't any bees in here."

Nina offered the biscuit and water to Naomi.

Naomi thanked her, took a bite of the biscuit and was about to take a sip of water when the thumb pressed down on her shoulder. She closed her eyes and tried to control the emotions that had gone haywire again.

A woman's voice that she hadn't heard before said, "Don't fret, I'm here with you now, and I'll stay until..."

"Naomi?" Helen's voice cut across what she was hearing.

Naomi closed her eyes and listened – "...comes." She wanted to say, "Until who comes?"

She kept listening for a few seconds longer until she heard Helen ask, "Naomi, what is it?"

The moment passed. She opened her eyes and said, "I'm sorry, I've just got a bit of a headache, that's all."

Charlotte and Nina stared at Naomi for a while, and then cast a questioning glance at one another and returned to their seats.

As Helen watched, she realised that things weren't all that they seemed with her new friend.

One hour later and on the return journey to her office, Naomi still hadn't been able to rationalise what had happened. She still felt on edge, and was aware that she was listening for any unusual sounds from within her car.

In the few seconds before the black shadow had rushed towards her, she'd been petrified by what was approaching from the rear. It felt dark and disturbing, as though some horrible thing had clawed its way up from the bowels of the earth and wanted to drag her back down. The primitive, instinctive fear that froze the blood in her veins had been palpable.

All sorts of questions were flying around her mind.

Was the woman in black Maria? Why hadn't she had any prior warning of the thing approaching her from the rear? And most of all, what the hell had been behind her?

# Chapter 15

*Monday 10<sup>th</sup> April 2006. High Farm Cottage,
Rushworth Moor*

At 8:10am, Ted Wylie and John Hayes from Walmsfield
Borough Council's Parks Department stopped the works van in
the drive opposite High Farm Cottage and hopped out. They
walked to the rear, removed the 'Works Ahead' signs, and
deposited three of them at fifty-yard intervals back up the lane.
They then positioned the diagonal white arrow on a blue
background sign in front of where they proposed parking, and
moved the van to that spot.

"Come on then," said Ted in his lilting Irish accent. "Let the
dog see the rabbit."

He and John hopped out and walked up to where there was
an obvious break in the low sandstone wall. They turned in and
stopped.

"What the fuck?" said John. He turned and stared at Ted and
said, "What's going on?"

"I've got no bloody idea," said Ted, "but we'd better get
Naomi down here straightaway."

At 9:30am, Naomi pulled in behind the works van and got out.
She'd received a message from the receptionist requesting her to
attend the High Farm Cottage site as soon as possible, and on
her way there, she'd wondered whether the guys had
experienced the same kind of spooky goings on with the foliage
that she'd had on her previous visit.

She walked up to Ted and John, who were waiting for her
by the small entranceway.

"Morning guys," she said as she approached. "What's the
problem?"

Ted indicated for Naomi to go through the gap and said, "See for yourself."

Naomi frowned, turned into the entrance, and stopped.

Every single scrap of foliage had been removed from around High Farm Cottage, the grass had been cut, and it stood like a pristine structure in a huge void.

"What?" exclaimed a mystified Naomi.

"It gets better," said Ted. "Go in and look closer."

Naomi walked towards the cottage and looked inside. The entire floor area appeared to be backfill. She walked through it and looked into the garden.

That too had been stripped of vegetation, and the backfilled remains of a one-metre wide by six-metre long trench spread diagonally across the full width of what had been the back garden. The only thing that appeared to be untouched was the small gravestone in the corner.

She walked to the gateway adjacent to the trees and was amazed to see that two one-metre square test pits had been dug and backfilled on the other side of that too.

She turned around and saw a baffled looking Ted and John behind her.

"This is a rum do," said Ted. "Nothing like this has ever happened to us before."

"Was some other company contracted in to do this instead of us?" said John.

"I'm as much in the dark as you are," said Naomi, "and nothing like this has ever happened to me before either."

"Well there's always a first time for everything," said a female voice from within the cottage.

Naomi and the two men turned and saw a large female figure appear in the doorway.

"The name's Gillorton," she said, "Hayley Gillorton, but you can call me Ms Gillorton."

She was dressed in a three quarter length dark blue woollen mix overcoat with a matching hat, black leather flat-heeled calf length boots, matching gloves, and a red woollen scarf.

Naomi's eyes narrowed. She walked across to Gillorton, extended her right hand, and said, "My name's Naomi Wilkes, head of Historic Research for Walmsfield Borough Council, and you can call me what you like."

Gillorton took the offered hand and gave it a feeble shake.

"Right, Ms Gillorton, I take it that you're responsible for this?"

"I am."

"And can I ask you why you did this instead of us?"

"You can."

Naomi waited for an explanation but none was forthcoming. She looked at her opposite number and said, "Why did you do this instead of us?"

Gillorton said, "Wait."

She reached into her coat pocket, extracted a piece of A4 paper, and opened it up. She read down it for a few seconds and then said, "Here we are, – we are researching people who lived in the locality and want to try to build up a picture of everyday life in the mid-1800s."

Naomi recognised the words that she had written in an email to the Christadar offices and realised that for some reason, Gillorton was being offensive and provocative.

She controlled her emotions and said, "Fine. It's nice to know, then, that we are both interested in the same things."

"Yeah, whatever," said Gillorton.

Naomi knew that going head-to-head with Gillorton would be playing into her hands, so she opted to remain as professional as possible.

"You were of course aware that we had planned to carry out this work ourselves, so what prompted you to do it?"

Gillorton removed the A4 paper from her pocket once again, looked at it and said, "We are researching people who lived in the locality and want to try to build up a picture of everyday life in the mid-1800s."

Naomi wanted to say, "You sarcastic cow!" but didn't. Instead she said, "Excellent. What did you discover?"

"Nothing."

Naomi frowned and said, "And didn't the geophys' reveal anything either?"

"The what?"

"The geophysical survey."

"No."

Naomi realised that she was talking to a non-professional, ignorant moron, and that she was getting nowhere, but she persisted.

"What about the interior of the cottage? What was causing that springiness underfoot?"

"What?"

Naomi took in a deep breath and said, "The springiness on the interior of the cottage, underfoot. What caused it?"

"Beats me," said Gillorton.

John, who'd been listening to the conversation, had had enough and said, "I'd like to beat you with rolled up newspaper, you objectionable twat."

Everybody spun around and looked at John.

"What did you say?" said Gillorton.

Naomi said, "John, no!"

But it was too late. John liked Naomi and wasn't about to let anybody talk to her with such contempt.

"You heard me, you old sow. Show a bit of respect."

Gillorton blazed and glared at John. She opened her mouth to speak but was cut off.

John turned to Ted and said, "Bloody wars, Ted. Look at that face – she has eyes like a shithouse rat."

Gillorton was caught offside again.

Naomi intervened and said, "Ted, take John back to the van and wait there for me please."

Ted nodded and led a grumbling John away.

Naomi turned to face Gillorton, who was still fuming, and said, "I'm sorry about that, I…"

Gillorton said, "Not interested. If you think that I'm going to stand here and be insulted by one of your lobotomised Council labourers, you can think again. This meeting is terminated and your permission to work here is withdrawn."

"Alright, I accept your decision," said Naomi, "and I apologise for my colleague, who will be dealt with for his unacceptable behaviour – but before you go, would you please tell me if we can proceed with the works at the bottom of Lark Hill?"

"That's been done too."

Naomi frowned and said, "But why?"

For a third time, Gillorton removed the piece of A4 paper from her coat pocket and started to open it.

Naomi saw what was happening and lost it too. She leaned closer to Gillorton and said, "You know what? John was right, you are objectionable, but you've crossed swords with the wrong person, and you'll live to regret it one day."

"Yeah?" said Gillorton, "Bring it on."

Naomi stared with defiance into Gillorton's face for a few seconds longer, and then turned and departed.

As she stepped into Cragg End Lane, she saw Ted remonstrating with John in the front of the van. She walked over to it, opened the door, and leaned in.

Both men fell silent, awaiting the backlash.

Naomi looked at John and said, "You were absolutely right about her, John; I couldn't have put it better myself. Now, pack up your gear and report back to base."

Naomi returned to her vehicle, reversed it into the drive opposite High Farm Cottage, and drove up to the top of Lark Hill. She checked her mirror and then pulled over close to where she had stopped on her first visit. She took out her binoculars, walked across the lane to the dry-stone wall, and looked down Lark Hill. She put the binoculars up to her eyes and tried to see if she could spot the remains of any digging near the side of the lake.

For several seconds she scanned the area, looking for signs of latent activity, and then every hair on her body stood on end.

The same gaunt looking figure that she'd glimpsed before stepped out of the trees at the bottom of the hill and looked right back at her through another pair of binoculars.

Her first instinct was to drop hers and to look the other way, but she was made of much sterner stuff. She kept them trained on him and waved. The man, whom she presumed to be the sinister and creepy Les Spooner, didn't respond but kept on looking.

Naomi tried waving again, but still drew no response.

The Chance family had throughout history, been known as the 'Iron Chances' because of their inherent resolve and tenacity, and some of that kicked in. She knew that she had permission to be on the site and, ignoring the voice in her head that kept repeating *'No, don't...'* she walked back to her vehicle, put the binoculars inside, and locked it with a steadfast determination to climb over the wall and confront the gamekeeper.

She turned to cross the lane and her heart leapt into her mouth.

Spooner was standing behind the wall that she had only seconds earlier been leaning on.

The shock of his appearance was so great that she jumped back, yelped, "Jesus Christ!" and banged into the side of her car. There appeared to be no way that he could have got to the wall in such a short time.

As her heart rate slowed, she stared at his fearsome appearance. He was wearing a long black coat and wide-brimmed hat, his skin was thin and pallid, and appeared to be stretched over his bony face and hands. His dark, sunken eyes looked weird, more like an animal than human and he looked as though he had been dragged out of a Victorian mausoleum.

In a raspy, hollow-sounding voice, Spooner said, "Don't you *ever* step onto this land again, or I'll shoot you where you stand..."

Trying not to look intimidated, Naomi walked across to him and said, "Charming. My name's Wilkes. I wrote to you last week..."

"Did you hear what I just said?"

"I have permission from your management company to..."

"Not any more you don't. It's been rescinded."

Naomi frowned and couldn't believe that Spooner already knew about the contretemps with Hayley Gillorton, but then figured that he could have been contacted by VHF radio or mobile phone.

"Alright, I accept that," she said, "but I'm trying to discover the whereabouts of Larkland Fen. Have you ever heard of it?"

Spooner leaned closer and said, "No. Now go away and don't come back."

Naomi looked up and saw Spooner's long, thin, wispy hair protruding from under the brim of his hat and said, "Is everybody on this estate so friendly, or are you all just having bad hair days?"

For the briefest of seconds Spooner looked as though he didn't know how to respond, but he recovered and said, "I'm warning you – don't ever attempt to set foot on this estate again, or you'll suffer the consequences."

"Nice, very nice," said Naomi, gaining confidence. "I think I'll get a photo of you for my office wall."

She turned and walked over to her CRV to retrieve her camera, but when she turned back, Spooner had gone.

She looked around but there was no sign of him; he had disappeared as mysteriously as he had appeared. Seconds later she got back into her vehicle, drove down to Ted and John, and pulled in behind their van.

As she walked towards them, Ted approached her with a curious look on his face.

"You did the right thing, disappearing," he said. "We've just had the spookiest experience ever!"

Naomi frowned and said, "How?"

"Seconds after you left, this weird looking guy appeared in the driveway opposite and just stared at us the whole time."

Naomi felt the hairs on the back of her neck go up.

"And did you speak to him?" she said.

"No. We nodded at him but he didn't respond – he just stood and stared at us until a minute or so before you arrived. We looked away for a second and when we looked back he'd gone."

"And what did he look like?"

Ted described Spooner perfectly.

Naomi opened her mouth to tell Ted about her experience but decided against it. She shook her head and said, "Hmm, – spooky indeed."

She didn't notice the return journey to her office at Walmsfield with all the odd things that had happened, but she was certain that she was edging closer to the truth about Whitewall.

Her parents, Jane and Sam, had arrived over the weekend, and she knew that her father was planning to visit Wordale Cottage Museum, so before leaving Cragg End Lane she'd called him on his mobile phone and asked him to see if Daphne Pettigrew could shed some light on the mysterious Les Spooner and the objectionable Hayley Gillorton.

She knew that her number one priority was the discovery of Larkland Fen, and that it must have been somewhere near High Farm Cottage, but she had no idea how to overcome the ubiquitous Les Spooner.

She needed to have an advantage; she needed the help of someone used to dealing with this type of problem.

Something clicked in her brain and she smiled. There really was only one person to contact, and she wondered why she hadn't thought of him before.

# Chapter 16

*22<sup>nd</sup> November 1871. Cheshire Lunatic Asylum, Parkway, Macclesfield*

Senior Ward Orderly Arnold Honeysucker walked lugubriously up to the reception desk, leaned over to the male receptionist, and said, "Where is 'e?"

The receptionist pointed to a man dressed in a plain, dark grey suit, white shirt, and blue tie, seated in the corner, leafing through a newspaper.

Honeysucker walked across the lodge and said, "Good afternoon. My name is 'oneysucker. I'm the Senior Ward Orderly. Are you Inspector Brewster?"

Brewster stood up, extended his right hand, and said, "Yes, Detective Inspector Brewster of Lancashire Constabulary."

"Begging your pardon, Inspector, but do you 'ave some proof?"

Brewster extracted his Warrant Card and showed it to Honeysucker.

"Thank you. Now, what can we do for you?"

"I'd like to know if you have any missing patients."

Honeysucker became defensive and said, "Not that I'm aware of."

Brewster paused for a few seconds and then said, "And without wishing to cause offence Mr Honeysucker, as a Ward Orderly, would you know the situation of *all* the patients in here?"

Honeysucker looked at Brewster trying to assess where the conversation was going and said, "Yes, more-or-less."

"And once again, not wishing to be offensive, 'more-or-less' doesn't exactly cover it, does it?"

Honeysucker's eyes narrowed. He said, "Alright, Inspector, why don't we cut to the chase? What do you want?"

Brewster wanted to speak to a more senior person, but was wise enough to know that being antagonistic to him would get him nowhere.

"Very well," he said. "We've received information that one of your allegedly missing patients is in hiding at a location somewhere in Lancashire."

On the opposite side of the lodge, the plumber and estate handyman Len Chapman was attending to a small leak from one of the radiators, and his ears pricked up when he heard the words, "in hiding at a location somewhere in Lancashire." He put down his metal spanners, picked up a rag, and feigned wiping around the joints as he listened to the rest of the conversation.

"And do we 'ave a name for this alleged patient, Inspector?"

"Yes we do – Maria Chance."

A cold shiver shot down two spines simultaneously, Honeysucker's and Chapman's.

Honeysucker stood still for a few seconds and then regained his composure.

"Maria Chance, eh? Right…" He paused, unsure of what to say. "Perhaps you'd like to wait 'ere while I go and make some enquiries."

He turned to go and then turned back again.

"Would you like a mug of tea and some biscuits while I'm gone?"

Brewster nodded and said, "Yes please – that would be nice."

Honeysucker nodded and then walked across to the receptionist to arrange for the tea and biscuits.

"Shan't be long," he said to Brewster as he departed. "Your tea will be 'ere in a jiffy."

Across the room, Chapman smeared some jointing compound around the top of the leaky joint, put his tools in his cloth bag, and wandered over to the receptionist.

"That'll be all right for a while," he said, "then I'll be back with the right sized spanners!" He shrugged his shoulders as if acknowledging a small blunder, smiled and left.

The disinterested receptionist said, "Right."

A few minutes later, Honeysucker rapped on the door of the Medical Superintendent Doctor Edwin Cobbold.

"Come in."

Honeysucker walked in and sat down.

"That sounded like a serious knock, Arnold. Anything the matter?"

"You could say that, Doctor."

Cobbold frowned as he looked at one of his most trusted employees because he knew that Honeysucker wasn't an excitable man.

"We 'ave a Lancashire Detective Police Inspector in reception, asking if we 'ave any missing patients by the name of Maria Chance."

Cobbold was stunned.

"What? How?" he said. "You haven't said anything have you?"

"No, of course not," said Honeysucker. "I arranged for 'im to 'ave a mug of tea while I made enquiries."

"Crikey, I don't like the sound of that," said Cobbold. "We'd better get Ida in."

He stood up from behind his office desk, walked across to a few bell sashes, and pulled one.

A couple of minutes later, the office door opened and Matron Ida Pinkstaff stepped in. She saw the concerned look on the faces of her colleagues and said, "Edwin, Arnold, everything all right?"

"We have a Detective Inspector in reception, asking if we have a missing patient by the name of Maria Chance," said Cobbold.

Pinkstaff walked to another chair and sat down as the men stared at her.

"Hmm," she said. "Tricky, but not insurmountable; we still have that patient with the memory loss up in Private Ward Nine. She, and everybody else up there, including the staff, believes that she is Maria Chance."

"But what if the real one turns up here? How will we explain that away?" said Cobbold.

"That's not likely, Edwin," said Honeysucker. "She disappeared from 'ere with nary a trace, so it's not likely that she'll turn up and admit she's a missing patient, is it?"

"Arnold's right," said Pinkstaff. "She'd know that she'd be vulnerable to re-incarceration if she hadn't been medically discharged."

Cobbold leaned back in his chair and stroked his chin.

"True enough," he said.

"So," said Honeysucker, "what do I tell the Inspector? That we know of no such person, or that we 'ave a patient by the name of Maria Chance 'oo isn't missing?"

"It's your call, Edwin," said Pinkstaff.

Cobbold looked from face to face for a second and then said, "We tell the policeman that we do have a patient by the name of Maria Chance, and that she is not missing."

"That would have been my choice too," said Pinkstaff. "There could be dozens of women with that name. Ours is here, safe and well, and we have no missing patients."

Honeysucker pulled himself to his feet and headed for the door. He turned, nodded to his colleagues, and said, "Very well, I'll tell 'im."

Senior Sister Florence Parks was sitting in a small anteroom off Ward One in the female epileptic unit, sipping a hot cup of tea, when the door sounded as though it had been hit by a train. She jumped and spilled some tea on her apron.

The door burst open and Len Chapman entered.

"Good grief, Len," said Florence. "Look what you made me do!" She pointed to the stain on her apron.

"Sorry Flo," said Chapman, "but there's a Peeler in reception asking if we have a missing patient by the name of Maria Chance..."

Florence put her cup down and said, "Oh, good Lord..."

"I overheard Honeysucker tell the Inspector – who was from Lancashire Constabulary, by the way..."

Florence said, "Oh no..."

"... that he'd go and make enquiries."

"And then what?"

"I made an excuse about having the wrong tools and rushed over to you."

Florence thought for a second and then said, "You need to get back over there and see what Honeysucker says to the policeman. After that, come and see me and we'll decide what needs to be done."

"All right, I'll go now." Chapman departed and almost ran back to the reception lodge.

Honeysucker ambled in and saw the policeman still sitting in the corner.

He walked over to him and said, "Sorry to keep you waiting Inspector..."

The door to the reception lodge burst open and everybody looked at Chapman as he blundered in. Thinking on his feet, he said, "Sorry! I just tripped over the boot scraper... Wasn't looking where I was going..."

An awkward silence ensued until the receptionist said, "Not your day, is it, Len?"

Chapman smiled, said "Sorry," once again, and returned to the leaky radiator.

Honeysucker continued to stare at Chapman for a few seconds and then shook his head. He turned back to Brewster and said, "'e's a good lad... generally."

Brewster nodded and said, "Quite."

"Now then, Inspector, I 'ad a word with the Medical Superintendent and the Matron, and they assure me that Maria Chance is still 'ere in one of our wards."

"Oh," said Brewster. "So you do have a patient by that name?"

"Yes, we do, and she is 'ere in our care."

"Well that seems to answer that then," said Brewster. "It would seem that we have a case of mistaken identity."

"It would seem so, Inspector."

"Very well, Mr Honeysucker," said Brewster, extending his arm. "You've been most helpful. Thank you for your time, and I hope that I haven't disrupted your daily routine."

"Not at all, Inspector," said Honeysucker shaking the offered hand. "Anytime."

Chapman watched and listened until the Inspector had departed, and then turned back to the leaky radiator with a heavy load off his mind.

Several hours later, Brewster walked back into Rochdale Police Station and saw Banks at his usual position behind the front desk.

Banks looked up and said, "Worthwhile trip, sir?"

"So, so," said Brewster.

"Did Parkway confirm that the lady was missing?"

"On the contrary – they confirmed that she was still in their care."

"A case of mistaken identity then," said Banks.

Brewster nodded and said, "Yes, I suppose so…"

He remained still as various possibilities went through his mind.

Banks noticed the Inspector ruminating and said, "Everything all right, sir?"

Brewster looked up and said, "I was just recalling the way in which that anonymous informant reported the whereabouts of the apparently missing Maria Chance, and how positive he sounded."

"He did that, sir," said Banks, recalling the incident himself.

"Well," said Brewster still pondering his options, "we won't actively pursue this line of enquiry unless he shows up here again, and then if he does, *I'd* like to talk to him."

"Very well, sir," said Banks.

Brewster turned to walk away and then stopped; something was nagging at him. He turned back to Banks and said, "I don't think that we've heard the last of this Graham. Be sure to let me know if there are any further developments. We may yet find ourselves going back up to Whitewall to see what's what."

Banks raised an eyebrow and said, "I bloody hope not…"

At 7:00pm the same night, Sister Florence Parks, and her husband Cornelius sat in front of Maria and Silas in their parlour at Whitewall. They'd been on numerous occasions since Maria's escape from Parkway, but each of those had been joyous events. This was not.

"This is a delightful surprise Flo," said Maria, "but what brings you and Cornelius out on such a cold night, and so far away from home?"

Cornelius saw his wife look at him and said, "Go on, tell her."

Florence turned to face Maria and said, "Len Chapman was working in the reception lodge at Parkway this morning and overheard a police detective asking Arnold Honeysucker, our Senior Ward Orderly, whether we had a missing patient by the name of Maria Chance."

Maria's eyes widened and she clapped her left hand over her mouth.

A shocked Silas said, "How the hell...?"

"I don't know," said Florence, "but he did."

"And what did your Ward Orderly say?" said Maria.

"Apparently Honeysucker went off to make enquiries and then returned to the policeman about twenty minutes later, saying that they did indeed have a Maria Chance in their care, and that she was safe and well; which, of course, is all news to me, because even after all this time, I haven't yet been told about the private wards above the admin block." Florence paused for a second and then said, "Mind you, that's not surprising if they really are keeping somebody there by the name of Maria Chance."

"That doesn't bear thinking about," said Silas, "because if it's true, who is it?"

"'If it's true' being the operative words," said Florence.

"That's why we thought we'd better come tonight," said Cornelius. "Those crafty buggers could be just saying that to mask their apparent ineptitude while they try to find you."

"And did the policeman say where I was supposed to be?" said Maria.

"No," said Florence. "He made a non-specific reference to you hiding somewhere in Lancashire."

"Oh, good Lord," said Maria. "Even the mention of Lancashire is too close for my liking. You don't think…?"

"We don't know," said Cornelius. "That's why we came."

Maria turned to face Silas and said, "What do you think – should we leave?"

"No, *we* shouldn't, but perhaps you should. You've been saying for some time that you'd like to see your cousin Grant in Gloucester, so maybe now's the time. If you leave on the early train tomorrow, you can stay for a week or so. That'll allow enough time to see if we get any unwanted callers."

Nods of agreement were passed around and it was settled.

Silas got up and excused himself; he needed to think. He walked out into the yard and recalled the exchange that he'd had with Harland over their tenancy a few days earlier, and the yell of "lex talionis, cabby" as he'd departed with his tail between his legs. He couldn't believe that Maria's nephew would be wicked enough to do such a dreadful thing to his own flesh and blood, but then again, nothing surprised him about the Chance family and Whitewall anymore.

He walked down to the outhouse, where his faithful dog Sugg lay on the floor.

Sugg leapt to his feet and stood to attention at his master's side.

"Good boy," said Silas patting the huge dog's neck. "We may soon have to be a bit more choosey about who we allow onto the land in the days to come."

Back in the parlour, Florence said, "How do you think that policeman got wind of you being an escapee from Parkway?"

"I don't know, Flo, but if your Ward Orderly told them that nobody was missing, maybe they'll drop it."

"True," said Florence, "but that doesn't answer my question. What, or who, alerted the police in the first place?"

Maria remained quiet for a few minutes and then, like Silas out in the yard, could only think of one person – Harland.

# Chapter 17

*Monday 10<sup>th</sup> April 2006. Wordale Cottage Museum,*
*Wordale Moor*

Sam Chance stepped out of his car and took in a deep breath. He was back on Wordale Moor where generations of his ancestors had lived and breathed before. It was invigorating and he loved it. He looked across at the museum and hoped that Daphne would be on duty. He locked the car, walked over and entered.

Nothing appeared to have changed since his last visit in May 2002. The glass cases with the stuffed and mounted wildlife set in countryside scenes were as he remembered them, and the 17<sup>th</sup> century ducking stool remained in its place with the rhyme extolling its virtue. One or two people milled about, peering in here and there, and listening to the small electronic information devices provided by the museum.

He walked further in and caught sight of an elderly couple talking to a female museum official. His heart dropped because, unlike the blonde haired Daphne that he remembered, this lady had dark ginger coloured hair. That was, until she spoke, and then he smiled, walked up to the back of her and waited until the elderly couple had finished, and moved away.

"I'll bet you had no mates at school with hair that colour."

Daphne wheeled around, looked at Sam from toe up to head, and then said, "Isn't it a basic requirement to have some hair before offering fashion advice, Samuel Chance?"

"Ooh, cruel!" said Sam with a smile on his face. "I still do have plenty of hair, you know."

"In that case, it's just a shame that none of it remained on your head."

Sam laughed and conceded defeat. He looked at Daphne, and as per his previous visit, she looked delightful. She was no more than five feet four inches tall, wore a cream cashmere figure-hugging jumper, a navy blue knee length skirt, black patent leather high-heeled shoes, and around her neck hung a silver medium length necklace with small glistening crystals.

"Now then, Sam," said Daphne, "what is it this time? More information on the Whitewall Estate? Of course it is."

Sam smiled again as he remembered Daphne's quirky way of asking questions and then answering them herself.

"Well, yes and no," he said. "It is related to the Whitewall Estate, but in a roundabout sort of way."

"And am I supposed to deduce what you want from that?"

Sam opened his mouth to speak but was cut off.

"No of course not!" she said.

Sam waited for just a nanosecond before responding, but even that was too long.

"Well, are we to stand here all day playing guessing games?"

Sam opened his mouth, but was again cut off.

"No, of course we're not, so spit it out!"

"Right," said Sam almost panicking to get out an answer. "I need to find the location of somewhere named Larkland Fen, on or near to Rushworth Moor."

Daphne frowned and said, "Larkland Fen? I can't say that I've ever heard of that before."

She stood stock still, trying to conjure up any reference to it, but nothing was forthcoming. She looked sideways at Sam and said, "Hmm, this requires my reference books..."

She led the way to her office behind the central displays, unlocked the door, and they stepped in.

That too was just as Sam had remembered it; various artefacts lay atop the work surfaces, piles of old books and papers lay beneath inspection lamps, innumerable unrecognisable curios lay scattered about the place and everywhere had a 'musty museum' smell.

For the next half hour, Daphne scoured all of her maps, and the Internet for any reference to Larkland Fen, but found none.

"Are you sure that it was Lark*land* Fen and not Lark Hill Fen?" she said, echoing the question posed by Dave Brown to Naomi earlier.

Sam waited for her to answer her own question, but she didn't and it caught him out.

"Sam, did you hear me?"

Sam opened his mouth but got caught out again.

"Well, of course you did – you're only feet away from me." Once again he paused, but upon seeing Daphne staring at him, he said, "Yes, I did hear you, and yes, we're sure that it's Larkland and not Lark Hill."

"Well, I'm sorry to disappoint you, but if I can't find anywhere named Larkland Fen on Rushworth Moor with all of the reference sources at my disposal, it isn't there."

"Perhaps it's somewhere nearby?" said Sam.

"No, it's not. I've very carefully checked that name with all the reference material on both Lancashire and Yorkshire, and it doesn't exist. There are one or two references to locations and/or businesses on the Internet named 'Larklands', but there is nothing with the specific name of Larkland Fen."

"Okay," he said. "We'll have to go back to the drawing board with that one. Now, – have you ever heard of a woman named Hayley Gillorton and a gamekeeper named Leslie Spooner?"

Daphne frowned and said, "The former, no; the latter, yes. He is the unusual and, I am led to believe, exceptionally sinister gamekeeper of the Cragg Vale Estate on Rushworth Moor, owned by Adrian and Christiana Darke."

Sam's mouth fell wide open.

"Adrian Darke? Are you sure?"

"Of course I am."

"Stone the flaming crows!" said Sam. "Just wait until Naomi hears that."

Sam saw Daphne raise her eyebrows in question. He explained who Naomi was, what she did for a living, and how she had led the research into the findings at Whitewall. He also told her that Darke had been one of the main suspects in most of the nefarious goings on relating to that research in 2002.

Daphne listened as Sam related the various snippets until she said, "Everything about Adrian Darke seems to be shrouded in mystery, but nothing more so than his gamekeeper, the curious Leslie Spooner."

She went on to explain that there had been numerous reports of Spooner being seen in two places at once, of his impossible ability to move from one location to another at either breakneck speed or 'magically', and of his inexplicable ability to be able to appear within minutes, wherever, and at whatever time anybody trespassed on any part of the Cragg Vale Estate.

Sam tried to think of rational explanations for all of those activities, but nothing came to mind.

"But the oddest thing of all about Mr Spooner," said Daphne, "is his age."

"His age?"

"Yes, quite so. According to the local census records, he appears to have been the sole occupant living at his domicile, Cragg Vale Cottage since 1832, which makes him a spritely one hundred-and-seventy-nine years old."

"A hundred-and-seventy-nine?" said Sam. "That's impossible!"

· "We know it is, but it changes nothing. Furthermore, the census records seem to be the only official reference to him anywhere.

"Because of his 'out-of-this-world' ability to do things, dozens of people have tried to research his life and history, but he has no driving licence, television licence, credit cards, debit cards, bank accounts, library cards or even medical history that can be viewed. He's never been seen in any shops, he doesn't own any kind of vehicle that we know about, he's never been known to visit any relatives – if he has any – and he has only, but ubiquitously, ever been seen on the Cragg Vale Estate.

"Furthermore, he has, for as long as anybody can remember, been the only gamekeeper *ever* at Cragg Vale, and in all of the people's recollections of him, he has always dressed in the same clothes and has always looked the same age."

Sam was amazed. "What about the police?" he said. "Can't you make any enquiries with them?"

"I once asked an old friend of mine, a now ex-police constable, to run a check on him, but he found nothing. It would seem that he has never done anything wrong either."

"Well, I guess that we can take comfort from that at least, because if he hasn't ever done anything wrong, there's nothing to be scared of, is there?"

He saw Daphne open her mouth to speak, but playfully caught her out at her own game. He said, "Of course there isn't!"

Daphne looked at him and raised an eyebrow.

Sam smiled and raised an eyebrow back. He looked at his watch and said, "As much as I hate to say this, I suppose that I'd better not hold you up any longer."

Daphne shot a glance at the clock on her wall and said, "No, I suppose not. There may be people out there waiting for me."

Sam pursed his lips and said, "Thanks for your help, and I'll keep my wits about me if I come into contact with that gamekeeper."

Daphne smiled at him with genuine affection and said, "I'm sorry that I wasn't able to help you any more, but if you ever do locate Larkland Fen, please give me a call or drop in, 'cos I'd love to know where it is." She paused for a second and then said, "Wouldn't I? Of course I would!"

Sam burst out laughing and said, "Touché!" He walked across to Daphne, extended his hand, and said, "Once again, it was a delight meeting with you."

Daphne shook the offered hand and said, "Look after yourself, Sam Chance, and be very careful around Leslie Spooner. There can't be all smoke and no fire, can there?"

Sam waited for the answer, but none came.

"There – got you!" said Daphne.

The two friends walked out into the car park and bid each other a warm farewell.

Sam got into his car and watched as Daphne walked gracefully back to the museum. He saw her turn and wave. He waved back and thought, "Oh, Daphne Pettigrew, in another life…"

Several hours later, within the warm confines of The Little Mill public house in Rowarth, Naomi, Carlton, Jane, and Sam sat mulling over the day's events following a very hearty and enjoyable early evening meal.

All four of them loved the ambience of the countryside pub. A log fire burned in the stone fireplace, the faint smell of burning wood pervaded the air, the furniture was big and comfortable, the staff were amiable and courteous, and the food and drinks had been excellent.

"Oh my word!" said Sam.

Everyone turned to look at him.

"I've only forgotten to tell you one of the most important bits of info that Daphne passed on..." He looked from curious face to curious face and then said, "The Cragg Vale Estate is owned by Christiana and Adrian Darke."

Naomi could have been knocked down by a feather.

"Oh my God," she said. "Doesn't that just say it all! The underhanded on-site activity, – that bitch Hayley 'Ms' Gillorton, and the spooky Les Miserables. I might have known!" She looked at her father and said, "Did you say Christiana Darke?"

Sam nodded.

"Christiana Darke, Christadar Property Holdings. I should have known."

"How could you?" said Jane.

Something else clicked in Naomi's head.

"The crest on the gates at the top of the drive opposite High Farm Cottage. I read the Darke family motto, 'Aquila non capit muscas' – 'the eagle does not catch mosquitoes', and thought that it looked familiar, but I never made the connection." She berated herself for missing a vital piece of information.

"Well," said Jane who couldn't stop herself being motherly, "I hope that you aren't planning to do anything foolish after your experiences with that creepy guy – and especially now that you know who owns the place."

"Don't worry, Jane, I wouldn't let her," said Carlton.

Naomi flashed a look at her husband and said, "And do you think that you could stop me if I wanted to?"

Carlton said, "I'd give it a damned good go."

"Do you think that I need help then?"

"Not with Hayley Gillorton I don't, but it sounds as though Les 'the-walking-dead' Miserables is a completely different kettle of fish."

"He's right," said Sam. "We all know what a fearless little powerhouse you can be when you set your mind to it, but it does sound as though we're dealing with something out of the ordinary with him."

"So you think that I could do with help, do you?" said Naomi.

Carlton cottoned onto a tone in Naomi's voice and realised that she was leading the conversation somewhere.

"Alright, that's twice that you've asked now. Where's this going?"

Naomi looked at her husband and was surprised that he'd latched on in so short a time. She said, "Well, you know that I've attempted to research Les Spooner along with Percy and Gasworks..."

"Gasworks?" interrupted Sam. "Who the hell is Gasworks?"

"Don't ask!" said Carlton.

Naomi looked at her father and said, "He's a friend of Percy's who breaks wind and then jokes about it every time it happens."

Sam shook his head and said, "Weird..."

"Yes. Now, as I said, I and numerous other people have tried to research Les Spooner without much success." Naomi turned to her father and said, "Including your friend Daphne Pettigrew. So I think that it's about time we gave ourselves an edge."

"An edge?" said Carlton, "What type of edge?"

"Somebody who could make a real difference."

Silence reigned for a few seconds until Carlton said, "Who?"

Naomi looked from face to face and then turned back to Carlton. She said, "Auntie Rosie."

"Rosie!" repeated Carlton, "But he's in Florida!"

"Yes, Rosie and maybe two of the guys from the sewing circle."

Carlton was incredulous and said, "Are you serious?"

He recalled numerous offers of help from his gay and flamboyant, ex-marine buddies, known to all as Auntie Rosie and the sewing circle. He'd saved three of their lives during The Falklands conflict, and they'd been invaluable in helping them in Florida in 2002, but to ask them to come to the UK was still 'a big ask.'

"Can you think of anybody better equipped to be able to deal with Adrian Darke and Les Spooner?" said Naomi cutting across Carlton's thoughts. "And to get us onto the Cragg Vale Estate?"

Carlton didn't answer at first and then said, "Okay, but even if you are right, there's no guarantee that he or any of the others will be able to come."

"I'm going to email that re-worked contrivance to Alan in Florida when we get home tonight," said Naomi, "so I can drop Rosie a line too."

Alright," said Carlton, "but don't get your hopes up. I know that it's been a while since any of them returned to Blighty, but whether or not they'll consider it is another matter."

He had a troubling thought and said, "Oh, Gordon Bennett!"

Everybody turned and looked at him.

"If they do come, Naomi Wilkes," he said, "I will be holding you, in person, responsible for keeping them well away from the Council Offices..."

# Chapter 18

*Tuesday 11<sup>th</sup> April 2006. The Farlington House, Dunnellon, Florida*

Alan Farlington looked down at the email from Naomi and read it for the second time.

"Hey Debs!" he called from his den, "Are you free for the next half hour?"

"Why?" called back Deborah from the kitchen. "I'm preparing dinner right now."

"We've just received another email from Naomi and…"

"Alan, Alan, I've got pans on the stove and I can't hear you – come on through."

Alan picked up the email and walked through to the kitchen.

"Sorry honey," said Deborah. "I couldn't hear you with all this going on. Now, what were you trying to tell me?"

"We got another email from Naomi, and she's asked us to look at the chest again."

"Again? We've already looked at it a thousand times. We know that there's nothing in there, so what on earth does she want us to look at it again for?"

Alan held up the email and said, "One of her conservator buddies reckons that she's cracked the contrivance that she sent us a couple of weeks back, and that if we find something, we could be getting some exciting news."

Deborah said, "Intriguing. Let me read it."

She stopped stirring the contents of one of the pans, took the email off Alan, and read it.

*"Hi Guys,*

*Sorry to trouble you again, but would you please re-examine the chest? This time carefully inspect in and around that indentation to the right-hand side of the carvings. A*

*colleague of mine believes that she has solved the contrivance I
sent to you on the 31<sup>st</sup> March. This is what she has come up
with:*

*'The first chest you must obtain, then seek the truth within
grain.*

*O' truth on topmost board, when first you order all
discord.'*

*Have a good look at it and tell me what you come up with,
because if you do find anything, I could be coming right back to
you with some very exciting news!*

*Love N xx"*

Like Alan minutes earlier, she read it a couple of times and then
said, "Hmm, I see what you mean."

"That's why I asked you if you are free for the next half
hour, so that we can look at the chest again."

Deborah glanced at the clock on the kitchen wall and said,
"I can turn the heat down and let the pans simmer for a short
while, but only for twenty minutes or so, tops."

"Okay," said Alan, "I'll go and get it. Is it still under the
bed?"

Deborah nodded and said, "As far as I know."

He made his way into their bedroom and reached under the
bed. He waved his arm about from left to right but felt nothing.
He lifted the edge of the duvet and leaned down so that he could
see under the bed. He moved one or two items around but saw
nothing. He gave up scratching around on all fours, stood up,
and humped the entire bed to one side. The chest wasn't there.

He frowned and then walked back into the kitchen.

"The chest isn't there – have you moved it?"

Deborah said, "No. It must be, did you check everywhere?"

"Yes, I shifted the whole bed to one side, and it isn't there."

Deborah stopped stirring the pan and tried to recall if she'd
put the chest somewhere else and had forgotten about it, but
within a few minutes she said, "No, I haven't moved it. Are you
sure that you put it back under the bed after the last time you
looked at it?"

This time it was Alan's turn to think, but within seconds he said, "I'm positive that I did, so you must have moved it when you were cleaning up or something."

Deborah took exception and said, "Hey mister, if I tell you that I haven't moved it, I haven't moved it, so quit with the accusations while you're ahead..."

Alan knew when to back down and said, "But if it isn't under there, where could it be?"

"Beats me. Maybe one of the kids has had it."

"But I thought that we told them not to touch the chest?"

Deborah looked sideways at Alan and said, "Come on, hon, it's a wooden box for pity's sake. I appreciate that it's a family heirloom, but it's lasted for over two hundred years already, so I'm guessing that it can stand the playful knocks and bangs of a couple of kids."

"But that's the point, isn't it? Its age and history means that it should be treated with care so that we can pass it on to our children to treasure. It's not for them to just take and use for God knows what. What if it gets damaged?"

Deborah said, "Okay, okay – let's check in all the usual places, then if we still can't find it, we'll question Elizabeth and Thomas, because Jacqueline and Christopher would have asked first." She paused for a second and then said, "Even then, I can't think what Elizabeth would want with it 'cos she's never shown any interest in it before, so my best guess would be Thomas."

"Fine," said Alan. "I'll go check in the garage, his bedroom, and anywhere else I can think of. After that we'll have to wait 'til he gets home and ask him then."

Just after 5pm, Thomas walked in and headed straight for his bedroom.

"Just one moment son," called Alan. "Come in here, will you?"

Seconds later, Thomas walked into the lounge, perched on the edge of the sofa, and said, "I'm in trouble, aren't I?"

"That depends on your answer," said Alan.

Thomas sat back on the sofa and waited for the hammer to fall.

"Now, son, you won't be in trouble if you're honest with me, but if you lie that'll be different, do you understand?"

"Yes."

"Have you removed Gran'ma's old chest from under our bed and used it for anything?"

Thomas couldn't believe his bad luck and the speed at which he'd been found out. His cheeks turned bright red; he looked down, and didn't answer.

"Well, I think that that answers that," said Alan. "Where is it?"

Thomas hung his head lower and kept quiet.

"Thomas!" said Deborah. "Answer your father."

Thomas remained quiet.

"Come on," said Alan. "What have you done with it?"

Thomas gathered up some courage, looked straight at his father and said, "You did say that I wouldn't be in trouble if I told you the truth, didn't you?"

Alan looked at Deborah and said, "I don't like the sound of this…"

Thomas repeated, "But you said I wouldn't be in trouble if I told you the truth."

Alan looked at his son and said, "Yes I did – so what is the truth?"

Thomas looked at his mother and then his father and then looked down and said, "I've lost it."

*"What?"* yelled Alan, "You've lost it? Where, and when? – And what the hell where you doing with it in the first place?" He was furious.

"I'm sorry, pa," said a woeful Thomas. "I didn't mean to…"

"That's not good enough! You know that you weren't meant to touch that chest! Now, what were you doing with it, and where did you lose it?"

Thomas stared down at his legs and, "I needed something to put my tackle in 'cos the lid on my fishing box broke."

"My God!" said Alan. "This just gets better and better, doesn't it?"

"There's no need to blaspheme in front him," said Deborah, "and you did promise that he wouldn't be in trouble if he told you the truth, right?"

Alan looked at Deborah without answering. He took in a deep breath and then turned back to Thomas.

"Okay, where did you lose it?"

"Taylor and me…"

"Taylor and I!" said Deborah.

Thomas looked at his mother and said, "Taylor and I took one of Kathy Dykes' boats out on the Withlacoochee for a couple of hours to go bass fishing. When we'd finished, we took the boat back to her place near the South Williams bridge. I picked up the fish and thought that Taylor had gotten all the gear, but when we got back to his place I noticed that the chest was missing."

"You hadn't dropped it overboard, had you?" said Alan in deep despair.

"No. Taylor missed it 'cos I'd stuffed it under the thwart to keep the lid shut 'cos I didn't want to have to carry that big key with me."

Alan raised his eyebrows, shook his head, and said, "Go on…"

Thomas looked at his father and said, "We went back to Kathy's place, found the boat on the rack, and saw that the chest had gone. We went in and asked her for it, but she said she didn't know what we were talking about 'cos she hadn't seen it either. Then, when I asked if I could go talk to Backbone, she told us to leave him be, and to hightail it out."

Alan placed his head in his hands for a few seconds, then looked up and said, "Just perfect! Kathy 'the psycho' Dykes, and Backbone – how many times have we told you stay away from them?"

"But they're the cheapest boats, pa…"

"Of course they are, because they're the crappiest!"

"Alan!" said Deborah. "Language!"

"But it's true!" said Alan.

"That's no excuse."

Alan looked at Deborah, apologised, and then turned back to Thomas.

"We've told you before that whenever the other boat operators take any of their boats out of service, Kathy Dykes buys them and puts them in her fleet."

"They may not be the prettiest boats on the river," said Thomas, "but they have to be sound 'cos of the crocs, so it's not like anybody's going to get hurt because of a bad paint job…"

"Can't argue with that logic," said Deborah.

Alan shook his head in frustration and realised that they were drifting away from the point.

"Alright, alright – that besides, are you positive that the chest was in the boat when you returned it to Dykes' Yard?"

"Yes, I am."

"So in your opinion, they must have it?"

"Yes."

"Right," said Alan. "She doesn't close until 8 o' clock. Get in the car; we're going back there now!"


Thirty minutes later, Alan and Thomas walked into Dykes' Yard office and rapped on the counter.

The dishevelled looking Kathy walked in behind the counter and said, "Yep?"

Alan swept Thomas towards the counter and said, "My son and his buddy hired one of your boats this afternoon, and he's left his tackle box, an old sea chest which is a valuable family heirloom…" He immediately berated himself for using the word 'valuable' in her company but it was too late, "…under the thwart, and we want it back."

Kathy looked down at Thomas, then looked back up to Alan and said, "I already told the kid we don't have it."

Alan stared in silence for a few seconds, unsure of how to respond and then said, "Where's Backbone? Perhaps he's seen it."

"He's gone home," said Kathy, "and anyways, he'd tell you the same."

"Yeah, I'll bet he would…" said Alan.

"Implying what?" said Kathy giving him a hawkish glare.

"Look – that chest has no monetary value but it belonged to my grandmother, so it means a lot to us."

Kathy fixed Alan with a steely glare and said, "How many more times am I going to have to say this? We don't have it!"

"Well, I'm sorry, but if my son said he left it in the boat, and that it was there when he returned it to the yard, then I believe him. So I'm giving you one last chance to give it to me, or I'm getting the Sheriff down here!"

Kathy shrugged and said, "Do I look like I give a shit?"

For a split second, Thomas saw a reflection in the glass cover of a notice on the counter. He turned around and saw Backbone climbing into a pickup. He jabbed his father in the side, pointed out of the door, and said, "Pa!"

Alan turned around, saw what was happening, and ran outside.

Backbone saw Alan rush out and heard him yell. He jammed his foot down on the accelerator and in a shower of dust and gravel sped out of the yard.

"Shit!" shouted Alan. He turned back to his car to give pursuit and stopped dead in his tracks.

Kathy was standing beside it, with the ignition keys in her hand.

"Now what, cowboy?" she said. "You gonna to make me throw these in the river, or are you gonna leave my boy alone?"

"Don't do anything stupid," said Alan. "That's the only set I've got."

"T'aint me who has to consider what stupid is now, is it?"

"Alright," said Alan. "Just give me the keys."

"And are you gonna leave my boy alone?"

"Yes, yes – now just give me the goddamn keys!"

Kathy stood looking at Alan for a second said, "Naw!" then turned and threw the keys into the grass twenty or thirty feet away.

"What the hell did you do that for?" shouted Alan.

"Two guesses, smartass," said Kathy, and then she turned and walked back to the office.

Alan ran across to where he thought that the keys had landed and scoured the area. To his good fortune they'd landed on a small clump of dried grass, and within ten panicky minutes he had them back.

He walked back to the car and found Thomas sitting inside.

He climbed into the driver's seat and said, "Why didn't you help me look for the keys?"

"'Cos I went and did some looking for myself," said Thomas.

Alan looked at his son and said, "What do you mean?"

"I went round the back while you were having that row with Kathy, and looked in Backbone's shed." He held up a few small items and said, "and I found these."

Alan looked at what Thomas was holding, and recognised his spare reel, gutting knife, and plastic box of beads and floats.

"They were in the chest," said Thomas.

Alan was furious. He grabbed the items off Thomas, jumped out of the car, and stormed back into the office. He banged his clenched fist on the counter and shouted, "Kathy! Kathy!"

Kathy re-appeared and said, "For Chrissakes! What now?"

Alan held up the items and said, "These were in the chest when Thomas brought the boat back, and he's just found them on Backbone's bench, so how do you account for that?"

Kathy looked at the items and said, "He had no right snooping around private property."

"And you had no right stealing my chest!" said Alan filled with indignation. "Now I demand that you return it immediately or I *will* call the Sheriff."

Kathy considered her options for a few seconds and recalled a not too distant brush with the intolerant, no-nonsense Sheriff about 'alleged stolen goods,' and she wasn't keen to repeat that.

"Alright," she said, "I'll see if Bernard…"

"Who?" said Alan.

"Bernard… Backbone, you all call him. I'll see if he's picked the chest up by mistake, and if he has, I'll bring it back in the morning."

"By mistake my ass!" said Alan.

"Do you want the chest or not?"

Alan nodded and said, "Yes I do. I'll be back here for it at 8:15am, and if it isn't here by then, I'll be on the phone to the Sheriff by 8:16am!"

# Chapter 19

*5<sup>th</sup> December 1871. Rochdale High Street, Lancashire*

Harland Chance looked left, then right, and then slipped a ha'penny into the eager hand of the butcher's delivery boy.

"And are you sure that it was Mrs Cartwright who took the delivery from you?" he said.

"Not atcherly took it from me mister, but it was 'er what told me where to put it."

"And when was this?"

"Before it was light this morning."

Harland looked at the open countenance of the young boy and decided that he was telling the truth.

"Alright lad, off you go."

The boy looked down at the coin in his hand and then said, "Do you want me to check again tomorrow?"

Harland half-smiled at the boy's ingenuity and said, "Maybe next week – we'll see."

The boy said, "Thanks mister," and skipped off down the road.

Harland ambled down the High Street in the opposite direction, deep in thought.

It had been two weeks since he'd reported Maria's whereabouts to the police, and nothing seemed to have changed. He knew that following his last disastrous visit to the police station he couldn't take the risk of going back to check progress, but he felt more and more incensed by their apparent lack of action as each day passed. He needed some way, any way, to get them off the Estate.

He was aware that his aunt and Silas were only tenants, but that was beside the point. If they could be encouraged, peacefully or not, to vacate, then he and his family could take up the tenancy and pursue the right of ownership from within his rightful inheritance.

But how to get them off was the tricky bit. It appeared that his attempt at having his aunt returned to Parkway had failed, so he needed another, more drastic solution.

Deep in thought, he sauntered off the High Street and meandered down a maze of back streets, not concentrating on where he was going, when all of a sudden, in front of him, the front door to a public house burst open, and a man flew out onto the pavement. Seconds later, he saw a bulky man sporting an ankle length apron appear in the doorway and yell, "Don't let me have to tell you again – keep out of my pub!"

He stopped walking and watched from a distance as the stricken man lay staring at the man who'd ejected him.

"Fucking potato-headed arsehole!" shouted the man in the doorway, and then turned and disappeared inside.

Tommy Bunn, or just Squat to his associates, was a bad-tempered dwarf with a very bad attitude. He was a thief, a rapist and he had crabs that constantly nipped at his filthy pubic regions. He never washed, he stank from every pore in his body, and he spent most of his waking hours drinking and getting into fights.

He staggered to his feet, made a foul gesture to the retreating back of the landlord, and then saw that his clothes were muddy and wet from being thrown into a large, dirty puddle.

"Fucking bastard!" he yelled at the closed door. "Just wait 'til the pastor comes back – you won't fucking pick on me then!"

He looked around to see if anybody had observed his humiliating ejection, and saw a dapper figure staring at him from a distance.

"And you can fuck off too, you fucking toff bastard!"

Harland was doubly stunned; first because the ejected man was a dwarf, and second by the man's sheer aggression. He didn't say anything; he just stared in disbelief.

"You heard me shithead," shouted Squat. "Walk away now, or I'll come down there and kick your fucking arse!"

Harland felt as though he was in some sort of surreal dream world occupied by nasty, aggressive half-men, and couldn't believe all of the ire being directed at him for just standing and looking.

A thought popped into his head.

"Right, cunt!" shouted Squat, "You asked for this…"

He set off towards Harland at a brisk rolling gait, determined to kick some upper class dandy arse.

Harland waited until Squat was within a few feet, and then said, "Why did that landlord throw you out?"

Squat stopped walking and said, "What did you say?"

"I said, buggerlugs, why did that landlord throw you out?"

Squat looked up at Harland in disbelief and said, "Do you want your fucking face rearranging, you nosy bastard? What business is it of yours?"

"It's my business because I made it my business," said Harland, as cool as a cucumber, "and if you don't like it, you can piss off back to the bridge you live under, you ugly little troll!"

Squat was stunned.

"What did you just fucking say?" he yelled.

"You heard me," said Harland.

Squat bent down, snatched a knife out of his left sock, stood back up, and stopped dead in his tracks.

Pointing straight at his throat was the long thin blade of a walking-stick sword.

"Now then, short-arse," said Harland. "Are you going to calm down, or am I going to have to cut you down to size?" He paused for a second and then added, "Not that you can afford much more of that…"

Squat stared with venom at Harland but didn't move.

Keeping the blade in place, Harland said, "Good. Now that I have your undivided attention, I'd like to ask you something."

Squat's eyes narrowed, he looked up, and said, "What?"

"When that landlord threw you out of his pub, I heard you say that he wouldn't pick on you when 'the pastor' comes back?"

"He fucking wouldn't!" said Squat.

"Yes, yes," said Harland, "I gather that. What I want to know is why he wouldn't pick on you if the pastor was back?"

"Just because he wouldn't!"

Harland started to lose patience. He pushed the point of his sword into the flesh of Squat's neck and leaned closer to his face.

"You're trying my patience, little man. Now, – why wouldn't the landlord pick on you if the pastor was here? Is it because he is a man of the cloth, or something else?"

Squat emitted a "Huh!" and thought about his friend for a second.

'The pastor', Robert Dogg, was as far from a man of the cloth as it was possible to be. He was a cold-blooded murderer who had gained the name from his associates in whom he had instilled an irrational fear. He had no family, always wore a small white dog-collar, quoted unauthenticated references from the Bible, and had the fearful habit of blessing and forgiving all of his victims before killing them.

Squat recoiled as he felt the sword point cut into his flesh; he tried to back away, but to no avail.

"Well?" said Harland, "Answer me."

"All right, all right!" said Squat. "It's because he's murdering fucking madman who'll cut your throat if you attempt to harm me. Are you satisfied now?"

"And do you know when the pastor is coming back?"

Squat looked at Harland and said, "Are you a Peeler, or a militiaman?"

"No," said Harland, "neither."

Squat paused for a second and then said, "He's coming back at the end next week, in time for Christmas."

To his shock, he saw Harland lower his sword and put it back into his walking stick. For a split second he considered lunging at him with his knife, but something made him hold back.

Harland's mind was filled with wild ideas. He looked down at the puzzled dwarf and said, "Would you allow me to buy you a drink? I have a proposal for you and your friend."

# Chapter 20

*Wednesday 12<sup>th</sup> April 2006. Naomi & Carlton Wilkes'*
*House*

"Good morning beautiful," Carlton whispered into Naomi's ear as he kissed her on the cheek.

Naomi opened one eye and saw Carlton leaning over her, almost dressed for work.

"You had a visitor in the night again."

Naomi glanced over at the bedside clock and saw that it was just after 7am.

"Morning darling," she said and then frowned. "What visitor? Who are you talking about?"

"Can't you smell it?"

Naomi sat up and took in a deep breath.

"Oh wow!" she said. "Violets!"

"Correct. So, what did Maria want last night?"

Naomi frowned again and said, "Nothing, well, no, not nothing... I mean, I didn't see her, so I've no idea."

"Well that must have been a disappointment for her, coming here only to find you sleeping and sawing off chunks of wood all night!"

"Hey!" said Naomi. "If anybody saws off chunks of wood while they're asleep round here matey, it's you, not me!"

Carlton smiled and said, "Okay. I give in, but nevertheless, it must have been a pointless visit for her." He stopped and thought for a second and then said, "Do you know, I've never given much thought to that side of things before. Can ghosts or spirits turn up somewhere expecting somebody to be in, – or as in your case awake – and find that they're not?"

The question stopped Naomi for a few seconds. She said, "I don't know..."

"Because," said Carlton, "what was the point of Maria turning up here last night and finding you asleep?"

Naomi was confounded too. She said, "Sometimes I wish you weren't so logical. You're going to have me puzzling that all day."

"Right pet, brekky time."

Carlton picked his tie up from the bed, leaned across and kissed Naomi on the nose, and went downstairs.

'But I haven't gone.'

Naomi wheeled around and looked behind her; nobody was there. She looked from left to right but still saw nothing.

'And I have no intention of going until…'

"Sweetheart," Carlton called up the stairs, "when you come down, could you please bring my watch?"

Naomi could have screamed. She didn't answer – she listened for the other voice, but heard nothing more.

"Mimi, did you hear me?"

Feeling frustrated Naomi called back, "Yes, I'll bring it when I come down."

"Thanks pet."

As with all of her psychic messages, Naomi didn't hear the voice as such, it was as though somebody had planted a memory that she could easily recall. She sat still on the edge of her bed trying to tune in to it again, but nothing was there.

That had been the second time that she'd thought that Maria had been trying to tell her something, and the second time that she'd not heard it. She resolved that it would not happen again.

With a resigned sigh, she got up and went into the bathroom.

Just after 10am, the phone rang on Naomi's desk and she answered it.

"Hi Naomi, it's Helen from the Vical Centre. How did you get on at High Farm Cottage on Monday?"

Naomi remembered that Helen had booked a couple of days of annual leave to visit a sick aunt prior to the pending Easter holidays, and hadn't heard anything about what had happened.

She said, "You won't believe your ears when I tell you."

"That sounds ominous," said Helen.

"I mean it, but it's best told face-to-face so I'll pop over and see you over the next couple of days."

"I've been doing some errands for Craig," said Helen, "and one of them is at the Council Offices, so if you're free, I could drop by for a cuppa and a catch-up."

"Excellent! I'll see you soon then."

Fifteen minutes later, there was a tap at Naomi's office door and Helen let herself in with two cups of tea.

Naomi regaled Helen with all of the events that had taken place. She spoke about the objectionable Hayley Gillorton, the disturbing Les Miserables, and how Ted and John had reported that they'd seen the mysterious gamekeeper in Cragg End Lane at the same time that she'd been speaking to him at the top of Lark Hill.

Helen remained silent the whole time, but jotted down one or two notes onto a small pad that she carried with her.

Naomi finished her narrative, sat back in her chair, and said, "Well, what do you think?"

"Gosh," said Helen. "Where do you want me to start? Everything about the whole set-up is so weird and unlikely that I'm kind of lost for words." She paused for thought and then said, "That Gillorton woman – did she ever show you any credentials?"

"No. The whole operation was so whitewashed that asking for credentials after the deed would have been beside the point."

"So you don't know if she's a genuine conservator or not?"

"No."

"So she could have been any old amateur acting under the instructions of a suspicious or disgruntled landowner who didn't want you snooping around?"

Naomi recalled her father's revelation about Adrian Darke and nodded.

"More than likely," she said.

"And she didn't disclose any information about anything found – any odd activity with the trees, what was underfoot in the cottage?"

"Nothing. She was as unhelpful as it was possible to be."

"Curious..." said Helen. A few seconds later she said, "I'd loved to have been with you when you met that creepy gamekeeper, and when you experienced that odd episode in the trees. I revel in trying to solve that type of conundrum."

Naomi remembered her camera.

"Does your laptop have a card reader?" she said.

"Yes, it does, but it's back at the Vical Centre."

Naomi extracted her camera from her briefcase, removed the memory card, put it in a small envelope, and handed it to Helen.

"Here you are," she said. "I can't help you with the gamekeeper episode, but if you check out the photos and footage on there, that'll give you an indication of what it was like that first time round in the trees."

Helen thanked Naomi, took the envelope, and promised to return it within a few days.

Four-and-a-half thousand miles away in Dunnellon, Florida, and in the early evening, Alan Farlington placed the recovered chest next to Naomi's email and a large magnifying glass on the kitchen table.

He took in a deep breath, looked across to Deborah, and said, "Here goes."

He placed the chest in front of him, picked up the magnifying glass, and positioned it over the indentation mark to the right-hand side of the carvings. He inspected it minutely but could see nothing embedded within the grain of the wood. He scraped at the surface with his fingernail, but once again saw nothing.

He gave a resigned sigh, turned to Deborah, and said, "Nothing's there."

Deborah said, "Let me see."

Alan slid the chest and magnifying glass over to her and watched as she repeated the same process.

Deborah turned to Alan, and with a resigned sigh said, "Sorry honey, I think you're right."

They both sat back in their chairs and lapsed into silence until Thomas walked into the room.

"Hi mom, hi dad. What are you doing?"

Alan explained what they were doing and showed Naomi's email to him.

Thomas read it and then said, "And you found nothing?"

Deborah said, "No son, nothing."

"What, nothing over the whole lid?"

Alan frowned and said, "No. We only checked the indentation because it looks as though something hit it there."

"But that's not what it says in the email, is it? Naomi said to check in and around the indentation. She didn't say to *only* check that."

Deborah looked at Alan and said, "He's right – we should check it all."

Alan repositioned the chest in front of him and looked at the aged surface of the wood and said, "Where on earth do we start? And how should we do it? Whatever could be in there could be anywhere, and if we abrade the whole surface we'll ruin the patina."

"And if something is in the grain, what would you expect it to be?" said Thomas.

"I don't know – a sliver of metal I guess..." He looked across to Deborah, shrugged and said, "I can't think of what else could be in there, could you?"

Deborah shook her head and said, "Me neither."

"Right then," said Thomas. "Just a mo." He ran out of the room.

Alan looked across to Deborah with a puzzled expression on his face, and then turned back as Thomas re-entered the room.

"Here we are!" he said. In his hand was a small but powerful bullet-shaped magnet.

"Son, you're a genius!" said Alan.

He took the magnet off Thomas, held it between his right forefinger and thumb, and moved it towards the indentation.

Straight away he felt the attraction. He let go of it and it stuck to the surface of the lid, over the top of the indentation.

"Whoa!" said Alan, "Look at that!"

Deborah and Thomas watched as Alan removed the magnet and swept it across the lid. Back and forth he went, hovering just above the surface. Nothing happened until he reached the indentation, and then once again he let go of it and it stuck to the lid.

"Good Lord," he said. "There's no mistaking that." He turned to Thomas and said, "Run to the garage and get my small toolbox."

Seconds later, Thomas returned with the toolbox and opened the lid.

For the next half hour, Alan scratched and scraped at the surface with a variety of files and knives until he exposed the top of a small shard of metal. He gripped the top of it with a pair of needle nosed pliers and pulled, but the metal stayed put.

"You must be careful with those pliers, hon," said Deborah. "If something's written on there, you don't want to be damaging it or making it illegible, so be patient and do it right."

Alan nodded and continued to expose more of the shard, taking care not to scrape it as he proceeded. Once a good deal more was exposed, he removed an old rag from his toolbox, placed it between the teeth of his larger pliers, and gripped the top. He wiggled the metal a few times and then pulled. It came out. He placed it on the table as Deborah and Thomas gathered around, then picked it up, wiped it with the oily cloth and looked at it.

Scratched into the surface of one side were the words 'Ashley Andrew', and on the reverse side the word, 'Charleston'. He passed it to Deborah and Thomas, who both read it and then handed it back.

"Ashley Andrew Charleston?" said Thomas, "Who on earth is he?"

Deborah looked at Alan and said, "Honey?"

"It's a new one on me," said Alan. "I don't ever recall anybody of that name in the family."

"It could even be Ashley Andrew from Charleston, or I suppose any other permutation from those three names," said Deborah.

Alan sat in silence for a few minutes and then said, "Okay guys, there's nothing more we can do for now..."

"I can check out that name on the net," said Thomas.

Alan looked at him and said, "You can, but after you've done your studying."

Thomas said, "But pa..."

"But nothing; homework comes first. I'll email Naomi and tell her about our discovery and see what she has to say about it. I'll also check out what she meant by having some exciting news for us if we do find something too."

Thomas went to his room in a state of high dudgeon.

Deborah got up, headed for the kitchen, and said that dinner would be on the table within the next half hour.

Alan replaced the tools in his box, locked the chest, and placed it on the floor next to his toolbox. He then picked up the metal shard and read the words again.

'Ashley Andrew Charleston. Ashley Andrew Charleston.' For some reason or other it sounded right, but try as he may, he couldn't glean another thing from it.

# Chapter 21

*Thursday 13<sup>th</sup> April 2006. Walmsfield Borough Council Offices*

At 9am Naomi sat down in her office chair and switched on her computer. The start-up process ran its course and the home page appeared. She then clicked onto her email page and pressed 'send and receive'.

She looked at the emails that appeared in her inbox and noted that they were the usual mix of enquiries – promotional and sales, historical requests, a few personal and several internal. As per her usual routine, she deleted the unsolicited sales and promo emails first, she dealt with the internal requests next and then she cast her eyes over the new enquiries. She turned her attention to three personal emails.

She opened up the first one and a large smiling mouth filled up her screen. She watched as the mouth opened and an effeminate voice said, "I thought you'd never ask!"

She stared in fascination as the mouth disappeared and Rosie's smiling face appeared on the screen. The camera panned backwards and revealed that he was dressed in an incredible costume, similar to those worn by the revellers of the South American Mardi Gras. It was a tight-fitting sparkly red bodice, below which was a tight-fitting ankle length sparkly red skirt with a full length split up the side, revealing red stockings and red suspenders. He had on red sparkly high-heeled shoes with small ankle straps, long red sparkly gloves that terminated in loops over his fingers, and on his head he wore a flamboyant, red feathery headdress.

Naomi watched in awe as Rosie leaned towards the screen and said, "Hi babe, doesn't your favourite auntie look just fabulous?"

There was a brief pause and then he said, "I got your email, had a word with the girls, and despite it taking us all of twenty seconds to weigh up the pros and cons, Kitty, Lola and I have decided to grace your shores and should be arriving on Friday 21$^{st}$.

"Hilda and Randy will have stay at Camp Stanley with Gloryhole Gladys and Hemline Harriet, but they send their love and wished that they'd been coming too, so tell Carol to break out the clean sheets and towels because his bestest buddies are on their way – and we're prepared to bend over backwards to help him in… Oops, sorry, I meant out!"

The camera panned in to Rosie's face; he puckered up his lips, blew a kiss, and finished by saying, "Bye bye sweetie – competition for that man of yours is on the way, so you'd best be heading to the designer shops for a few new frocks!"

Naomi leaned back in her chair with a huge grin on her face. She thought about how Carlton was going to react and then sniggered to herself. All she could think was, 'Oh, my, God!'

Auntie Rosie and the 'sewing circle' ran a specialised security service and a gay revue bar named Camp Stanley in the art deco section of Miami.

Rosie, in real-life ex-Colour Sergeant Rob McCloud of the SAS and two other ex-marines, Lola – aka Lloyd Masters – and Hilda – aka Henry Boxer – had all been saved by Carlton whilst on active duty in The Falklands.

Along with two other ex-marine buddies, Randy – whose real name was Pete Kincaid, and Kitty, real name Kevin Langdon, – were about as outrageous and flamboyant in one guise as they were dangerous in their other.

In 2002 they'd foiled a plot by some of Adrian Darke's American associates to hijack Valentine's reproduction chest, and then they'd delivered it intact to Miami where Naomi, Carlton, Naomi's brother Ewan and the Farlingtons had been in attendance when it had first been opened.

The memories came flooding back into Naomi's mind and she couldn't help smiling at the prospect of what was about to come.

Following several seconds of speculation, she leaned forwards in her chair and opened up the second email from Alan in Florida.

*'Hi Naomi,*

*We found a piece of metal hammered into the grain on the top of the lid! On one side it said, 'Ashley Andrew' and on the other it said, 'Charleston'.*

*We haven't had time to do anything about it yet, but we've speculated that it could be Ashley Andrew Charleston – i.e. someone's name – or even Ashley Andrew, or vice versa, from Charleston.*

*Anyway, I thought I'd let you know so that you could send me the "exciting news" you mentioned in your last email.*

*Love Alan xx'*

She stopped and thought about it for a few moments. The next thing to do would be to send Valentine's second contrivance, but something held her back. She decided to email Helen with the news of the discovery and to listen to what she had to say first.

She replied.

*'Hi Alan,*

*That was exciting news in itself, congratulations!*

*I want to check something out before sending the other info, but I promise to be in touch after the Easter weekend.*

*Love Naomi xx'*

She opened up the third email from Helen at the Vical Centre.

*'Hi Naomi,*

*I've downloaded the content of your camera card reader onto my PC and though you explained the spooky aspect of it to me, it doesn't come across like that when you see it. I guess that you had to be there to get the full effect.*

*However there is something on there that teases my inquisitive mind, and it has nothing to do with anything that you've told me before.*

*Drop me a quick line and tell me when you are next free so that we can arrange a meeting.*

*Best,*

*Helen.'*

She replied.

*'Hi Helen,*

*I'm a bit tied up today, but I'll call round on Tuesday afternoon (18$^{th}$) after the hols, unless I hear otherwise from you.*

*I've heard from Alan in Florida and they've found a piece of metal hammered into the lid of the chest with 'Ashley Andrew' on one side and 'Charleston' on the other.*

*Perhaps this in conjunction with the second contrivance will help to assuage your desire to solve conundrums during the Easter break!*

*Regards N.'*

She clicked the 'send mail' icon on her computer, and then got up from her desk with a smile on her face to break the news about Auntie Rosie's arrival to Carlton.

Several miles away at the Darke Industries H.Q. in Manchester, Adrian Darke was coming to the end of a small and very select meeting prior to the forthcoming Easter weekend.

He looked across to Hayley Gillorton and said, "Are you sure that we've stopped the Wilkes woman prying about at Cragg Vale?"

"As sure as I can be," said Gillorton.

"You don't sound positive."

"Well, how can I be? We did everything you instructed us to, and she buggered off. What else can I say?"

Adrian looked across to Dominic Sheldon and closed his eyes for a second. He, along with everybody else at Darke

Industries didn't like Gillorton's coarseness, but she was good at what she did.

"And Dominic, – my wife, are you positive that…"

"She has no idea?" said Sheldon, "No A.D., none."

"Where does she think that you are right now?"

"I told her that I needed time off to see my orthodontist."

Adrian nodded and then turned to Garrett Hinchcliffe, his Chief Operations Manager, and said, "This is a very busy weekend, Garrett. Are we ready?"

"Yes A.D."

"And Les Spooner?"

"Yes A.D.," said the taciturn Hinchcliffe.

An audible sound was uttered by Gillorton that attracted everybody's attention.

"Do you want to say something Hayley?" said Adrian.

"No, not really."

"Not really?"

"Are you going to want me to go to Cragg Vale again?"

"It depends, maybe… Why?"

"Because that Les Spooner puts the fu…" Gillorton looked at the assemblage and saw the looks of disapproval. "… Because I don't like being anywhere near Mr Spooner. He bothers me."

Once again, Adrian cast a quick glance at Sheldon and then said, "But that's the point, Hayley – he's supposed to do that."

"Maybe to strangers and trespassers, but he's not supposed to upset other members of staff." She stopped speaking for a second, frowned, and then said, "And where on earth did he come from? A fucking horror movie?"

Mutters of disapproval came from around the table.

Adrian said, "Please curb that language around this table, Hayley. We all try to act like ladies and gentlemen here."

Gillorton turned and looked at Adrian's personal bodyguard and Head of Security, Leander Pike, and said, "If that's so, how do you explain him?"

Pike's eyes widened and he stared at Gillorton. He was six feet eight inches tall, was very broad, had a bald head, two large protruding ears, and was nicknamed F.A. Cup, but only by those of whom he approved. He always dressed in black – suit, shirt, tie and thick-soled black leather shoes, and he had a strange habit of sniffing, and sometimes licking, the faces of those people who antagonised him.

And Gillorton just got added to the list – and that wasn't good at all.

Adrian saw what was happening and said, "F.A., no, she's new to…"

"F.A.?" interrupted Gillorton. "I thought that his name was Leander Pike?"

"It's short for F.A. Cup, his nickname," said Sheldon. "But…"

"F.A. Cup?" said Gillorton. "Now there's a surprise! Christ Almighty that's'…"

Pike leapt to his feet and leaned over Gillorton like a huge, hovering harpie.

"What the fuck?" said Gillorton trying to back away.

"F.A.!" said Adrian, "Enough!"

Pike ignored Adrian and leaned down to Gillorton's face, sniffed it, and then licked it.

Gillorton was traumatised.

"What the fuck is this – a fucking freak show?" she yelled. She wiped the side of her face on her coat sleeve and tried to back away from Pike. But he remained hovering above her like a church roof gargoyle.

"Get the fuck away from me, weirdo!"

"Leander! Sit down!" called Adrian.

Pike turned and looked at Adrian for a second, and then went back to his seat.

"Fucking hell," said Gillorton turning to face Adrian, "and I thought that all the loonies were in the asylum!"

Pike grunted, causing Gillorton to whip around and stare at him in alarm once again.

"Gentlemen, lady!" said Hinchcliffe, "Enough! Let's get on with the meeting." He turned and nodded to Adrian and said, "A.D.?"

Adrian felt like a man trying to control a bucket full of eels; he looked from face to face and remained silent until he was satisfied that a semblance of calm had returned.

"Right," he said. "If we can all at least *try* to get on…" He looked at Gillorton first, and then Pike.

Neither responded but remained silent.

"Very well," said Adrian. "It's imperative that we're ready for the Reading and Leeds Music Festivals in August, so we'll get Easter out of the way first, and then we'll gear up over June and July in readiness. All agreed?"

Nods of approval were received from all around.

"Very well, that's that," said Adrian, relieved at being able to call an end to such a fiasco. He was about to announce the termination of the meeting when a thought crossed his mind.

"Hayley," he said, "did you find anything following your digs at High Farm Cottage?"

"Nah," said Gillorton in a way that rubbed everybody up the wrong way. "But then again, most of it was just for show. We never got a digger in or anything like that. We got the foliage cleared by one of the estate gardeners with his hedge trimmer and chainsaw, and then a couple of the boys dug a diagonal trench right across the back garden, but it was only a foot deep."

"And was there anything inside the building?"

"No idea, 'cos we just dumped half a truck full of earth over the existing floor and rolled it flat."

Adrian nodded and said, "And near the lake?"

"We never went anywhere near there 'cos of you-know-who." She resisted the urge to make any 'freak' comments in case it resulted in another disgusting face licking.

Adrian paused for a few moments, and found to his surprise that he would have been interested to discover what had attracted the Wilkes woman in the first place.

He shrugged it off and said, "Okay folks, have a nice Easter, and I'll see you all sometime next week."

Everybody except Leander got up and left.

"Sorry boss," he said.

Adrian looked at his faithful bodyguard and said, "No worries F.A. I don't like her either."

Leander leaned forwards and said, "Do you want me to…"

"No," said Adrian, "maybe later…"

# Chapter 22

'Pastor' Robert Dogg and Squat sat by the fire in a quiet corner of the Monkey Pit with Harland Chance. The combined smell of ale, tobacco smoke and body odour hung in the atmosphere, and the light from the flickering lamps did little to illuminate the darkest corners of the public bar. And if ever any three men preferred their faces to remain in shadow, it was they.

Squat leaned over to Harland and said, "The moon will be just right tomorrow night, so we're going then."

Harland knew that he hadn't made any mention of Sugg, and wanted to make sure that they'd be prepared in case he put in an appearance. He looked around and then said, "And you'll both have side arms?"

The pastor patted his jacket pocket with his right hand, leaned forward, and said, "I call it Saint Peter's finger, brother, and I never go anywhere without it."

Harland frowned and said, "Why do you call it Saint Peter's finger?"

The pastor leaned forward again and said, "Because whoever it's pointing at is just one step away from paradise."

Harland shuddered and cast a furtive glance at the pastor.

He was five foot six inches tall, slim, had a dark, sly looking face, slits of eyes, and a couple of bad front teeth. He wore black clothing that appeared to be dusty all the time, dirty black leather shoes, and he sported a makeshift white dog collar in some sort of vain attempt to fool people that he was a man of the cloth. He had a huge, deep scar that arced from his left cheekbone to his jaw line, and a large black cross tattooed in the centre of his forehead.

Harland had only met him on two occasions since his first encounter with Squat, and though Squat had seemed to be a bit unhinged with an explosive and violent temper, he had seemed like a normal human being compared to his partner-in crime. There was something disturbing about the pastor; something that worried him at a primal level.

"And then again," said the pastor patting his left-hand pocket, "I might prefer to use Santa Maria's finger, it depends on the circumstances."

Harland almost didn't dare ask, but felt obliged to when he saw the wild look of expectancy on the pastor's face. He said, "Santa Maria's finger...?"

"Yes, brother, Santa Maria's finger." He leaned closer to Harland and said, "It's my jabber – my beautiful Italian mistress, my stiletto. It makes the experience of assisting wayward members of my flock through the pearly gates more personal, more enjoyable, and it isn't too quick neither."

Not for the first time, Harland realised what a dangerous and unstable man the pastor was. He wanted to get off the subject as soon as he could, but was beaten to it by Squat.

"Are there any nice young girls on the estate?"

Harland turned to face Squat and said, "What? There's a young dairymaid and farm boy lives up there, but I hope that you aren't forgetting why you're going..."

"Nobody's forgetting anything, brother," said the pastor. "We'll do the job, and then afterwards Squat can have his fun."

Harland reached into his jacket pocket and extracted the silver chain that he'd stolen from Maria and Silas. He threw it onto the table and said, "Once you've finished what I'm paying you for, there'll be lots more of that stuff lying around, so do a good job and you could end up with a fine haul."

"And maybe a good fuck," said Squat, feeling the customary movement in his breeches as he thought about it.

"Just one thing left, brother."

Harland looked at the pastor and said, "What?"

"You said you'd tell us which estate it was tonight."

"Yes, I did, didn't I?" said Harland. He took a deep breath and said, "It's the Whitewall Estate on Wordale Moor."

If Harland had dropped a ticking bomb onto the table between them, the effect could not have been more profound. Both men reacted as though they'd been stung.

Squat blurted out, "Whitewall? *Fucking Whitewall?*"

"Are you crazy, brother?" said the pastor. "That's the Johnson's place!"

"You must be off your fucking rocker if you think we're going anywhere near that place!" said Squat.

"Haven't you heard about the Johnsons?" said the pastor. "Especially Caleb! Holy Christ, Brother Squat and I have our faults, but we're saints compared to that crazy bastard."

Harland looked around to see if the sudden outburst had attracted any attention, but all looked normal.

"They don't live there anymore," he said, "Abraham was found dead a couple of years ago, and Caleb disappeared not long after."

"Doesn't mean he won't come back though," said Squat, "and if he ever found out what we'd done…" He stopped speaking for a second, turned to the pastor, and said, "Do you remember what he and Abe did to those four…"

"Stop, – please…" The pastor frowned and made the sign of the cross on his body. "…don't speak about it, brother," he said. "I've been trying to block out that memory for years."

"He's not coming back because he's wanted by the police for murder," said Harland, "and the people who live there now are tenants."

"So why do you want *them* gone?" said the pastor.

"That's my business."

The pastor looked at Squat and then shrugged. He caught sight of the silver necklace on the table, scooped it up, and said, "All right, brother, consider it done. We'll meet back here two nights from now and let you know how we got on."

Just before midnight the following day, Squat halted the cart a quarter of a mile from the drive to Whitewall, clambered down, and secured the horse's reins to the dry-stone wall on the roadside. The pastor hopped down and joined him.

"It's fucking freezing," he said.

"Make the most of it, brother," said the pastor, "'cos we aren't getting any younger, and I guess that it's going to be bloody hot where we'll end up."

"I thought you had a place reserved in Heaven – you being the pastor and the like?"

"Bless you, Brother Squat, and I shall reserve a place for you next to me."

The two men made sure that the horse and cart were secure and continued up Wordale Moor in the light of the waning half-moon.

"That dandy-prat had better be right about the Johnsons," said the pastor, "'cos we'd be dead as dodos if we crossed them."

"And he'll be as dead as a dodo if he's crossed us," said Squat.

"Do you remember that monster of a dog they had?"

"How could I ever forget?" said Squat. "Bastard thing was taller than me!"

Both men reflected for a few seconds as they approached the gateposts to the Estate.

"Best put these on our boots," said the pastor as he handed two Hessian bags to Squat.

Both men sat down by the roadside and secured the bags over their footwear with twine, and then, satisfied that all was well, set off down the drive.

The pastor patted both of his jacket pockets to make sure that his saint's fingers were with him and then turned to Squat. He said, "This drive's longer than I thought it would be…"

Squat nodded and kept on walking.

As they approached the entrance to the courtyard they stopped and looked around; everywhere appeared to be in darkness.

Squat looked up at the moon and saw that the sky was crystal clear. He looked at the buildings and noted that the living quarters were just as Harland had said, on the right-hand side. On the left were storerooms and work places. The courtyard was wet underfoot and he could see reflections of the moon in some of the small puddles. He scanned the windows and saw a ground floor one half open, near the living quarters.

"Let's check that one out," he whispered.

The pastor nodded and they crept into the yard.

They had gone no more than fifty feet when Sugg exploded out of his room, barking and snarling like something possessed. He saw them, and ran straight at them with huge bared fangs.

Squat, who'd regretted not emptying his bowels before setting off, immediately addressed that situation. The sight of the monster running at him made him lose complete control and he felt it deposit into his pants. He stood rooted to the spot in terrified silence and awe.

"Holy fucking Christ!" said the pastor as he grabbed for the pistol in his pocket.

*"Holy fucking Christ...!"* he repeated as the dog sped closer towards them, making a fearful, hell-sent racket.

He yanked the gun out of his pocket and fired. The shot flew over the top of Sugg's head and made him veer off to the left.

The pastor turned to run, but saw Squat immobile and staring into the yard. He slapped the back of his companion's head and said, "Quick short-arse – run!"

The slap shook Squat into action and he ran up the drive as fast as his short legs would carry him.

Up in the master bedroom, Silas was out of bed and staring into the yard with his service revolver in his hand. He'd heard Sugg's sudden outburst followed by the sound of a shot, but he couldn't see any kind of movement or activity from where he was standing. He turned to face Maria who was sitting bolt upright in bed.

"Wait here, lock the door when I've gone, and don't open it unless you hear my voice.

Maria nodded.

Silas pulled on his boots, grabbed an overcoat, and ran out of the room.

Three windows along, Simeon Twitch was out of bed and doing the same thing.

Having first bolted for cover at the sound of the gun being fired, Sugg reappeared in the yard. He'd been shot twice before and was in no hurry to repeat the experience. He checked to see if he could see the two men, and then ran towards the drive. Seconds later he set off in pursuit, snapping and barking at the retreating figures.

Squat could feel the mess in the back of his trousers squelching, but he didn't care. He could see the pastor running in front for all his worth, and could see him gaining ground. He glanced over his shoulder and saw the monstrous, ugly hound racing up the drive behind him. He thought that his heart was going to give out, but kept pumping his legs for all they were worth as the top of the drive came into view.

Another twenty yards and he was out. He turned and headed back towards the cart and could hardly believe his luck when he realised that the dog hadn't followed him down the road. As he got to the cart, he saw that the pastor had untethered the horse and was waiting for him.

The pastor saw Squat running full tilt towards him, leaned over and extended his hand.

Squat grabbed it and was hauled bodily into the seat.

The pastor turned the rig around and set the horse off at a gallop down the side of the moor.

Back at the top of the drive, Silas and Simeon arrived at the same time. Silas had his revolver in his hand and Simeon was sporting a double-barrelled shotgun.

"Did you see who it was?" gasped Simeon.

"No," said Silas. "I only caught a fleeting glimpse of one of them, and he looked as though he was a circus midget or something…"

"What do you think they were up to?"

"No idea," said Silas. "They could have been trying to find something to steal maybe…"

Sugg was barking non-stop in the direction of the retreating men until he felt Silas' steadying hand and heard his voice.

"Good boy, Sugg. You saw those thieving bastards off didn't you?"

Simeon looked down at Sugg and patted him too. He then looked up at Silas and said, "I'll bet those buggers won't forget this lad in hurry."

# Chapter 23

*Tuesday 18<sup>th</sup> April 2006. The Vical Centre*

Following the now customary light banter with the workmen, Naomi stepped into the Conservation Suite, bade the girls a 'good afternoon', and walked across to Helen's workstation.

"I'm so pleased to see you," said Helen, "because I think that I've solved one mystery, but I may have created another."

Naomi sat down on the stool that Helen had pulled up and said, "Sounds interesting; which mystery have you solved?"

"The Ashley Andrew Charleston one."

"Wow, I'm impressed. I've been mega-busy with existing projects so I appreciate all the help that you can give me. What have you come up with?"

"The first thing that I did was to put 'Ashley Andrew Charleston' into an Internet search engine, and it came up with what I believe to be the most plausible answer. An answer, I might add, that would not have been as available or researchable to anybody in history, or indeed to anybody without the aid of the Internet."

Naomi nodded in agreement.

Helen said, "The search engine picked up on Old St. Andrews Church on the Ashley River Road in Charleston, South Carolina. It was founded in 1706; it is the oldest church in use in Carolina, and would have been in situ whilst Valentine was alive. Charleston is also a seaport that was used extensively in his day, and the Ashley River runs past the church, down to the port.

"I then ran a check on the church graveyard directory and found this name." She opened her notepad and pushed it in front of Naomi.

"Good grief!" said Naomi. "That's amazing!"

Written on the notepad was the name 'Chance Mathewes'.

She looked at Helen and said, "If the ruby hasn't already been found, it's got to be buried in that grave."

Helen flicked back the page of her pad and pointed to the 'go below 'mid soil and seed' reference in the second contrivance and said, "This can't mean anything else."

Naomi looked at the notepad for a second and then said, "But one thing still puzzles me. It was your attention to detail in the first contrivance that led us to solving it. You pointed out Valentine's use of the hyphen after the words 'First the' leading us to read 'The first', and he was clear in his instruction to 'order all discord', so if he was that meticulous about how he wrote down the clues, what do you think he was driving at when he wrote 'Grandfather's name 'after deed'?"

Helen faltered for a few minutes, made several attempts to answer, and then said, "Frankly, I don't know."

Naomi pointed to the script and said, "The 'after deed' words have inverted commas around them too, so it must be significant."

Helen sat in silence pondering Naomi's comment until something came to mind.

"Hang on," she said. "What if it didn't say deed, but dead? i.e. 'Grandfather's name 'after dead'. That would make sense. Maybe we read it wrong or Valentine spelled it incorrectly..."

Naomi read the contrivance again and said, "But 'dead' doesn't rhyme with 'seed' or 'proceed.'"

"And 'discover' doesn't rhyme with 'river'," replied Helen.

It was Naomi's turn to lapse into silence and ponder. A second or two later she said, "Maybe you're right, maybe not, but I think that we need to contact Alan in Florida and tell him what we know. The Chance Mathewes grave has to be his starting point, and if that draws a blank or we think of something else, he can look into that too."

Helen gave an approving nod and then said, "Now, have you viewed the footage that you took of your first visit to High Farm Cottage?"

Naomi frowned and said, "No I haven't."

Helen flipped open her laptop, switched it on and said, "You need to look at this."

Naomi watched the footage as it played and was surprised to see that the filmed version of what happened didn't convey any of the atmosphere. The rustling and what she had considered odd behaviour of the trees and foliage appeared to be the result of the breeze and nothing more.

"Now watch this bit," said Helen.

Naomi moved closer to the screen and watched as the camera fell out of her hands and came to rest in the grass. It bounced, blurring the image, and then came to rest facing the small gravestone. It stayed pointing there for a few seconds, was then snatched up in a blur of movement, and went blank as it was switched off.

"There," said Helen. "Did you see?"

Naomi frowned and said, "See what?"

"The gravestone."

"Yes, but what about it?"

"Look," said Helen. "I'll play it again."

She slid the movie bar icon on her laptop until it neared the end of the footage and then clicked 'Play' once again.

As before, the camera fell and came to rest facing the gravestone.

Helen clicked the 'freeze frame' icon and the film stopped with the gravestone in view at the end of the garden. She clicked onto the 'zoom' feature and zoomed in to it.

"There now," she said. "See what I mean?"

Once again Naomi frowned and said, "I don't know what you're driving at. All I can see is a blank gravestone."

"Right!" said Helen. "A blank gravestone!"

Naomi gazed at it, devoid of understanding. She could hear how animated Helen was, but whatever had switched her lights on hadn't done the same for her. She looked at Helen and said, "And that means what?"

Helen turned to Naomi and said, "What would be the point of it?"

Naomi didn't answer, she just frowned.

"Why go to all the cost of having a gravestone in your own back garden and then put no inscription on it? It doesn't make sense."

Naomi turned back to the screen and looked closer still; the gravestone was indeed blank.

"But there could be any number of reasons," she said. "For example look at the size of it – it could be a pet grave."

"And wouldn't that have had an inscription on it?"

Naomi began to feel frustrated. She could see Helen's point, but it was such a minor issue that it felt as though she was being distracted from the bigger picture.

"I, – I suppose so," she said.

"There's no 'suppose' about it," said Helen, labouring the point. "Given the size of the cottage, we have to assume that the occupiers were not wealthy people. So if they went to the expense of having a gravestone erected in their own back garden, surely they would have had an inscription put on it."

"But what if they could only afford the stone and hoped to get it inscribed at a later date?"

"That's a possibility, I'll grant you," said Helen, "but I wouldn't put money on it."

"And is this the mystery that you think you've created?" asked Naomi. "A blank gravestone?"

Helen picked up on Naomi's negativity and said, "Well yes – in part. I appreciate that I have a pernickety mind, but to me these things are important."

Naomi didn't comment; she turned back to the screen, looked once more at the gravestone, and put her fingers up to her mouth in thought. All of a sudden the thumb pressed down on her left shoulder and a female voice said, "See the name."

Without thinking she repeated, *"See the name?"*

Helen looked at Naomi and said, "Yes, precisely."

Naomi realised that she'd spoken out loud and tried to proceed as though nothing had happened.

"See the name…" the voice repeated inside Naomi's head as the pressure from the thumb continued. She looked back at the laptop and said, "So, if there was a name, why can't we see it?"

"Ah!" said Helen oblivious to the voice in Naomi's head. "That's why I said 'in part' when you asked me if the blank gravestone was the mystery that I had created."

Naomi turned back to Helen, shook her head and said, "Go on…"

"To me, this is the interesting bit. Just because we can't see any inscription on the stone doesn't mean that there isn't one."

"What?" said Naomi. "You're not inferring that it's eroded, are you?"

"No, not at all," Helen paused for a moment and then said, "but what if that's the back of the stone?"

The pressure of the thumb lifted from Naomi's shoulder. She turned to look at the screen again and asked Helen to pan out.

"But that makes even less sense than having no inscription on it at all," she said. "Why would anybody go to the expense of inscribing a gravestone and then turn it to face the wall?"

"Now we're on the same wavelength!" said Helen. "Why indeed?"

Naomi looked at Helen with a renewed respect and said, "You're right. You have created a new mystery. I need to get back to High Farm Cottage and have a look."

"What about that gamekeeper and the Gillorton woman?" said Helen.

Naomi thought for a second and then remembered that Rosie and co. would be arriving on the 21$^{st}$. She smiled and said, "I'll drive up there early tomorrow morning and try on my own. Maybe I can slip into the garden without attracting anybody's attention and have a quick peek at the other side of the gravestone. If I don't manage it, I have some friends arriving on Friday who may be able to help me get past those creeps."

"Would you like me to come with you? I have the day off tomorrow."

Naomi thought about it for a few seconds and then said, "No, not tomorrow. I appreciate your offer of help, and I'd love to have your company, but I think that it would be better if I went alone on this occasion."

"Okay," said Helen, feeling disappointed, "but promise to give me a call as soon as you've finished.

"I will," said Naomi. "I promise, I will."

# Chapter 24

*Wednesday 19<sup>th</sup> April 2006. Rushworth Moor*

There was a bitter chill in the air as Naomi walked down Cragg End Lane just before 8am. The piercing cold northerly wind forced her to pull her dark grey overcoat tighter, pull her black woollen beanie hat over her ears, and to fluff her black scarf up over her nose and mouth. In her pocket, her leather-gloved hands gripped her digital camera.

As she approached High Farm Cottage, she tried to imagine the excitement Alan would feel in Florida when he read what Helen had discovered. She'd given some thought to suggesting to Carlton that they go to Florida to be with him when he visited the church in Charleston. But it had been late when she'd sent the email, and Carlton had been asleep.

She'd slipped out of the house early in the morning, had left him a note informing him that she'd had to attend 'a meeting', and that she would see him at home after work. She'd known how Carlton would have reacted if she'd told him where she was going, and even more so if she'd said that she would be unaccompanied.

Due to the narrowness of Cragg End Lane, she'd left her CRV some distance away and she'd walked down to High Farm Cottage, hoping to slip in unnoticed.

Apart from the cold wind, everywhere was as quiet as the grave. She encountered no vehicles or lone dog-walkers, and even the early morning birdsong seemed to be in short supply. Her soft-soled leather boots made no sound as she rounded the final bend and made her way down to the familiar entrance.

She stopped, looked back and forth, and then stepped in.

The thumb pressed down on her left shoulder and a female voice said, "No!"

She stopped walking, reached up and rubbed it with her right hand, and looked around.

The voice became more urgent. "No," it said. "Don't go in – *leave now*!"

She stood still for a few seconds and listened; there was nothing out of the ordinary. She looked across to the cottage and saw that it was tantalisingly close.

Just a few small steps, she thought, and I'll have it.

"No, don't go in!" repeated the female voice.

She took her gloves off and stuffed them into her right-hand coat pocket. She then removed the camera from her left pocket, switched it on, and made her way through the cottage into the back garden.

The gravestone was there. She took three or four steps towards it when, from behind a tree just beyond the gravestone, the gamekeeper stepped out.

Naomi yelped and stopped dead in her tracks.

"I told you that you were no longer welcome here!" said Spooner in his weird raspy voice.

Naomi said, "But…"

"I told you not to come back or you could get shot." He opened the front of his long black coat and exposed a sawn off shotgun.

Without thinking, Naomi turned and ran. With a wildly beating heart she charged through the open cottage, got to the other side and stopped dead again.

Spooner was standing in front of her.

"I told you that you weren't welcome here!" he shouted. "I told you that you could get shot!"

Once again he opened the front of his coat, but this time he reached in for the shotgun.

Naomi was petrified and let out another cry of terror. She had no inkling of how he could have got past her, yet there he was. Once again she turned and ran. She bolted into the cottage and saw to her shock and horror that he was standing in the doorway opposite with the gun in his hand.

She felt her legs weaken with fear as terror gripped her heart. For what seemed like an eternity, she stared at Spooner's contorted and evil face, as he appeared to be studying her. She heard a clicking sound, looked down, and saw that he'd cocked the shotgun.

"Please, no…" she begged.

Spooner lifted up the shotgun and aimed it at Naomi's chest. Coldly and callously he said, "Time to die, missy."

He pulled the trigger.

The thunderous boom of the shot echoed across Rushworth Moor, causing all birdsong to cease and the odd dog to bark in the distance.

The sound receded, and within a few minutes the only things to be heard were the icy gusts of the cold north wind, and the sound of Naomi's body being dragged through the open gates of the Cragg Vale Estate.

At 7pm that night, Carlton looked at his watch for the umpteenth time and wondered where Naomi was. He redialled her mobile number but as before it only connected to her voicemail. He telephoned Jane and Sam who were out for an early evening meal and asked them if Naomi had been in contact, but he received a negative response from them too.

"Is something wrong?" said Sam.

Jane picked up on Sam's words, put down her glass of water and frowned at him.

"I don't know," said Carlton. "According to a note that I found this morning, she was going to a meeting somewhere, but she didn't say where. She never returned to the office, nobody's heard from her, and she still hasn't shown up here."

"I don't like the sound of that," said Sam.

Jane couldn't contain herself any longer and said, "Sam! What is it?"

Sam covered the mouthpiece of the phone and said, "Wait, I'll tell you in a minute." He then removed his hand and said to Carlton, "So, what do you propose doing?"

"I don't know. I could give her another half hour I suppose, but…"

Jane was beside herself. She stared at Sam and said, "Sam! What's going on?"

Sam excused himself from Carlton and said, "Naomi's missing…"

"What!" said Jane, "And what are you doing about it?"

"We haven't…"

Jane snatched the phone off Sam and said, "Carlton, phone the police. With all the weird goings on that Naomi's experienced the last few days, anything could have happened to her. Now get off the phone to us and phone the police."

Carlton was taken aback by Jane's fortitude, and said, "Okay."


Two hours later, Naomi still hadn't shown up. Jane and Sam sat in Carlton's house, and as a uniformed officer sat checking the details of Carlton's statement, the front doorbell rang.

Sam jumped up and opened it.

There in the doorway stood the familiar figure of Bob Crowthorne, the policeman who had led the investigations at Whitewall Farm in 2002.

"Good evening Mr Chance," said Crowthorne. "I'm sorry that we're meeting again like this."

"Chief Inspector," said Sam, "it's good to see you…"

"Superintendent now, sir," said Crowthorne.

"Sorry – *Superintendent* Crowthorne," said Sam with respect. "Do come in."

"I came as soon as I received the report about Mrs Wilkes," said Crowthorne. "Under normal circumstances we don't react to 'missing persons' reports for at least twenty-four hours, but given these circumstances and past history, I thought it best not to waste time."

"And we really appreciate that," said Sam, leading Crowthorne into the lounge.

As soon as Carlton saw Crowthorne, he jumped up and extended his hand.

"Bob," he said, "you're a most welcome sight. Do you have any news?"

Crowthorne shook Carlton's hand and said, "Not right now, Carlton. We've asked all of our duty officers to keep a lookout for her, and her vehicle, but so far we've received nothing back.

Now, please tell me everything that you know and leave nothing out, however insignificant you may think it is."

As Crowthorne listened, his ears pricked up at the mention of the Cragg Vale Estate.

"Cragg Vale?" he said. "Of course, you know who owns that place, don't you?"

"Adrian and Christiana Darke," said Carlton.

"Correct," said Crowthorne. "So what was Mrs Wilkes' interest in the place?"

Carlton explained how new evidence had emerged relating to Naomi's family history that had led her to High Farm Cottage, and her encounters with the mysterious gamekeeper.

"The ubiquitous Leslie Spooner," said Crowthorne.

"Oh, you know about him?" said Jane.

"Indeed we do Mrs Chance," said Crowthorne. "And a lot more besides."

"Then can you send a car up there to see if he had anything to do with Naomi's disappearance?" said Sam.

Crowthorne leaned back in his chair and said, "Tricky…"

"What's tricky about it?" said Jane.

Crowthorne looked at Jane and said, "Any number of things. For example, we don't actually know whether she's missing or not yet…

"That's preposterous, Superintendent," said Sam.

"Not so, sir – there still could be a rational reason for her absence…"

"But…" said Jane.

"Please Mrs Chance, you know that I'm taking this seriously otherwise I wouldn't be here, but right now Mrs Wilkes could turn up with news of a vehicle breakdown and the loss of her mobile, and then we'd all look ridiculous rocking up to the Cragg Vale Estate and asking them questions about her possible whereabouts."

He paused for a few seconds and then said, "And furthermore, Cragg Vale Estate is already the subject of – what shall we say, er, – closer police interest?"

"All the more reason for going on up there then!" said Jane.

"No, on the contrary," said Crowthorne. "It would be better if we were able to keep away for the time being."

Jane opened her mouth to object, but was cut off by Carlton.

"It's obvious that there's more to this than meets the eye, so perhaps we'd better leave things to Bob – don't you think?"

Crowthorne turned to Jane and said, "Carlton's right, Mrs Chance. There is more to this than meets the eye, but you may rest assured that I shall be doing everything in my power to locate Mrs Wilkes."

Just after 11pm, Crowthorne sat in his car, talking on an unlisted mobile phone. He looked around and said, "What time do Phobos and Deimos switch on tonight?"

"Phobos is 23:44 or 01:02, and Deimos is 00:17 or 01:40, sir."

"Very well. I'm about to transmit a text message to you. Make sure that they both receive it."

"I will, sir."

# Chapter 25

*January 4th 1872. The Monkey Pit Public House, Rochdale*

In the dark interior of the bottle store at the rear of the Monkey Pit, the pastor pushed the blade of Santa Maria's finger just far enough into the skin of Harland's stomach to draw blood, whilst Squat pressed into his legs and held onto his penis and testicles through his trousers with a vice-like grip.

"You nearly got us killed, brother," hissed the pastor, "and I keep on asking myself the same question – was that your intention?"

"And I shat my favourite pants, you fucking bastard!" shouted Squat.

The pastor looked down at Squat and said, "What do you think, Brother Squat? Should we cut his balls off after we kill him, or before?"

Harland couldn't speak because the pastor's free hand was clamped like a vice over his mouth.

"Just gut him and let's get the fuck out of here," said Squat. "We can take all his stuff and have it pawned before anyone knows he's missing."

The pastor looked into the eyes of Harland for a second, then looked down at Squat and said, "Before we kill him, do you want to fuck him? I've been told that all the toffs have smooth white skin like young girls."

Harland saw Squat look up at him as he digested the question and, despite being petrified at the prospect of being maimed or killed, the thought of a stinking dwarf buggering him was even more horrendous.

The pastor saw the look of growing panic in Harland's eyes and stared at him without compassion.

To his utmost horror, Harland felt Squat start to tug at his trouser belt and fly buttons.

"Let's have a look at his cock then," said Squat with mounting lasciviousness.

Harland started to struggle and weave around in an attempt to halt Squat's progress, but felt a violent blow to his lower stomach as Squat punched him hard.

"Keep fucking still," he shouted, "or I'll cut it off when I've finished with it!"

Now Harland was as revolted and terrified as it was possible to be; he looked at the pastor and started making indiscernible, but appealing sounds.

"Stop, Brother Squat," said the pastor. "I think that Brother Harland wants to say something."

He turned to face Harland and said, "If you try to attract any attention once I let you speak, you'll feel Santa Maria's finger ram through your gut, clean to your backbone. Is that clear?"

Harland nodded.

"Now then, brother," said the pastor removing his hand. "What have you got to say for yourself?"

"Let me go. I'll double your money and I'll kill the dog. Also you can keep anything you find, and Squat can fuck the dairymaid if he wants."

Squat looked up at the pastor and didn't speak.

"And this would require us to go back up to Whitewall again?" said the pastor.

"Yes," said Harland.

The pastor looked down at Squat and said, "Carry on, brother. I'll hold him still whilst you pull his pants down."

"Wait!" said Harland. "I'll treble your money and guarantee that you don't get caught after the job's done."

The pastor looked down at Squat and said, "Stop, brother…"

"Make your fucking mind up," said Squat with growing irritation. "I'm getting a hard-on and you know how fucked off I get if I can't satisfy it."

"Patience, brother. I just have to ask Harland one question and then we shall decide once and for all."

He turned back to Harland and said, "And just how could you guarantee that we won't get caught?"

"Because," said Harland thinking on his feet, "I'll tell the authorities that I was in hiding there when the attack was carried out, and that I saw who did it. Then I'll say that at least three different-looking people did it."

The pastor and Squat looked at one another again.

"And you'll treble our pay, let us keep anything we find and you'll kill the dog before we get there?" said the pastor.

"Yes, and let Squat have the dairymaid, after which you can do with her what you like."

A tremor of excitement ran through the pastor's body at that thought. He looked at Squat again and said, "What do you think, brother – should we trust him?"

"We did before and we nearly got killed."

"But you'll have a clear run at it next time," said Harland. "I'll make sure of it."

Once again, the pastor and Squat exchanged glances.

"Alright," said the pastor, "but now we require a deposit."

"What kind of deposit?"

"Everything that you have on you – notes *and* coins – and maybe then we'll let you go."

Harland nodded in agreement.

"And today's Thursday," said the pastor. "We'll give you until Saturday night to sort things out. After that the new moon will make it impossible to see."

"Saturday?" said Harland. "But that's only…"

"Not my problem, brother, but if you haven't kept your part of the bargain, or you try to double-cross us, I'll hunt you down and cut out your liver. Do you understand?"

"But that's only two days from now!" said Harland.

The pastor pushed the blade into Harland's stomach again and clenched his teeth.

"Like I said, not my problem. Now, hand over the cash, and to use Brother Squat's vernacular, – *fuck off.*"

He yanked Harland away from the wall and pushed him towards the centre of the room.

Harland emptied the contents of his pockets and wallet, and handed them to the pastor.

"And the pocket watch," said Squat.

Harland knew better than to argue, and removed the watch from his waistcoat pocket.

Squat snatched it out of Harland's hand, opened it, listened to it for a second or two, and then stuffed it into his trouser pocket.

Harland noted which pocket it had gone into in case the opportunity arose to retrieve it.

The pastor took the money, looked at it, and said, "Now go in peace, brother, whilst we thank the Lord for your bounteous gifts." He paused for the briefest of seconds and then said, "Saturday night, don't forget – and you'd better pray that things go right this time…"

Harland exited the bottle store and ran down the street. He'd been reading earlier in the day, and as he put as much distance as he could between himself and his co-conspirators, he recalled some of the words from one of Amelia Opie's poems.

> 'Now his swift wings the sea-bird lowers,
> For well he reads the angry skies,
> And 'ere the storm its fury pours,
> For shelter to the rock he flies.'

The following morning, just after 6:30am, Matty Shield, the butcher's delivery boy, knocked on the front door of the Whitewall Estate living quarters.

The door opened and Maria smiled at him.

"Morning Matty," she said. "Put it in the cold store, there's a good lad."

Matty smiled back and said, "Yes, Missus."

He walked down towards the barn with a spring in his step for two reasons. First was the shiny thre'penny bit that he'd received from the gent, and second, because he'd taken a shine to Sugg, he was going to enjoy feeding him the tender meat that the gent had given him because it was his birthday.

He took extra care not to mention any of it to the Missus because, as the gent had said, she wouldn't have approved of giving a farm dog such a good cut of meat.

As he heard approaching footsteps, Sugg came bounding out and stopped when he recognised the young boy.

Matty was still unsure of Sugg because of his sheer size and appearance, but once he'd seen him stop, he gained confidence.

He glanced back to make sure that the Missus wasn't watching and then said, "Happy birthday, boy – I've got a real treat for you…"

He reached into his bag, pulled out the brown paper parcel with the strychnine-laced meat, and waived it at Sugg.

"Come on into the barn, or the Missus might see us and take it off you."

Sugg wagged his tail and followed the boy into the barn.

Matty undid the string, opened up the paper, and exposed the choice cut of meat.

"Matty!"

Matty whirled around at the sound of the Missus' voice. He heard her approaching, looked about, and saw that there was nowhere to conceal the meat.

"Sorry, boy!" he said, and then threw the whole package into a far corner of the barn behind some farm equipment.

"Ah, there you are," said Maria. "Have you been petting Sugg?"

"Yes, Missus," said Matty.

"You'll be turning him soft if you carry on!" Maria paused and looked at the perplexed look on the boy's face and said, "But I'm sure that he'll survive you. Now," she said holding out a couple of letters, "when you go back into town, will you please take these to the Post Office for me? There's a farthing in it for you…"

"Yes, Missus," said Matty taking the letters and coin.

"Now go and put the meat in the cold store and be off with you."

"Yes, Missus."

Matty cast a quick glance in the direction of Sugg and then a furtive one at the corner in which he'd thrown his meat. He hadn't done what the gent had paid him for, but he'd never admit to that.

He looked down at the extra coin and smiled. It had been a good couple of days.

A couple of minutes later, Silas appeared in the barn and called over to Sugg.

"Come on lad, it's quarter-to-seven," he said. "Time for our morning constitutional."

Sugg looked into the corner of the barn, then turned and looked at Silas. The meat could wait; he had other duties to attend.

Within a few minutes, silence fell upon the barn. In the corner, the poisoned meat lay on the floor. The first animal to find it was one of the numerous wild farm cats that haunted most country estates. It sniffed at it and then started eating. And then another cat appeared, and then another.

"And are you absolutely positive that you gave that meat to Sugg?" said Harland a couple of hours later, "because I'm very fond of him, and I'd be very annoyed if I found out that you'd taken it home for your family."

Matty looked up at the stern face of the gentleman and said, "Yes, I did, mister."

"And did he enjoy it?"

Matty felt his cheeks flush but kept calm and said, "Yes, mister."

"And he ate it all?"

"Yes, mister."

Harland smiled and patted Matty on the head. He retrieved a ha'penny from his wallet and handed it to him.

"Well done, lad," he said. "I knew that I could trust you."

Matty looked down at yet another coin and then added it to the others in his coat pocket.

It had been a very good couple of days indeed.

# Chapter 26

*Thursday 20th April 2006. The Cragg Vale Estate*

Naomi looked around the room of her cell. The walls and ceiling were painted in a mid-green gloss and the concrete floor was covered in a rubber-backed mat. Her bed had a single bottom sheet, a pillow and two blankets, and in the corner of the small windowless room stood a commode. She had no washing facilities, food, nor water, and a low-wattage single white light shone from behind a glass cover in the centre of the ceiling.

She'd been given two sparse meals and some bottled water, and due to that alone guessed that it must now be the day after her encounter with Spooner. She'd re-lived the horrifying experience over and over again, but she had no notion of what had happened to her after he'd fired the shotgun; indeed the only thing that she was sure of was that the gun must have been loaded with blanks, because there were no signs of injury anywhere on her body.

Her musing was interrupted as the bolt slid back on the other side of the door. As per each of her previous visits, a figure dressed in black, complete with full-face balaclava, stepped into the room with a tray. She saw that it contained a few cereal bars, some chocolate, a packet of crisps, and a mug of hot tea. Additionally, and to her relief, there was a packet of moist wipes.

For the briefest of seconds, she considered snatching up the tea and throwing it into the face of her guard, but she dismissed the idea as being impetuous.

The figure in black deposited the tray on the end of her bed and removed the bucket from the commode. He or she deposited it outside the door and then placed a clean bucket back in its place.

She watched in silence and noted the lack of sound as the figure moved around. She glanced down and saw that the guard appeared to be wearing some sort of flat-soled ballet shoes or similar.

Once the bucket had been replaced she expected the person to depart, but instead, he or she went to the door, looked left and right, and then returned to where she was perched.

The figure leaned close to her left ear and then in a hushed tone, a male voice said, "Is your name Wilkes?"

Naomi nodded.

"Very well," said the man. "I'm a friend, and I'm going to get you out of here. Don't do anything impulsive, keep strong, and wait for my signal."

He looked through the eye slit in the balaclava until he was sure that his ward had understood, then nodded his head and departed.

Silence descended upon the tiny cell once again, but this time Naomi set about the food and water with a renewed vigour.

Sixteen miles away in Manchester, Adrian Darke sat puzzling with Pike, Sheldon, and Hinchcliffe in the board room of his offices.

"But *why* had she gone back to the cottage?" said Adrian. "There must be something there that attracted her."

"No idea," said Hinchcliffe. "Spooner loosed off a blank and she fainted dead away. After that, you know the rest."

Adrian sat with a perplexed look upon his face and said, "I wish I'd never put that bloody Gillorton woman on to her case..."

Sheldon reached into his briefcase and retrieved Naomi's email; he read it and then said, "Her email states that they were carrying out a routine research into 19$^{th}$ century lifestyles, etc. Isn't that a good enough reason?"

"It might have been if she hadn't come back," said Adrian, "but for her to return early in the morning after two encounters with Les Spooner, she must have been looking for something important."

"I could get the answer out of her in no time, boss," said Pike.

Adrian turned and said, "Not on this occasion, F.A."

A silence descended on the room until Hinchcliffe said, "Sorry if I'm being a bit insensitive, A.D., but why does it matter what she's looking for? She obviously hasn't found whatever it is, and if we finish her, she never will…"

"And Gillorton has trashed the site and rendered it useless with her indiscriminate excavations and soil dumping," added Sheldon.

Adrian looked at the two men and nodded. He didn't want to bring up how Naomi had nearly exposed a fraudulent land deal by one of his ancestors that could have cost him millions, but when he'd heard via Gabriel Ffitch the town clerk, that her research had something to do with the Chance family history again, he'd become ultra-sensitive and ultra-curious. He also harboured reservations about whether she might have shared her reasons for the research with anybody else too.

"So if we just…" Hinchcliffe made the throat slitting sign with his right hand, "… that would be the end of your problems, wouldn't it?"

Adrian remained silent.

"And if anybody else turns up prying about, we can see them off too."

"What about her vehicle?" said Adrian.

"That's already been crushed, along with all of her personal belongings, – handbag, phone, etc."

"Alright," said Adrian. "Wait until this evening then get one of the guys at Cragg Vale to do it. He can dump her body in the lake at the bottom of Lark Hill. If the police turn up, be cooperative, but keep them well away from Spooner's cottage."

Several miles away, at Rochdale Police Headquarters, there was a knock on Crowthorne's door.

"Come in," he called.

The office door opened and Detective Sergeant Pete Caulfield walked in.

"Yes, Pete?"

"We've picked up a '212RF90' from Deimos."

Crowthorne, who was momentarily distracted said, "Sorry Pete, could you please repeat that?"

"Yes, sir – we've just picked up a '212RF90' from Deimos."

Crowthorne looked at his watch and saw that it was 4:37pm. He thought for a minute and then said, "Right, we need to be ready; activate two armed response units and ask the duty Inspector to come and see me." He paused for a second and then said, "What time is Phobos due to switch on today?"

"21:46 or 01:13, sir."

"Damn, that's no use," said Crowthorne. "It looks as though Deimos will have to go it alone."

"If he'd known who Phobos was, he might have been able to turn to him for help..." said Caulfield, "... which, of course, makes you consider whether we made the right decisions a few months ago."

Crowthorne emitted a humming sound and said, "What's done is done." He thought for a few seconds and then said, "I know that the topography of Cragg End Lane is tricky, but get the armed response guys in unmarked cars, out of sight at least an hour beforehand – even if they have to park in people's drives, etc. We need to be ready to assist Deimos if he needs it."

"And what would you like me transmit to Phobos, sir?"

"Just acquaint him with the circumstances. By the time he switches on, it could all be over."

Caulfield looked down for a second and then said, "We could have done without this, sir; it could ruin everything."

Crowthorne took in a deep breath and said, "Priorities, Pete, priorities."


At 7pm that evening on the Cragg Vale Estate, the Team Leader spoke to his subordinate.

"Are you quite clear on what you have to do?"

"Yes boss."

"It's James Miles, isn't it?" said the Team Leader.

"Yes, boss."

"Right, James – tell me."

"Take the occupant from the green room to the bottom of Lark Hill, terminate her, and sink her body in the centre of the lake."

"Right," said the Team Leader. "And you have no problems with those instructions?"

"None, boss."

"Excellent." The Team Leader paused for a few seconds and then said, "Let's get it done."

Miles looked up at his boss and said, "Are you coming too, sir?"

"Of course I am. I wouldn't miss this for the world; and furthermore, I'll be able to keep any prying eyes diverted if I need to."

"Oh," said Miles. "You'll be…"

"Yes. Now you pick up one of the silenced pieces from stores and take the woman to where we discussed. I'll meet you there in fifteen minutes."

"Yes, boss."


Five minutes later, the door to Naomi's cell opened and a black-clad figure walked in. He walked across to Naomi and said out loud, "Put your palms together in front of you."

Naomi obeyed and held out her arms.

Miles placed a large black cable-tie over her wrists, threaded it, and pulled – but not tight enough to stop her wriggling her hands out if she tried.

He leaned close to her ear and whispered, "Keep calm and do exactly as I say."

In a loud voice he said, "Stand up." He then wrapped a gag around her mouth. Seconds later, he grabbed her by the wrists and dragged her down two bunker-style concrete corridors until they reached a lift.

Naomi noted that there were only two levels, and that she must have been on the lower one.

The lift carried them up, the door opened and Naomi was pushed across a small room, through a metal door, and out into a yard containing several electric quad-bikes, that were being charged from sockets on the wall.

Miles pushed her into the seat of an unconnected one and pressed the pedal on the floor. The vehicle sprang into action and headed for a large metal gate. As they approached it, it opened, and they sped out.

Naomi was amazed at the speed and ease with which the small, silent, electric vehicle handled the terrain and realised how the gamekeeper had been able to move around so quickly.

The silence was broken as Miles said, "Time is of the essence. As soon as we get to the lake, get out of the vehicle, and lie face down on the ground. And don't move if you hear anybody else. Do you understand?"

He looked at Naomi and saw her nod.

The vehicle exited a group of trees, and Naomi saw the familiar looking lake at the bottom of Lark Hill. They drove to within twenty-five yards or so of it, the vehicle stopped and she heard her rescuer order her out. She jumped out and dropped down onto the ground as she'd been instructed.

Minutes later a second vehicle pulled up and she heard another man ask, "Is it done?"

She didn't hear a reply, but then heard the second man say, "Good – I'll take the cable ties and weights across to the boat and get it in the water whilst you drag her over."

To her utmost horror, she realised what was supposed to have happened to her and terror gripped her heart.


At the top of Lark Hill, one of the armed response units was sitting in an unmarked police car just inside the gates of High Farm. The driver and co-driver were awaiting instructions when there was a gentle tap on the driver's window.

The driver saw the amiable face of Dave Brown standing next to the car with two steaming mugs of tea. He wound down the window and said, "Hi."

"I thought that you lads could do with a cuppa while you waited," said Dave.

The driver looked at the tea and smiled.

"You're not wrong there," he said as he opened the door and got out.

At the bottom of Lark Hill, events seemed to erupt in a flash.

Miles waited until his Team Leader's back was turned, and then whipped out the silenced handgun and brought it crashing down on his head.

The Team Leader fell into a heap on the floor.

Miles sprinted back to Naomi, yanked her to her feet, and said, "Quick, get..."

"Hey!" A voice yelled from a nearby copse.

Up in the yard of High Farm, Dave and the two plain-clothes policemen heard the shout and turned to face where it had been coming from.

Miles and Naomi whipped around and saw Spooner standing a short distance away with his shotgun in his hand.

"Not so fast, Miles." Spooner looked at Naomi and called, "You, girlie, move to one side."

Miles looked at Naomi and said, "Do as he says."

Naomi started to move away.

"Now, drop the piece," called Spooner.

Naomi saw Miles hold out his hand as though he was about to drop the weapon, when suddenly he dropped to one knee, aimed at Spooner and fired.

She heard the muffled shot and spun around to look at Spooner, but he appeared to be unmoved. She looked back at Miles and saw him looking in disbelief at the handgun.

When she looked back at Spooner, she saw that he was aiming the shotgun at her rescuer.

"You two-timing bastard," called Spooner. "This is what happens to scum like you."

He pulled the trigger and hit Miles full in the chest.

Naomi gasped as she saw blood appear from multiple wounds.

Without speaking, Spooner walked up to Naomi and hit her on the side of the head with the butt of his gun, knocking her unconscious. He was about to drag her across to the Lake to finish the job, when in the stillness of the night he heard the sound of voices at the top of the Lark Hill. As quick as a he was able, he manhandled Miles' and Naomi's bodies into the cover of the trees.

Dave and the two policemen looked down into the darkness. One of the policemen shone a high-powered torch down the hill and scanned it from side to side but saw nothing.

"Send for back-up," said the policeman with the torch.

"Could have been a poacher," said Dave. "We get a few round these parts…"

The second policeman looked at the first and raised his eyebrows.

The first policeman thought for a second and then said, "Best not to take any chances – go and do it."

The second policeman nodded and ran back to the police car.

# Chapter 27

*Friday 21ˢᵗ April 2006. Naomi and Carlton Wilkes'*
*House*

Just after 8am, Crowthorne sat in Carlton's kitchen holding a cup of fresh coffee. Carlton, Jane, and Sam listened to what was being said.

"We have two highly-trained undercover officers working within Darke's organisation at Cragg Vale, and yesterday afternoon we picked up something called a '212RF90' from one of them.

"The 'RF' indicates red flag; this is an emergency exit signal and the number preceding it indicates the number evacuating – therefore, the '2RF' code meant that two people were going to be exiting. The numbers around that refer to hours in a day. The inside two i.e., the one and nine, are the planned start time, and the outside numbers the planned conclusion time. So to sum up, the signal meant that our man would be attempting an emergency exit with one other between the hours of 19:00 and 20:00 hours last night."

"And did he?" said Sam.

Crowthorne turned to face Sam and said, "No, sir, he did not."

"And did he give any indication who would be with him?" said Jane.

Crowthorne turned to Jane and said, "No, he didn't." He saw Jane open her mouth to speak and said, "And though it would be tempting to presume that it was Mrs Wilkes, we shouldn't."

"Do you think that something happened to him?" said Carlton.

Crowthorne looked at Carlton and said, "It's impossible to say. When our chap was as specific as he was about the exit times and then didn't show up, it could have meant that something had cropped up to stop him trying. Or, it could be something less palatable."

"And how will we get to know which it was?" said Carlton.

"Each day our man has two specific three minute windows when he switches on an unlisted mobile phone. The next one is at 18:02 this evening. The response we get will determine our course of action."

Sam, who had for the most part been listening in the background, said, "Superintendent, can you tell us why you have a couple of undercover guys working on the Cragg Vale Estate?"

Crowthorne looked down and considered his response for a couple of seconds. He said, "I shouldn't be saying this, but given the unique circumstances, I'm prepared to divulge some very sensitive information if I can have your word that it will not leave this room?"

Everybody agreed.

"Very well," said Crowthorne. "For several months now we have been aware that Adrian Darke has been producing a large amount of illegal substances in an underground facility located below his gamekeeper's cottage."

"What, the creepy guy that Naomi told us about?" said Carlton.

"That 'creepy guy', as you name him, isn't all that he seems," said Crowthorne.

"We know," said Carlton. "We've all heard the stories."

Crowthorne looked from face to face and then said, "That 'creepy guy' is several creepy guys. At any one time, there are at least six on duty posted at the most publicly accessible areas of the Estate, each dressed the same, and each equipped with VHF radios, and high-speed electric quad bikes. The whole of the estate is monitored by an elaborate array of CCTVs, located on high-level posts, trees, buildings – you name it – and the 'creepy gamekeeper' can be directed to any possible trouble spots within seconds."

"Good grief," said Carlton. "That sounds a serious set-up."

"It is," said Crowthorne. "And it also explains how several people have been able to report seeing the gamekeeper in two places at the same time."

"So if you know all this, why haven't you gone in and cleaned it up?" said Jane.

"Because according to our undercover chaps, there's supposed to be a meeting of some of the UK's top drug barons at Cragg Vale, next Tuesday. We already have enough intelligence to go in and break up Darke's operation, but we've been waiting until the 24th to try and capture the regional bigwigs too."

"But what if that's our daughter's life you may be risking?" said Jane.

"Well, there's the rub; and not wanting to alarm you, one of our armed response units heard some shouting and a gunshot at around the time of the planned exit last night."

"You don' think…" interrupted Jane.

"We don't *think* anything Mrs Chance," said Crowthorne. "That would be unprofessional and speculative, but we did react. Following the sound of the gunshot, we sent a patrol car to investigate. The officers spoke to staff at the estate and found nothing unusual…"

"Oh, surprise, surprise," said Jane.

Crowthorne stared at Jane for a second and then continued, "And the 'gamekeeper' informed them that he had seen off a couple of men who'd been poaching rabbits."

"So what now, Bob?" said Carlton.

"We wait until six o' clock tonight, see what our man has to say, and decide upon our best course of action."

"But what if Naomi is in danger?" said Jane.

"I'm sorry if this upsets you Mrs Chance, We don't know if it was Mrs Wilkes that was about to be extracted, but we are keeping an open mind about it and we have apprised our other man of the existing situation. And if it's of any comfort to you at all, he's the best that we've got."

A short silence ensued until Carlton looked up and said, "Bob, if you do decide to go in tonight based upon the intelligence that you may receive, how would you feel about being offered some professional help?"

In the stark light of the small cell, Naomi sat with her eyes closed on the edge of her bed. The right-hand side of her face was cut, swollen, and very tender, and she had difficulty seeing out of her right eye. All-in-all, she felt as though she'd been hit by a train.

The pain though was something that would pass. The prospect of what was about to come was altogether more worrying. She recalled the callous way in which her erstwhile rescuer had been killed, and she couldn't allay the feeling that the clock was on a countdown for her too.

Her mind strayed across to Carlton and her mother and father. She knew that they'd all be desperate to find her, but because she hadn't told them where she'd planned to go, they wouldn't know where to look. She didn't think that she could feel any lower.

Then the thumb pressed down on her shoulder, and a sudden aroma of violets pervaded her senses.

"Don't fret dear," said the voice that she believed to be Maria. "One of our boys will soon be coming to get you."

Naomi mistook the meaning and said, "No! I don't want to go; I have a life here, I…"

"No, no," said the voice. "I don't mean that. I mean that one of our boys is coming to help you."

There was a sudden bang on the outside of her cell door and a male voice shouted, "Stop whining, bitch, and think yourself lucky you got an extra day!"

Naomi realised that she'd spoken out loud and that her guard must have mistaken her meaning. For the first time ever, she tried replying with her mind. She couldn't see anybody or anything, but turned in the direction of the voice and tried to think, "Who's coming, and when?"

She sat in silence until she heard the voice say, "Did you hear me, dear?"

She realised that 'thinking' words wasn't going to work, so very softly she said, "Yes I did. Who's coming, and when?"

"Brandon, one of our boys, very soon, so be patient."

Naomi was comforted and said, "Please don't leave me."

"Of course I won't," said the voice, "but I want you to give Brandon a message from me. – Tell him to go left, when he has a choice to make."

Naomi repeated, "Tell him to go left, when he has a choice to make."

"Yes. Now lie down and try to rest for a while. I'll stay by your side."

Naomi didn't even try to question what was going on. She lay down, shut her eyes, and fell into a short, restful sleep.

At 6:30pm, Carlton was still in his office at Walmsfield Borough Council, waiting for the call from Crowthorne. Everybody had gone home and everywhere was silent. He got up and paced around the main open-plan office adjacent to his small office, and realised that he hadn't had anything to eat since breakfast. He caught sight of the vending machine in the corner and decided to treat himself to a chocolate bar and a hot coffee.

He walked across to it, inserted the appropriate coins, and lifted his hand to press the buttons when the phone burst into life on his desk. He ran back to his office, oblivious of the numerous items that he sent flying on the way.

He snatched up the phone and said, "Wilkes."

"Carlton, Bob Crowthorne here. We've received no communication from the officer who sent the exit signal yesterday, but ominously, we've received an urgent extraction request for two from our other chap."

"What's the difference?" said Carlton.

"An exit signal tells us the officer is attempting to break cover and come out. An extraction request is asking us to go in and help him get out."

"Good God – has he indicated a time?"

"Yes, sunset is at 20:05 tonight, so he has signalled then."

"Can I do anything?"

"Yes. Remember that offer you made to me this morning? I've had a word upstairs and we'll take you up on it."

"Okay," said Carlton. "Give me a mobile number and I'll ask them to liaise directly with you from now on."

Carlton made a note of the number, said goodbye and dialled the Duke of Lancaster's Regiment, 4th Battalion Garrison HQ at Preston, and spoke to Rosie and co. who had arrived earlier in the day, and who had been despatched there pending his call.

"Yes Carlton, Rob here…"

Carlton barely recognised the voice of Rosie when he was being official, and couldn't remember the last time that he'd been called Carlton by him.

"It's a go!" he said.

He passed on the contact info, promised to meet them on Rushworth Moor after the operation and put down the phone. He picked up his coat and was about to leave, when the phone rang again. Believing it to be either Bob Crowthorne or Rosie, he snatched it up and said, "Wilkes."

The Council receptionist, Karen Morecraft, said, "Mr Wilkes, it's Karen from reception. I'm glad that I've caught you…"

Carlton interrupted and said, "Is it urgent? I'm in a terrible rush."

"I have a lady named Helen Milner on the line who has been trying to contact your wife all day, and she wants to know if she can speak to you."

Five minutes later Carlton dialled Crowthorne's direct number and said, "Bob, Carlton here. Naomi went to High Farm Cottage early yesterday morning…"

# Chapter 28

*January 7<sup>th</sup> 1872. Wordale Moor, Lancashire*

As the horse and cart carrying the three co-conspirators approached the top of Wordale Moor just after midnight, Squat jabbed Harland in the side and said, "You'd better be right about that fucking dog, 'cos if you ain't, it's you who'll be shitting your pants."

Harland looked up. The moon was partially obscured by a light cloud cover but there was still enough light to be able to see. He hated being on Wordale Moor so late and so close to Whitewall, and even more he hated being with Squat and the pastor.

"Are you listening to me?" said Squat, jabbing Harland for a second time.

Harland turned around and said, "What do you want me to say? The butcher's boy fed the meat to the dog, he saw him eat it all, and when he went back there this morning, there was no sign of him."

"He could've been out with the farmer," said Squat.

"I doubt it. The lad said that the farmer took the dog out regular as clockwork at a quarter-to-seven."

"And how would a boy like that know what hour it was without a timepiece, brother?" said the pastor.

"Because every morning he heard the farmer say the same thing, – 'Come on lad, it's quarter-to-seven, time for our morning constitutional.'"

"What about this morning?" said Squat.

"No farmer, no dog."

"And did the boy ask after the dog?" said the pastor.

"No, – because he didn't want to attract any attention to himself."

The pastor thought about things for a few minutes. He knew that Harland's conviction that the dog was finished wasn't proof, but this time they were armed and ready, and if necessary they'd shoot the dog and anybody else who got in the way.

All things considered, the potential rewards, cash and goods, and a young dairymaid to have fun with afterwards justified the risk.

And this time they had 'the toff' in tow as a form of insurance.

A plan started to form in his mind, and a few minutes later he said, "Just to be on the safe side, this is what we'll do…"

Down in the estate buildings, Sugg was muzzled and lying on the floor next Silas in the barn. Detective Inspector Jack Brewster sat opposite on a bale of hay with his service revolver close to hand, listening for any unusual sounds.

Sergeant Banks sat in the darkened parlour with Maria. A police marksman with a cocked Snider-Enfield rifle sat in one of the upstairs bedrooms with Simeon and Martha, and four other armed officers were concealed in different places around the courtyard, watching and waiting.

"We'll look chumps if nobody turns up," said Silas in a hushed tone.

Brewster looked back and said, "Some days you bite the bear, some days the bear bites you."

"Nevertheless…" said Silas.

"It's all about odds in the end, sir. Our suspicion that something was going on was first raised when we received an unfounded report that you were harbouring an escaped lunatic – though the Lord only knows how that relates to any of this."

He paused for a second as the conundrum struck him again, but then dismissed it and looked back at Silas.

"Then within a few short weeks the dog here foils a robbery, and two days later the butcher's lad tries to poison him…"

"The boy didn't know that the meat was poisoned," interrupted Silas. "It was only me finding all those dead cats and the Missus recalling seeing him acting odd with Sugg that got us questioning him."

"And fair enough, he did come clean and do his bit," said Brewster. "But for whoever is behind this, to attempt to get the dog poisoned within two days of a foiled robbery – if indeed that was the intention – they must be desperate to get the job done."

He stopped speaking again and listened for any signs of abnormal activity. He then turned back to Silas and continued.

"It's a new moon on the tenth and the sky will be as black as a rook's backside. No experienced ne'er-do-well would operate in conditions like that, – so because the attempt was made on the dog a couple of days ago, with whoever behind it questioning the lad this morning, I'd put money on them returning tonight or tomorrow."

"It's a good job that we told him what to say," said Silas.

"A sensible precaution, sir, as was your decision to call us as soon as you did. And we'll soon see if the lad did as he was told."

"I hope so," said Silas. "I hope so..."

As per the pastor's earlier conceived plan, Squat edged closer to the courtyard with Hessian sacks wrapped around his boots and a cocked pistol in his hand.

Thirty yards behind him, the pastor followed with wrapped shoes and a cocked pistol, and like Squat in front, he only had one thing on his mind – Sugg.

The empty courtyard opened up in front of Squat. He stopped and listened for several seconds but heard nothing. His heart was beating so fast in his chest that he half-wondered if it could be heard outside. He looked at his gun and checked for the umpteenth time that all of the chambers in the cylinder contained bullets. Satisfied that all was in order, he bent down, picked up a small stone, and tossed it into the courtyard.

In the barn, Sugg reacted and stood up.

Brewster picked up his revolver with his right hand, turned to Silas, and touched his left forefinger to his lips.

Silas nodded and kept Sugg quiet.

Up in the bedroom, the armed policemen heard the sound too; he lifted the rifle up to his right shoulder and peered out of the partially open window.

Simeon picked up the shotgun, covered the breech with a pillow, and snapped it shut.

Following several seconds of total silence, Squat retrieved another small stone and tossed it further into the courtyard than the first one. Once again he stood stock still, listening for the slightest sound, but none was forthcoming.

He turned around and gestured for the pastor to follow.

As stealthily as a cat, he placed one silent foot in front of another until he reached a third of the way in. There he stopped and turned to see how far behind the pastor was, and to his amazement, saw no sign of him. He frowned and looked in other places but saw nothing.

Ten yards up the drive and out of sight of Squat, the pastor too was straining his ears for the faintest sound. His breathing was steady but controlled, and he was being ultra-careful not to step onto any loose stones.

He edged forwards another three or four yards with his eyes fixed on the path when, without a second's warning, a big hand clamped over his mouth and the barrel of a revolver was pressed into his neck.

He heard a voice whisper into his ear, "Throw your gun over the wall and keep still, or I'll shoot."

The pastor saw part of a black police uniform and recognised it. Cursing his own stupidity for not paying enough attention around him, he threw the gun over the wall.

In the courtyard, Squat remained still, half expecting the pastor to appear, but when he didn't, he turned and started to creep back. He took two or three steps when a voice commanded, *"This is the police; drop your weapon and put your hands in the air."*

Squat spun around and fired in the direction of the voice. Out of nowhere, he saw a couple of policemen appear with their weapons aimed at him and in a reflex action fired several shots at them. Most of the bullets flew into the air but two whined off the hard sandstone wall of the dairy as the startled policemen ducked back for cover.

Up in the bedroom, the marksman with the Snider-Enfield rifle took aim and waited for the optimum moment. He saw Squat turn, took in a deep breath, held it, and then squeezed the trigger.

The cartridge smashed through the bridge of Squat's nose, and killed him on the spot.

Back in the drive, the sudden violent action distracted the policeman and he looked in the direction of the firing.

The pastor felt the grip on his mouth loosen. He dropped straight down, snatched Santa Maria's finger out of his jacket pocket and rammed it hilt deep into the policeman's small intestine. As quick as a flash, he yanked it out and then rammed it hilt deep into his stomach.

The policeman groaned and dropped to his knees.

The pastor turned to run up the drive, but in a fit of cold-hearted blood lust couldn't resist stabbing the injured policeman one more time.

"Bless you, brother," he said drawing back the blade, "rest in peace."

He then rammed it into the back of the policeman's left lung.

With a cruel grin, he watched his victim fall face forwards, and then he turned and ran for all his worth up the drive.

Up on the road, Harland was petrified. He'd heard the shooting, but almost as soon as it had started, it had finished. He strained his eyes in the darkness, and awaited even the smallest of glimpses to reassure him that everything had gone according to plan.

Brewster, Silas, and the unmuzzled Sugg were the first to arrive at the drive; they looked up it and saw the policeman lying face down. Further up, they saw a man running away.

Silas unleashed Sugg and shouted, "Take him, boy!"

The pastor turned at the sound of the voice and couldn't believe his eyes. The monster was behind him. The bastard toff had betrayed him again... In his panic-stricken mind, he imagined that Sugg was the Hound of Hell, sent to drag him kicking and screaming into everlasting damnation.

Fear and masses of adrenaline leant wings to his feet. He reached the top of the drive and started to run towards the horse and cart.

Harland caught sight of the pastor. At first he couldn't make out any detail, but he knew that something wasn't right. He saw the pastor look over his left shoulder. He looked further up the road, and to his utmost horror, saw Sugg running straight at them. In blind panic, he snatched up the reins and attempted to turn the cart around.

In an instant, all hell let loose. As the horse started to turn, it caught sight of the monster dog and reared up in panic.

The pastor arrived and launched himself into the cart landing face down onto Harland's legs, knocking him back off the seat.

Seconds later, Sugg leapt in and buried his huge fangs into the pastor's right side. He snatched his head away, tearing off flesh, muscle, and clothing. He wheeled his huge head around and buried his teeth into Harland's left shoulder, breaking his collarbone and puncturing his shoulder blade.

The panic-stricken pastor was oblivious to the pain as Sugg repeatedly bit into his back. He tried to lash out with his knife, but then Sugg clamped his huge jaws over his upper arm, crushed his humerus, and severed his brachial artery. He screamed out in agony and then saw Harland staring at him in total terror.

Through clenched teeth, he said, "You bastard..."

Within seconds, Sugg bit into the back of his head, wrenched it to one side, and snapped his neck.

Harland looked in horror at the unbelievably fearsome monster as it wheeled around to face him. It lifted its bloodstained and streaked head upright in the moonlight, and for a split second their eyes locked.

It was like looking into the face of Satan himself. Copious amounts of saliva slavered out of Sugg's mouth, steam emanated from his sweat and blood-drenched fur, and his black-soulless eyes showed not one speck of compassion as he stared into the eyes of his prey.

Raging with blood lust, he opened his massive jaws and came in for the kill.

Harland knew that it was futile, but he rolled himself into a tight ball as Sugg ripped into his flesh over and over again, until all went black.

Silas and Brewster ran out into the road, turned right, headed for the horse and cart, and then stopped dead and stared in shock and horror. The scene in front of them was like something out of Dante's *Visions of Hell*.

In its blind panic, the horse had attempted to leap the drystone wall and had become trapped halfway over. It was kicking and trying to free itself from its restraints, whilst whinnying like something possessed. Its snorting, vaporous breath blasted into the night sky, causing it to look like something out of a Viking nightmare. In the cart, a terrifying blood-soaked Sugg flailed about, growling and ripping at human flesh and bone in furious frenzy.

Neither man dared to move in case the hound turned on them, but after several minutes and a few loud commands from Silas, Sugg calmed down.

Brewster was then able to bring the panic-stricken horse under control.

Bracing themselves, they ventured a look into the bottom of the cart. The gruesome sight burned itself into their memories forever.

They stared in horrified silence until Silas recognised one of the savaged, blood-soaked bodies; he said, "Oh my God, I know who that is..."

He jumped into the cart and lifted up the mauled and disfigured head of Harland. He could hear his laboured breathing and knew that he didn't have long to live.

He leaned down close to his face and said, "Why, Harland? Why did you do this?"

Harland opened one horribly disfigured and bloodied eye. He looked at Silas, and with his dying breath gasped, "Lex talionis, cabby."

# Chapter 29

*Friday 21ˢᵗ April 2006. The Cragg Vale Estate,*
*Rushworth Moor*

"Naomi, Naomi!"

Naomi wakened up and said, "What?"

The voice said, "It's time – goodbye dear."

She opened her mouth to speak, and then heard a muffled thud outside her cell door.

The bolt on the outside was drawn back and the door opened. A man dressed in black pulled in the body of another similarly dressed man.

Once inside, he pushed the cell door to, turned towards Naomi, and said, "My name's Leo. I'm here to help. Now, get undressed while I get these off him."

He started to pull the unconscious man's balaclava hood off, and then his black jumper.

For a second Naomi didn't move.

Leo turned towards her and said, "Don't just sit there, – get a move on!"

Naomi snatched at her clothes and took everything off except her underwear and boots.

Leo looked up and said, "Good, put these on."

He threw the unconscious man's jumper, trousers, and hood across the room.

Within less than a minute, Naomi had put all but the hood on. She watched as Leo dragged the unconscious body across to her bed leg, stuffed one of his socks into his mouth, and then secured a large cable tie across his open mouth and around the back of the bed leg. He then pulled the prone man's hands behind his back, secured a smaller cable tie around wrists, and another around his ankles.

Leo then leapt up and pushed Naomi into a sitting position on the edge of her bed. He looked at his watch, noted that it was 19:53 and said, "Now we wait, but not for long."

At 20:05, a Terradyne Ghurka armoured car, armed with a short battering ram, crashed through the gates of the Cragg Vale Estate, followed by eight officers in two cars from the Lancashire Police Firearms Unit and twelve officers in two vans from the Operations Support Unit.

They sped down the central drive towards the main house until they reached a junction where the Ghurka, cars and one of the vans veered off towards the gamekeeper's cottage, whilst the other van continued on to the main house.

In the Cragg Vale underground sound-proofed Control Room, panic had broken out. Several perimeter alarms had burst into life and the overweight controller, who'd been sipping a cup of red-hot tomato soup and poring over a men's magazine, hadn't known which way to turn first. At first, he'd thought that a fault had developed, but when he'd seen all the vehicles surging in, he'd attempted to put down the soup, caught the base of the mug on the edge of his desk, and had poured the scalding hot liquid over his thighs. He'd leapt up, knocked his chair over, and had tried to brush the soup off his trousers with the back of his hands, but in doing so, had taken a couple of paces backwards and fallen over the overturned chair. The back of his head had hit the concrete floor with such force that it had knocked him unconscious and had left everybody else unaware of what was going on.

In Naomi's cell, Leo looked at his watch and frowned; it was 20:07 and nothing had happened. He knew that his boss was a punctual man and that if he'd said they'd be breaching at 20:05, they would. He looked at his watch again – 20:08, and the alarms should have been going off big time.

He turned to Naomi and said, "Wait here, and keep quiet."

He poked his head out of the cell door, looked left, and right, and then slipped out. He closed the door but didn't bolt it, turned left and crept to the end of the corridor, removed a tiny mirror from his pocket and positioned it so that he see down the next stretch. It was empty. He crept down to the security office and then straightened up and walked to the window to ask 'Bounce', the security guard, to open the door.

At first he frowned when he saw the empty office, but seconds later saw Bounce lying on the floor. This was impossible – there was no way to access the lift unless the security guard released the door, and the only other escape routes were two fire escapes that were alarmed.

In a secret underground passageway leading from the main house to the factory, and unknown by Christiana, Adrian Darke, having lied to his wife about having to make an important call, unlocked the security door to which only he had a key, and entered No. 3 Processing Room. He nodded to a few surprised, white-coated employees, strolled across to the Packaging Room, and entered. There he walked across to the door that lead to the corridor in which Leo was standing and banging on the Control Room window.

Up on ground level the Ghurka, driven by a Marine Commando from the Duke of Lancaster's 4$^{th}$ Battalion with another Marine, a Lieutenant, Rosie, Kitty, and Lola inside, rounded the front of the cottage, and swept down the side of a high sided steel fence, followed by the cars. The Operations Support Unit van stopped at the front and discharged the officers, who took up pre-arranged positions at the front and sides of the cottage.

The Ghurka drove around to the rear of the steel fence and without stopping, veered left, and crashed through the steel gates into the yard containing the electric quad bikes.

One police car stopped inside the gates, the armed officers alighted and arrested two 'Les Spooners' who were about to go on patrol. The other police car stopped outside the gates and discharged the armed police who ran across to the Ghurka.

In accordance with known intelligence and an agreed plan of action, the Marine Lieutenant ordered the two Privates, Rosie, Lola, and Kitty, armed with Heckler & Koch G36

Carbines, to secure positions around the rear of the compound, leaving six armed policemen to enter the building whilst he and two other armed officers remained in the yard.

On the floor below, Adrian opened the door of the Packaging Room and was confronted by the sight of one of his Tactical Ops staff banging on the Control Room window.

"What's going on?" he said.

Leo spun round, saw Adrian, and said, "I don't know, boss. It looks as though Bounce has had an accident and is unconscious on the floor."

Adrian looked through the window, saw the prone figure, and said, "This is preposterous! What the hell happened to him?"

"I don't know, boss. I was about to remove the woman and found him just before you arrived."

"So does this mean that everybody is stuck down here until that man regains consciousness, for God's sake?"

"Yes boss," said Leo. "We couldn't even use the fire escapes in case the alarms or auto-destructs are still active, unless, of course, you know of some other way out?"

Adrian didn't want to give anything away and said, "No, of course I don't."

He looked back into the Control Room and saw Bounce stir.

"Ah," he said, "he's moving…"

Leo spun around and saw Bounce getting up whilst rubbing the back of his head. He watched the big guy turn, and saw the look of panic on his face. He saw him mouth something, but couldn't hear a thing because of the soundproofing.

Adrian watched the lumbering security guard as he staggered across to a corner of the room, with his arm outstretched.

In an instant, the whole building erupted as alarms went off, red lights flashed and sirens screeched from numerous places.

Bounce grabbed the microphone off his desk and shouted, "We're being raided!"

For a few seconds neither man moved. It was as though they had been frozen in time, and then Adrian shouted, "Shit! They can't find the girl – go and get her!"

Leo said, "Yes, boss," and set off down the corridor, knowing that Naomi was still dressed in the unconscious guard's clothes. His mind was ablaze.

Adrian had a terrible thought – a thought that would mean a small but necessary sacrifice, but one that would solve his problem.

"Stop," he shouted to the retreating Leo. "On second thoughts, bring the girl to me."

"Yes, boss."

Leo ran around the corner into the cell, looked at Naomi, and said, "Our extraction team has arrived, so we'll be surrounded by armed police. Darke doesn't know I'm helping you, but he's asked me to bring you to him. Put your overcoat on, put the hood in your pocket and let's hope that he doesn't notice what you've got on underneath…"

"You won't leave me, will you?" said Naomi

"No, of course not, but until we know what he wants, let's go along with it."

Naomi nodded.

Throughout the underground facility, the employees began to pour into the central corridor to make their way to the emergency exits.

This was contrary to what Adrian wanted. He gestured for Bounce to open the Control Room door, he entered and snatched up the microphone.

"This is not an emergency," he announced. "Return to your workstations until you are called. I repeat, this is not an emergency, return to your workstations until you are called. Anybody disobeying these orders will be dismissed."

The milling staff stopped where they were and then shuffled back to their individual posts to await further instructions.

Adrian turned to Bounce and said, "Can I count on you?"

"Yes, boss – of course, boss."

"And you will do what I say without question?"

"Yes, boss."

"Good man. Then switch off the fire escape alarms and do as I say, the minute that I say it, understood?"

"Yes, boss."


Leo appeared at the window with Naomi and said, "Your instructions, boss?"

Adrian looked first at Naomi, then turned to Leo and said, "It looks as though our number is up here, so let's not make matters worse by having anything happen to her. Take her up EE1 into the yard, and hand her over."

Feeling relieved by Adrian's apparent concern, Leo nodded and said, "Yes, boss."

"Alright," said Adrian. "Go now and when we've seen you hand her over, we'll come out in an orderly fashion – and tell those trigger-happy flat feet to keep their safeties on."

Leo said, "Yes, boss", and then set off down the corridor towards the fire door.

Adrian waited until they were out of earshot, turned to Bounce, and said, "Quick, activate AD1."

Bounce looked shocked and said, "But that will…"

Adrian's eyes blazed.

"I thought I could fucking count on you!" he said.

Bounce looked into the fearsome eyes of his boss, said, "You can", lifted up the red plastic cover of AD1, and pushed the button.

Inside the stairwell of emergency exit one, half a dozen variously sited invisible beams switched on at the top of the steps.


Leo held Naomi's hands behind her back as he pushed her back down the corridor.

They got partway down and Naomi felt the thumb press down on her shoulder.

"Which way are we going when we get to the end?" she said.

"Through emergency exit one," said Leo.

"Yes," said Naomi, "but which way are we going – to the left, or to the right?"

"To the right."

Naomi looked up and said, "You've got to go left."

Leo looked down and said, "What?"

"You've got to go left…"

"I don't under…"

"If your name is Brandon, we've got to go left!" Naomi felt an almost imperceptible change in her captor.

Leo saw Naomi looking up at him and said, "How? What?"

Naomi had no time to waste and said, "You have to trust me in this, – if your name is Brandon, we *have* to go left."

They reached the end of the corridor, went through the fire door, and stepped into the corridor. Leo looked at Naomi, frowned, and then propelled her to the left.

Adrian exited the Control Room and retraced his steps to the underground passage that led to the house. He entered, locked the door behind him, and broke out into a run. Partway along, he turned left at a junction, continued for another three-hundred yards, and then sped up a flight of steps to a locked wooden door. He put his ear to it, listened for a few seconds, unlocked it, and stepped into a small wooden hut situated in the trees a couple of hundred yards from the house.

"We've got seconds," said Leo letting go of Naomi's arms. "Quick, run!"

"Where does this go?" said Naomi.

"To emergency exit two. Now shush, and keep on running!"

They reached the end of the corridor, turned left, ran to a flight of steps, and charged up them. At the top they opened a metal door and stepped into a small enclosure disguised as an outdoor electricity compound, one-hundred yards away from the cottage.

Leo ran across to a small upright storage unit next to a quad bike, opened it, and retrieved two 'Les Spooner' long black coats and wide-brimmed hats.

"Quick," he said, turning to throw one across to Naomi. "Put these on and…"

Naomi saw Leo staring at a point behind her right shoulder. She turned and saw whom she believed to be Les Spooner standing behind the open door, with a raised sawn-off shotgun in his hand.

"And where are you two going in such a hurry?" said Spooner.

Naomi remembered a trick that her father had once taught her, pointed up in the air above him and shouted, "Look out!"

She saw Spooner look up, and then kicked him hard in the crotch.

As the shocked gamekeeper crumpled to his knees, Leo jumped on him, disarmed him, and knocked him unconscious with the butt of the gun. He secured his arms behind his back with a cable tie and then strapped another round his ankles.

"Good grief," he said turning to Naomi. "Remind me not to upset you when we get out of here!"

Naomi looked at the prone figure and said, "I've had to put up with enough nonsense from that idiot."

Leo picked up the gamekeeper's gun, snapped open the breech, and extracted the cartridges. He saw that they were live No. 4's. He turned to Naomi with a renewed respect and said, "Cool Mrs Wilkes – very cool."

In the compound behind the cottage, one of the armed policemen approached the door to emergency exit one. He listened at it for a few seconds, and then opened it. The interior was dimly lit, but he could see steps going down.

He turned and called out, "Sarge, I think this is another way down!"

The Sergeant called, "Okay, wait there – I'll get another couple of guys."

The armed policeman nodded his acknowledgement and then turned to look down the steps. He reached into his utility belt, extracted a small but powerful torch, switched it on, and stepped inside the door. He took two more steps towards the top of the flight, and then walked through one of the electric beams.

The blast was horrendous.

A quarter of a mile away, and deep in the estate woods, Adrian was beginning to wonder why he hadn't heard anything when the tremendous explosion rent the air.

"Yes!" he thought, "Problem over," and smiled at the prospect of never having to worry about Naomi Wilkes again.

# Chapter 30

*Saturday 22$^{nd}$ April 2006. Route 61, Charleston, South Carolina*

Deborah and Alan Farlington, with son Thomas and daughters Jacqueline and Elizabeth, sat looking for Old St. Andrew's Episcopal Church on the Ashley River Road as they cruised along in the mid-morning sunshine.

Brother Christopher had opted not to go, figuring that a party at his vacant parents' house was a far better prospect than scratching around an old graveyard.

Elder sister Jacqueline might not have gone too, except for one thing – JP.

Jean Paul, or JP as he was known to all, sat next to his younger brother Jordan in the rear of the Robiteauxs' car, directly behind them.

The two families could not have been more different. The Farlingtons lived in Dunnellon, where Deborah was a waitress at a local Golf Club and Alan was a self-employed handyman; the Robiteaux's lived in Gainesville where multi-talented mom Julie was a college Professor, a published author and accomplished artist, and dad Steve, with an equally dazzling array of talents, was an English Professor and Emmy Award-winning film producer to name but two. Regardless, something gelled between them and when it came to vacations and excursions, they were one-another's first choice of friends to go with.

They'd set off the day before. They'd driven to Jacksonville, picked up the I95 north until it intersected Route 17 forty miles north of Savannah, and had then driven to a nice hotel in Charleston's French Quarter.

Alan could still recall the buzz that he'd felt when he'd received Naomi's email informing him about 'El Fuego de

Marte'. Naomi and her friend's Internet research into the 'Andrew Ashley Charleston' conundrum had mirrored that of the eager Thomas, and though he'd not been able to help speculating how a discovery of that magnitude could impact their lives, he'd kept his feet on the ground believing inside, that it would be most unusual if a ruby of that size and importance had not been long discovered and ferreted away. He'd had no hesitation in telling the Robiteauxs about the stone either, because having first slept on the knowledge, he'd considered the likelihood of it being there even less likely the next day.

He'd accessed the church's website and an excerpt from the 'History' section quoted, *The surrounding area suffered greatly from Indian, Spanish, French, and British wars, as well as a number of hurricanes (the most famous being Hugo in 1989). A historic preservation effort to ensure the proper restoration and to guarantee the architectural integrity of the building resulted in a $1.5 million renovation of the church building, completed in time for Easter 2005.'*

He couldn't imagine that during all of those occurrences, a rare and valuable ruby had remained undiscovered. But none of that had diminished the excitement of anybody except Christopher, and nothing could have stopped them going for a look-see.

Now, refreshed and with full stomachs, they were on their way and ready to search for the mysterious 'Chance Mathewes' grave.

They drove up Route 61, following the instructions from the Church's website. They passed the large Church Creek Shopping Plaza on their left, continued for another half mile or so, until Thomas shouted, "There, pa, on the right!"

Alan saw the church through the trees, indicated right, and then drove down to the car park, followed by the Robiteauxs.

"I've just got to see inside, honey," said Julie to Steve as she stepped out of the car. "I've heard that it's beautiful."

"I'm sure that everybody feels the same," said Steve. "We'll make sure that the kids remember where they are, and then we'll all go and take a look."

Following a small inter-family agreement over rules of behaviour, everybody set off and entered what was one of America's oldest churches.

They entered the white painted interior and their mouths fell open; it was more than beautiful – it was exquisite.

A red terracotta coloured stone-paved floor led between white-painted compartments of high-backed pews, through two small transepts, past an ornate, fenced-in mahogany pulpit, and up to the chancel containing the altar. The walls, arched ceiling, and woodwork were painted pure white, and several flags had been placed in various locations around the interior.

The two families proceeded up the aisle, noting the comparative lack of wall ornamentation until they reached the transepts.

Jordan gave his brother a nudge and said, "Hey, JP, check this." He pointed down to a large "X" set in the central nine paviours where the aisle and transepts crossed and said, "X marks the spot! You don't suppose…"

"Course not, dumbass."

Julie whipped around and hissed, "JP!"

JP looked up and said, "Sorry mom", and gave Jordan a sharp dig in the side.

They all walked up to the wooden altar which had hand-hewn Cypress tablets set into the Reredos which, Deborah informed everybody, had been installed in 1723. They displayed the Lord's Prayer, the Ten Commandments, and the Apostles' Creed in gold lettering.

After soaking up the history and atmosphere of the serene and beautiful place, Alan said, "Okay guys, let's go, and do what we came for."

They filed back down the nave and under a wooden gallery until Jordan spotted another large "X" on the right-hand wall. He opened his mouth to comment but stopped when he saw JP looking at him with raised eyebrows.

"Don't even think about it!" said JP.

They stepped back out into the warm Charleston sunshine and gathered around Alan.

"The graveyard directory states that the name of the grave is that of 'Chance Mathewes', but it doesn't list any further info, so if there's a headstone, and it dates from the beginning of the nineteenth century, please be aware that the engraving could be very worn, or in part, not even legible. Let's do this properly, and remember, – this is a place of rest and sanctity. Whilst we don't want to draw attention to ourselves, we should be sure to check every grave that we pass."

"And what if we find it, pa?" said Elizabeth.

"Then come to me and tell me about it, don't shout it across the full width of the cemetery."

Nods of agreement were passed around and Alan said, "I suggest we go in twos..."

"I'm with Jordan!" said Elizabeth.

"And I'll team up with JP," said Jacqueline.

Steve shot a knowing glance at Alan and said, "Okay, off you go – and remember what Uncle Al said – keep it dignified."

Julie and Deborah teamed up and set off in one direction, Alan teamed up with Steve, and Thomas wandered off on his own, keeping well clear of his two sisters and their crushes on JP and Jordan.

During their meanderings, Steve noticed a middle-aged man tending a grave not far from the church. He nodded an acknowledgement as he wandered past. The man gave a cursory nod of his head, looked straight down and carried on with his work, making it plain that he didn't want to be disturbed.

For the next three quarters of an hour, they all wandered around reading the inscriptions, and commenting on how well the graveyard was kept, until Alan realised that they had all probably overlapped one-another's search area without success. One-by-one, he attracted their attention and signalled for them to come to him.

Once the group had gathered, he received confirmation that nobody had seen the grave, and that the kids had been ultra careful not to miss any gravestones by being distracted by whom they were with.

Julie opened a downloaded copy of the Old St. Andrew's Graveyard Directory, and saw no reference to the Chance

Mathewes grave being obscured by anything. She said, "Sorry guys, there's no other conclusion – somehow we've missed it."

A collective groan went out from the younger members, who made it plain that Charleston offered many more attractions suited to their tastes than hawking around a graveyard two times on the trot.

"Alright, alright," said Deborah, looking at her three children. "We know what you want, but we did come to Charleston to help your pa find this grave, and if we have to look one more time, then I'm sorry, but so be it."

"Can't we ask that guy over there if he knows where it is?" said Jordan.

All eyes turned to the man tending the grave by the church.

"I don't know," said Alan. "He didn't seem very friendly when your dad walked past him earlier."

Steve said, "Uncle Al's right – and do we want to alert him to what we're looking for anyway?"

"What difference would it make?" said JP. "There must be hundreds of people visiting this church over a year, and lots of them would be looking for specific resting places. That doesn't mean that the guy over there would suspect that a rare ruby was buried in one of them."

"He's got a point," said Julie.

Alan looked at the expectant faces of the younger members and reluctantly said, "Okay, okay, I'll ask him. You guys wait here."

He walked across to the attendant, stopped at the edge of the grave and said, "Hey buddy, sorry to disturb you, are you a contractor here?"

The man looked up and said, "Nope. I'm the graveyard attendant and this is my place of work."

Alan nodded and said, "In that case, you may be able to help us. We're trying to locate the grave of a long-dead relative, but can't seem to find it. Could you help us with that?"

"Maybe. What name are you looking for?"

"Chance Mathewes."

The attendant froze. He stared at Alan for a few seconds and then climbed out of the hole. He considered his response and then said, "I might be able to help, but I need to check something out first. Wait here for a few minutes and I'll be back." He then disappeared into the nearby parish house.

More than five minutes later, Alan saw the others looking at him and he shrugged back at them.

Steve ambled over and said, "Is there a problem?" But before Alan could respond, he saw the attendant emerge from the parish house. He watched with a curious expression on his face, as the attendant appeared to be taking his time coming back. He looked at Alan and said, "Something's not right."

In the distance, they became aware of the sound of a police siren and watched in fascination as a patrol car sped into the church approach road and stopped.

The attendant walked across to the female Sheriff, said something to her, and then pointed towards Alan.

Everybody was mesmerised by the turn of events and gathered around Alan as the Sheriff approached.

"Good morning, sir," said the Sheriff. "I'm Sheriff Bonnie-Mae Clement. I understand that you've been enquiring about the Chance Mathewes grave. Is that correct?"

"Yes ma'am," said Alan.

"And may I be permitted to know what your interest is in that particular grave?"

"I believe that the guy laid to rest there was a distant relative of mine." Alan faltered as he realised that he was acting upon sketchy information received from a nineteenth century riddle, and that the name too, was the wrong way round. He said, "In reality, we aren't one-hundred-percent sure, but we'd heard about this lovely old church, so we figured that we'd come and take a look while we were here anyways."

Sheriff Clement nodded as she digested the information and then said, "So you didn't come to Charleston just to find this grave?"

Alan was aware that everybody was watching him, but blatantly said, "No."

Sheriff Clement nodded again and then extracted a small notebook and pen from her shirt pocket. She said, "And what is your name, sir?"

"Farlington, Alan Farlington – but the guy in the grave is believed to be an ancestor on my grandmother's side."

"And your address and contact number?"

Alan gave the Sheriff his details and then said, "What's all this about, Sheriff? Surely we haven't violated any by-laws by just looking around the graveyard have we?"

"No, sir, you haven't," said Sheriff Clement, "but it sure is strange you all turning up here today."

"Why?" said Alan.

The Sheriff looked from face to face, and then said, "Because that's the grave Casey's working on, and two nights' ago it was desecrated."

# Chapter 31

*January 15ᵗʰ 1872. The Whitewall Estate*

Adeline Chance sat in the parlour at Whitewall and watched as Maria poured the tea. She saw Silas playfully nudging Eveline, her youngest daughter, as Stephanie, her eldest, watched with a smile on her face, and she knew that her newborn baby boy was sound asleep in the dining room.

She'd put on her best but ageing dress and bonnet for the trip to see Maria and Silas, and couldn't believe her luck when they'd invited her in and made her feel welcome.

A hearty fire burned in the fireplace and in between teasing Eveline, Silas toasted some thick slices of bread ready to eat with butter and jam.

"There we are, Addy," said Maria, placing a cup of hot tea next to her. "The toast'll be ready soon, if Silas can leave Eveline alone!"

Adeline looked at Maria and smiled. A second later the smile evaporated, she looked down and said, "I'm so sorry, May – I still don't know what to say to you both."

"Stop it," said Maria. "You have nothing to apologise for. Silas and I know that you had no part in Harland's..." she thought about the two girls for a second and then said, "... business."

"You are too kind," said Adeline shaking her head.

"Pish," said Maria. "It's all over now and things have more-or-less got back to normal." She paused and thought about Adeline's plight, and said, "At least for us, that is..."

"But," said Adeline, "for Harland to have gone to such awful lengths to try to oust you and Silas, was completely unforgivable."

Maria reflected for a second and then said, "But he paid the ultimate price for his folly, and I hope that he is now at peace."

She paused and then said, "Tell me, who chose your son's name?"

"What, Talion?" said Adeline.

Maria nodded and said, "Yes. I ask because it's so unusual."

"It was Harland's choice," said Adeline. "He told me that he wanted to start a tradition – one that would see all the first born sons in our family, going from father to son ad infinitum, named Talion until we reclaim Whitewall. A fanciful notion, if you ask me," she paused and then said, "And why he chose the name Talion is quite beyond my ken."

"It is a contraction of the Latin 'lex talionis,' which means 'an eye for an eye.'"

Maria looked across at Silas and saw him shake his head.

Adeline frowned and said, "Why on earth would Harland have chosen such a name?"

Silas looked up and said, "Why indeed?"

The agreeable smell of warm toast started to pervade the atmosphere; he turned to the girls and said, "Toast's nearly ready, do you need to wash your hands?"

Adeline negated any potential protests and said, "Uncle Silas is right – away with you to the kitchen and wash them."

"And there's soap and a clean towel by the sink," added Maria.

The girls got up and walked into the kitchen.

"I've been listening to your apologies Addy," said Silas, "and I agree with May, you have nothing to apologise for."

He cast a quick glance in the direction of the kitchen and said, "But when that police Inspector arrives, I don't think that the girls should be made to listen to what he might have to say about their father, so I've arranged for Matt and Sim to entertain them for an hour or so. They can either play a couple of parlour games, or if they feel up to it, Sim has offered to give them a guided tour on the new trap."

Fifty minutes later, following a light but enjoyable meal of jam on toast and more tea, the assemblage heard a loud knocking. The girls were packed off to see their Auntie Matt and Uncle Sim, and Maria made her way to the front door.

"Inspector Brewster," she said, "please do come in."

Brewster smiled, removed his bowler hat, and stepped inside.

Maria showed him into the parlour, reacquainted him with Adeline and Silas, and offered him a seat.

Following the introductions and the refusal of a cup of tea, Brewster said, "If you don't mind, Mrs Cartwright, I'll get right down to business."

Maria and Silas exchanged glances at the Inspector's terseness, but figured that he was probably under a good deal of pressure. They watched in silence as he removed a few sheets of paper from a file.

"Right," he said. "We have now completed our investigation, and because you are all fully aware of the horrific events that occurred in the early hours of January the 7$^{th}$, there is no point in raking over them again."

He slipped the top sheet of his notes to the bottom, cleared his throat, and said, "But now, the dwarf. His name was Thomas Alouicious Bunn, aged thirty-seven, and of no fixed abode. He was wanted for robbery, rape, buggery, and assault by no less than five police forces, including our own – and the post-mortem examination on his body showed that he was infected by syphilis, gonorrhoea, and gout, and that he was infested by head and body lice."

"Good Lord," said Maria. "What a loathsome creature!"

"Precisely, madam," said Brewster. "His accomplice, Robert Iain Barrington Dogg, aged forty-one, again of no fixed abode, was wanted in six counties for no less than nine counts of murder directly attributable to him, and another fourteen for which he was the chief suspect."

"Unbelievable!" said Silas. "How in blazes did he remain free for so long?"

"Because he was so elusive, sir," said Brewster. "The police only have limited resources, so if a suspect can outrun our Bobbies, like as not he can get away. I have been pushing for a reform of our working practices, one that would see better communications being established between the various forces, but to date my suggestions have been ignored. But if ever there was a case that highlighted the need for improved cooperation, it was Robert Dogg's, because when it came to elusiveness, he was as good as it got."

He paused for a few seconds to allow everybody to digest his words, and then continued.

"He was also wanted for assault, drunkenness, robbery, immolation…"

"Immolation?" said Adeline.

Brewster turned to Adeline and said, "Yes, ma'am – he killed two people by setting fire to them."

"Good God, Inspector," said Silas. "It sounds as though Sugg did us all a favour a couple of weeks ago."

Brewster put the paperwork down and said, "He did that, sir." He paused for a few seconds and then said, "I don't think that we need to go any further with this particular train of conversation. You can see the type of person that he was, and I am unashamed to say that the world is now a better place without him."

He turned and looked at Adeline and said, "Now, ma'am, your late husband. Harland Archibald Chance, date of birth February 25th 1819, and up until his demise, resident with you in Bell Lane, Bury."

Adeline nodded.

"I think that it would be far less distressing for all present if I was to just say that he died as a direct result of injuries sustained on that fateful night, and to leave it there." He stopped, looked around, and saw nods of consent.

"As you might already have assumed, there will be no need, nor indeed point, in pursuing the cases of these three individuals, given the tragic and unfortunate outcome, but, and I hesitate to say this, the positive identification of Mr Chance has presented us with a dilemma."

Everybody stared at the Inspector, but nobody spoke.

"When the late gentleman's body was brought in for post-mortem examination, we were able to identify him as the man who somewhat mysteriously reported that an escaped patient from the Cheshire Lunatic Asylum at Parkway, Macclesfield, was residing here at Whitewall."

An uncomfortable atmosphere started to manifest itself in the parlour as everybody sat riveted to the Inspector.

"And the name of the wayward patient, according to him, was Maria Chance..." Brewster looked from face to face and then said, "...and since we have discovered that his name was Chance, that his aunt was named Maria, *and* that the Whitewall Estate was historically owned by his family, it has left me with some very awkward questions indeed.

Now I should be fair and tell you that I paid a visit to the Asylum where the Senior Ward Orderly, one..." he reached down to his file, leafed through a few papers, and then said, "... Arnold Honeysucker informed me that they did have a Maria Chance in their care and that she was safe and well, but what I can't fathom is this. What possible benefit could Mr Chance have gained by informing the police that one of his relatives, a certified lunatic no less, was in hiding here at Whitewall if he knew that she wasn't? And if part of his overall plan had been to rob this place with his criminal associates Bunn and Dogg, why on earth would he walk into a police station with a ridiculous tale like that, and attract our attention to him and it in the first place?"

Silence descended on the room until Maria said, "I presume that was a rhetorical question, Inspector?"

Brewster looked across the room, hesitated, and then said, "Yes, of course, ma'am, but being a detective of many years' experience, my alarm bells sound when I believe that I'm missing a vital piece of evidence, and right now they're ringing loud and clear."

Silas opened his mouth to speak, but thought better of it.

Following a few more seconds of contemplative silence, Brewster turned to Adeline and said, "Could you shed any light on your late husband's unusual behaviour, Mrs Chance?"

Adeline shifted uncomfortably in her seat and said, "I'm sorry, Inspector, no."

Brewster nodded and said, "Hmm. Is this your first visit to Whitewall?"

"Yes, it is."

"And you've never met Mr and Mrs Cartwright before this regrettable affair?"

Silas began to see a subtle change in Adeline, and knew that Brewster would be picking up on it too.

Adeline looked at Maria before answering; an almost insignificant act in itself, but one that was inconsistent with spontaneous veracity.

"No, Inspector," she said with the first hairline cracks appearing in her conviction. "I haven't."

Once again Brewster nodded and emitted a long "Hmm." He turned to Silas and said, "Mr Cartwright, I understand that you have in your employ a Mr and Mrs Simeon Twitch. Is that correct?"

Adeline started to feel the walls closing in and had to get out. She stood up and said, "Please forgive me, Mrs Cartwright, I need to pay a visit. Could you tell me where to go?"

"Please call me Mary, or May," said Maria, jumping at the opportunity to reiterate her married name.

Adeline smiled and said, "Thank you. Given the circumstances, that is very gracious."

Silas felt the need to take the pressure off himself too, and said, "You stay put, May. I'll show Mrs Chance where to go."

Adeline responded by saying, "And you must call me Adeline, too."

Seconds later, she and Silas departed.

Brewster looked at Maria for a few seconds, and then opened his mouth to say something, but before he could, Adeline's baby boy started to cry.

Maria listened to see if somebody would attend to him, but when it became obvious that nobody was, she said, "Excuse me Inspector; I'll just call one of Adeline's daughters to sort this out."

"Oh," said Brewster. "I hadn't realised that they were here too."

"Yes, they're with Matt and Sim. We thought it best not to include them in this meeting."

Brewster nodded and said, "Yes, very considerate."

Maria nodded and smiled, walked across to the door, and called out, "Girls – could one of you come here please?"

She heard a muffled response, closed the door, walked back to her chair, and sat down.

Within less than a minute, Eveline opened the door and said, "Yes, Aunt Maria?"

# Chapter 32

*Sunday 23rd April 2006. Naomi & Carlton Wilkes'*
*House*

Naomi, Carlton, Sam, Rosie, and Kitty sat waiting for Crowthorne to sum up the Friday night's operation, whilst Jane finished clearing up in the kitchen, after a major breakfast and tea making exercise. Lola had opted to go outside and service the Wilkes' car.

Naomi smiled as Carlton cast a caring glance in her direction, and then saw him shake his head. She knew that he was livid about the injuries that she'd suffered, and would have loved to be given a few minutes alone with the guy who'd done it to her.

"Are you positive that Lola doesn't want to hear what Bob has to say?" said Sam.

"We'll tell her later," said Rosie, with all signs of his professional persona now gone. "She's much better with something big and hard in her hands, than listening to small talk."

Carlton looked at Rosie with disapproval as Crowthorne cleared his throat.

Rosie saw and said, "Stop worrying about the policeman, love – he's a big boy, and I'm sure that he's had to take things into his own hands many a time."

Crowthorne raised an eyebrow and wasn't sure how to respond. The last time that he'd seen Rosie, Kitty and Lola they'd been in full Army assault gear, and he couldn't reconcile the huge difference.

"Rosie, stop teasing," said Naomi. "You know what Cal's like."

"Naomi Wilkes," said Rosie with mock surprise, "it's *Auntie* Rosie, if you don't mind! And yes, I do know what Carol's like, why do you think that I do it?"

Crowthorne shook his head and said, "Gentlemen, lady, if we could get back to the matter in hand..."

"Ladies!" admonished Rosie.

Crowthorne looked at Rosie in puzzlement and said, "Er, yes – whatever."

"Come on Rosie, love" said Kitty. "We don't want the Super getting distracted and reaching for his helmet, do we?"

Rosie gave Crowthorne a full once-over and said, "Oh, I don't know..."

Carlton said, "Come on, guys, give Bob a chance."

Silence descended. Crowthorne looked at Rosie and Kitty waiting for a response, but when none came, he reached down to his briefcase, extracted a few notes, and put them on his lap.

He watched as Jane entered and then sat back in his armchair.

He said, "Right, first things first; as you are aware by now, one of our officers was killed by an explosive device detonated at the top of one of the fire escapes. We have the person responsible for arming it in custody, but he insists that he was acting under the direct instructions of Adrian Darke."

"Bastard!" said Kitty.

"Quite," said Crowthorne. "The man, a security guard, has been charged with murder, but so far, Adrian Darke has not been apprehended. We've posted alerts at all the UK exit points, but we know how resourceful he is, and truth-be-known, he could be anywhere by now."

"You wouldn't care to hire us to find him for you, would you, Superintendent?" said Rosie, in a cold and formal tone.

"Tempting," said Crowthorne, "but no. That besides, we have smashed his illegal substance production operation; we have arrested every member of the staff from the underground factory, and we've arrested five of the six known 'Les Spooners.'"

"Did you get the one that killed the man trying to help me?" said Naomi.

"The man that tried to help you," said Crowthorne, "was an undercover police officer operating under the codename of Deimos. Leo, the chap who got you out, was another under the codename of Phobos."

"The two moons of Mars," said Naomi. The name 'Mars' brought to mind the Farlingtons, and she wondered how they were getting on with their search for 'El Fuego de Marte'.

"Correct," said Crowthorne. "But in answer to your question, we don't know whether we have Deimos' killer or not, because nobody is saying a word."

"Was anything found at the house?" said Carlton.

"We arrested Christiana Darke and an extensive search of the property is still underway, but so far nothing has been discovered there."

"Was Darke's wife in on it too?" said Jane.

"We don't think so," said Crowthorne. "She appeared to have no knowledge of the underground facility, and she seemed genuinely shocked and horrified by the death of our officer. She's been cooperative since her arrest, and I'm inclined to believe that she is innocent."

"Will you keep her in custody?" said Sam.

"Unless we find anything linking her to any of her husband's illegal activities, she will be released this afternoon."

"And what about Leo?" said Naomi. "Will I be able to thank him for saving me?"

Crowthorne considered that for a couple of seconds and then said, "Didn't you get the opportunity to last Friday?"

"No," said Naomi. "We made our way into a small compound, Leo grabbed two Les Spooner outfits from a cupboard and instructed me to put one on, and then that explosion went off. He told me to wait where I was and to keep quiet, and then he slipped away. The next people I saw were officers from your Operations Support Unit. They whisked me away in a car and I never saw Leo again.

"I don't even know what he looks like because he had a balaclava on the whole time, and I never saw his face."

Crowthorne said, "Hmm, perhaps I can arrange for you to meet him at a later date, if you would like that."

"Yes please – and I'd also like your permission to have a quick look at the property across the road, High Farm Cottage."

Crowthorne frowned and said, "Why?"

"Because that was why I was there in the first place. I've been trying to discover the whereabouts of somewhere named Larkland Fen, and my investigations led me there."

"Larkland Fen?" said Crowthorne. "I've been a policeman round here for more years than I care to remember, but I've never heard of that place before."

"It's a long story," said Naomi, "but if I can have your permission to go, I may be able to enlighten you."

Crowthorne thought for a few seconds and then said, "Do you think that 'Larkland Fen' is there?"

"It sounds unlikely, but unless I can check it out, I won't know." She opted not to mention anything about the gravestone.

"Well, I can't see what harm it would do," said Crowthorne. "So yes, that's fine." He paused for a second longer and then said, "None of this would have anything to do with Whitewall, would it?"

Naomi looked at Carlton, who appeared to be looking at her with concern.

"It may," she said.

"Stone the crows, Naomi," said Rosie. "You've not found some more clues, have you?"

"I may have. A letter dating from the nineteenth century was discovered in an old solicitors' bricked-up wall safe, informing the recipient to conceal incriminating Whitewall documents within the confines of somewhere named Larkland Fen, and it was addressed to a woman who lived at High Farm Cottage. She was later murdered there by Caleb Johnson, the guy who dispossessed our family in the late eighteen hundreds."

*"Within the confines of somewhere named Larkland Fen?"* repeated Crowthorne. "That makes it sound like an enclosure."

Naomi hadn't considered that before, and her mind went into overdrive. An enclosure conjured up all sorts of possibilities.

"And did you know that Adrian Darke owned that land?" said Crowthorne, cutting across her thoughts.

"Not at first, but then I met a dreadful woman named Gillorton…"

"Not Hayley Gillorton?" said Crowthorne. "Because I've had my eye on her for some time…"

"Yes it was, and she was so objectionable, scuppering my plans to carry out a small survey there. At first I couldn't understand why, and then I learned that the land was owned by Darke and it explained a lot."

"You're not referring to the stuff that went on in 2002, are you?" said Crowthorne.

"Can you put any other explanation on it? We deduced four years ago that his ancestor may have illegally purchased some land from the Whitewall Estate in the eighteen-hundreds, and that Giles Eaton, the old town clerk, may have been blackmailing him to keep quiet about something that could have harmed him – so what if that's still the case, or at least if he still perceives it to be?"

Crowthorne sat forwards, put his elbows onto his knees, and rested his head on his hands. Following a few seconds of silence he said, "Mrs Wilkes, I've got to hand it to you. Here was I, a simple copper, believing that all of this was about drugs; and now, in one fell swoop you have put the cat, once again, amongst the pigeons." He paused for a second and then said, "And I just know that my life is about to get a whole lot more complicated."

"That's our Naomi for you," said Rosie.

Crowthorne nodded and said, "Okay – you'd better tell me everything that you know."

For half an hour, everybody sat listening to Naomi's account and revelations. Even Carlton hadn't been aware about all of it. Crowthorne took down the odd note in his pocket book, and one or two questions were fired at her, but everything remained calm until she told them about the concealment of the huge ruby in Charleston.

Kitty interrupted the proceedings and said, "Why on earth didn't you tell us, Naomi? We'd have loved to have gone up to that church and done a reccy for you."

"Because it was Alan's distant relative Valentine who buried it at St. Andrew's, so it was only right that he should go and check it out first."

"And what did he find?" said Rosie.

"I don't even know if he's been there yet. I only wrote to him late Wednesday night telling him what we'd come up with..."

"You and the conservators at the Vical Centre?" said Crowthorne.

"Yes," said Naomi, "and as you know, I've been somewhat indisposed this last couple of days, so I haven't had a chance to check my emails."

Crowthorne leaned down, replaced his files into his briefcase, and said, "Alright, I think that I've got everything I need for now. I'll make some enquiries about Larkland Fen and I'll let you know if I come up with anything." He paused and then added, "One of my PCs will be here this afternoon to take statements, and we'll keep you posted about ongoing developments."

"And you'll arrange for me to meet up with Leo to thank him in person?" said Naomi.

"I'll see what I can do."

Crowthorne got up, said his goodbyes, and was escorted to the door by Carlton.

"Keep an eye on that wife of yours, Carlton, she's a bit of a firebrand," he said as they shook hands.

"That's easy for you to say," said Carlton. "Doing it, however, is something else..."

# Chapter 33

*Monday 24th April 2006. The Historic Research Dept.*
*Walmsfield Borough Council*

Naomi sat staring at the screen of her computer in total shock. She re-read the email to make sure that she hadn't misunderstood any of it.

*'Hi Naomi,*
*Don't ask me how, but somebody beat us to it.*
*We visited St. Andrews on Sat. last with some good buddies of ours and following an unsuccessful search, we approached a guy working on a plot. When we asked him for his help he told us he needed to check something out and disappeared for a few minutes. The next thing we knew, the local Sheriff arrived with blue lights flashing!*

*It turned out that the plot being worked upon by the guy was the Chance Mathewes grave, and that it had been desecrated two nights earlier.*

*After lots of questioning, the Sheriff did accept our story of "just visiting the grave whilst in the area", but it was touch and go at first. She took down my details and let us go, but I guess that if we ever have to go back there it could be viewed as very suspicious.*

*After the Sheriff had gone, we slung the gravedigger a cold beer and he told us that when he'd arrived he'd found nothing more than a hole in the ground. He said that there had been no sign of a casket, bones, or anything – just soil.*

*Later that day we grilled the kids and they assured us that they'd spoken to nobody about the planned visit, so given the ridiculous possibility that somebody just decided to desecrate that grave by chance, (sorry about the pun!) – I would be*

*interested to hear if you can come up with an answer about how*
*somebody else knew about it.*
   *Regardless of your findings however, – the result is the*
*same, the dream has gone. No 'El Fuego de Marte', no secret*
*hoards of cash, and back to work on Monday!*
   *I hope that you had a more successful weekend than we did.*
   *Love Alan xx'*

In shock and disbelief, she printed out the email and took it up
to Carlton's office.

Carlton read and re-read the email, and was just as
surprised.

Following one or two questions he said, "But if Alan is to
be believed, and if it is a hard fact that his kids said nothing,
then somebody from the UK must have leaked that info."

"Impossible!" said Naomi. "And not only is it impossible,
it's implausible too."

"Well, there's a contradiction in terms," said Carlton.

"Oh, you know what I mean," said Naomi.

"Yes, but implausible doesn't rule out possibility."

"Maybe so, but I just don't believe that it's any of us. Think
about it – we've only told Rosie and co, mum and dad, and Bob
Crowthorne. Which one of them would want to contact
somebody in America to arrange a desecration? Come on!"

"What about the girls at the Vical Centre? Could any of
them have alerted somebody to the ruby's whereabouts?"

Naomi stopped and thought for a few seconds, and then
said, "I grant you that we haven't dealt with this as though it's a
matter of high security, because none of us really believed that
anything would be found; but having said that, I can't believe
that careless chatter in a pub or whatever would result in
somebody contacting somebody else in America to ask them to
drive to a high profile church in Charleston and desecrate a
grave! And all of this since last Tuesday? No, – it doesn't make
sense!"

Carlton nodded and said, "It is pushing the levels of
believability." He thought for a few seconds longer and then
said, "Could anybody have gone into the Conservation Suite and

accessed the information from a laptop or a notepad whilst nobody was there?"

"That's a possibility," said Naomi, thinking about the proximity of the rest of the workforce, "but it's clutching at straws. I know that Helen has been responsible for solving the contrivances, etcetera, but jotting down notes to help her, and leaving them lying around doesn't mean that she had written down that a valuable ruby was located under the Chance Mathewes grave in Old St. Andrew's Church graveyard in Charleston, South Carolina – and with such conviction that somebody felt compelled to alert somebody in America to go and look for it."

Carlton sat back in his chair and expelled a deep breath.

"Well," he said, "somebody knows something, that's for sure." He paused for a second and then said, "And whoever it is isn't working with us."

Carlton's last comment got Naomi thinking; it implied that somebody could be working against them.

She thought about Adrian Darke and recalled that he had been linked to illegal activities in America in 2002, but nothing had ever been proven; and besides, on this occasion, all of his shady activity had been centred on his drug factory. She also thought about the objectionable Hayley Gillorton who, according to Crowthorne, was still at large, but she dismissed her too.

In short, she couldn't think of anybody, and concluded that the leak must have emanated from one of the Farlington children.

She looked up at Carlton and said, "It can't be one of us, it must have be one of Alan's kids spilling the beans to somebody. And thinking about it logically, it must have been one of their friends at school or somewhere, 'cos only somebody in America would have been able to get to that grave so quickly."

Carlton sat in silence as he digested Naomi's comments. He then shrugged and said, "I wonder if they found anything?"

"I doubt it, but even if they had, they wouldn't have been able to announce its discovery for fear of being exposed. A ruby like that would have to be disposed of on the black market, or, be spirited away into a private collection somewhere."

Carlton nodded and added, "And it's like Alan said – the end result is the same. We don't have it now, and we never will."

Naomi sat back in her chair and sighed.

"It was a nice dream while it lasted though, wasn't it?"

"Yes, darling it was. Now, I've got lots to catch up on and you've got some old documents to find, so unless that poor injured face of yours is hurting too much, I suggest that you go and find them!"

"Yes," said Naomi reaching up and touching her bruises. "Onwards and upwards. I'm off to High Farm Cottage this afternoon."

"This afternoon?" said Carlton. "Given what you've just been through, are you happy about returning there so soon?"

Naomi got up and headed for the door.

"Wild horses couldn't keep me away!" she said.

At 3pm, Naomi and Helen turned into Cragg End Lane and headed for High Farm Cottage.

During the journey they had talked about Naomi's abduction, imprisonment, and escape, about the inconvenience of having all her credit cards and other personal stuff destroyed, and about how much she missed her beloved CRV. They also discussed and exhausted all the possibilities of a security leak about the ruby, and Helen had assured Naomi that she had been very careful not to leave anything sensitive lying around. She stressed that all of her notes had been taken home with her, and that she hadn't ever discussed their business with anybody outside of the Conservation Suite.

And as Naomi had listened to Helen, she'd become even more convinced that the leak had to have come from the Farlingtons.

As Naomi's hire car approached High Farm Cottage, Helen said, "I can't wait to see this place!"

"I gathered that by the way you bunked off work this afternoon!"

They drove down the lane until they reached the gates of the Cragg Vale Estate, and pulled up in the drive.

"Are we okay to park here?" enquired Helen.

"Yes – we aren't going to be long and there's enough room to pass us if anybody wants to get in or out." Naomi reflected for a second and then said, "That's if anybody who lived or worked here is out of jail yet…"

The two women got out of the car and Naomi locked it. The warmth of spring was in the air and everywhere smelled fresh and new. The birds sang and the sun shone through the budding branches of the trees.

They walked arm-in-arm across Cragg End Lane and through the small gateway to High Farm Cottage.

"Oh wow," said Helen as they approached the cottage. "It still looks kind of spooky, but it's nothing like the footage I saw on your camera."

"I'm not surprised," said Naomi. "That ignorant Gillorton cow stripped most of the flora and fauna away."

They walked into the cottage, and Naomi shivered as the memory of Les Spooner rushed into her mind.

"It was here that I thought that creep had shot me," she said.

Helen gripped Naomi's arm tighter and said, "It must have been terrifying. I don't know what I'd have done." She looked around one more time and then said, "Come on, – let's see if we're right about the gravestone."

They walked across the small garden towards the tilted gravestone, and Naomi realised that her heart was beating quicker than normal. At first she put it down to her horrifying encounter with Spooner, but as she got closer, the thumb pressed down hard into her shoulder. She reached up and said, "Ow!"

Helen turned, looked at her, and said, "Are you okay?"

It dawned upon Naomi that she hadn't had any kind of psychic contact since the lady whom she had presumed to be Maria had said goodbye to her before Leo had arrived.

She turned to Helen and said, "Sorry, it's nothing. I just cricked my neck."

They walked across the garden until they reached the stone. Helen turned and said, "I'm almost afraid to look."

"Why?"

"Because my life as a conservator includes trying to solve conundrums and formulate theories from sparse pieces of data, and I really love doing it, but every now and then there comes a delicious moment when my logic is put to the test and it will be proved right or wrong. And now is just such a moment."

"Well, standing there talking about it won't prove a thing," said Naomi.

Helen smiled and said, "You're right – here goes."

She rested her left hand on the gravestone and leaned over to view the rear.

"Oh my God," she said. "I was right!"

# Chapter 34

*Sunday 21<sup>st</sup> January 1872. Cheshire Lunatic Asylum, Parkway, Macclesfield*

At 6pm, the horse-drawn, prison carriage rumbled across the access bridge of Parkway Lunatic Asylum.

Maria sat bowed in the rear, handcuffed to a uniformed officer, whilst Inspector Brewster sat with Sergeant Graham Banks in the driving seat.

The carriage proceeded up the drive and stopped outside the reception block.

Brewster jumped down from the seat, straightened his clothes, and walked up the steps to the reception room.

Chinny Nesbitt, the night receptionist, loved Sundays; there were very few staff on duty to watch and pester him, no patients were ever moved after 8pm, and nobody was at work in the adjacent admin offices. Most of the time he was left blissfully alone to read his newspaper and to take sneaky swigs of whisky from the concealed hip flask that he wouldn't dare to bring in on any other day.

He'd arrived at 5:30pm, taken over from the daytime receptionist, placed his favourite Lancashire cheese sandwiches and a newspaper on his desk and, having double-checked that everything was in order, he'd decided to take his chair across to the fireplace and to put his feet up in front of the roaring fire. He bent down to pick it up, and then heard somebody enter.

With a frown on his face, he walked through from his small office to the front desk and watched as a dark-suited man approached.

"Good evening," said Brewster. "I am Detective Inspector Jack Brewster of the Lancashire Constabulary, and I am returning one of your escaped patients."

"What?" said Nesbitt. "What are you talking about? We don't have any missing patients."

"Oh, I think that you'll find you do," said Brewster.

Nesbitt looked at Brewster and said, "Wait here."

He walked into the office and picked up the desk diary that left him daily instructions, opened it, and found nothing but routine material. Next, he picked up his clipboard and flicked through correspondence from the various offices, but found nothing informing him about any missing patients. He put down the clipboard, checked the loose paperwork on his desk, and then walked back out to the front desk.

"I'm sorry, Inspector," he said, "but you've made a mistake. We don't have any missing patients."

"Hmm," said Brewster. "Maybe I am wrong, but let's just make doubly sure." He walked across to the front door, opened it, and called, "Sergeant, will you and the Constable bring the patient in here please?"

Nesbitt heard a voice call back, "Very good sir", and watched until two uniformed officers brought a handcuffed woman up to the desk.

"Now then, ma'am," said Brewster. "What is your name?"

Maria looked up, said, "Maria Chance, sir", and then dropped her gaze.

Nesbitt felt as though a steel band had been placed around his head and tightened.

"And would you care to tell this gentleman here what you told me two days ago?"

Maria looked up again and said, "I was put in here on Wednesday the 30th of June 1869, sir, and escaped a few days later with the help of some friends on Friday the 9th of July."

Nesbitt started to feel the first signs of panic because he'd been the receptionist on duty when she'd escaped, and the resultant backlash and recriminations had been something that he'd never wanted to experience again.

Oblivious of the growing panic in Nesbitt, Brewster said, "And which ward did you escape from Miss Chance?"

"From Private Ward Nine, sir."

"Well, there we are then," said Nesbitt. "It's clear she's off her rocker, because we don't have any private wards in this asylum. She must be thinking of somewhere else."

Brewster nodded his head and said, "Ah, perhaps that explains things then." He turned to Banks and said, "Sergeant, it's clear that we don't have the right place, so would you please escort the lady back to the carriage?"

"Right you are, sir," said Banks.

Nesbitt couldn't believe his luck. He watched as the prisoner was walked to the door, and then he heard Brewster say, "Wait!"

Brewster turned to face Nesbitt and said, "The last time I was here, your Mr Honeysuckle informed me that you had a patient here named Maria Chance. Is that correct?"

"Mr Honeysucker," corrected Nesbitt. "People's always making that mistake, and he gets right touchy about it."

"Yes, yes," said Brewster. "But is it true that you have a patient here by that name?"

"I'm sorry, Inspector; I'm not at liberty to divulge the patient's names. Only the senior Nursing Staff could do that."

"Well, before we leave," said Brewster, "be a good chap and call one. You of all people know that we have to be very thorough when dealing with vulnerable patients, don't we?"

Nesbitt felt cornered; the panic level started to rise again.

"I… I… I'm not allowed to leave this post," he said lamely.

Brewster removed his pocket watch from his waistcoat and flicked open the cover; it was 6:20pm.

Nesbitt didn't know what to say, or what to make of it. The whole experience felt out of his control, and for once in his life he didn't know what to do.

The reception door opened and Senior Sister Florence Parks walked in.

Nesbitt closed his eyes and hoped that the floor would open up and swallow him whole.

"Chinny," said Florence, "what's going on?"

Nesbitt said, "The Police Inspector here thought that he had an escaped patient of ours; said she was from Private Ward Nine – but as you know, we don't have any private wards, do we?"

Florence turned to face Brewster and said, "Chinny's right, Inspector – we don't have any private wards at Parkway."

Nesbitt felt his equanimity start to settle and said, "There, Inspector, you heard her, and Sister Parks is our Senior Nursing Sister, so I guess that settles that."

Brewster nodded once again and said, "Alright Sergeant, take the lady back out to the carriage."

Nesbitt drew in a deep breath, smiled and said, "Sorry you gents had a wasted journey."

Banks turned to Maria and said, "Come along, miss."

Maria looked up and said, "I didn't like it up there anyway, with the noise of those typewriters clacking away."

Florence turned and looked at Maria and said, "I beg your pardon? What did you just say?"

"I said that I didn't like it up there because of the noise of the typewriters."

The smile disappeared off Nesbitt's face quicker than a mouse in a room full of cats.

Florence said, "Whereabouts up there?"

Maria pointed and said, "Through that door, and up the stairs on the left."

"But that's only admin offices…"

"Not up on the left it isn't."

Nesbitt cut in and said, "Take no notice, Sister – she has a screw loose anyhow."

Florence turned to Nesbitt and said, "Mr Nesbitt, that's no way to talk about patients!"

Nesbitt dropped his gaze and said, "Sorry Sister, but as I said, t'aint nothing but admin offices up there."

"Perhaps we'd better see," said Brewster.

Nesbitt felt his panic level rise and said, "I'm sorry, Inspector, but you have no right."

"No, but I do," said Florence. "Please pass me the keys."

"But, but…" said Nesbitt.

"But nothing, Chinny," said Florence. "Just give me the keys."

"Just do as the Sister says," said Brewster. "There's a good chap."

In a last desperate attempt to halt things, Nesbitt said, "I'm sorry, I can't let him in, 'cos he's a Lancashire peeler, and this is Cheshire."

Brewster nodded, walked over to the reception door, removed a whistle from his pocket, and blew it. Seconds later, a Cheshire Police Superintendent, an Inspector, and five uniformed Constables filed in.

He turned to the shocked Nesbitt and said, "Perhaps now you'll do as the Sister bids?"

As a crestfallen Nesbitt retrieved the keys, Florence walked across to Maria and saw that Brewster was removing the handcuffs.

"I hope that they didn't hurt too much," she said.

"No, the Inspector only fastened them lightly, but it had to look real, or we may never have got that denial out of Mr Nesbitt in front of so many witnesses."

Brewster handed the cuffs to the 'Constable' who had accompanied Maria in and said, "That uniform suits you."

Simeon Twitch looked down and said, "Blimey O'Riley – if any of my old mates could see me now, they'd think they was losing their marbles!" He thought for a second and then said, "And it wouldn't have mattered much if Chinny had refused to hand over the keys, 'cos I've still got the set I used to spring Maria two year ago!"

Brewster raised an eyebrow and said, "Perhaps the less said about that, the better."

He looked around and saw Nesbitt leading the Cheshire Police officers along the corridor towards the illegal wards and said, "I think that we can go now. Cyril…that is, Superintendent Tunnicliff, – is an old friend of mine, and he's very thorough. If anything untoward is going on here, he'll get to the bottom of it."

"And I'm free to go?" said Maria.

"Yes, of course, and thank you for helping us to set this up. We may need to take more statements, but that should be it. We'll get your incarceration order quashed, and you can start calling yourself Maria again."

Maria thought about it for a few seconds and then said, "I like being Mrs Mary Cartwright; I think that I'll stick with that."

Simeon smiled, because he knew that Silas would have approved, and said, "Well, Mary, before we set off, I think that we should celebrate your new found freedom with a pint of ale!"

All eyes turned to Brewster who smiled and said, "Sounds good to me!"

# Chapter 35

*Monday 24<sup>th</sup> April 2006. High Farm Cottage*

Helen moved to one side and said, "Here, have a look."

Naomi leaned over the small tilted gravestone and read the worn but legible inscription.

> *'Patch – a faithful friend.*
> *Departed this earth 11<sup>th</sup> April 1822.*
> *Sadly missed by*
> *Annabel and Frank Elland'*

She removed a small notebook from her handbag, wrote down the words, and replaced it. She said, "It's curious that the inscription is facing the wall, why do you think that could be?"

"Look at it," said Helen. "It's years old and badly tilted. It could have been uprooted from its original site and placed against the wall, – and time could have done the rest."

Naomi shrugged and said, "I suppose so."

Helen caught sight of the small gateway in the back wall and stared into the dense foliage.

"Is this what it looked like when you first arrived?" she said, pointing into the trees.

"More-or-less," said Naomi, "but it felt a lot more claustrophobic."

Helen continued to stare into the trees and said, "I wonder where it goes."

"It's overgrown now, but maybe it once led to a small vegetable, or herb garden."

Helen shrugged, turned, and looked at the result of the 'Gillorton surveys'.

"And is this what she did?"

"It is," said Naomi, "and I'd bet a pound to a penny that it was just for show."

"If you were given the opportunity, would you like another shot at carrying out a survey here?"

Naomi paused before answering and then said, "For some reason, I think that the grave is the relevant thing here. Maybe it..."

The thumb suddenly pressed down on her shoulder, but she got nothing more.

She hesitated whilst waiting until Helen said, "Maybe it what?"

"What?" said Naomi.

Helen looked at her and repeated, "Maybe it what?"

Naomi remembered what she'd meant to say, and said, "Sorry, maybe it's trying to tell us something."

The minute that she'd uttered the words, the pressure from the thumb stopped.

"What on earth could it be saying, other than that a pet dog was laid to rest somewhere near here in 1822?"

Naomi said, "I don't know, it's just a feeling."

Helen looked at Naomi for a second and then said, "What's the chance of having a quick squiz at Cragg Vale House?"

Naomi considered the request and said, "I can't see what harm it would do. It's unlikely that anybody's back in residence yet, and even if we do bump into somebody, we can explain the reason for our visit."

"Fantastic," said Helen, "let's go!"

The two women linked arms, walked back through High Farm Cottage, and crossed Cragg End Lane. They walked through the gates of the Cragg Vale Estate and headed down the central drive towards the house. Along the way, Naomi pointed out 'Les Spooner's cottage, and commented on how old and innocuous it looked considering that it was the main entrance to an ultra-modern underground drug manufacturing plant. She showed Helen the small compound from which she'd been rescued, and she tried to explain what it was like being imprisoned and in fear of death.

Helen shuddered and said, "I hope that I never have to go through anything that!"

They arrived at the front of the main house.

"It looks very grand," said Helen. "Imagine living somewhere like this..."

Naomi didn't answer at first, but thinking about Adrian Darke said, "Or, even worse – imagine owning somewhere like this and never being able to live in it for fear of being arrested."

Helen nodded and then propelled Naomi forwards.

"Let's have a closer look while we're here," she said.

The two companions started to walk towards the front door, when to their surprise it opened, and an elegant dark-haired lady appeared in the doorway.

The lady waited until Naomi and Helen were within talking distance and then said, "Can I help you?"

Naomi said, "I'm sorry if we're intruding, but my name is Naomi Wilkes. I was rescued by the police after being held prisoner here a couple of days ago, and we thought that nobody would be home."

The lady nodded and said, "I am Christiana Darke, and I cannot possibly apologise enough for my husband's deplorable behaviour. I had no idea what was going on." She paused for a second and then said, "Please do come in – the least I can do is to offer you a cup of coffee."

Helen turned to Naomi, smiled, and said, "Better and better!"

Over the next three quarters of an hour, Naomi and Helen listened to Christiana and became convinced of her innocence and honesty. She admitted that she knew her husband capable of manipulation and ruthlessness, and she spoke about his disagreeable habit of controlling and often brow-beating others to domineer, but when she'd been informed that Adrian had given the order to arm the explosive device that had killed the innocent policeman, she'd been profoundly shocked at his callousness and utter disregard for human life.

"And as far as I am concerned," she had concluded, "I may always love him in some small way, but I could never forgive him. It is over between us, and I shall be instigating divorce proceedings as soon as I am able."

Naomi wasn't sure what to say. She felt sorry for Christiana's plight, but then again she didn't know her, and she had to consider that she might be lying. She was wrestling with her emotions when Helen broke her train of thought.

"Can we see the remains of the old building by the lake at the bottom of Lark Hill?"

Christiana turned to Helen and said, "Yes, of course, but why do you want to go there?"

Naomi explained that it was her desire to investigate the ruins by the lake, and the High Farm Cottage site that brought her into conflict with Adrian, Gillorton, and one of the 'Les Spooner's, but she omitted to say that it had anything to do with the Larkland Fen conundrum.

Christiana recoiled at the names of Gillorton and Les Spooner.

"Did you know that there were six of those Spooner creeps?" she said.

"Yes," said Naomi, "and I believe that one of them is still unaccounted for."

"And Gillorton," said Christiana.

"What an objectionable old battle-axe she was," remarked Naomi. "I wouldn't be sorry to never see her again."

Christiana smiled and her face lit up, her perfect white teeth shone out through her full, ruby red lips and for the first time Naomi and Helen saw just how beautiful she was.

"Come on," she said. "We can use some of my husband's toys." She stood up and gestured for Naomi and Helen to follow her.

Fifteen minutes later, all three women were racing through the trees of the estate on electric quad bikes. They reached the bottom of Lark Hill, dismounted, and sauntered over to remains of the old building which lay just within the trees and set back one-hundred-and-fifty yards from the lake.

Naomi half-expected to feel something on her shoulder but didn't, and almost before looking, she had dismissed the site as being nowhere of importance.

"It doesn't look as though that Gillorton woman did any work around here," said Helen.

Christiana walked over and said, "You're welcome to carry one out."

Without thinking, Naomi said, "I don't think that will be necessary, because..."

She stopped speaking; a flash of movement in the trees caught her eye and she stared in its direction. One by one she felt the hairs on the back of her neck start to stand on end, and a cold shiver ran down her spine.

Christiana and Helen saw Naomi staring, and looked too.

"What is it?" said Helen.

Naomi remained stock-still and didn't say a word. Suddenly the thumb pressed down on her shoulder and a voice in her head yelled, *"Run!"*

She reacted instantly, turned, and shouted, "Quick, get out of here – *now!*"

A shocked Christiana and Helen remained rooted to the spot with frowns upon their faces.

*"I said, get out of here now!"*

Before either woman could react, the remaining Spooner stepped out from behind a tree, raised his shotgun, and fired.

Naomi threw herself into both women, knocking them off their feet.

Helen screamed in panic as a second shot was fired in their direction.

"It's a double-barrelled shotgun," said Naomi. "He has to load. Run to the bikes and go!"

"What about you?" said Helen.

Naomi looked into the eyes of her friend and said, "Do as I say! Go!"

Helen grabbed hold of Christiana's sleeve and started to pull her towards the quad bikes.

The Spooner stepped out into the open and, with a cruel grin on his face, levelled his shotgun at the backs of the retreating women.

Naomi caught sight of one or two heavy stones, snatched one up, and threw it straight at Spooner's face.

In a blinding flash of pain, and at the instant he pulled the trigger, the stone struck him hard on his left cheekbone. The effect was twofold; the blow stunned him and disorientated him, whilst the recoil of the shotgun knocked him flat onto his back. For a few seconds he didn't know what had happened. He shook his head, scrambled to his feet, and put his hand up to the searing pain; he withdrew it and saw a lot of blood.

"You fucking bitch!" he yelled. "You'll pay for that!"

He reached down and snatched up the shotgun.

Up by the quad bikes Helen turned and looked. She saw no sign of Naomi but completely out of character yelled, "Leave her alone, you fucking freak!"

The Spooner turned in her direction and yelled, "Yeah? You want some of this do you?"

He raised the shotgun, aimed it at Helen, but at the same instant, was hit on the left eye-socket by another huge stone.

The second blow was even more painful than the first; his head jerked backwards, he screwed up his eyes and yelled, "Fuck!"

He dropped the gun for a second time, but on this occasion he wasn't so lucky; the end of the barrel hit the ground and toppled over, with the butt facing away from him. The stock hit the ground, and the hairline trigger fired.

The full force of a number four cartridge shattered his left kneecap and shredded the flesh and bone of his lower legs. He dropped face down onto the ground as they were blown from under him.

In an instant, Naomi leapt out of the trees and jumped onto his back.

Up by the quad bikes, Helen and Christiana couldn't believe their eyes. Their friend, the normally reserved historic researcher was on top of their aggressor and tying his hands behind his back with her coat belt.

Helen ran down to them, grabbed the shotgun, and threw it into the nearby bushes.

Naomi yelled at Christiana to phone for an ambulance, and within ten minutes they were speeding back to Cragg Vale

House with their injured captive secured to the back of one of the quad bikes.

# Chapter 36

*Thursday 27<sup>th</sup> April 2006. The Historic Research Department, Walmsfield Borough Council.*

Just after 9:30am, the phone rang on Naomi's desk. She answered it and heard the familiar voice of Helen on the other end.

"Ah, you're back," she said. "I wondered if you'd stay off the rest of the week."

"No," said Helen. "It would have been nice to have the extra time off, but that little episode at Cragg Vale House on Monday and the time spent giving statements, etcetera, on Tuesday, had thrown my work schedule right out, so I put in an appearance yesterday afternoon."

"So you're not suffering with any after-effects, then?"

"No, on the contrary; once I'd realised that you were alright, I found the whole thing very exhilarating, and I still can't get over seeing the change in you! The way you leapt onto the back of that Spooner guy was amazing; you looked so fearless, just like an old warrior queen."

Naomi smiled and thought about Rosie and co when she heard the term 'queen'. She knew that they'd planned to return to America after the May Day holiday, and decided that a weekend barbecue would go down well if the weather held.

"Do you, Nina, and Charlotte fancy coming to our house for a barbecue this weekend with your partners?"

Helen said, "Hang on a mo."

Naomi heard muffled speaking at the other end of the phone, and guessed that Helen was asking the others.

Seconds later, Helen said, "That sounds great to Nina and me, but Charlotte is off today so I'll have to ask her tomorrow."

"Okay," said Naomi. "I'll fill you in with the details as and when I know them."

"Right," said Helen. "Now, – I've two reasons for calling. First, I wondered if you'd given any more thought to the Larkland Fen project?"

"No, I haven't. I've had a couple of other assignments and a mountain of filing and cross-referencing to do, and with everything that's gone on, I've got way behind. How about you?"

"Same with me. Craig has been away at another site, and he's left me in charge, which, I might add, doesn't equate to a promotion, only a heap more work!"

Naomi said, "Hmm, tell me about it."

"Now," said Helen, "the second thing. You're going to think that I'm stupid here, but I was watching one of the old James Bond films on Tuesday night and I saw him do the trick where he stuck a hair across one of his hotel dresser drawers. Then, yesterday afternoon, I got to thinking about how somebody had beaten your cousin to that grave in Charleston. Just for fun, I purposely left one of my notebooks on my desk before leaving last night and I copied James Bond. I stuck a hair down at the bottom of the book and onto the top of my desk.

Charlotte and Nina had already gone so I was the last to leave the office. I locked up and went home, and when I returned this morning, the notebook was exactly where I'd left it, but the hair had gone."

"And was there no sign of it on the desk at all?" said Naomi.

"No, nothing. I checked the surface of the desk and the notebook with a fine toothcomb, but there was no sign of it."

"And are you positive that it was there before you left?"

"I'm certain. In fact the hair was so well stuck down, I wondered whether it would snag the opening of the book and alert somebody to it, but obviously it didn't."

Naomi thought for a second and then said, "Are you trying to tell me that you now believe somebody may have come in to your office and looked at your notebook?"

"How else would you explain it?" said Helen.

"What about office cleaners?"

"No, they come in on Friday night, and anyway, I double-checked with the guys down below, and they reported seeing nobody go up there."

"That's weird," said Naomi.

An idea started to form in her mind, "Are you free for half an hour this afternoon if I come over?"

"I can be," said Helen.

"Good. Then I'll see you about 2:30pm."

At 11am on the dot, Naomi heard a knock on her office door. She knew who it would be, because he was always punctual.

"Come in, Percy," she called.

The door opened and Percy walked in with Gasworks.

"Morning, my dear," he said. "I hope that you don't mind me bringing Ga... Pat, because I think that he may be able to help you some more with your research into High Farm Cottage."

Naomi smiled and said, "No, of course I don't mind." She gestured to the chairs and said, "Would you both like a cup of tea?"

Percy sat down and said, "Yes please – white, no sugar. I'm..."

"I know," said Naomi, "you're sweet enough."

She watched as Pat lowered himself down, and then heard a suspect sound.

"That's got the engine working," said Pat. "Now I'll try the lights."

Naomi couldn't help sniggering and said, "Would you like a cup of tea, Pat?"

Pat looked over his left and right shoulders, and then gestured for Naomi to come closer.

Naomi leaned towards him.

Pat looked left and right once more and then patted his jacket pocket.

"Not whilst I've got this," he said.

Naomi frowned and opened her mouth to speak, but saw Percy gesturing for her to say nothing. She raised her eyebrows and leaned back up.

Pat nodded and touched the right-hand side of his nose with his right forefinger.

"Good girl," he said. "It's obvious that you know what it's like."

Naomi was more confused than ever. She nodded towards Pat, paused for a second, and then said, "Right – I'll get the tea."

Several minutes later and having returned from the drinks dispenser, Naomi said, "Okay Pat, what have you got for me?"

Pat cast a suspicious looking glance at Percy then turned back to Naomi and said, "Nothing – should I have?"

"But…"

"Naomi means what have you brought her by way of information," said Percy.

"Oh, I see," said Pat. "I thought…"

Naomi sat back in her seat and shook her head. She wondered if she'd ever get to grips with Percy's friends.

"It's nothing much really," said Pat, "but I met an old-timer who used to live and work around Cragg End Lane in the 1950s, and he knew about High Farm Cottage. Said in its day it used to be a bit grand…"

Naomi frowned – there was nothing whatsoever grand about what she'd seen.

"He also said that following a recent visit, he was surprised to see how overgrown the place had become since he'd last been there, and that there was hardly a sign of the old place now."

Naomi's perplexity deepened. She said, "Sorry to interrupt you, Pat, but what was he talking about, it's obvious where the cottage is, and you couldn't call it grand."

It was Pat's turn to frown. He stayed silent for a few seconds and then said, "Has something happened there then?"

"Like what?"

"Like have the trees and stuff been cleared away?"

"Yes, a couple of weeks ago, why?"

"Well, that would explain it then," said Pat, "'cos *I* could hardly see it when I went there at the end of last summer."

Naomi was bewildered. She said, "I'm sorry Pat, but I have no idea what you're talking about because it's so darned obvious. Several of us have seen it plain enough and I've even been inside it!"

Pat sat back in his chair and stopped speaking. He stared into Naomi's eyes for a couple of seconds and then leaned forwards and said, "We are talking about the same place are we?"

"High Farm Cottage in Cragg End Lane," said Naomi.

"Right," said Pat. "So when you say you've been inside it, I take it that you mean within the old perimeter walls?"

"No, I mean that I've literally been inside it – within the four walls."

Pat stopped talking again and looked at Naomi in an odd way.

Percy stepped in and said, "There seems to be some confusion Pat. What's the problem?"

"Well, the lass here is saying that she's been within the four walls of High Farm Cottage, which makes it sound as though they're still standing, but not one of them is above two foot high at best and it's confusing me."

"What do you mean, none is above two feet high?" said Naomi. "They're full height, and the roof is still on."

Pat turned back to face Naomi and said, "Now I know that we aren't talking about the same place."

"Where is your High Farm Cottage then?" said Naomi.

Pat described the route down Cragg End Lane, and then explained how the entrance was opposite the gates to the Cragg Vale Estate. He then went on to say, "You go through the one-post gateway, past the old gatekeeper's lodge…"

"Wait!" said Naomi. "What old gatekeeper's lodge?"

"The golden sandstone lodge – looks more like a small… Oh, wait a minute, I get it now," said Pat. "Did you think that the lodge was High Farm Cottage?"

Naomi nodded and said, "Yes – isn't it?"

"No," said Pat. "High Farm Cottage is further into the trees beyond the garden wall which, by-the-way, isn't the original one, then through a small gate…"

"Next to the gravestone," interrupted Naomi.

"Yes, you have to go through that and keep on going for about another hundred-and-fifty yards or so, and then you'll start to see the remains of the old cottage."

Naomi couldn't believe what she was hearing; that meant that both she and Hayley Gillorton had made the same mistake, and that no excavations had taken place at the real cottage. Furthermore if the garden walls weren't the original ones, it explained why the gravestone appeared to be facing the wrong way.

Oblivious to what Naomi was thinking, Pat continued, "That side of Cragg End Lane used to be the High Farm Estate, owned by the wealthy Elland family. Annabel and Frank originally lived at High Farm until they had the cottage built in 1829. Frank died there in the 1839, and when their only daughter Daisy married William Hubert in 1842, Annabel moved back to the farm to give them a place to live. Within a couple of years of Daisy's murder however, Annabel had it raised to the ground."

"And did anybody live in the gatekeeper's lodge?" said Naomi.

"They may have done at one time, but when the cottage was still standing, it was used as a storehouse."

Naomi sat back in her chair, half-listening to Pat whilst trying to assess whether or not to approach Christiana Darke for permission to carry out another survey.

Pat said, "Following Daisy's death, her body was put into the Elland family mausoleum alongside her husband William, at St. Peter's Church in Elland."

"What – there's a place named after them too?"

"Yes, my dear," said Percy. "It's a small hamlet a bit over six miles from here, originally named after Frank's grandfather Gilbert."

"And the church and mausoleum are still there too," added Pat.

The thumb pressed own on Naomi's shoulder, but she heard nothing. She was sure that Pat had said something significant, but she wasn't sure what. She reached into her desk drawer, removed her notepad, and jotted down the names of Annabel and Frank Elland, and then St. Peter's Church in Elland. For several seconds she deliberated in silence until she realised that Pat had stopped talking. She looked up and saw him looking distracted.

She shot a glance at Percy and then said, "Is everything alright, Pat?"

Pat leaned forwards in his chair and indicated for Naomi to come closer. As before, he looked left and then right over his shoulders and then said, "I've just thought of something."

Naomi sat with a quizzical look on her face until she realised that Pat wasn't going to respond. She raised her eyebrows and said, "What?"

"It's nearly half past eleven."

Silence descended on the small office as odd glances were exchanged but no words were spoken until Naomi said, "And...?"

"I should have picked up my machine at half ten."

Before she could stop herself, Naomi said, "I thought that you were collecting it with Percy a couple of weeks ago?"

Pat turned to Percy and said, "Do you want to tell her, or should I?"

Percy looked lost and said, "Tell her what?"

"What those idiots did!"

"I don't know what those idiots did," said Percy, "and, come to think of it, I don't know who the idiots are either."

"The dopes who cocked my machine up!"

It took a lot to faze Percy, but he looked bewildered.

Pat saw his look of confusion and said, "I told you about it the last time we met. They bent a retaining nut on one of the splines and buggered it up..."

He stopped speaking, waited for a response from Percy but then gave up and said, "Anyway, they said they'd fix it and I was supposed to pick it up at half ten."

"It's not a problem," said Percy. "We can pick it up after our visit with Naomi."

"No, sorry, no can do. I'm otherwise committed because of that trouble with the parking meter. It'll have to wait until Tuesday now."

Naomi mouthed, "Parking meter?" to Percy, and saw him raise his eyebrows and shrug his shoulders.

Percy decided to change the subject and turned to Naomi.

"I have something for you," he said, reaching into his jacket pocket. He pulled out a piece of paper, spread it out on Naomi's desk, and said, "'Dat Deus immiti cornua curta bovi', means, 'God gives short horns to the cruel ox'."

Naomi sat back in her chair and recalled the carving of the cow's head with pollarded horns on the lid of the Farlington's chest, but like Alexander Chance in his 1829 letter, couldn't begin to understand what bearing it had on the Whitewall Estate.

She saw the look of puzzlement on both men's faces and decided to explain. She took a photocopy of Valentine's letter out of her drawer and read it to them, omitting the reference to the ruby.

When she'd finished reading, she put the copy letter back in her drawer, and said, "So you see, that now leaves me stumped. I can't think how that Latin saying would have any bearing on his inheritance either."

Percy said, "One of my older reference works states that the maxim was a polite way of saying that 'angry men would always be punished for their wrongs', but I too cannot see how that would relate to…"

One-by-one, small pieces started to drop into place in Naomi's and Percy's mind at the same time.

They looked into each other's eyes and both said, "Unless…"

Percy said, "Are you thinking what I'm thinking? That the recipient, Valentine, was being punished for some reason?"

"By being bequeathed an empty promise. Which," said Naomi with growing conviction, "could explain why Valentine warned his descendants not to open the chest because it was cursed? Maybe the curse was that there was no inheritance?"

Percy sat and thought for a second or two and then said, "But if Valentine knew that no inheritance was in there, why would he write to his father asking the meaning of the aphorism?"

Naomi sat and thought some more, and then said, "Maybe Valentine didn't know that there was no inheritance in there. What if *he'd* been duped and told not to open the chest so that something could be kept a secret from *him*? That would explain him writing to his father and saying that he had no recollection of his father ever mentioning what was inside the chest, and of his subsequent surprise at discovering the contents."

"That makes a lot more sense," said Percy. "Why indeed would Valentine write to his father to ask for that meaning?"

"My God," said Naomi. "So that would have meant, that one of Valentine's close forebears knew that they either couldn't, or never had any intention of leaving Whitewall to Valentine in the first place."

"But didn't you once inform me that Whitewall had at one time been jointly owned by one of your great-aunt Maria's forebears, along with his twin brother?"

"Yes," said Naomi. "Maria's great-grandfather, John Chance, owned it with his twin brother Matthew, Valentine's grandfather."

"So Valentine could only ever have been left half of the Estate in the first place?"

Naomi nodded but didn't answer. The Whitewall conundrum seemed to be plumbing new depths.

"And," continued Percy, "let us say that either Matthew or Valentine's father Alexander had, for some reason, no intention of leaving Whitewall to Valentine; that must have been because they either had other plans for it, or that they were already in no position to be able to leave it to him."

Naomi sat in silence, pondering like crazy. Percy's conjecture made good sense and it felt right, but if it were true, the prospect would have had the direst of consequences on her great-aunt Maria's quest for ownership. It would have meant that all of her labours would have been doomed to failure from the outset, particularly if some hitherto unknown skulduggery had occurred on Matthew's side of the family without her side ever knowing about it.

She said, "I'd love to get my hands on Daisy's documents. They might explain everything."

She saw Percy nod in agreement and then said, "You know, this Whitewall mystery drives me crazy. Every time I think that I'm getting a handle on it, another layer opens up. It's like trying to get to the base of a lotus. Every time you lift up a petal, you find another one underneath."

Pat, who'd remained silent the whole time, interrupted and said, "That's odd."

Naomi and Percy turned and looked at him.

"What is?" said Percy.

"I was just kicking things about in my mind when I thought of something."

Naomi and Percy watched as Pat looked from face to face. At length he said, "Do you know that 'Larkland Fen' is an anagram of 'Frank Elland'?"

# Chapter 37

*2:30pm. The Vical Centre, Newton*

At 2:30pm, Naomi screeched to a stop in the Vical Centre visitors' car park in a shower of dust and stones, attracting the attention of the nearby workmen. She switched off the engine, jumped out of her car, and headed for the familiar steps to the conservation suite.

"Hey beautiful," called one of the guys. "You go up and make yourself comfy; I'll come in a couple of seconds…"

Naomi stopped, turned, and called back, "And what's your name, big guy?"

The workman turned and smiled lasciviously at his listening mates and called back, "Big guy!"

Chuckles of laughter broke out all around.

"Well 'big guy', you've just confirmed what the girls in the local pub told me."

"What's that? That I'm a very big guy?"

"No," called back Naomi. "That you come in a couple of seconds!"

A huge peel of laughter and ribbing burst out from all around, and one or two of the workmen applauded.

With a satisfied smile on her face, Naomi ascended the steps and entered the conservation suite.

"Good grief," said Nina. "What was that all about?"

"Just the usual," said Naomi, as she headed to Helen's desk with a smile on her face.

"You're still having fun with the cavemen then?" said Helen.

"They're harmless enough," said Naomi, "and like I said before, I enjoy a bit of banter every now and then." She perched down next to Helen, waited until she saw the other girls resume their work, and then said in a hushed voice, "Can you think of an excuse to come out with me for half an hour?"

Helen frowned and said, "I don't need an excuse, but why?"

"I'll explain when we get in the car."

Helen raised her eyebrows and said, "Intriguing." She said to Nina, "I'm just popping out with Naomi for half an hour. I'll see you when I get back."

Nina stopped what she was doing and said, "Okay. Perhaps you could pick some milk up while you're out?"

Helen agreed, and within ten minutes they were stopped in a quiet back street.

"Now, what's with all the cloak and dagger stuff?" said Helen.

"Two things," said Naomi. "First, you got me thinking when you told me about sticking a hair on your notebook and finding it gone next day, and I'd like you to repeat that exercise tonight."

"Tonight?" said Helen, "Why tonight?"

"Because you told me that Charlotte was off today, so that only leaves you and Nina in the office."

"You're not suggesting that it could be any of us, are you?" said Helen. "Because if you are, I'd find that most offensive. I've worked with Charlotte and Nina for years, and I'd trust them with my life."

"It isn't my intention to offend you, but offensive or not, you'd like to know who looked at your notebook, wouldn't you?"

"But they'd only have to ask, and I'd show them whatever they wanted to see; we don't have any secrets from one another."

"So if they're both innocent, there'll be nothing to worry about and they'll be eliminated from our search."

"But..."

"But nothing," interrupted Naomi. "You know that our line of work involves eliminating all sorts of possibilities in our quest for the truth. This is just more of the same."

"No it isn't," said Helen. "They aren't only trusted work colleagues, they're personal friends. Why, only this morning you invited us all round to your house for a barbecue."

"I know, but the second reason for coming to see you is because I have some electrifying information, and I want to be sure that we can all trust each other."

Helen sighed and said, "I don't like it, and I don't agree with it, but if it'll make you happy and absolve my friends, I'll go along with it. Now, what's the electrifying information?"

Naomi looked at her friend, and then turned in her direction.

"The cottage that we saw in Cragg End Lane was a gatekeeper's lodge, not High Farm Cottage. *The* High Farm Cottage is further into the trees beyond the boundary wall which, by-the-way, isn't an original wall, and explains why the gravestone was facing the wrong way..."

Helen couldn't help herself and said, "Oh my God..."

"Wait," said Naomi, "it gets better. Do you remember the names on the gravestone?"

"Annabel and Frank Elland? Yes."

"Well, it seems that they're laid to rest in a mausoleum about three miles away from the cottage in a hamlet named Elland."

"I've heard of there," said Helen, "but..."

"Larkland Fen."

Helen stopped speaking and frowned at Naomi. She said, "What? Are you trying to tell me that Larkland Fen is in Elland?"

"No, I'm telling you that Frank Elland is."

"I don't understand," said Helen. "What are you driving at?"

Naomi couldn't contain herself any longer; she looked straight into the eyes of her friend and said, "Larkland Fen is an anagram of Frank Elland."

For a split second nothing registered with Helen, and then she let out a shriek of delight.

"Oh my God!" she said. "Oh, my, God!"

"I knew that you'd be excited," said Naomi.

"Excited? That doesn't begin to cover it! We have to get over to Elland and gain access to that mausoleum, and see what we can discover."

"Alright," said Naomi, "but perhaps we'd better leave it until next Tuesday after the Bank Holiday. That way it'll give me some time to find out what's involved in gaining entry to an old mausoleum, etc."

"Right," said Helen feeling a bit disappointed, "but I hope you realise that you've spoiled my long weekend? I'm going to spend the whole time looking forward to going back to work!"

"Also," said Naomi, "we might get a result from what I want you to do…"

Helen sat and listened to Naomi as she explained her plan.

Half an hour later, Helen breezed into her office and said, "You're not going to believe what Naomi has just discovered!"

Nina looked up from her workstation and said, "Did you get the milk?"

Helen lifted up a plastic carrier bag and said, "Yes, and a cake each. Wait 'til you hear what I've got to say."

Nina looked at her watch and said, "Alright, give me twenty minutes and I should be finished here. You put the kettle on."

"Okay, but I'm just going to scribble down some notes in my book, before I forget all the details." Helen watched the back of Nina and saw her nod her head as she continued to work on one of her projects.

She opened her notebook and wrote down;

*'Valentine Chance wasn't referring to his own grandfather's name; he was referring to the name of his son's grandfather on their maternal side.*

*Valentine married one Agnes Andrew, whose father was named Ashley, and he was buried at Old St. Andrew's in Charleston.*

*A new search is to be instigated at St. Andrew's within the next two weeks to see if a tomb with the name Ashley Andrew can be located.'*

Twenty minutes later, Nina walked across to Helen's desk and said, "I'm sorry, H, but I haven't finished with that dating material and I need to get it sorted before I go." She picked up her offered cup of tea and cream cake and said, "Can you tell me whilst I scoff this down?"

Helen opened her mouth to respond, but then feigned surprise and looked down at her watch.

"Oh no, I should be picking my sister's kids from school in ten minutes time!" She grabbed her coat from the back of her chair, and said, "Sorry Nina – gotta go. I'll explain tomorrow."

Nina raised her eyebrows and said, "Okay – watch the traffic on the main road. It's hell around this time."

Helen said, "Thanks!" and reached for the door handle.

"And don't worry if you can't make it back. I'll lock up tonight."

Helen swished out, turned, and said, "Thanks hon, I'll take you up on that. See you tomorrow."

She rushed down the steps to her car, got in, and turned the engine on. She put the car into gear and drove towards the site exit.

She checked left, right, left, before joining the adjacent road, and then cast a last quick glance up to the office where her notebook with the stuck-down hair lay innocently atop her desk.

# Chapter 38

*12<sup>th</sup> October 1890. St. George's Church, Hyde*

Adeline Chance sat in silence with daughters Stephanie and Eveline in the fourth row of the pews as the pallbearers carrying Maria's coffin walked in reverent silence past.

On the outside she was calm and composed, but inside she was blazing with pent-up anger. She cast a quick glance towards the door, but it had been closed, and two ushers stood with their heads bowed waiting for the service to commence.

In a hushed voice, Stephanie said, "Where's Tal, mother?"

Adeline turned to her left and leaned close to her daughter's right ear.

"I have no idea, but by the blood of the saints themselves, if he lets us down today I'll never forgive him!"

The pallbearers halted in front of the catafalque, lowered the coffin from their shoulders, and laid it to rest. They each took a pace backwards, bowed their heads in a reverent gesture and then dispersed to their seats.

Adeline felt the emotion rise in her chest and cast a glance towards Silas. She saw that his head was bowed and that he was crying. Either side of him sat Martha and Simeon Twitch, to whom Silas and Maria had become so close, and they too were moved by the sadness of the occasion.

Nearby sat other members of Maria's family and friends, including Sister Florence Parks and her husband Cornelius, and even ex-Police Inspector Jack Brewster was in attendance with his wife Joyce.

Anton Rubinstein's haunting 'Melody in F' ended and the sombre Reverend Trevor Morecraft looked up from his position in the pulpit and said, "We are gathered here today to witness the…"

*Bang!*

The heavy church door flew open with such force that its momentum was only halted by it crashing into the stone frame.

A male figure stood in the doorway. He was dressed in a pair of black pantaloons, black calf-length boots and a white silk shirt that was tucked in at the back, but hanging out at the front.

Adeline knew who it was, and her heart sank.

Although most eyes were upon him, for a brief moment in time it appeared as though he was going to do nothing, but then he raised a bottle to his mouth, swigged down a deep draught, and cast it outside, causing it to break on the stone steps.

"Murderer!" shouted Talion Chance. "You black hearted murderer, Cartwright!"

Everybody was stunned as Talion lurched a few paces up the aisle in a half-drunken state.

"Did you hear me, Cartwright?"

Adeline leapt to her feet and said, "Talion, how dare you? This is your Aunt Maria's funeral – show some respect!"

"Yes?" shouted Talion. "Respect, you say? And what respect did that murdering bastard show my father as he was being ripped apart by his dog?"

The two church ushers rushed forwards, grabbed Talion, and tried to manhandle him back towards the door.

Talion wrestled free and shouted, "Are you listening to me, Cartwright, you murderer?"

Silas rose up from his seat, turned, and stared at Talion with diamond hard, ice cold eyes.

Martha Twitch grabbed hold of Silas's arm and said, "Silas…"

Silas shrugged her off as though she was a child and edged his way out of the pews. Despite being sixty-eight years old, he was still big and bulky and he was as strong as an ox.

All eyes were fixed upon him, and nobody moved.

"I see that I have your attention at last, you hypocrite!"

Unable to control herself any longer Adeline shouted, "Talion, stop this at once!"

Talion ignored his mother, and watched as the bulky figure of Silas filled the aisle and glared at him.

"This," said Silas in a threatening tone, "is the funeral of my beloved wife, Maria. Any problems that you have with me we can take up later, but as God is my witness boy, if you don't leave now, I will not be held responsible for my actions. Do you understand me?"

"And what are we supposed to do – weep for the passing of your wife? Did anybody weep for the passing of my father whilst he was being savaged to death by your dog?" He took a couple of faltering steps backwards and then shouted, "Well? You murdering, hypocritical bastard!"

Up until two years before, Maria and Silas had often socialised with Adeline and her children – on numerous occasions at Whitewall, on trips to the park or seaside, to the shops, at church functions and festivals, and on all of their birthdays without fail. In a sad way, the death of Harland had brought them closer together.

But once Talion had reached the age of seventeen, he had gone completely off the rails.

His descent into baseness had commenced once he'd started drinking in the less salubrious public houses of Rochdale. One bad place had led to another, always on the way down, and in the end he'd become a regular drinking member of the scum of society. He hadn't thought for one minute that he was only being tolerated by them, because he was the one who paid for most of the drinks, but as the time had progressed, and his slide into profligacy had escalated, he'd bumped into an old acquaintance of 'the pastor' who'd known about how his life had ended.

He'd then learned of his father's part in the plans to rob and murder at Whitewall in an attempt to reclaim what he'd considered to be his rightful inheritance, and the more that he'd learned, and pieced together his motives for adopting such an extreme measure, the more he had become sympathetic. In the end he'd not seen his father as a pathological, ruthless murderer, but as a crusader attempting to return a God-given birthright to its rightful heirs.

He'd broached the subject with his mother but had been left in no doubt how she'd felt; she had never forgiven his father for his ruthlessness and cold-hearted desire to possess Whitewall, and nor had she ever forgiven him for leaving her alone to cope with three young children.

And, she'd pointed out, if on more than one occasion it hadn't been for the kindness and compassion of Maria and Silas, they would have found themselves in more than a few terrible fixes.

But his mother's resolute stance had not, in the end, been a good enough reason for him to agree with her, and now he wanted what he considered *his* rightful inheritance, and a reckoning for the killing of his father.

Through a whisky-fuelled haze, he saw Silas start to bear down on him, and he lost some resolve. He backed up a few paces more and then shouted, "What are you going to do? Kill me, like you killed my father?"

The old policeman in Jack Brewster came to the fore and he leapt to his feet.

Joyce grabbed hold of his sleeve and said, "Be careful, Jack – he's got a right wild look in his eyes."

Brewster ignored his wife and said in a stentorian voice, "All right, young sir, that's quite enough now."

Talion looked to his right and saw Brewster exiting the pews.

"Please, Silas," said Brewster. "Leave this to me."

Silas ignored the request and continued walking towards Talion as he backed further away. Over Talion's shoulder he saw the two ushers positioning themselves to be able to grab him from the rear.

Brewster caught up with Silas and said, "Please don't do..."

"You don't think that you can scare me, do you?" shouted Talion, and then he jammed his hand into his jacket pocket and pulled out a pistol.

Everybody froze except Silas and Brewster.

Talion waved the gun in the air and shouted, "Back away, Cartwright!"

The level of hysteria rose as he yelled even louder. "How do you think your precious friends would feel if they saw the contents of your head all over the fucking floor?"

Adeline, Stephanie, and Eveline were mortified. They'd known that Talion had become unbalanced through drink, but they'd never witnessed anything like this, and they hadn't an idea what to do. They sat in appalled, embarrassed silence.

A shot rang out as Talion fired into the air. Several women screamed, and a shower of plaster and lathe fell from the vaulted church ceiling.

"I mean it," shouted Talion. "Keep away, or the next one'll be for you."

Brewster stopped walking and adopted a defensive posture.

The two ushers who'd positioned themselves behind Talion turned and ran out of the open door. Several other members of the congregation dived for cover below the level of the pews.

But not even the devil himself was going to stop Silas. With a gritted jaw and steely determination he kept on walking towards the object of his blind rage; it mattered nothing when he saw Talion point the gun at his face and fire. He saw Talion look in disbelief at the gun for a few seconds, and then raise it, and fire again.

The bullet swished past his face and took a chunk of flesh out of his right ear, but he didn't even notice it. He lurched forwards, and smashed the gun out of Talion's hand sending it slithering across the floor. He then grabbed hold of the boy's shirtfront with his left hand, clenched the big gnarled fist of his right, and drew it back to shoulder height.

In blind panic Talion shouted, "Do what you like, – we won't ever give up 'til Whitewall is ours!"

Silas loosed the blow; a blow loaded with all the pent-up passion of years of anger, of wondering who would be the next to threaten his and Maria's life, of putting up with insulting and obnoxious comments from both him and his father, and knowing that this day, his last day on earth with the woman that he loved most, would be marred forever by the memory of the scum in front of him.

In a mighty, jarring crash, his fist broke Talion's nose and shattered his right cheekbone. He drew his hand back a second time and wanted more than anything to keep on pounding away until he could hit no more.

But then out of nowhere, he suddenly heard Maria say, "Silas, that's enough."

He wheeled around, half expecting to see his wife standing behind him, but she was not. He looked left and right, but to no avail.

Brewster saw Silas stall, rushed over, and grabbed hold of his withdrawn fist.

"Alright, Silas," he said. "Leave it now, there's a good lad."

Silas looked at Brewster's face and felt the anger drain away. He released his grip on Talion, watched as he fell unconscious to the floor, and then succumbed to the gentle hands that guided him back to his place in the pews.

# Chapter 39

## *Sunday 30<sup>th</sup> April 2006. Naomi & Carlton Wilkes' House*

The barbecue was in full swing, the wine was flowing, the food was plentiful, and even the weather was playing its part in providing everybody with a wonderful sunny afternoon. Rosie, Kitty, and Lola had returned the day before, following brief visits to friends and family at various locations throughout the UK and, much to Carlton's relief, they had appeared at the barbecue in normal hetero clothing, and appeared to be behaving themselves.

Naomi couldn't help harbouring some disappointment because she had explained what they could be like to her mum and dad, Jane and Sam, and they too had hoped for a bit more of a show, but when they'd questioned Rosie about his plans, he'd explained that because of the next day's early scheduled flight back to Orlando, they'd had to pack up most of their clothes in preparation.

She cast a quick glance in the direction of Carlton who was at his 'manly' place overseeing the barbecue, and they exchanged blown kisses. In one corner of their garden she saw the three girls from the Vical Centre, and sauntered over to join them.

"Hi girls!" she said, as she approached.

All three girls turned and greeted her.

"Have you got plenty to eat and drink?"

Once again she got nods of approval, as they smiled and held up loaded plates and glasses.

"We've been lucky with the weather," said Nina. "The last barbecue I went to, we all stood inside whilst my friends' partner insisted on cooking outside under an umbrella."

"Men, eh?" said Charlotte, "What are they like?"

"Can't live with them, can't live without them!" said Nina.

Naomi smiled and saw Helen looking at her with an odd look in her eyes; she frowned and said, "Everything okay?"

"Can I have a word in private?" said Helen.

Naomi nodded and said, "Sure, let's go indoors."

She led Helen into her front room, where more food was on display on a table in the corner of the room. She helped herself to a few nibbles and then said, "Anything wrong?"

"It's about that plan of yours with my notebook. It's backfired."

Naomi frowned and said, "How?"

"I got into the office before the other girls on Friday, and was shocked to see that the notebook had gone. I obviously considered other possibilities such as workmen, cleaners, and even Craig putting in an appearance, but I don't mind telling you that I was appalled at the prospect of having to broach the subject with Nina. But I needn't have worried. As soon as she walked in, she told me that she'd put my notebook in my desk drawer, so that it wasn't a temptation to prying eyes."

Naomi cocked her head to one side and opened her mouth to speak.

"I know what you're going to say," cut in Helen, "that that could have been a ruse to cover up her tracks, but it is not conclusive evidence of anything underhand, and we're going to have to come up with something better than that old James Bond hair trick."

Naomi leaned over the table, picked up a stick of fresh celery, and started nibbling on it.

"And I did tell you how distasteful that I find all this spying on my friends, didn't I?"

Naomi nodded and said, "You did, but it is necessary, I'm afraid."

"But how do we know that the leak didn't come from your end of things?"

"Anything's possible," said Naomi, "but my circumstances are different to yours. I don't share an office with anybody else, all of my notes are either locked up at night or taken home with me, and I alone have the keys to my filing cabinets. The only people who know about the ruby are the Farlingtons, Carlton and you three, and being head of my own department, I don't have to report to anybody else either."

"Alright," conceded Helen. "I suppose that it does make more sense that it could have come from our end, but we'll have to think of something more reliable than that old trick."

Naomi stood pondering the various possibilities, until Helen spoke.

"And it's not even as though we have any security cameras or CCTV that could help us…"

Naomi nearly spit out her mouthful of celery.

"Ah!" she said. "I've got it. A couple of days ago my dad showed me a pen of his that appears to be normal, but it contains a pinhole camera that's capable of recording sight and sound for a full five hours per charge."

"And then what?" said Helen.

"You stick it into a USB port on a computer. It plays back and recharges at the same time. Why don't I ask him if we can borrow it before he goes back to Bournemouth?"

"And you want me to set it up so that it spies on my friends – is that what you're saying?"

"Yes. I know that it's unpalatable, but it's simplicity itself. If you leave the office at 5:30pm and set it up in a suitable location, it'll keep on recording until half past ten or so. That should be long enough to see what's what."

"Unless someone comes into the office in the early hours."

"Then we'll have to think again, and make other plans."

Helen said, "I'll do it, but I don't like it."

A plan of action was agreed, and then they moved back into the garden to join the others.

Almost as soon as they returned to the other girls, their pact was put into jeopardy.

Nina saw them approaching and said, "I've been dying to ask you – Helen told me that you'd found something significant out. What was it?"

Charlotte jumped in and said, "What's this? You never told me!"

Naomi took control. She looked at Helen and said, "It's two things; one is to do with the 'El Fuego de Marte' in America, and the other is about our mysterious Larkland Fen."

She looked from face to face and saw that she had their undivided attention.

"But I'm going to ask a favour of you. Please don't push me for info on the ruby, because although new information has come to light, it is as yet unsubstantiated and may not be accurate. Furthermore, we still aren't sure how somebody was able to get to that grave before us, so it's best that we keep our cards close to our chest until we discover how that could have happened."

Charlotte said, "Can you give us a clue?"

Naomi raised an eyebrow and said, "So much for not pushing me!"

Charlotte grinned and said, "Pretty please – just a tiny clue?"

Naomi took in a deep breath and said, "Alright, just this and no more, okay?"

Charlotte nodded and said, "Yes, I promise."

"We may have been looking in the wrong location at St. Andrew's in Charleston."

Nina immediately said, "No!"

"So it could still be there?" said Charlotte. "And whoever went there before the Farlingtons got it wrong too?"

"Yes," said Naomi. "Now, please remember, you promised not to push me further."

Nina looked at Helen and said, "Is that what you were writing down in your notebook the other night?"

A look flashed between Naomi and Helen.

Helen said, "Yes, Naomi did confide the full extent of the new info in me, but because I respect where she is coming from with this, if you don't mind I'll keep mum about it too until we know more."

Naomi watched as both girls nodded, and noted an almost imperceptible shift in Nina's demeanour.

"So what's the other bit of news?" said Charlotte.

"As you are aware, Helen and I have been trying to establish the whereabouts of the mysterious Larkland Fen."

Nina and Charlotte nodded.

"We recently discovered that the building we thought to be High Farm Cottage in Cragg End Lane, was in fact just an old gatekeeper's lodge, and that the real High Farm Cottage was located much deeper into the trees. Furthermore, we found out that it had at one time been owned by a Frank and Annabel Elland, who are lying in a mausoleum at St. Peter's church in the hamlet of Elland – and yes, before you ask, the names are related."

"And what has this to do with Larkland Fen?" asked Charlotte.

Naomi turned, looked at Charlotte and Nina, and said, "Larkland Fen is an anagram of Frank Elland."

For a few seconds silence ensued until Nina said, "Oh my God in Heaven! So it's just possible that those documents could be concealed in that mausoleum?"

"Correct," said Naomi.

"And what next?" said Charlotte.

"I've been in touch with Jean Dickens, the wife of the Rector of St. Peter's, and she has told me that providing there are no living relatives of the Ellands who could object, her husband should be able to give me permission to enter it."

"Wow," said a captivated Helen. "It's as simple as that?"

"More or less," said Naomi. "The Rector will have to run the proposal past his Diocesan Registrar, their kind of legal bod, and if he has no objection either, we're in."

"And when will you find all of this out?" said Nina.

"Mrs Dickens has asked me to call her husband this coming Thursday."

Helen grabbed hold of Naomi's arm and said, "And listen to me, Naomi Wilkes, don't even think about going there without me – do you understand?"

"What about us?" said Charlotte and Nina in harmony.

Helen raised her eyebrows, turned to face them, and said, "Rank's a bitch, isn't it?"

No more work related topics were discussed for the rest of the day, and as more and more friends and neighbours arrived, Rosie, Kitty, and Lola disappeared. Thirty minutes later, all hell seemed to break loose in the house. One-by-one, everybody's heads turned to face the apparent mayhem and then Rosie, Kitty and Lola flounced into the garden in full drag and performed a comic version of the film theme tune 'Nine to Five'.

Within minutes everybody seemed to have been co-opted in to helping out with the song, and even Carlton gave in as Rosie pulled a mini-skirt over his shorts.

Naomi ran into the house, retrieved her camera, and took just enough embarrassing photos of him to be able to blackmail him into new pairs of shoes for years! And just when she didn't think it could get better, Rosie got hold of her dad and tried to get him to dance too, a skill that had eluded him for his entire life!

Then something happened that took everybody by surprise. Just after 5pm, the front door bell rang. Naomi opened it half-expecting it to be another neighbour or friend, but standing in the doorway was a young girl unknown to her.

"Can I help you?" she said.

"I understand that you have a bit of a party going on today, and a close friend of mine told me that I'd be made welcome if I called."

Naomi was taken aback; the girl looked well-dressed and pleasant enough, but she'd never been faced with a dilemma like that and she didn't know what to say.

"My friend also said that maybe you could put me up for the night too," said the girl.

Naomi frowned and said, "Who is your friend?"

"Well, he's more than a friend; he's more of a fiancé."

"And who is he, this fiancé of yours?"

In a blur of movement her brother Ewan leapt into view and shouted, "Me!"

You could have knocked Naomi down with a feather. To the best of her knowledge, her brother had been crewing on super-yachts in and around Baja, California.

The entry of Ewan and his new fiancée Catherine made everybody's day, and the only negative comment came from Rosie who, following hearty congratulations, admonished him by saying, "I'll forgive you this time Yolanda, but you know my views on mixed marriage!"

Because of Rosie and co's early departure time next day, the party didn't go on too late into the night, and therefore, soon after 1am Naomi climbed into bed and turned off the bedside light. She turned to her right, kissed Carlton on his lips, and told him that she loved him. She heard him tell her that he loved her too, and then heard him fall fast asleep.

She wasn't sure what time it was when she awoke, but as she emerged into the world of reality, she could still see what part of her dream had awakened her.

In the dream she had answered her front door and been confronted by a delivery driver with a huge wooden crate. She'd queried whether or not he'd been given the right address, but the deliveryman had assured her that he had. He'd manhandled the crate into her hallway and had laid it onto her floor.

At first she'd wondered whether Carlton had ordered something that he hadn't told her about, a surprise maybe, but in his absence, curiosity had got a hold, and, with the aid of a crowbar from his tool shed, she prised open the lid.

Inside had been another box. She'd removed that from the crate and opened it too, only to be confronted by another box. One-by-one she'd opened subsequent boxes until she'd come to the last one; it had been roughly the size of a cigar box, and it had been secured by a simple eye and hook.

She unlatched the hook and opened the last box. Inside, lying on the bottom, and looking diminutive, was an old-fashioned, discoloured cigarette card. She picked it up and looked at it; one side was blank but on the other, was the single mysterious word, 'Malaterre'.

She had no idea what that meant, and so that she wouldn't forget, she opened a drawer next to her bed, removed a pad and pen, and wrote it down. She then placed it back and resumed lying down in the darkness. For some inexplicable reason, she felt alarmed and half-wondered whether it was some kind of portent. The thought of a box-within-a-box-within-a-box, etc., carried with it many more negative thought-provoking processes than positive ones, and though she couldn't explain it, she didn't like it.

Following an unknown length of time, she took herself off to the bathroom, spent a penny, had a small drink of water, and returned to her bed.

Within minutes she was sound asleep again.

# Chapter 40

*Tuesday 2<sup>nd</sup> May 2006. The Historic Research
Department, Walmsfield Borough Council*

Halfway through the afternoon, Naomi sat in her office pondering the grave desecration in Charleston. With all that had gone on in such a short period of time, she hadn't given a lot of thought to it but now, alone and in the quiet, she had a strong feeling that she'd been missing something. And she felt that it was similar to something that she'd experienced before, but for the life of her she couldn't put her finger on it.

She was plagued by worrying thoughts about who had passed on the information, and the more she thought about it, the less she liked it. What was indisputable was that somebody who had been a party to all of the shared secrets about 'El Fuego de Marte' had informed outsiders about its possible presence in Charleston, and had been able to mobilise an operation to search a grave within just four days of solving both contrivances.

But therein lay the rub. If somebody had chanced upon any single part of the information, such as Valentine's letter to his father or maybe the metal shard recovered from the lid of the chest – two individual parts of the same puzzle located in two separate continents – that would not have been enough information to lead them to the Chance Mathewes grave. And that is why she felt convinced that any odd person, workman, cleaner, etc., who may have been lucky enough to see and understand some information left lying around in the conservation suite, couldn't have been to blame for what went on in America. They wouldn't have had enough to go on.

No, she considered – whoever went to St. Andrews had to be in possession of *all* parts of the solved clues.

And only eleven people knew those, the six members of the Farlington family, she and Carlton, Helen, Charlotte and Nina. The informant had to be one of them.

She could rule out herself and Carlton, and she could rule out Deborah and Alan Farlington, because they obviously wanted to be the first people to discover their forebear's legacy.

That left the four Farlington children and the three Vical Centre conservators.

But then there was another problem; what could any of the four Farlington children have said to anybody with such conviction that it had occasioned a team of adults to respond with such speed and fortitude, to carry out an act of desecration in a country so fiercely religious?

And even if any of the children had been believed, whom had they told? Other children? Friends? Strangers? And could, or would, any of them have acted upon the information in such an extreme way? Not likely.

That left the three Vical Centre conservators – and that's why the more she thought about it, the less she liked it.

As she sat deliberating, the telephone rang on her desk. She glanced at the clock on her wall and noted that it was just after 4pm.

She picked up the receiver and said, "Good afternoon, Walmsfield Historic Research, Naomi Wilkes speaking."

"Good afternoon Naomi," said a familiar voice. "How are you today?"

Naomi recognised the distinctive voice of Superintendent Crowthorne and said, "I'm very well thanks, Bob, how are you?"

"I'm very well too, thank you. Now, would you be free anytime tomorrow?"

"I could be, why?"

"I have somebody with me whom I believe you'd like to meet."

Naomi was caught off guard and said, "Who's that then?"

"Our man Phobos – or, as you know him, Leo."

Naomi could have jumped for joy. She said, "I most certainly would like to meet him, and to thank him for saving my life."

"I gathered so. Just one moment, please."

Naomi heard muffled conversation, and then Crowthorne spoke.

"Would you be happy enough meeting him alone, or would you like to be accompanied?"

"Does it make a difference?"

"Just one moment…"

Again more muffled conversation.

"Because of his particular line of work, Leo says that he would prefer it if you were alone."

Naomi said, "That's fine. Where and when?"

Muffled conversation.

"Leo says that there's a public house name the Cragg Vale Inn at the start of Cragg End Lane. If it suits you, he'll meet you in the lounge bar at 1pm."

"And how will I recognise him?" said Naomi.

"You won't, but he'll recognise you."

Naomi closed her eyes and felt stupid, she said, "Yes, of course, sorry," and the time and location were set.

At 5:15pm the same day, at the Vical Centre, Helen removed her white coat and positioned herself in such a way that neither Nina nor Charlotte could see what she was doing. She pressed the micro-switch on top of Sam's pen camera and waited until the tiny, telltale blue light came on, on the opposite side to the pinhole lens. She then hooked the pen into the top pocket of her coat, and hung the coat on her hanger in such a way that it would record any movement anywhere near her desk.

Still unable to suppress a feeling of horrid sneakiness, she cleared up and prepared to leave.

Once again, she placed her notebook on top of her desk, and left it in plain view. This was a ploy that she had questioned, but both she and Naomi had reckoned that she could get away with it just one more time.

"Who's locking up tonight?" she said.

Both girls looked up, but Nina spoke first.

"I can. I'm still not finished with these cursed dendro samples, so if you guys want to head off, that's fine."

Charlotte said, "I'll go when you do Nina, 'cos I'm not finished yet either."

"Alright, guys," said Helen, scooping up her lightweight jacket and heading for the door. "I'll see you tomorrow."

As the time approached 5:30pm, Nina said, "Okay, done."

She stood up and caught sight of Helen's notebook.

She walked over to her desk, picked it up, and said, "My God, what is H like? That's the second time she's left this lying around."

She then put it into the top drawer of her desk.

She shook her head and said, "I don't know – she'll be forgetting her head next…" She paused and said, "Are you nearly done, Charlie?"

Charlotte said, "So close that I'm touching. I'm going to stay on for a few minutes longer so that I won't have to complete this tomorrow, so if you want to go, I'll lock up."

Nina said "Okay" and tidied up her workstation.

She switched off her laptop, put it into her bag, picked up her coat and said, "Right hon, it's all yours. Don't do anything I wouldn't!"

Charlotte looked over her shoulder and smiled.

"I won't," she said. "I'll see you tomorrow."

# Chapter 41

*Wednesday 3rd May 2006. The Vical Centre, Newton*

At 08:05am, Helen sat with a horrified look upon her face, staring in disbelief at her computer screen.

For the whole of the previous evening, she had not been able to take her mind off the pen cam quietly recording away in her white coat pocket. She'd seen the time approach 10:15pm, and knowing that the pen would have switched off; she'd wondered whether it had captured anything. Her obsession with it had caused her to have a very fitful night, and when she'd awakened at 5:30am, she'd not been able to go back to sleep. She'd arisen, showered, dressed, and killed time until she could stand it no longer, – and at 7:15am, had entered the office.

For a full ten minutes she'd procrastinated. She'd stared at the pen in her pocket without touching it, she'd made herself a cup of tea, and then she'd ordered her desk, and switched on her laptop. She'd removed the pen from her coat, unscrewed the top half exposing the USB connector, and had plugged it in. The picture had only been small, but it had been remarkably clear, and the sound quality had been excellent.

She'd watched the first fifteen minutes, noting the innocent exchanges between Nina and Charlotte; she'd seen Nina leave, and Charlotte continue to work at her desk. Twenty minutes later, she'd watched as Charlotte had put away her stuff, tidied up her desk, and collected her coat. At first, she'd thought that Charlotte would just lock up and go, but what she'd seen had shocked her so much that she'd moved the film's progress indicator back to a pivotal point and had paused it.

She checked the time, saw that she had a good twenty minutes before either of her colleagues were due to arrive, and pressed 'Play' again.

Charlotte walked across to the office window and looked out for a few seconds. She then walked over to the office door and locked it from the inside. She walked across to Helen's desk, opened the drawer, and removed the notebook. Next she collected an A4 notepad from her desk, flicked through the various pages of the notebook until she saw what she wanted, and then copied it.

Helen had been horrified enough at what she'd seen, but what she saw next shocked her even more.

Charlotte removed her mobile phone from her handbag and dialled a number.

Helen tapped the 'volume up' icon on her keyboard and listened once again.

*"Could I speak to Mr Sheldon please?*

*"Mr Sheldon? It's Charlotte Southwell from the Vical Centre.*

*"I know, but...*

*"I have some new information about the grave in Charleston, it...*

*"...but...*

*"...Mr Sheldon, please let me speak, it's important!*

*"Very well but you will be interested in what I have to say. Now, do I take it that we could still have the same arrangement?*

*"Yes, and I was just as disappointed as you were. I betrayed the trust of my friends and still ended up with nothing to show for it, so this time I want something up front before I reveal any new information.*

*"And what would be the point of that? I know that you're not fools and I need the cash, so I'm not going to drip feed you rubbish.*

*"Three hundred pounds, and the rest if you find it.*

*"No, don't insult me, that's not good enough, and if you don't accept my terms I'll take my business elsewhere."*

There was a long pause.

*"Very well – send it to my office tomorrow by courier in a parcel marked 'handle with care,' and address it to me personally. Once I have the draft, I'll call you with the name.*

*"Yes I understand,- and I hope so too. Goodnight Mr Sheldon."*

Helen pressed the pause button and the recording stopped. She was mortified; she looked at her watch and knew that Charlotte would arrive very soon.

She hated confrontation and she hated being betrayed. She considered Charlotte not only to be a great co-worker, but a good friend of many years standing, and now she'd placed her in this intolerable position. And in truth, she didn't know what she liked least, knowing that a supposed friend was disloyal and dishonest, or that she had sunk to the base level of spying on her. But now the Rubicon had been crossed, and it was far too late.

At 8:40am, the office door opened and Nina stepped in.

"Morning Helen," she said. "What brings you here so early? Did you fall out of bed?"

Helen smiled and said, "Ha-ha, chuckles," but she was in turmoil. She didn't know whether to confide in Nina, whether to confront Charlotte as soon as she walked in, or what to do.

She opted to keep her own counsel until she'd spoken to Naomi.

At 8:45am, Charlotte walked in and said, "Wow, I'm not usually the last to come in!"

"And H isn't usually the first in," said Nina playfully, "but today she fell out of bed…"

"Alright, Coco the Clown," said Helen. "For that you can make the tea."

Nina and Charlotte exchanged glances and smiled as Nina picked up the kettle and took it over to the sink.

"I'm hoping to arrange a meeting with Naomi this morning to mull over some stuff," said Helen.

"I'm beginning to think that you should apply for a job at Walmsfield Borough Council instead of working here," said Charlotte. "You're over there that often…"

Almost in a revelation, Helen realised that she did enjoy working with Naomi more than she did at the Vical Centre, and it set off a hitherto unconsidered train of thought.

She said, "I suppose it must look like that, but I never let it interfere with my schedule here, and this morning I have to head over that way anyway. I thought that it would save time to pop in and see her to discuss our options in case we find anything in that mausoleum."

It was the best that she could think of at such short notice.

"It must be nice to have such autonomy, you lucky devil," said Charlotte. "I'd love to be coming with you."

Helen thought about the conversation that she'd heard from the pen cam, and wondered how Charlotte would react if she tried to lure her out before her 'special delivery' arrived.

"Are you really busy today?" she said.

Charlotte looked up and said, "Not particularly. I stayed late last night to finish my most pressing project, but as you know, there's always another and then another."

"But nothing that couldn't wait for a couple of hours?"

Charlotte frowned and said, "I don't suppose so..."

"Well, why don't you come with me to see Naomi? We'd value your input, and Craig isn't due to check in until tomorrow, so if you worked late last night, you deserve a small break every now and then."

"Hey! What about me?" cut in Nina. "Don't I deserve a break too?"

"Of course you do," said Helen, "but we can't all leave the office, and I know that you're still up to your neck cataloguing those latest finds."

Nina pursed her lips for a second and then said, "Just now and then I wish that you weren't so damned logical!"

Helen smiled and turned towards Charlotte. She saw that for the briefest seconds she appeared to be at loggerheads with herself.

"Well, what do you think?" she said. "Do you want to come?"

For a couple of seconds Charlotte remained silent. She then looked at Helen and said, "I can't believe that I'm saying this, but I'll stay here. I'm expecting an important parcel this morning and I want to be here when it arrives."

"Can't Nina take delivery of it?"

"No, I need to sign for it."

Helen paused, despising the game that she was playing.

"It sounds intriguing. What is it?"

"It's a present I've sent for, for Stuart. It's his birthday this weekend and I want to make sure that he gets it on time."

Helen nodded and said, "Okay, but don't say that I didn't offer."

"I thought that Stu's birthday was in August," said Nina.

Charlotte's cheeks flushed. She said, "No, whatever gave you that idea?"

"I could have sworn that you said you'd be celebrating Stuart's birthday when you went to Barbados last year."

Charlotte shook her head and said, "Maybe I said something that gave you that impression, but if I did, I'm sorry. It still doesn't alter that his birthday is on Sunday."

Helen turned the screw.

"Are you having a party?"

Charlotte felt herself sinking into a quagmire. She could have kicked herself when she'd said that it was Stuart's birthday. Now she had to dig herself out.

Theatrically, she flung both arms up in the air and said, "Alright, alright, you've caught me out. It isn't Stu's birthday – I was lying." She turned to Nina and said, "It is in August, sorry."

"But why…?" said Nina.

"Because… because," Charlotte looked at both her friends and then said, "I'm going to propose to him this weekend."

"Oh my God!" said Nina.

A line by Sir Walter Scott flashed through Helen's mind.

'*Oh what a tangled web we weave, when first we practise to deceive!*'

"And do you think that he'll say yes?" said Nina.

"I hope so," said Charlotte, "otherwise I'll kill him!"

Helen wanted to end the farce, and said, "Okay, well, good luck with that. Sorry if I seem a bit distracted, but I've got a lot to do before I meet Naomi, so if you don't mind?"

Both girls nodded as Nina continued to interrogate Charlotte about the hows, whens, and wherefores.

At 11:20am, Naomi sat in her office with an astonished expression upon her face. She too had been horrified to find out that Charlotte had been the one to give away the secret of 'El Fuego de Marte'.

She digested everything that Helen told her and then said, "Are you sure that you heard Charlotte use the name Sheldon?"

"Positive – why?"

"Because she may have been talking to Dominic Sheldon the Estates Manager of Christadar Property Holdings – one of Christiana's top guys."

"You're not suggesting that Christiana had a hand in any of this, are you?"

Naomi paused for thought and then said, "I hear what you're saying, and it does seem too much of a push to suggest that she's involved, especially after what we went through together, but Dominic Sheldon is her Estates Manager."

Helen thought for a second and then said, "Maybe it's a different Sheldon."

Naomi gave Helen a sideways look and said, "And is that likely?"

Helen expelled a long exasperated "Oh!" and then said, "And I liked Christiana too! I thought that she was one of the good guys."

"Like Charlotte?"

Helen looked with despair and shook her head.

"Look," said Naomi, "as far as Christiana is concerned, let's not jump the gun; she may be perfectly innocent..."

"But we can't ask her outright, can we?"

"No, and she isn't our top priority either. I need to ring Alan Farlington in America to ask him to alert the authorities that there might be another attempted desecration."

"But the grave is a fictitious one," said Helen.

"I know that, but whoever hit the last one doesn't, and it would be my guess that not too long from now, some people may descend upon that graveyard late one night and start scouring the gravestones in search of that name."

Helen sat for a few moments and then said, "Whoa! I've just thought of something."

Naomi raised her eyebrows.

"You know what this means, don't you?"

"No – what?"

"It means that 'El Fuego de Marte' wasn't found by Charlotte's contacts."

Naomi hadn't given that a moment's thought and said, "Wow! You're right!"

"So, if it wasn't found in the Chance Mathewes grave, it was either removed at some time in the past, or we've all been looking in the wrong place…"

Naomi sat back in her seat and said, "Good Lord, this means that it's 'game on' again!" She glanced up at her clock and recalled her lunchtime meeting.

"I'm sorry to have to say this, Helen," she said, "but I've got another appointment…"

Helen looked at her watch and said, "Me too. The girls are already making comments about me coming here so often, so I suppose I'd better be getting back."

Naomi nodded and said, "You do know how much I value your support and friendship, don't you?"

"I do," said Helen, "I do."

She got up from her seat and headed for the office door. She paused, turned around and then said, "And don't forget to ring Alan before your appointment."

Naomi smiled and waved goodbye as Helen departed. She noted that the time was approaching 12 noon, and knew that it would soon be 7am in Florida. Seconds later she reached for the phone and dialled Alan's number.

# Chapter 42

*The Cragg Vale Inn, Rushworth Moor*

At 12:50pm Naomi wandered through the chairs and tables of the lounge in the Cragg Vale Inn, purchased herself a drink, picked an empty table, and sat down. She believed that Leo would be somewhere in his thirties, but apart from that, she had no idea what to expect. As she sipped her drink, she cast her eyes around the half-filled lounge, but saw nobody that looked a likely candidate. The thumb pressed down on her shoulder and she knew that she was no longer alone.

"That looks nice. What is it? Sauvignon Blanc?"

Naomi whirled around and saw a man's midriff behind her. She looked up and noted that he was slim, dressed from head to foot in black, and was familiar looking.

"It's an Italian Pinot Grigio," she said.

"Hmm, okay, I'll try one."

For some reason unknown to her, Naomi looked down at the hemline of her mini-skirt and then looked up again, but he was gone. She looked along the bar for the stranger but could see no sign of him. She studied all of the men and not one of them was dressed only in black.

"Do you mind if I join you?"

For the second time she whirled around and he was there again, this time with a glass of wine in his hand.

Naomi looked up and said, "How did you do that?"

"Ah," said the man, "it's all part of my elusive qualities." He walked to the opposite side of the table, pointed to the empty chair, and said, "Do you mind?"

Naomi suddenly filled with doubt; she had been so pre-occupied with the thought of meeting Leo, that she hadn't entertained the possibility that a complete stranger may act the same way in the presence of a lone woman.

The man saw the look of indecision on Naomi's face and said, "If I was going to bite, I'd have done so twelve days ago in your underground cell."

Naomi stood up, rushed around the table, and threw her arms around the man's neck.

"Leo!" she said. "I'm so pleased to meet you at last."

"Steady on, old girl," said Leo putting his hands lightly on Naomi's waist. "You'll get the natives talking!"

"I don't care," said Naomi letting go and returning to her seat. "You saved my life, and I can't thank you enough."

Leo looked around to see if they had attracted any attention, and being satisfied that they hadn't, said, "It was my pleasure."

"Well, the least that you can do is to let me buy you lunch."

Leo hesitated and then said, "It's a most generous offer, but that's not why I came."

"I know," said Naomi, "but I want to." She saw the look of uncertainty in Leo's eyes and said, "That is, unless you have to be somewhere else?"

"No, no – it's just that being a guy of the old school, I usually buy the lady her food and drinks, not vice versa."

"Are you accusing me of being a lady?" said Naomi with a smile on her face.

Leo smiled back and his whole countenance lit up. He had beautiful clear white teeth, set into an almost perfect mouth. He was clean-shaven, had short but not cropped dark hair, and his almost perfect skin was suntanned. There was also the hint of a very agreeable, after-shave scent around him.

"Okay, I give in," he said.

Over the following hour-and-a-half, the couple got acquainted. Leo learned about Naomi's profession, her marital status, her general likes and dislikes; and Naomi learned that Leo was single, a career policeman within a specialist unit about which he would not elucidate, that he liked holidaying in Italy, and that his favourite pastime was drinking Danzante Pinot Grigio whilst painting watercolour scenes of Mediterranean marinas just before sunset. The only thing that was not mentioned was any reference to their first meeting, but Naomi changed all of that.

Out of the blue, and unrelated to anything else, she said, "Did you know the guy who was killed trying to help me escape the first time?"

Leo put down his double espresso, paused, and then said, "Yes, we'd worked together on other assignments, but until I was told who had been killed, I had no idea that he was working in that facility."

"Wouldn't it have helped you, knowing that you had another undercover colleague working on the same case?"

"Well, yes and no; I did suspect that another undercover officer may have been in there, and of course it would have been a comfort knowing that I wasn't alone, but on the other hand, by not knowing, there was no chance that I could have let anything slip under pressure."

"And what about the policeman who got blown up – did you know him?"

"Not personally, but I knew of him."

Naomi looked around to see if they were being overheard, but seeing other disinterested and preoccupied faces deep in their own conversations, she realised that it was her own suspicious mind that had made her look.

"Now, that was a classic giveaway," said Leo, "and a trained cop would have spotted that look a mile off!"

Naomi blushed and said, "I wouldn't be a very good policewoman. I'd believe every sob story and I'd be inclined to let everybody off!"

Leo smiled.

Naomi leaned closer and said, "Has Adrian Darke been apprehended yet?"

For the first time since they'd met, she saw a change in Leo's demeanour. His face hardened, and she caught a cold and steely glimpse of his professional side.

Leo leaned forwards and said, "Not yet, but we may be getting close."

"He has a lot to answer for, said Naomi, "and not just with the latest goings on, but for other stuff dating back to 2002."

Leo frowned and said, "I don't understand."

Naomi gave Leo a clipped history of the Whitewall affair, including who she was by birth, but she said nothing about the American side of things. And it was when she was airing her suspicions about Darke's involvement in all of the murders that a penny dropped.

She recalled her previous day's deliberation about the grave desecration in Charleston, and her vague feeling that she had been missing something – now she knew what it was.

In 2002, the ex-Mayor of Walmsfield, Tom Ramsbottom, and his wife Peggy had been killed whilst holidaying in Florida. At first, all of the suspicion had been directed towards their ex-town clerk Giles Eaton, but the one thing that had baffled everybody had been the speed and efficiency with which the operation had been carried out in such a far off place. Nobody had been able to believe that their own town clerk had had the kind of clout in America to be able to pull off such an action. Now she knew that he hadn't; – the common denominator was Adrian Darke.

Her temporary obsession with her sinister thoughts blanked out a realisation that Leo had gone quiet.

Remembering where she was, she snapped out of her brooding silence and looked across the table.

She saw the change in his demeanour and said, "I'm sorry for laying some of my intense family history onto you. It wasn't polite lunchtime conversation and I shouldn't have done it."

"On the contrary," said Leo. "You couldn't have said anything more interesting."

Naomi frowned and said, "Why? Was it the mention of Adrian Darke?"

"No, it was the mention of your birth name, and all of that diverse family history."

Naomi smiled and said, "Is family history something that interests you too?"

"Not just any family," said Leo, "but Chance family history does."

Naomi raised her eyebrows and said, "Why?"

"Because my surname is Chance too." He paused for a second as he saw the look of shock appear on Naomi's face and then continued, "I've been intending to delve into it for years on-and-off, but to date I've not given it much time."

Naomi was dumbstruck. She couldn't get past the possibility that she could be sitting next to a distant family member, and one that had saved her life less than two weeks before. At last she found her tongue.

"I don't know what to say! I'm awestruck. You may be a direct relative of mine, and up until two weeks ago, I'd never even heard of you – yet here you sit, and after having saved my life!"

She sat back in her seat as she tried to digest things and then said, "Weren't you around in 2002 when the Whitewall affair kicked off?"

Leo thought for a second and then said, "No. In 2002 I was working in Northern Ireland."

"Well, trust me, it was big news around these parts, and although nothing was ever proven, Adrian Darke's dirty hands were thought to be well and truly in the mix."

Leo nodded and said, "In that case, we should cross fingers that it won't be too long before justice catches up with him."

The couple lapsed into temporary silence as each thought about how pivotal their lunchtime meeting had been.

The seconds ticked by until Naomi said, "So, Cousin Leonard, if it doesn't compromise anything within your profession, I could try to see if we have a direct family link. All I'd need to get me going would be the names and birthdates of your parents."

Leo looked at Naomi and said, "Leonard? Who said that my name was Leonard?"

"I'm sorry. I just presumed when you said that your name was Leo that it was a contraction of Leonard."

Leo smiled and said, "My name is actually Brandon…"

"Brandon?" said a shocked Naomi as she recalled what the voice in her cell had said. "I thought that you said your name was Leo?"

"It is, but it's a contraction of my awful middle name, because I got fed up with people calling me Brandy!"

"I see," said Naomi. "So your middle name isn't Leonard, then?"

"I should be so lucky!"

"Why, surely nothing can be worse than Leonard?"

"Oh, yes it can," said Leo. "I've been stuck with a hideous moniker that has been passed down from father to first-born son for generations, and apart from it being an embarrassment, it puzzles the hell out of me too."

"Why," said Naomi, "what is it?"

Leo leaned forwards in his seat and said, "I'll tell you if you promise never to use it, and never to tell anybody!"

Naomi smiled and said, "Cross my heart and hope to die."

Leo looked theatrically left and then right and said, "Very well – my middle name is Talion."

# Chapter 43

*2:35am Eastern Daylight Time, Thursday 4th May 2006.*
*Old St. Andrew's Church, Charleston*

Following the shocking telephone call from Naomi, Alan Farlington had acted at breakneck speed, but no more so than the Charleston Police after they'd been informed that another attempted grave desecration might be about to take place at Old St. Andrew's. They'd left nothing to chance, and once the church floodlights had turned off at midnight, they'd concealed armed police officers with bullhorn loudspeakers in numerous locations around the graveyard.

Commanding the operation from within the church was the mega-feisty Sheriff Bonnie-Mae Clement, and she was not in a happy mood.

"Keep your eyes peeled, boys," she said following her individual radio checks. "If those son-bitches show up in our graveyard again, I want their asses well and truly nailed – out."

Because of their cooperative nature and previous help, Sheriff Clement had allowed Alan Farlington and one of the senior church officials, Deacon Del Morrison, to stay.

She turned to Alan and in a hushed tone said, "Could be a long night, Mr Farlington, but if your contact in England is correct and we do catch the callous bastards who had the gall to carry out an act like that in our backyard, it will be well worth it."

As Alan sidled up closer to the Sheriff, she turned towards him and her face was temporarily illuminated by the light from the waxing moon; at once he saw how attractive she was, yet at the same time, how determined she appeared to be. He'd heard that she was not a woman to be fooled with, and it showed every inch on her high-cheekboned don't-screw-with-me face.

Feeling meeker than normal in the presence of such a woman, he said, "I did tell you that the information we'd fed out was related to a fictitious grave, so another desecration is not going to happen."

"That, sir," said Sheriff Clement, "is entirely beside the point. If anybody turns up in this graveyard, in the middle of the night with a shovel or pick in their hand, they will not have come here to tend a loved-one's plot. They'll be here with the sole intention of unlawfully taking or possessing human remains and/or funerary objects. That is against the law. And even worse, – in this county, – that is a crime against God."

Alan gulped.

"But what I don't get," said the Sheriff, unaware of Alan's undermined resolve, "is why, after all of these years, anybody would *want* to desecrate any of our graves?" She turned to face Alan full on and said, "Unless, of course, you could enlighten me on that subject?"

Alan took in a deep breath but didn't know what to say.

The Sheriff saw Alan's uncertainty and said, "And, sir, please don't go assuming that I have missed any connections. I am naturally grateful that you have been public spirited enough to come forwards to warn us of possible perpetrators, but I am not unmindful that on both occasions, you were either indirectly, or in this case, directly involved."

She paused and gave Alan a long, lingering look and then said, "And make no mistake, – sir, – I will be doing all in my power and jurisdiction to get to the very bottom of things in due course."

Alan felt uncomfortable and realised that it wasn't going to be long before he would have to face a lot of demanding questions.

"Charlie Papa One, this is Charlie Papa Seven, over."

Sheriff Clement turned away and lifted the tiny mike of her VHF headset up to her mouth. She said, "Charlie Papa Seven, this is One – what's up Lennie?"

"We got movement over here, Bonnie-Mae."

"Roger that, keep alert and don't make a move until I say, got it?"

"Got it, out."

"Charlie Papa One, this is Charlie Papa Two, over."

"Charlie Papa Two, this is One, over."

"We got movement too, Sheriff."

Sheriff Clement covered up her mike, turned to her Deputy Wayne Parker and said, "Holy cow, we got two insurgencies!"

"Charlie Papa One, this is Charlie Papa Five, over."

The Sheriff frowned and replied, "Charlie Papa Five, this is One, over."

"A vehicle just pulled up and dropped another three guys by us, over."

Alan saw a look of concern appear on the Sheriff's face, turned to Deacon Morrison, and raised his eyebrows.

Deacon Morrison shrugged his shoulders; he was in unchartered waters.

"Charlie Papa One, this is Charlie Papa Three, over."

The Sheriff said, "Not you too, Dean?"

"Yes Ma'am – we got three guys coming in over here."

For the first time in her entire police career, Sheriff Clement was thrown. She pulled the mike down from her mouth and froze. She saw Wayne staring at her for instructions, but the status quo had rapidly deteriorated.

"Bonnie-Mae?" said Wayne.

The Sheriff brought the mike up to her mouth and said, "Seven – how many guys have you got there, Lennie?"

"Three – two with shovels and picks, one with a shotgun."

"Two, what about you, Harve?"

"Same set up as Lennie, Bonnie-Mae, three."

The Sheriff did a quick mental calculation and realised that she was dealing with at least twelve men, four of whom were armed. She had six officers in different locations around the graveyard, herself, and Wayne, and two civilians in the church. The situation was becoming untenable.

"Charlie Papa One, this is Charlie Papa Four. We just got another three, over."

With an increasing sense of concern, the Sheriff said, "Okay, roger that, Jim. Now, – everybody hold your position until I say; out."

The numbers cascaded through her mind like herd of wild horses – fifteen intruders consisting of ten diggers and five armed guards arriving in five vehicles, and entering the graveyard from five separate places. That represented one hell of an operation, and the only officer to have remained quiet was her only female deputy, Eleanor Drake on Charlie Papa Six. She decided to call her.

"Charlie Papa Six, this is One, over."

No response.

"Charlie Papa Six, this is One, over."

A horrible sense of foreboding started to creep over her as Eleanor failed to respond.

"Charlie Papa Six – Ella, are you there? Over."

No response.

Now filled with uncertainty, Sheriff Clement stared at the moon through the window, and being deeply religious, thought, 'Lord, if you were of a mind, I sure could do with some help right now…'

Almost at once, the silence was broken by Deacon Morrison.

"Might I be allowed to make a suggestion?" he said.

The astonished Sheriff turned around, looked at the Deacon, and said, "Sure thing, Del – what?"

Deacon Morrison reached into one of the enclosed pews, picked up a kneeling cushion with a hardwood base, and offered it to the Sheriff.

"Why don't you try throwing this through the window?"

The Sheriff frowned but didn't question. She was overcome by a feeling that she was now being helped by a higher authority. She took the kneeling cushion, raised the VHF mike up to her mouth, and said, "Charlie Papa One to all units, unholster your sidearms and standby with your horns."

Without further ado, she flung the kneeling cushion through the nearest window.

In an instant, floodlights switched on all around St. Andrew's; they illuminated every elevation of the church, the parish house, the car park, and the graveyard. Seconds later multiple sirens burst into action and sent out high pitched wailing sounds similar to speeding police cars, and groundkeeper Casey Peters' bad tempered dog raced across the open ground from his nearby house, and started biting everything that moved.

Out on Highway 61, a Highway Patrol car which had been heading towards Charleston arrived at the junction opposite St. Andrews just as everything kicked off. The two officers couldn't believe their eyes; they added to the cacophony by switching on their blue lights and siren, and turning into the car park.

Inside the church, the Sheriff ordered, "Right guys, make your announcements."

All around the panic-stricken intruders cops appeared, armed and yelling into bullhorns, "This is the police – drop your weapons and raise your arms in the air!"

Such was the unexpected enormity of what had happened that most of the stunned intruders complied and remained still. The only ones who didn't were the ones who were being arbitrarily snapped at by Casey Peters' dog.

Even the stoic Bonnie-Mae Clement was astounded by what had happened – the sudden appearance of the Highway Patrol car, and the amazing turnaround success of her operation.

On her way out of the church she caught sight of the cross on the altar. She shook her head, and said, "Sweet Jesus, – you sure don't do things by half…"

# Chapter 44

*10:20am British Summer Time. Walmsfield Historic Research Department*

The telephone rang on Naomi's desk; she picked it up and said, "Walmsfield…"

"Mrs Wilkes?"

Naomi stopped speaking for a split second.

"Mrs Wilkes, is that you?" said a male voice.

"Yes it is, I…"

"Excellent. This is Terry Dickens, Rector of St. Peter's in Elland."

Naomi perked up and said, "Good afternoon, Rector!"

"What's that?"

"What's what?" asked Naomi.

"You said something about a tractor, did you?"

"No, I said…"

"I'm afraid I can't allow anything like that into my graveyard."

"No," said Naomi, "I'm not planning to use a tractor…"

"Because that would be out of the question; my architett would have a fit."

"Your Archie what?" said Naomi.

"My architett; he's in charge of the Graveyard Committee."

Naomi puzzled a second and then said, "Reverend Dickens, I think that we've become distracted through a minor misunderstanding."

"Have we?" said the Rector. "My hearing isn't what it used to be."

Naomi paused and waited for the Rector to continue, but only silence ensued. She gave it a few seconds longer and then opened her mouth to speak.

"Did you hear me all right?" said the Rector.

"Yes, yes, thank you," said Naomi.

"Well, what is that you want?"

Naomi frowned and said, "I don't want anything. You…"

"Why did you ring me then?"

"I didn't…"

"Oh, I'm so sorry. I'm still on an old-fashioned party line here. We must have got our wires crossed. Goodbye."

Naomi stared in disbelief at her handset as the line went dead. She gathered her wits, looked up the Rector's number, and dialled it.

"Terry Dickens, Rector of St. Peter's."

"Reverend Dickens, it's Naomi Wilkes from Walmsfield Historic Research Department…"

"Ah, yes, I've been trying to contact you."

Naomi resisted the temptation to refer to any of their previous conversation and said, "Is it about the Elland family mausoleum?"

"It is. I've completed my research into the family and it would seem that there are no living relatives. I then contacted the Dossisan Registrar…"

Naomi thought, 'Dossisan?' but said nothing.

"… and he has no objection to you entering the mausoleum, so if you'd like to come along at a time suitable to us both, we can open the place up."

"Excellent!" said Naomi, "Would tomorrow morning at 10·30am suit you?"

"Just one moment please, I need to check my diary."

Several minutes passed as Naomi listened with amusement as the Rector carried out a bizarre but distant conversation with his wife.

*"Jean, have you seen my diary anywhere?"*

*"What do you want one of those for? You don't wear them anymore."*

*"What?"*

*"I said what do you want one of those for?"*

*"One of what?"*

*"Ties."*

*"What on earth are you talking about?"*

*"Ties."*

*"What are you talking about ties for?"*

*"You brought it up!"*

*"No I didn't."*

*"Well what do you want, I'm in the conservatory trying to prick out here."*

*"I want my diary!"*

*"Why didn't you say so, – it's under the phone."*

*"Oh, yes – right, thank you."*

*"What did you say?"*

*"I said... oh, forget it. I've got somebody waiting on the phone..."*

Naomi heard a few pages being turned and then the handset being picked up.

"Now," said the Rector, "where were we?"

"You were going to check to see if I could meet you tomorrow at 10:30am."

"Yes, yes, of course..." There was a brief pause and then the Rector said, "Where was it again?"

Naomi wanted to say, "Under the phone," but resisted and said instead, "At St. Peter's."

"At 10:30am, you say?"

"Yes."

"That will be fine. Now bear with me whilst I make a note of it in my diary, otherwise I'm likely to forget. My memory isn't what it used to be, you know."

Naomi wanted to get off the phone, but having experienced just a small time with the Reverend Dickens, she too thought that it would be worthwhile waiting until she was sure that he had it written down. She heard him say, "Excuse me one moment, please – I seem to have mislaid my pen."

*"Jean!"*

No answer.

*"Jean!"*

*"Yes?"*

*"Have you moved my pen?"*

*"Where to?"*

*"What did you say?"*

*"I said, where to?"*

*"What do you mean, where to?"*

*"Exactly what I said – where have you moved your pen to?"*

Naomi couldn't help herself; she started to giggle at the ridiculous exchange, and had to cover up the mouthpiece to mask it.

*"I haven't moved it, I..."*

*"Well why did you tell me that you had?"*

*"I didn't tell you that I'd moved it; I asked you where you'd moved it to."*

*"I haven't moved it!"*

*"Well where is it then?"*

*"How should I know? Isn't it in that little container next to the phone?"*

*"Ah, yes, I've found it. Thank you, dear."*

Naomi regained some equanimity and then heard the sound of the phone being picked up.

The Rector said, "Hello Mrs, er…"

"Wilkes."

"Yes, that's right. Now, that's all booked in for 10:30am tomorrow, and you'd better bring some bolt-cutters."

"All right, I will. Thank you Reverend Dickens."

"Until tomorrow then – goodbye."

Naomi leaned back in her chair and smiled. She thought that Percy and his oddball friends were bad enough, but she couldn't wait to tell Helen about who they'd be meeting the next day.

# Chapter 45

*Friday 5th May 2006. St. Peter's Graveyard, Elland*

At 10:35am, Naomi and Helen looked around as they heard the beep of a car horn. They watched as the Reverend Dickens pulled up in the car park, exited the car and started to walk over to them – then they saw him change his mind, walk back to his car, extract a piece of paper, and then head back in their direction.

He was a handsome looking man who appeared to be at least six feet tall. He had a shock of white curly hair and was bulky and strong looking. Not a bit like Naomi had envisaged following her conversation with him on the telephone.

Both women got out of the Naomi's temporary hire car and walked over to meet him.

"Reverend Dickens," said Naomi extending her hand, "thank you so much for giving us this opportunity to carry out our research." She paused for a second and then said, "This is my friend and work colleague, Helen Milner."

The Rector, Naomi and Helen exchanged handshakes and general niceties until he said, "Before we enter the mausoleum, I would ask you to sign this piece of paper; it's a simple document asking you to respect the sanctity of where we're going, and to ask you to treat everything with due reverence."

Naomi smiled and said, "Of course, I'd be happy to."

She took the offered piece of paper and pen, looked for where she had to sign, and saw that she was holding a shopping list.

"I seem to have the wrong piece of paper, Reverend," she said.

"What? What do you mean?"

Naomi handed the paper back and said, "This appears to be a shopping list."

"Oh for goodness' sake!" said the Rector, "That means that the memsahib's probably on her way to Sainsbury's with your form." He shook his head and said, "I didn't have my specs on when I picked this up, so I expect I'll be in for a bit of an ear-bashing when she gets back..."

"Will it hold things up?" enquired Helen.

"Well, I don't know about that, but I'll bet that the old girl will forget my crunchy-nut peanut butter."

"No, Reverend Dickens," said Naomi, "Helen didn't mean..."

"The name's Terry – please call me that. Things used to be different in my day but the church has gone all-informal now. I'm embracing the change, – it's supposed to be good for the soul, you know."

"Thank you, Terry," said Naomi, "but I think that Helen was referring to us being held up here."

"Oh?" said the Rector. "Why is that – are you waiting for somebody else?"

"No, because of us not being able to sign the form."

"Oh, that, no, no, it's more of a request than a legal requirement. We can move on up there any time you like."

"We'll go now then," said Naomi, full of enthusiasm.

"Very well – and you did bring your bolt-cutters, didn't you?"

"I did," said Naomi as she opened up the boot of her car. She removed her travel bag and a small pair of bolt-cutters, locked up, and said, "Okay, we're ready."

The Rector led Naomi and Helen around the left-hand side of the church, and the mausoleum came into view. It dominated everything; it was the only one in the graveyard, but it was huge, austere, and very imposing.

It was rectangular in design, constructed out of limestone that had become heavily patinated with fungal deposits and it had a domed roof topped off with an ornate, carved stone cross. The side and rear elevations were fenestrated with single small rectangular stained-glass windows, and the front elevation contained two small lancet-arched stained-glass windows either side of a lancet-arched doorway.

As they got closer, Naomi saw that they were double doors, painted black with ornate carvings on their top halves, and simple blank panels on the lower half. Each door was adorned halfway down with a long black wooden handle, similar in appearance to a small towel rail, but tipped at each end with a tarnished but ornate brass finial. Through both of the handles was a sturdy length of chain secured by an old padlock.

Above the door was a large limestone ashlar engraved with the family name Elland.

"Here we are then," said the Rector.

Naomi and Helen stopped and half-wondered whether Terry would say a small prayer or something, but he seemed not to be so inclined.

Naomi stepped up with the bolt-cutters, lifted them up, and then stopped when she saw a small brass bell to the right-hand side of the doorway.

The Rector saw her looking and said, "A vivid memento of taphephobia."

Helen said, "I beg your pardon?"

The Rector turned to Helen and said, "Taphephobia – the fear of being buried alive. Lots of 19th century graves and mausolea were fitted with such devices because the Victorians were obsessed with the idea that they might waken up after being interred, and be unable to escape."

Helen shuddered at the thought of being buried alive and said, "Ooh, perish the thought…"

"Yes, me too chief," said the Rector.

Naomi shot a glance at Helen, and then turned her attention back to the chain. She attempted to snip through one of the links, but try as she may, nothing happened.

Helen watched Naomi for a few minutes and then said, "Here, let me have a go."

She couldn't cut through the link either.

"Try cutting the shackle of the padlock," suggested Naomi.

Helen tried that, but once again with no luck.

"It's no good," said a dejected Helen. "We'll have to come back with bigger cutters."

Naomi took the bolt-cutters off Helen and tried to cut through the padlock shackle, but she too had no luck.

She turned to the Rector and said, "I'm sorry, Terry, we'll have to come back another time with some more sturdy cutters; these don't seem to be making any impression at all."

The Rector looked down at them and said, "They look alright to me. Let me have a go."

He stepped up to the doors, placed the cutter blades over a chain link, and cut through it as though it was made out of paper. He then snipped the other side of the same link and the chain and padlock fell to the ground with a crash.

Naomi and Helen were astonished at the apparent ease with which he'd cut the chain.

The Rector saw their faces, smiled, winked, and said, "That's crunchy-nut peanut butter for you. Builds up the muscles, you know!" He then looked up at the stone cross on the roof, nodded upwards, and said, "And every now and then, I get a bit of help from Head Office."

Naomi and Helen smiled, and warmed to him.

Naomi took a deep breath and stepped up to the doors. She placed a hand on each handle and pushed. Nothing happened. Once again she pushed, this time harder, but to no avail. She then tried each door in turn, but neither moved.

She turned to the Rector and said, "Do you think that something could be blocking the doors on the inside?"

"Or that the occupants have barricaded themselves in? Not likely pud. Have you considered pulling?"

Naomi looked at Helen and mouthed, "Did he just call me 'pud'?"

Helen raised her eyebrows, smiled, and shrugged.

Doubting her ears, Naomi turned back to face the doors. She placed a hand on each handle and pulled. The doors opened part way, but snagged on the stone step.

"They've probably distorted a bit over the years," said the Rector. "Give 'em a good old yank!"

Naomi placed both hands on the right door handle and gave it a hearty pull. The door opened enough to allow them entry.

She turned to the Rector and said, "Do we need to observe any rights before we go in?"

"Not unless you have a preference to do so, otherwise you're at liberty to enter. I'll wait here until you've completed your investigation."

Naomi thanked the Rector and gestured for Helen to follow her.

Inside the mausoleum, the atmosphere was musty and dank; cobwebs adorned everything. The dirty stained-glass windows let a limited amount of light in, but the morning sun gave them enough to be able to see.

The coffins were sited around them in two horizontal rows of niches, and each had a brass nameplate attached to the door that housed them.

At the far end of the of the mausoleum, and below the rear stained-glass window, was a small Portland stone altar complete with a stone cross, set behind an indented area that was formed to hold flowers or offerings.

Naomi and Helen accustomed themselves to the solemnity of their surroundings, and then turned their attention to the task in hand.

Starting at opposite sides, they brushed away dust and cobwebs, and checked the names of the deceased at waist level. Frank Elland wasn't there. Next they moved to the upper level and repeated the process.

"Oh my God," said Helen.

Naomi turned around to face her and said, "Have you found it?"

"No, but I've found Daisy Hubert."

Naomi walked across and looked at the inscription. She felt odd.

"It sends shivers down my spine seeing her here after all of the things that we've been through," she said.

"Me too," said Helen.

Both stared at the brass plate for a while, and then Naomi turned her head to the left.

There it was; the last resting place of Frank Elland.

His wife was on one side of him, and his daughter was on the other. The simple inscription stated,

*'Frank Elland*
*29<sup>th</sup> January 1796 -*
*10<sup>th</sup> May 1839'*

"It's here," said Naomi.

Helen stopped what she was doing and looked too. She was lost for words.

Naomi stared at the inscription for what seemed like an age. Her heart was thumping and she felt a real sense of presence. Without saying a word, she reached up and turned the handle. Years of dust and cobwebs parted as the creaky, stiff, door opened.

She looked into the pitch-dark interior and noted that the end of the coffin appeared to be positioned over to the right-hand side, allowing her a clear view down the full length of left-hand side. She removed a small but powerful pen torch from her bag and shone it in. Nothing was there.

She turned to Helen and said, "I hope to God that we don't have to look inside the coffin."

"I doubt that we'll be able to anyway," said Helen. "Decaying bodies in wooden caskets used to putrefy the wood too, so most mausolea burials were made in zinc lined coffins."

"But that doesn't mean that all of the lids were sealed."

"True," said Helen, "but I'm with you anyway. I don't relish the idea of opening one either."

Naomi looked one last time at Helen and said, "Okay, cross your fingers."

She placed her torch back in her bag and then positioned her hands at the foot of the coffin. She exerted some pressure, and it rumbled over to the left. She moved her head to the right and looked.

Something was there.

Not daring to breathe she grabbed her torch from her bag, switched it on, and shone the light into the niche.

With her breath coming in short gasps, she turned to Helen and said, "Look."

Helen leaned around the door and looked in. Next to the coffin, illuminated in the torchlight, was small wooden box.

She looked at Naomi and said, "Oh my God!"

Naomi was overwhelmed. She stayed rooted to the spot, not daring to believe that she could be on the verge of discovering the most important and significant find of her life; documents that had been searched for by her great-great-great-aunt Maria, and countless other members of her family, for well over one-hundred-and fifty years.

"Well, go on," said Helen, seeing Naomi's temporary immobility. "That may be it. All you have to do now, is to reach in and get it."

Naomi looked at Helen and nodded. She pulled on a pair of cotton gloves, retrieved the box, and placed it on the stone altar. She then repositioned the coffin in the niche and closed the door.

"Are you going to have a peek inside?" said Helen, brimming with curiosity. "The atmosphere in here seems to have suited the preservation of the woodwork."

Naomi looked at it.

The weight and colouration of the box led her to consider that it could be constructed out of rosewood or walnut, but it had a deep coating of dust on it which could have discoloured the grain over time. The base was larger than the rest, which appeared to be about twenty centimetres long by twelve centimetres wide and six to seven centimetres deep. There was a small keyhole set into the panel below the centre of the lid, but the lid appeared to be secured by a hook and eye.

"Well?" prompted Helen again.

"No way," said Naomi. "The conditions in here with that door open are much different to those of a sealed niche for a hundred plus years. We are going to be so damned mega-careful with this that it'll be painful. It mustn't be shaken, knocked, jarred, or opened until we're in laboratory conditions."

Helen knew that Naomi was right, and that she'd let her excitement blur her professionalism.

"Of course you're right," she said. "I wasn't thinking straight."

For the next fifteen minutes the two colleagues wrapped the box in numerous layers of bubble wrap, and then sealed it within a large polythene travel envelope.

They then exited the mausoleum and explained what they were doing to an excited Rector. They promised to keep him informed about their progress, and then carried the wrapped box across to Naomi's car, where they placed it in a plastic container ready for the next leg of their journey.

They then returned to the mausoleum and closed the doors. The Rector promised to have them secured and reminded them that if they wanted to keep their bodies fit and healthy, that they should consider adding crunchy-nut peanut butter to their diets.

Naomi and Helen smiled and bid him a very warm farewell, with a promise to return.

In a gesture of thanks and reverence, both colleagues bowed their heads towards the Elland family mausoleum and departed.


Two hours later, Naomi and Helen, dressed like pre-op surgeons, stood in the atmospherically controlled laboratory of Rochdale University, staring at the box.

Helen turned to her friend and said, "Good luck, Naomi. I hope that the documents you want are in there."

Naomi thanked Helen and said, "Me too." She stepped forwards and slipped the hook out of the eye. "Now, let's see if it's locked."

She took a hold of the lid and exerted a small amount of upwards pressure.

The box opened, and the contents were exposed for the first time in one-hundred-and-thirty-seven years.

# Chapter 46

*12 noon Eastern Daylight Time. Police H.Q.,*
*Charleston*

Alan Farlington sat with Deacon Del Morrison in Sheriff Bonnie-Mae Clement's office as she read through their statements. From time-to-time she stopped and made a note on a pad, and then continued reading. At length she laid the statements to one side and looked at Alan.

"I see from your statement, Mr Farlington, that you were not entirely honest with me upon the occasion of our first meeting."

Alan looked down at his knees because he knew that he had not been 'entirely honest' with her in his statement either. He had made a reference to the possible existence of a buried family heirloom, but he had not been specific about what it was.

"No Ma'am," he said.

"So once you'd established the existence of the Chance Mathewes grave on…" She paused as she turned a few pages of her notebook, and then continued, "…on the 22$^{nd}$ of April this year, had it been your intention to return late one night and desecrate it too?"

Alan looked up and said, "No Ma'am! Our sole intention of visiting was as you said – to establish its existence."

"And then what would have been your intention?"

"We would have approached the South Carolina Department of Health and Environmental Control for permission to disinter, under Rule 9 of their Code of Practice, once we'd received permission from the Rector of St. Andrew's."

The Sheriff sat back in her seat and pondered the information for a second or two. She stared at Alan as she tapped her front teeth with the end of her pencil and then leaned forwards and said, "And what first alerted you to the possibility of something being buried in that grave?"

Deacon Morrison turned to face Alan, wanting to hear the answer too.

"It's complicated, Ma'am..."

"We have all day sir, – take your time."

Alan looked down as he gathered his thoughts and then said, "A long lost and previously unopened letter was discovered a few weeks ago by a distant cousin of mine in England. It was dated from 1829, and was written by my great-great whatever grandfather Valentine Chance, to his father Alexander in England, informing him that he had secreted a family heirloom of great value in a grave near to where he lived, but he didn't state where it was. He'd set up some sort of riddle for his sons and father to work out so that it wouldn't be easy for just anybody to find. Over the next couple of weeks, my cousin in England thought that she'd worked out the riddle and asked us if we could find a grave at Old St Andrew's bearing the names Matthew or Chance, or any derivation of either, and we'd discovered that there was indeed a grave with the name Chance Mathewes there. My wife and I went with a couple of our children and some family friends a couple of weeks ago to see if we could locate it – and you know the rest."

"No, sir," said the Sheriff with furrowed eyebrows. "I do not know the rest. I do not know how somebody else got to learn about that grave and carry out that foul act of desecration, and I do not know why, once having perpetrated such a heinous act, a whole shit load of people should have arrived in such force to carry out another one."

She realised that the Deacon may have taken offence at her language, turned to him and said, "Please forgive my unrestrained outburst there, Del. I allowed my passion to run away with me."

The Deacon nodded and said, "There's nothing to forgive Bonnie-Mae, and I applaud your emotional fortitude."

Alan drew in a deep breath; he'd gathered that his ordeal wouldn't be easy, and he hadn't been wrong.

He said, "Following the shock of finding out that some people had beaten us to the grave at St. Andrew's, my cousin in England learned that the discovery of the heirloom..."

The Sheriff stopped the conversation.

"Forgive me for interrupting your most interesting narrative, Mr Farlington, but you keep on referring to an heirloom without being specific about what it is."

"Ah," said Alan lying through his teeth. "The 1829 letter wasn't specific about it either; it just referred to a family heirloom of great value."

The Sheriff nodded and said, "Fine. Please do continue."

"Okay, as I said – my cousin in England finally discovered that the possible whereabouts of the heirloom had been leaked by a dishonest colleague of hers to some other folks, and in order to prove that it was her, and to flush out who had received the info, she set a trap by informing her that more information had come to light, and that we had been looking for the wrong grave."

"And then you hightailed it up from Dunnellon yesterday to inform us," said the Sheriff.

"Correct, and I also told you that she'd fed the name of a fictitious grave so that there wouldn't be any possibility of another desecration occurring."

Deacon Morrison, who'd been digesting all of the information, said, "Do you mind if I make an observation?"

The Sheriff, who continued to be in awe of the Deacon following his suggestion, with or without God's guidance, the night before, said, "No, sir, not at all."

The Deacon said, "I understand Mr Farlington's English cousin's reasons for creating the illusion to flush out the bad guys, but this highly curious situation does lead us to one inescapable fact."

The Sheriff looked at the Deacon and said, "That being?"

"That Mr Farlington is being conspicuously economical with the truth."

Alan and the Sheriff were both stunned by the Deacon's assertion.

"I've got to hand it to you, Del," said the Sheriff. "I was not anticipating that." She shot a glance in the direction of the troubled looking Alan, turned back to the Deacon, and said, "But what leads you to that conclusion?"

"In my humble opinion Bonnie-Mae, I think that it would be impossible to motivate anybody to carry out such a serious endeavour, unless at least the person in charge was aware of what might actually be found." He paused for a second and then added, "Because, let's face it, why would any one person, let alone a highly organised gang of armed men, even attempt such a desperate act unless they were sure that the heirloom was worth taking the risk for?"

Alan felt a sinking feeling in his stomach. He saw the Sheriff turn towards him.

"An interesting point, wouldn't you say, Mr Farlington?"

"Okay, okay," said Alan. "The heirloom is an eighty-plus carat ruby known as 'El Fuego de Marte' – 'The Fire of Mars'. It was recovered from a Spanish shipwreck off The Marquesas Quays in the early 1800's and given by an old indigenous indian woman to my great, great whatever grandfather Valentine in payment for an act of kindness. He buried it sometime in 1829, and left us the clues to its whereabouts."

Deacon Morrison and the Sheriff were now stunned into temporary silence.

"So are you trying to tell us," said the Deacon, "that that ruby could still be buried somewhere in St. Andrew's graveyard?"

"That's the general consensus," said Alan.

"My, my," said the Deacon. "Now I can see what all the fuss is about."

"And I can see yet another occasion when you were withholding the truth," said the Sheriff acerbically.

Alan looked down at his feet and didn't reply.

"Why didn't you just simplify things and ask us to help you?" said the Deacon.

"Because we still aren't sure where the ruby is located or even if it is still there. After all of these years anything could have happened to it."

"But I thought that your English cousin had solved the riddle?" said the Sheriff.

"Not definitively," he reached into his pocket and pulled out a piece of paper with the second contrivance written upon it. "Here," he said, pointing to the words. "Read for yourself."

The Sheriff and Deacon read the now familiar lines.

*'Grandfather's name 'after deed,' 'tween here and there and then proceed, to go below 'mid soil and seed. Now at last the gift discover, oh joyous day beside the river.'*

The Sheriff was the first to speak.

"Well it's obvious from that 'soil and seed' reference that it is indeed buried, but St. Andrew's is hardly beside the river."

"Not now it isn't," said Alan, "but in Valentine's day, it may well have been."

The Sheriff nodded and said, "Hmm, I guess I can understand your desire to find anything with either Matthew or Chance written upon it, but what do you surmise that the 'after deed' 'tween here and there' reference is referring to?"

"Nobody knows," said Alan. "None of us can make head or tail out of it."

"Well," said the Deacon, "if I ever come across anything with the name Mathew or Chance upon it, either in the graveyard or the old records, I'll be sure to let you know."

Alan picked up a pen from the Sheriff's desk, wrote his contact number on the contrivance, and handed it to the Deacon.

"That," he said, "is my number; please call me anytime, if you do."

The Sheriff looked across at Alan and said, "And I shall be expecting full and *honest* exchanges with you if that ever happens!"

She saw Alan acknowledge her and then said, "Alright, Mr Farlington, you are now free to leave."

Alan breathed a sigh of relief and said, "Thank you, Sheriff". He turned to the Deacon and said, "And thank you Deacon."

The Deacon smiled and said, "Calling me Del's just fine, and I have to say that despite all that's gone on, you sure have added a whole new level of interest for me in Old St. Andrew's!"

Alan thanked the Deacon and then turned to the Sheriff.

"Before I leave, was your female Deputy all right?

The Sheriff nodded and said, "Yes, thank you for asking. Some of the insurgents were standing very close to her concealed position in the graveyard, so she'd switched off her radio not to give away her presence."

"And was the operation a complete success last night?"

"Not entirely," said the Sheriff. "but thanks to Paul's suggestion we managed to arrest thirteen of the fifteen men who entered the graveyard, and I'm sorry to say that several of them had been recruited from our own local dregs of society."

She paused, shook her head, and then continued. "The men behind the operation were employed by a company operating out of Miami known as GFK Logistics – a company that has long been suspected of a string of illegal activities.

Acting upon our information, a series of dawn raids were carried out this morning by the Dade County Police and all of GFK's senior men were arrested and taken into custody.

"Additionally, a known and wanted Englishman was also arrested at the home of GFK's top executive, Grant Fitkern, and extradition proceedings are underway."

Alan looked up at the Sheriff and said, "Are you at liberty to tell me the name of the guy who is being extradited?"

The Sheriff looked at her notes and then said, "Yes, sir. His name is Adrian Darke."

# Chapter 47

*12:30pm British Summer Time. Rochdale University*

In the controlled laboratory of Rochdale University's Historical Conservation Department, Helen watched as Naomi opened the small box that she'd removed from the Elland family mausoleum.

Standing on the clinically clean work surface, it looked unremarkable and diminutive, and it was not dissimilar to any number of old boxes that could have been found filled with nuts, bolts, bits, and bobs in countless sheds and attics across the country.

Naomi opened the lid and looked inside. There appeared to be at least three envelopes. Before removing any, she took two photos of the interior of the box. Next she placed a small plastic spatula under the first envelope and lifted it to see if it had become attached to anything below. The envelope lifted freely and appeared to be in good condition. She then laid it down on a muslin-covered worktop and turned back to the box.

Another envelope was in there. She took two photos of the interior once again and repeated the process. She then laid the second envelope next to the first.

In the box was a third envelope, and the process was repeated for a third time.

Helen remained quiet as she watched Naomi emptying the box. There was something at once exciting yet frustrating about the process; it was exciting because they still had no idea what was in the envelopes, yet it was frustrating because her base instincts, derived from all of her birthdays and Christmases, instilled within her a desire to grab hold of the envelopes and tear them open to get to the contents.

Naomi returned to the box and looked inside. There was a fourth envelope. Once again she repeated the careful removal process and laid the fourth envelope next to the other three. She then looked inside the box and saw that it was empty.

Not daring to breathe, she picked up the first envelope in her gloved hands and removed the document from within. She saw that it was an original 'Fee Simple Absolute' copy of the Deeds to the Whitewall Estate written on parchment, a true indicator that the document predated the mid-1800's, describing the joint ownership of the estate between John and Matthew Chance.

She felt as though somebody had placed their palms against her temples, and was squeezing.

She picked up the second envelope and saw that it too was in good condition. She removed the document, and opened it up. It was Matthew Chance's copy of the original 1747 'Fee Simple Determinable' Freehold Tenancy Agreement, once again written on parchment.

Now she had it. Proof at last that the Chance family had been the undisputed owners of the Whitewall Estate at the commencement of the Tenancy Agreement, and that by virtue of being able to issue a 'Fee Simple Determinable' document to the Grantee, James Montague Lincoln and his subsequent heirs, it meant that the Agreement was of a legally determinable time, after which the Freehold reverted back to the Grantors, John and Matthew Chance, or their heirs or assignees in 1845.

Maria and her father had been proven right at last.

Unable to control her raging emotions, Naomi put her hands up to her face as the tears streamed down her cheeks.

Having been unable to read the words from where she was standing, Helen said, "What's wrong? Isn't it what you wanted to find?"

Still with her hands clasped over her mouth, Naomi nodded.

"What?" said Helen. "It was or it wasn't?"

"It was what I wanted to find. We now have proof absolute that my great-great-great Aunt Maria had been right."

Helen stared at Naomi for a few seconds unable to believe that they had succeeded in their quest.

She then said, "Wow – so does this mean that you now legally own all of that land?"

Naomi didn't know how to respond. She was nonplussed by the whole situation.

She shook her head and said, "I don't know…"

Helen looked equally flummoxed, and said, "So, what's in the other two envelopes?"

Naomi shrugged and said, "I've no idea. Let's see…"

"Wait," said Helen. "Swap gloves with me; yours might still be damp from your tears."

Naomi exchanged gloves with Helen and walked back to the worktop. She opened the third envelope and extracted yet another document written on parchment.

As she started to read the words, it felt as though somebody had delivered a physical body blow to her. In shock and disbelief, she saw that it was a Common Law, 'Absolute Bill of Sale,' in which the seller, Matthew Chance, had sold to the purchaser, James Montague Lincoln, 'in the Year of Our Lord seventeen-hundred-and-sixty-two, that parcel of real property known as the Whitewall Estate on Wordale Moor in the District of Hundersfield, over which he had full and lawful possession.'

She didn't think that she could have been rendered so mentally ineffective, but following the revelations of the two previous documents, her brain had gone into overload and shut down. She stared at the words in front of her, but nothing registered.

In a daze, she turned around, walked straight past Helen, and stepped into the corridor outside the lab.

Helen looked on in amazement, as Naomi walked passed and went outside. For several seconds she didn't know how to respond. She reached into the box of gloves, extracted a new pair, and put them on. She then picked up the content of the third envelope and stared at it in equal disbelief to Naomi.

The Bill of Sale was very clear in describing Matthew Chance as the sole owner of the Estate, which could only have been indicative of two things; either he had been the sole owner legally because he had at some time obtained the full rights to Whitewall, or, – much less likely, – he had dishonestly claimed to be the sole owner of Whitewall, and had sold all of it anyway.

Regardless, the outcome appeared to be the same for Naomi; despite all of hers, and in the nineteenth century, her Aunt Maria's efforts to learn about and to secure the ownership of Whitewall, it had according to the document in front of her, all been for nothing.

She turned around and looked at the shaken Naomi, and considered that it wasn't surprising that she had been so shocked and upset.

She turned back to the worktop and saw the fourth envelope as yet unopened. She ignored it and walked into the corridor to Naomi.

Naomi saw Helen approach and shook her head. "I take it that you've seen it?" she said.

"I have," said Helen.

"It can't be true," said Naomi. "Surely somebody in the last two-hundred-and-forty odd years would have known something."

Helen remained silent as something started to niggle.

"Maria and her father rigorously pursued ownership of Whitewall, believing that once the Tenancy Agreement had expired, they would regain ownership and tenure. Her side of the family was directly descended from Matthew's twin brother John, so why would they have continued with their quest, if they hadn't been convinced that they would inherit?"

Helen looked at Naomi and said, "But didn't you tell me that until you'd received a call from Alan in America, you weren't even aware of Matthew's half-ownership of Whitewall?"

"Not quite," said Naomi. "Just before Alan's call in 2002, my dad's cousin John had surprised us all by informing us that he had discovered that the Estate had at one time been in joint ownership, but despite being in possession of all of the numerous documents passed down by Maria, he couldn't ever recall seeing any reference made to that joint ownership by her."

"Are you saying then that Maria believed that she was the sole inheritor of the estate?"

"I suppose so."

"But that's equally bizarre," said Helen. "On the one hand you have Maria believing that she is the sole heir by virtue of her descent from John Chance, and on the other, a completely different line of descendants believing the same because they were related to Matthew; and yet here we are in 2006, in receipt of a document that states that at the time of the sale, Matthew had full and lawful possession. It doesn't make sense.

Why would Maria have spent so much of her life trying to secure possession if she hadn't believed that one day she could? It's almost as though her side of the family knew nothing about Matthew and his joint ownership."

Naomi's raging emotions had come under control, but she too was puzzled, and then the thumb pressed down onto her shoulder. A heavily accented male voice that she'd never heard before said, "Open t'other envelope."

She put her hand up to her shoulder and turned to Helen.

"Let's see what's in the other envelope."

The two colleagues walked back into the lab and across to the worktop.

Naomi picked up the fourth envelope and extracted the contents. It was a letter. It was written on paper, and it had a custom wax seal at the top, indicating that it had not been despatched in an envelope.

She opened it up, spread it out on the muslin-covered worktop, and read the following;

'To James Montague Lincoln,
    Dunsteth Hall,
    Rochdale.


Under this, my hand and seal, and following the agreed disbursement for the Whitewall Estate in its entirety, I hereby give my surety that I shall not ever assist or otherwise give support to any claim of rightful ownership for the Whitewall Estate situate on Wordale Moor, in the District of Hundersfield, made against James Montague Lincoln, his heirs or assignees, by any member of the Chance family in the event of contestation of said ownership.

*Furthermore, I shall not ever challenge, or otherwise dispute, any assertion or declaration, either at present, or at any time in the future, that the Whitewall Estate was originally mortgaged to James Montague Lincoln, by me and my late brother John Chance in the month of March, in the Year of Our Lord 1747.*

*Dated this 20<sup>th</sup> day of December, in the Year of our Lord 1762.*

*Signed by the hand of:*
*Matthew Chance, Vendor in Toto*
*In the presence of:*
*James Montague Lincoln, Vendee*
*And Witnesseth by:*
*Wilberforce Harrison Hubert, Attorney-at-Law'*

Naomi and Helen both read the letter several times until Helen spoke.

"Does this mean…?"

"That Matthew Chance duped his family and illegally sold Whitewall to James Montague Lincoln in 1762?" said Naomi. "Yes, it does!"

The thumb pressed once more on her shoulder and the male voice said, "I'm sorry lass, I…"

"But the repercussions are enormous!" said Helen, cutting across Naomi's thoughts.

Naomi had to gather her wits, and though feeling frustrated that the voice had been cut off, she shook her head and said, "My brain feels fit to explode. There's no way that I'm going to be able to take all of this in right now, let alone fully comprehend it."

"But the fraud couldn't be more obvious," said Helen. "One document is a copy of the Tenancy Agreement of 1747 signed by John and Matthew Chance, clearly describing the conditions, and that is followed fifteen years later by a letter promising James Montague Lincoln that Matthew won't dispute any assertion that he and John had mortgaged the estate to him in 1747!"

Naomi ordered her thoughts for a few seconds and then said, "The only possible explanation could be that John had, at sometime between 1747 and 1762, transferred or sold his share of the estate to Matthew."

"No," said Helen. "I disagree. If John had been aware of what was going on in 1762, why would Matthew have needed to write a letter to Lincoln promising not to contest any assertion or declaration that Whitewall had been mortgaged to him in 1747?"

"My God," said Naomi. "We're looking at a plain and simple case of fraud, aren't we?"

"Yes, and these are the documents that Daisy's brother-in-law asked her to secrete in 'Larkland Fen' because they were the damning evidence needed to bring the Johnsons to justice."

Naomi frowned and said, "Wait, wait; now, that doesn't make sense. If James Montague Lincoln had purchased the estate one way or the other in 1762, then the Johnsons – the direct and only surviving descendants of Lincoln by marriage – would have been the legal owners of Whitewall after all."

"But the sale by Matthew was a fraudulent one," said Helen.

Naomi closed her eyes. The almost immeasurable permutations that could result from the discovery of the documents were overwhelming. Once more her mind went temporarily blank.

Helen broke the silence and said, "Any suggestions?"

Naomi opened her eyes and said, "No, not right now. Let's just put those papers back in the box and take them to my office."

"Okay," said Helen. "It'll give us some breathing space, and I've been far longer than I intended anyway. If Craig ever saw how much time I spent with you, I'd be out of a job."

Out of the blue, Naomi said, "And if you ever did lose your job at the Vical Centre, would you consider coming and working with me at Walmsfield?"

Helen was stunned.

"Are you offering me a job?" she said.

"Yes I am," said Naomi. "Only last week I was given permission to start recruiting because of my ever-increasing workload, and even though I say it myself, the offered salary would be tempting. – Plus, of course, you would have the added advantage of working with me full time!"

Helen burst out laughing and said, "Are you sure that that is an advantage?"

"Come on," said Naomi giving Helen a mock-sardonic look. "You get the box and I'll put the documents back in their envelopes ready to transport, and maybe later we could discuss my offer over a drink?"

The door to the lab opened and one of the resident forensic archaeologists, Dr. Uri Tal walked in.

"Hi girls," he said. "Did you find anything interesting?"

Naomi told Uri about the phenomenal and surprising finds, and then informed him that they were going to take them back to the Historic Research Department at Walmsfield Borough Council offices.

Uri nodded, pulled on a pair of cotton gloves, and picked up the box. He studied it from all angles, opened the lid, and then frowned. He inspected it for a few seconds longer and then said, "Would you have any objection to me keeping this for a few days?"

Naomi said, "Has something caught your eye?"

"Maybe," said Uri, "but I'd prefer to reserve judgement until I've had a proper look."

"Oh, come on, spoilsport," said Helen. "Give us a clue!"

"No," said Uri. "I know how impatient you can be, Helen Milner, but you'll just have to wait!"

Both colleagues smiled at Uri, and with exasperated sighs, turned their attention to preparing the documents for transportation to Naomi's office.

Fifteen minutes later, and following the departure of Naomi and Helen, Uri looked again at the keyhole in the box. He opened the lid and frowned once more; now he definitely knew that something wasn't right.

# Chapter 48

*Wednesday 10<sup>th</sup> May 2006. Rochdale Police Headquarters*

"We have looked through the copies of the documents that you gave us, Naomi," said Superintendent Crowthorne, "and you were right when you told us that the implications were extensive. Indeed, they were far more extensive than we at first imagined."

He cast an eye across to another officer in plain clothes and said, "So with your permission I'd like to hand you over to Detective Chief Inspector Mark Simmonds."

Simmonds smiled, nodded, and said, "Before we proceed, Mrs Wilkes…"

Naomi interrupted and said, "Please call me Naomi."

"Very well, Naomi – before we proceed, why did you bring these documents to us? Surely they could have been examined by the Legal Department of your own Council, or a firm of solicitors specialising in land ownership, perhaps?"

Naomi considered her answer and then said, "A huge amount of history surrounds these papers, Chief Inspector. Time and again, people spanning hundreds of years have been duped or misled, threatened, intimidated, and even murdered because of them, and their influence has always seemed to attract the worst in corruptible people. So, not wishing to let history repeat itself, I decided to bring them to whom I thought would be the incorruptible – yourselves."

"Well, that's very flattering of you," said Simmonds, "and I trust that we won't give you any reason to doubt our veracity."

"If in the end, you advise me to take them to a firm of solicitors, I will, but it will be in the knowledge that nobody else will be able to use the information contained in them to feather their own nests, because they'll have been made aware that you've already seen them."

"I understand," said Simmonds. He placed the photocopies of the documents in front of him and said, "Right – it is complicated, but try to bear with me. If you have any questions as I proceed, just fire away."

Naomi nodded.

"Thanks to the generosity of Wordale Cottage Museum, we were given access to historical maps outlining the boundaries of the Whitewall Estate since the 1600's, and as you could imagine, there have been several changes. But not one of them, including the 19th century map, showed any kind of boundary line separating what could have been Matthew's half of the estate, compared to John's. Therefore, we can only assume in the absence of documentation from the Land Registry Office that the division of land between Matthew and John had been by mutual agreement instead of lines drawn in the mud.

There are no formal or informal recorded acts of 'livery of seisin' performed by their father after 1747 when they jointly inherited, and there is nothing at all to indicate who owned what, where."

Naomi looked at Crowthorne who raised his eyebrows and shrugged.

"In short," said Simmonds, "what Matthew Chance did was to massively blur the edges. When he legitimately sold his half of the Whitewall Estate to James Montague Lincoln in 1762 and unlawfully sold his dead brother's half too, he made it impossible for subsequent researchers to fathom out which part he had owned and which he had not. Which, of course, may have been his ploy all along."

"So," said Naomi, "when Abraham Johnson sold off two sections of the estate in 1868 and 1869, are you saying that even if he'd been aware of Matthew's actions one hundred years earlier, it would still have been impossible for him to determine whether the sales had been illegal or not?"

"In effect, yes," said Simmonds, "but in reality, we still have to be aware that George Hubert had been warning his sister-in-law Daisy to conceal the documents from the Johnsons.

Therefore, it would be safe to assume that they knew that something was amiss, particularly if they were being informed by your old Aunt Maria that she had proof of their wrongdoings."

Naomi sat back in her chair in astonishment and said, "This is both amazing and bizarre. On one hand, the sales may have been completely legal – on the other, completely illegal!"

Simmonds nodded and said, "Bizarre indeed. Even thinking about the permutations could drive you crazy."

Naomi sat in stunned silence until other awful consequences started to come to mind. She looked up and said, "And because my side of the family were never made aware of Matthew's dreadful act and his side had relocated to America, my great Aunt Maria would have assumed that the estate should have reverted to them upon the cessation of the 1747 Tenancy Agreement?"

"Right," said Simmonds, "and that's what I meant when I said that Matthew had massively blurred the edges."

"My God," said Naomi. "He left one hell of a legacy, didn't he?"

"He did indeed," said Simmonds.

Silence fell on the office for a few minutes longer as each person pondered the information.

A few seconds later Crowthorne said, "Good Lord, I've just thought of something else."

Naomi and Simmonds turned to face him.

"This means that all of that skulduggery in 2002 had been for nothing too." He paused, waiting for a response, but when nobody spoke said, "Think about it; we always presumed that your ex-town clerk, Giles Eaton, had been blackmailing Adrian Darke by threatening to scupper his plans to sell a piece of his land on Hobbs Moor to the Highways Agency, – and similarly we also believed that the Chance family were being denied access to the documents by Eaton because he had discovered that some of the land owned by Walmsfield Borough Council may have been illegally purchased and prone to a possessory Court hearing, but knowing what we know now, none of that could ever have been proved."

"And," said Naomi, "because Matthew did what he did, not one single part of the land could ever have been reclaimed by the Chance family because nobody had ever recorded which part of the estate had been sold legitimately?"

"Right," said Crowthorne, "and though it's true what the Chief Inspector said, that you could now take the documentation to a firm of specialist solicitors to sort out, I'd hazard a guess that the costs of litigation would be so prohibitive that they'd probably advise you not to even attempt to proceed."

Naomi sat in a daze. She thought about her Aunt Maria, Carlton, her father Sam, mother Jane, brother Ewan, the Johnsons, Postcard Percy and his band of oddball friends, of Auntie Rosie and the sewing circle, Adrian and Christiana Darke, the Farlingtons in America, Helen, Nina and even the now shamed and jobless Charlotte – indeed all of the diverse people who had become so entangled in the centuries long mystery of land ownership at the Whitewall Estate, and how that one incredibly selfish and wicked act by Matthew Chance in 1762 had rendered it all valueless. She looked up and saw Crowthorne and Simmonds looking at her.

"Penny for them?" said Crowthorne.

Naomi looked at both men and said, "What more can I say? He has caused it all to crash and burn. The pursuit of truth by generations of my family had resulted in threats, intimidation, physical abuse, the incarceration of my Aunt Maria in a Lunatic Asylum for God's sake, and even murder – but every last one of them had considered it all worthwhile.

And now I know that it had all been for absolutely nothing." She paused and shook her head. "The quest has been expunged; it has gone forever, and along with it the excitement, the anticipation, and the exhilaration. And all thanks to the Matthew Chance legacy."

The two policemen nodded and waited for Naomi to resume speaking, but when she did not, Crowthorne said, "On a different note, there is one good piece of news at the end of all this."

Naomi looked at him and said, "What?"

"Adrian Darke was extradited to the UK yesterday, and has been charged with the murder of Constable James Munro on the 21$^{st}$ of April at the Cragg Vale Estate."

Naomi thought about that for a few moments, and about all the other scheming and deaths that he may have had a hand in.

"Good," she said, "and I hope that they keep that callous bastard behind bars for the rest of his life."

Later that evening, whilst celebrating Sam's birthday in a nearby restaurant, Naomi broke the news to her immediate family. Everybody sat in shocked silence, until she'd finished what she was saying.

"So every last chance of claiming Whitewall has now gone?" said a stunned Ewan.

Naomi nodded and said, "Yes, it has. In the absence of documentation describing Matthew's share of the Whitewall Estate, it is impossible to determine which part he had legally sold, and which he had not, so how could anybody lay claim to a parcel of land which they only believed they may at one time have owned?"

Carlton shook his head and said, "It may have all gone, but it would make one hell of a story to pass on to future generations."

"And you're getting close to being put out to pasture, dad," said Ewan, ever the joker. "Maybe you could give it a go?"

"Yes," said Naomi. "You told us endless stories as we grew up, – you should think about it."

"No," said Sam. "Even for me that would be a daunting task."

"You never know, though," said Jane. "If you were able to make it exciting enough, you might be able to interest a publisher one day."

"Or even better, have it made into a film!" said Catherine.

Sam sat back in his chair, thought about it for a few seconds and then said, "Hmm, maybe, but because of all that's gone on, I'd never be able to use my real name. I'd have to adopt a nom de plume."

"Like what?" said Naomi.

"Oh, I don't know," said Sam. "It'd have to be a good old northern name."

"Like what?" said Ewan.

"Like, er... Clegg, maybe," said Sam. "Yes, that's it – I'd call myself Stephen F Clegg."

"And what would the 'F' stand for?" said Carlton.

"Frank," said Sam, "after my old dad."

# Chapter 49

## *Thursday 11th May 2006. St Andrew's Church, Charleston*

Deacon Del Morrison opened the storehouse door and sighed. It was to be the eleventh birthday of one of the church elders' grandchildren, and he, and several volunteers had promised to decorate the parish house in preparation. He looked at the mish-mash of jumble and junk and just knew that the box containing the birthday drapes and regalia would be at the bottom of it all.

One-by-one he lifted the various boxes and bags, posters and picture frames, and other bits of unidentifiable paraphernalia, until he reached the birthday box. Clearing away the final few items, he bent down, scooped it up, and took it outside into the hot South Carolina sunshine. He then went back into the even hotter storehouse, looked around and decided to tidy up so that the next time anybody needed it, it wouldn't be such a pain to get to.

As he busied himself with the task, he saw some Hessian sacking covering an obscure looking object in the corner of the room. He couldn't recall seeing it before, so he walked over to it, lifted it, and peeked underneath.

To his surprise, he saw that it was two old headstones and a small memorial stone. He inspected the headstones first, but age and weather had taken their toll. He saw nothing to indicate whose graves they had once stood sentinel over. The other stone appeared to be a small paviour measuring two feet long by one foot wide, and though it had at one time been engraved, the only legible carving was, *'ews P. F.'*

Curiosity sated, he replaced the sacking and resumed tidying up the storehouse.

"Howdy Del, – need a hand?"

The Deacon turned around and saw Casey Peters standing in the doorway.

He smiled and said, "That sure would be good. It's hotter than a Glassblower's ass in here, and as you can see, things have gotten a bit out of hand of late."

Casey nodded and said, "I've been meaning to tidy this shit up for a while, but each time I've tried, something else always cropped up." He walked in and started putting things on shelves, and in neat piles, and within twenty minutes, order had been restored.

"Now, I owe you a cold beer," said the Deacon. "It would have taken me twice as long without your help."

Casey walked across to the Deacon, tapped the side of his nose, and said, "We don't have to go too far for that. Follow me."

He led the Deacon to his work shed, opened the door, and stepped inside. He removed one or two boxes and revealed a small refrigerator.

He turned to the Deacon and said, "Grab yourself a box and take the weight off."

He then removed two small cans of Budweiser Light from the fridge and handed one over.

The Deacon raised his eyebrows and said, "I didn't know that you were so well catered for…"

Casey was suddenly unsure of whether he had done the right thing; he turned around and said, "There ain't no need to go telling Rector Hughes, is there?"

"No," said the Deacon. "Your little, er, oasis will be our secret." He paused for a second and then said, "And who knows – we may find ourselves in need of some light refreshment at some other time in the future…"

Casey smiled and said, "For you, sir, the door is always open."

The two men sat in the work shed, sipping their beers and making small talk, until the Deacon mentioned the old gravestones in the storehouse.

"They were removed about fifteen years back," said Casey. "The two headstones used to be near the centre of the car park as it is now, and the gravestone used to be between the posts of a small gateway through a low wire fence."

"What was the fence for?"

"It was the original boundary fence for the graveyard, but as the congregation grew and more folks got themselves automobiles, it was decided to remove the stones and fence to enlarge the car park."

"And I suppose that nobody could have objected because…"

"They didn't have anybody left to object."

The Deacon frowned and said, "How could you know that? – I looked at the stones, and apart from a few letters on the small one, there were no legible engravings to indicate who they once belonged to."

"From the old graveyard directories."

"You keep those things, do you?"

"Sure," said Casey. "They're in one of the boxes we just tidied up." He paused as he took a sip of beer and then said, "We were able to get the names of all the folks whose stones we'd removed, but despite all the Rector's efforts to find living relatives he couldn't, so a few weeks later they were removed and put in the storehouse in case anybody ever did turn up."

The Deacon nodded as he sipped his beer.

"I can still remember their names, even after all these years," said Casey in a matter-of-fact way.

The Deacon turned towards him and said, "You must have a good memory."

"No, not really" said Casey. "I can remember 'em because we were all saints together."

The Deacon frowned and said, "How do you figure that?"

"We were all named after New Testament saints. Everybody knows me as Casey but that's not my real name. My old momma was very religious and named me Simon 'cos she thought it sat nice with Peters – you know, Simon Peter?"

The Deacon nodded and said, "Yeah, I get that."

"Then when we removed the old stones, we found out they were saints too. There was P.F. Matthews, Mark Soames, and Luke Smith – Matthew, Mark, and Luke, see?"

The Deacon nodded, but something stirred in his memory. He recalled his promise to Alan Farlington a week earlier and said, "P.F. Matthews, you say?"

"Yes sir." Casey paused, and then said, "Well no, not exactly – it was 'Matthews P. F.' to be exact, but I suppose it makes no never mind one way or the other."

"And where did you say his grave was?"

Casey pointed towards one of the trees adjacent to the car park and said, "Just to the left of that tree aways."

"No, I didn't mean that," said the Deacon. "I meant where was it before the car park was extended?"

"I told you – in the gateway of the old fence."

Something started to peck away at the Deacon. He had a sudden desire to go home and look at the copy of the old clue that Alan had given him.

"Casey," he said at length, "I've got to go home for half an hour, but I'll be back after that to help put up the decorations in the parish house."

"Fine by me," said Casey. "I ain't going nowhere."

Fifteen minutes later, Del spread the piece of paper out on his table and read the clue once more.

*'Grandfather's name 'after deed,' 'tween here and there and then proceed, to go below 'mid soil and seed. Now at last the gift discover, oh joyous day beside the river.'*

He looked at it and knew that somehow it was right – the references all seemed to make sense: 'go below 'mid soil and seed' – obvious, 'joyous day beside the river'. St. Andrew's wasn't located by the Ashley River anymore, but he recalled Alan's comment that it may have been in the past. 'Tween here and there' could have been a reference to the grave being located at the boundary of the graveyard, or the link between Heaven and earth; and the grandfather's name was there. The only part that remained a puzzle was the reference to grandfather's name 'after deed.'

Like Helen before him, he stared at the single quotation marks around the words 'after deed' and couldn't make sense of it. He then wrote down the name 'Matthews P. F.' below the clue and tried to make a link between 'after deed' and 'P. F.', but nothing registered.

As he continued to stare at the clue, he caught sight of his wife's laptop on the table nearby. In a flash of inspiration, he brought up the Google search engine and keyed in "P. F." He saw abbreviated references to computer science, to French Polynesia, the capital letters of organisations, references to 'phonetic form', and almost everything in between, and he was about to give up until his eyes alighted upon Latin abbreviations and references. There he saw the reference "P. F. – post factum."

His heart rate increased as he read the literal translation of 'post factum', and saw that it was 'after deed.'

The clue was definitively solved! – "grandfather's name 'after deed'", or put another way, – "Matthews P. F."

All he had to do now to discover an incredibly valuable and rare ruby was to confirm its exact location in the car park, and to ring Alan Farlington on the number that he'd written below the clue.

For a long time he stared at the telephone. He reached out several times to make the call, but in the end, he didn't pick it up…

# Chapter 50

*Friday 12<sup>th</sup> May 2006. Walmsfield Historic Research Department*

At 10:20am, Naomi heard a knock on her door. She lifted up her head and called, "Come in."

The door opened and Doctor Uri Tal walked in.

"Hi Uri!" said Naomi. "What brings you here?"

"Seeing that you haven't been answering my calls for the last few days, I thought that I'd better bring these over to you."

Naomi looked at the small pile of memos that had been left on her desk and blushed.

"I'm so sorry, Uri," she said. "I've been out the last few days and my calls have built up…"

"Well, I'm here now, so the least that you can do is to get me a cup of coffee in a nice plastic cup, and then I'll show you what I've brought."

Naomi smiled and said, "Of course – how do you like it?"

"White, no sugar."

Naomi went out to the drinks dispenser and then returned a couple of minutes later with two white coffees. As she approached her desk, she saw the small box from the Elland family mausoleum sitting there.

She placed the drinks down and said, "You've brought my box back." She recalled Uri's mysterious behaviour the last time that they'd met and said, "Are you going to tell me what bothered you now?"

"I'll do better than that, but first I want you to look at the box."

Naomi frowned, then reached over and picked it up. She inspected the outside, opened the lid and looked inside, but saw nothing unusual. She hooked the hook back through the small metal eye, lifted the box to face level, and looked again.

Something triggered in her mind. She unhooked the hook, opened the box, and looked at the upper front rim. Despite there being a conspicuous keyhole below the hook and eye, there was no sign of any visible locking mechanism to the lid.

"Ah," said Uri, "now you see it."

Naomi continued to inspect the exterior of the box and then said, "Good grief – because I was so distracted by the contents, I missed this. You must think that I'm very unprofessional..."

Uri smiled and said, "I won't tell anybody if you don't."

Naomi nodded and said, "So go on, tell me..."

"I ran the box through our scanner and saw that it had a false bottom..."

"No!" gasped Naomi.

"Yes."

"And was anything in there?"

"One thing at a time!" said Uri. "Next I had to get a locksmith in to open the lock, not a difficult task by all accounts, but he managed it within a short period of time. Once he'd finished, we turned the box upside down, and the false bottom dropped out."

Naomi was beside herself with anticipation.

"And?" she said.

"And," said Uri reaching into his bag, "we discovered two items. First was this." He placed an object on the desk wrapped in discoloured linen.

Naomi picked it up and unravelled the delicate material. Inside was a medium-sized bronze key. It was ten centimetres in length, and consisted of a five centimetre long cylindrical shaft, a two centimetre bit, and a three centimetre bow. All unremarkable, except for one thing – set into the interior of the bow was the capital letter 'M'.

She studied it for a few minutes, looked up and said, "Curious. Any idea where it came from?"

Uri reached into his bag and extracted a small cardboard box. He opened it and said, "No, but this was in with it."

He turned the box upside down and let the contents fall onto the desk in front of Naomi.

The thumb pressed down onto her shoulder with such force that she let out an involuntary "Ooh!" and rubbed it.

"Are you okay?" said Uri.

Naomi grimaced and said, "Yes, sometimes I get a spasm."

*"No!"*

A voice yelled into Naomi's consciousness. She heard a scream and then another anguished yell.

*"No, please let us go..."*

Naomi fought to control her emotions as she saw Uri staring at her with a look of concern upon his face. She heard the sound of crying, and more screaming. Then she heard a man's voice pleading, *"No, please, not the girls..."*

She closed her eyes and tried to shut out the sounds of torment.

"I'm sorry," she said. "I have to spend a penny."

She left her office and went to the ladies' washroom. She gulped down a plastic cup full of cold water and stood with her back to the wall. The sounds diminished, so she splashed some water into her face, dried herself on a clean tissue, and then took another drink of water.

Feeling more under control, she returned to her office, sat down, and said, "Sorry Uri, when you've got to go..."

Uri smiled but said nothing.

Naomi looked down and her heart nearly stopped.

Lying on the desk was a small, discoloured cigarette card, exactly the same as the one in her dream. Hardly daring to breathe, she picked it up and turned it over.

The word seemed to spring off the card and dash itself into her face. The intense emotion drained her as the all-powerful might of destiny took a hold and changed her life forever from that second on.

Written on the card was the single word 'Malaterre' – a word that would become the one that she most despised, because it would rob her of one of the most precious things that she had ever had.

Unaware of Naomi's raging emotions, Uri said, "Those two items must be related because of the letter 'M' in the bow of the key. Have you ever heard of anywhere named Malaterre before?"

Naomi felt as though her heart was going to burst. It was racing ten-to-the-dozen. She sat in silence until she was able to speak without emotion.

She looked at Uri and said, "No, I haven't, but I believe that I soon will."

# Epilogue

Naomi burst through the front door of her house and shouted, "Cal, Cal!" She listened for a couple of seconds and realised that he wasn't there. She looked down at her bloodied hands and wiped them on her top.

Outside the suspicious taxi driver had waited until Naomi had run indoors, and had contacted his control room to get the police.

Indoors Naomi didn't know what to do first. She saw the phone lying on her kitchen table and snatched it up. She was about to dial 999 when it rang. She nearly dropped it and said, "Bugger!" The phone rang a second time.

She clicked the button and said, "Yes – who are you?"

"Shit, Naomi?" said a flabbergasted Helen. "Is that you? We thought that you were dead!"

"What? Why? And where's Cal?"

"I thought that he was at home, that's why I was calling."

"He's not."

"Maybe he's at Dunsteth."

Naomi was confused. She said, "Why? What the hell is he doing at Dunsteth?"

"Christ," said Helen. "Have you no idea what's happened at Malaterre?"

"Course I haven't! What has happened?"

Helen said, "You need to get to a TV and switch it on to BBC North West now."

"What?" said Naomi. "Why?"

"Just do it and ring me back on my mobile, and I'll call the police for you."

Naomi stared in disbelief as she realised that Helen had terminated the call.

With a puzzled expression on her face, she walked into her lounge, dropped down onto her sofa, picked up the television remote, and clicked onto BBC North West.

The news reporter appeared to be on the verge of tears.

"This is terrible," he said. "In all of my years reporting, I have never witnessed anything like this."

The camera panned around and showed horrified onlookers gathered around the southern edges of the Dunsteth Reservoir, staring at the smoking tower of the recently revealed Malaterre Estate.

Naomi watched in amazement as she saw three rib-type police launches pulling people out of the water and gesturing to others to keep clear.

Without warning, a loud rumbling penetrated the air and everybody looked up.

"Oh no, please God, not again..." shouted the reporter.

Nothing appeared to happen for a few seconds, and then in frozen silence, a huge section of the upper level of the building became detached.

Directly below was a police rib with two occupants staring upwards too.

Men and women started screaming at them to move, but it was too late. In what looked like slow motion, a massive section of masonry broke free and crashed down onto the rib.

People screamed as they watched more panic-stricken individuals in the water, thrashing about in all directions.

"No, no, no..." sobbed the reporter.

The thumb pressed down onto Naomi's shoulder and a voice said, "I'm sorry, he's gone..."

Naomi leapt to her feet and said, "No, not him..."

She dropped the remote onto the floor, ran towards the door, and a searing pain shot through her lower abdomen. She gasped and bent double as the excruciating feeling spread into her back. She clutched at her stomach, dropped to her knees, and the last thing that she saw before all went black was the shadowy outline of a man staring in through the front window...

*If you enjoyed this novel look out for book three:*

# The Emergence of Malaterre

www.stephenfclegg.com